I0587885

THE OLD LOVE AND THE NEW

Alistair Caradec

First paperback edition November 2021

Book design by Eliott Griffen
Cover art by Amalas Rosa
Editing by Kate Nascimento
Sensitivity read by Nadhira Satria

ISBN 978-1-7776-3480-3
www.alistaircaradec.com

CONTENT WARNING

Dear reader,

Thank you for your interest in Sid's story. Before you carry on, please be aware of the following.

The Old Love and the New is set in an oppressive police state. It depicts and describes abuse, self-harm, suicide, and mental illness including schizoaffective disorder, depression and anxiety. It contains strong and derogatory language, alcohol and drug use, graphic sex between two men, and graphic violence.

I took my foot entirely off the brakes because sometimes, the brakes aren't even there to be stepped on anymore. However, this means we will be driving full speed into the good things as well as the bad.

The Old Love and the New also depicts love and friendship, identity and passion, trust, hope, and unconditional support in the face of adversity.

So here's to figuring ourselves out. Here's to sharing the bad and the good, here's to pulling each other back up, here's to laughter, here's to love, and here's to you.

Don't forget your seatbelt.

A.

To my dad

1

I wanted to stay home, but Jamie asked, so I went.

Kelly's is crowded and loud, always fucking loud, and smells like a hangover.

It's not quite sunset yet. It's not started. The telly on the wall's trying to give everyone a seizure. I hear static and what sounds like the distant voices of the presenters, only that's not possible cos the mute symbol's blinking on the top right corner of the flat screen.

The tip of my shoe scrapes against the floor and taps on the counter.

'. . . splits his infinitives all over the fucking shop, but . . . Alright, Sid?'

I pull a smile from the corners of my mouth. 'Fine.'

Jamie's hands flail about when he speaks, when he gets this way, when the spark lights behind his eyes and his accent gets thicker and he's letting loose. Second or third pint?

He gives the next page a little slap and I find myself

wondering once more why he bought the fucking book in the first place.

'The man can't tell an Oxford comma from an intoxicated koala bear!'

'Maybe he's got the metaphors down,' I say.

'That wasn't a metaphor, mate,' he says.

'No?'

'Not even a little bit.'

'Well, I'm not the writer.'

He snorts. 'Neither am I, evidently.' And he takes a swig.

'What was his name again?' I ask.

He closes the book to check. 'Nathaniel Flair.'

'Please tell me that's an alias.'

'Fucking romance fucking novelist eejit pen name, for fuck's sake.'

I shrug and tip my empty glass. 'Maybe that's what you need. A pen name, I mean.'

'What I need is to write fluff.'

He's looking at the ceiling. I check, in case there's something up there, but no.

You're losing it, Robinson.

I swing my head sideways to shake the voice out.

Jamie barely registers it.

'Escapism,' he says, like he's about to puke, like the word is reaching down his throat and pulling itself out. 'People want escapism. "Sorry, Paddy, your stuff's too serious."'

'They call you that?'

'Pretty sure one of them thinks it's short for Paddington.'

'Paddington Flair. That's good, you should make a note.'

He chuckles. 'Right!' Then, with a wave in the general direction of the barman, 'Want another?'

Sand crunches in my mouth, rough and dry. I just nod. Sometimes it's safer to just nod, cos sometimes the wrong word comes out, and Jamie has to ask again, and that's just awkward for everyone.

Then the barman asks 'What can I get you?' and the whole thing comes back to bite me in the arse.

Jamie orders a Guinness, which means he's either had one too many or he's decided to steer into the skid. I order a lager – their cheapest. The barman says 'You got it,' and I see him glance at Jamie over his shoulder as he pulls the pints.

'Where's Tom?' Jamie asks.

'I told him seven,' I say.

'You told me six o'clock.'

'I told him seven.'

'Right.'

The barman trots back over. 'It's me birthday,' he tells Jamie, all flirtatious, all smitten, and slides the Guinness over.

'Is it?' Jamie says, and turns back to me. 'Too serious, my arse. Fucking ostriches, the lot of them.'

'Have we moved on from koala bears, then?'

He takes an impressive swig from his glass and his fist tightens on his lap. 'Just look at them, fucking jerking each other off!'

My body tenses with the spike of stress. The song springs out in response, mechanically, like a jack-in-the-box.

'*It's raining men . . . hallelujah, it's—*'

'Shh,' Jamie says.

'Sorry,' I say.

Wimp.

I swing my head left, trying to make it seem like I'm just tucking a strand of hair behind my ear.

Jamie sees, and asks with his eyebrows, without asking.

I tell him I need a piss and shuffle off.

Some bloke watches from behind the pages of the *Mail* as I walk past. I keep my head down until I'm out of sight and make a right through the door with the triangle character.

One of the reasons I like this place, that sign. Owner never took it down. Fuck knows, he could get into trouble for that. It's a stupid thing to do, pointless, reckless, idiotic, but you've got to admire the guy's nerve. Jamie would call it hypocrisy. That's not taking a stand, he'd say. That's a cop-out, he'd say, a small gesture to feel better without actually trying anything real. Me? I probably shouldn't be trusted to decide what's real or not.

'*Hallelujah, it's raining men, every specimen.*'

I check every stall – no one here.

'*Tall. Blond. Dark. Lean. Rough and tough and strong and mean.*'

The water from the sink scalds. I rub until my hands are red and raw, and stare at my reflection for a while. Someone's scrawled 'FUCKIN KILL YOU ALL YA CUNTS' across the mirror in black marker. I stare at that. Then I dunk my head under the tap and lap up the burning water to stave off the headache.

Back in the bar, some melodramatic fucker's belting out '*The Wild Rover*' on the stereo in a forced Dublin accent. As I approach, I catch Jamie mouthing the words, gazing at his Guinness, and I smirk.

'Nostalgic?'

'You're joking, right?'

I nod in the general direction of the barman. 'He's playing it for you.'

Jamie waves me off. 'He's not.'

But then we both look and the barman gives him a wink.

Jamie turns back to his pint. 'Fuck me.'

'Nah, you're not my type.'

This earns me a laugh and a playful nudge. I take a swig of my lager and wipe my mouth with the back of my hand.

'Anyways,' he says. 'What's new with you?'

I shrug. 'Nothing.' Then I decide to make at least a bit of an effort. 'Got a Hawaiian in my bag.'

He makes a face. 'Aw, mate, that's gross.'

'From work.'

'I'm getting chips on the way home.'

'Pizza's free.' I shrug.

'Why d'you always have to go for the weirdest shit?'

'Exotic.'

'I can't fucking stand pineapple.'

'Free pineapple,' I say.

'Getting chips,' he says.

I'm about to reply, but I don't, cos all of a sudden everyone has gone quiet. A voice has risen from the stereo.

A woman's.

She's singing '*The Wind that Shakes the Barley*'. The recording is old and it screeches and cracks and we're all holding our breath.

'*I sat within the valley green,*

I sat me with my true love.
My sad heart strove the two between,
The old love and the new love.'

The sound sweeps up and meanders down. It echoes, glides effortlessly.

My head begins to spin in time with the rise and fall. I listen for the next trill, the next deep vibration. I can almost see her, her mouth, her throat and the vocal cords inside. I can almost see the sound. It's green and earthy brown, like a tree, sort of.

Then, slowly, a guy in one of the booths raises his glass. Another follows, and another, and soon half a dozen glasses are up.

'The old for her, the new that made me
think on Ireland dearly'

I feel the prickle at the back of my neck, the tremor in my hand. My brain's getting sweaty and my mind's slipping out of its grip. If it gets away, if it gets away I won't be able to catch it again.

'While soft wind blew down the glen
And shook the golden barley.'

And as she sings, as she sings, I start again too, inside, under control. *Humidity's rising, barometer's getting low*, and the pounding beat from inside clashes, discordant, with the melodic lilting. *According to all sources, the street's the place to go.*

Jamie's fingers close around his own glass.

He makes a move.

I grab his wrist.

Don't.

He releases the glass and I release his wrist and I'm starting to hum out loud, *it's raining men, hallelujah, it's raining men*, but I'm already slipping away.

'Jamie, let's go, mate,' I whisper, but it's too late.

'Alright, that's quite enough now, gentlemen!'

They're in the doorway, three of them – always three, three by three. I spot the batons and guns at their hips. They notice me noticing.

The leader – always a leader – sighs and gives us the disapproving head shake.

The barman pops the record out and he's laughing as he addresses us. 'Oh come on, fellas! Who called 'em?'

Everyone mumbles.

'Did you call 'em, darlin'?'

Jamie chuckles into his beer. 'Right, that sounds like me.'

I try to kick him under the counter, miss, and my foot slams against the hardwood. I bite the inside of my cheek for a while.

'I didn't mean offence with those Irish tunes, ya know?' says the barman.

'I know you didn't,' Jamie says.

'Nobody called us, Reg, we just happened to walk by.'

Well that's fucking likely. Bloke in the corner's still reading the *Mail* like nothing's going on.

'Alright, this establishment is going to close down for the evening, if everyone would please step out.'

'Come on, now! Not like I'm hurtin' anyone, eh?'

'You know I would, mate, but it's your third in three months. I let you off again and I'm looking at suspension time. You have to help me out here.'

For a second Reg seems about to protest again, but the look in the officer's eyes shoves the words right back down his throat.

He turns to us. 'Sorry, fellas . . .'

And that does it. The crowd breaks into grunts of disappointment. The guys all stumble to their feet. One of them trips and nearly spills his pint down Jamie's back.

They usher us out with emphatic waves and a tad more pushing than strictly necessary – someone's hip against mine, a raspy voice in my ear.

Reg spews a constant stream of apologies. 'Sorry, sorry! That's the way it goes, eh, lads? Why don't you go ahead and keep the glass, Frankie. Just bring it back round tomorrow, alright?'

Tomorrow. I guess that's hope for you.

As they escort him away, I watch his foot catch on the threshold, his fingers stroke the frame of the door. His mouth is still smiling; the rest of his face is not.

Some fucker's pissing his beer on a lamppost outside. Some people have no sense of decorum.

I reach into my jacket for a fag. Jamie shoots me that look with the eyebrows and the tongue just barely visible between his teeth, ready to argue. Smoking kills, I get it, Jamie, I really do. But then again, I light up and take a drag and hold the smoke there for a while, and love every second of it. My lungs expand. My body's busy, and it feels fucking brilliant. Jamie looks like he might start. He looks like he might, but then he doesn't.

'Home, then?' he says, instead.

I exhale smoke into the cold. It sort of hangs there in front of us and I swear there's a stale, Nathaniel

Flair-tier metaphor in there somewhere. 'The address is starting.'

'Fuck the address,' he says.

'Fuck the address,' I mirror.

Here's a thought. We could have stayed home and avoided the whole ordeal altogether.

We make our way through the streets.

Stale feels about right. Like some sort of ironically ill-organised God hit pause and lost the remote. The twat's probably halfway under the sofa looking for it right about now. I hope he chokes on the dust.

An old church collapsed in Marylebone, last winter. Killed twelve people. It was all over the news for a week, to ensure everyone had a chance to display appropriate degrees of outrage. Now everyone's clean forgotten about it and some of the city's oldest buildings are lined with scaffoldings, as if it'll hold the crumbling pieces together.

Langley's younger, twenty-five-years-ago voice blares out from the Tower, from every pub door, from every shop window. It sounds like the wailing of an emo teen who thinks their violin rendition of '*Stairway to Heaven*' is just transcendent. The man's got precisely the amount of flamboyance needed for politics, you have to give him that.

Jamie plugs his ears with his fingers every time we pass a speaker.

'*. . . our comrades, our equals and a vibrant segment of our society . . .*'

I was too young to remember of course, but it's been everywhere since. On the radio, on the telly, in the newspapers. Quotes from it on huge patriotic billboards, slapped against the Union's red, white and blue, every fucking month at sundown, year after year, until you find yourself mouthing the words along with it and it's too late to develop an opinion.

'. . . *a question of health and safety . . . '*

I've seen it. A delivery job means I get a sneak peek inside people's homes. After a few weeks of painful boredom, you have to either quit or warp it into a bit of a hobby. A sick, twisted, voyeuristic hobby. Quitting was not a viable option.

As we cruise by, I casually check them out through the windows. Jamie calls it the 'zombie menagerie'. Me? Well, I'm not sure what menagerie means, but I'll tell you one thing: the zombie part is hard to dispute.

You've got your cheap beer and dirty sweatpants types who treat it like it's Wimbledon, your 'religious experience' types, holding hands on the floor with lit candles and I swear to God I once saw a pentagram. Then you've got those who actually know. The old ones, nursing their scotch on the rocks, staring at their framed pictures. You recognise them as soon as they open with the 'my boy', the admittedly fantastic tips. Address night is a shift not everyone is willing to cover.

'. . . *priority is, and has always been, to protect the citizens of our country. God save the King.'*

Applause and cheers from back then – some of it pre-recorded. The fuckers bought into it. They clapped and whooped and whistled like Langley was a fucking war hero, ready to pull them out of the massive shit they'd stumbled into. Jamie's dad probably stood in that crowd. My dad sat at home, uninvolved, content to let it happen. I suppose the apple didn't fall too far from the spineless, self-serving coward.

'Sid!' Jamie calls.

'What?'

He hums a few notes.

'Was I?'

He's not allowed to make fun of me for it. Not that he would. Tom would, likely enough, but what Jamie does is slap his arm around my shoulder and leave it there until I've become completely hyperaware and the heat and pressure are nearing on too much.

'Could you—' I start.

'You hear that?'

Two blokes are shouting at each other down St Anne's Court.

Jamie just dives in before I have time to say 'Don't just dive in.'

The shouting gets louder as we approach, and the content more colourful. There's a bike on its side with the headlight on and a minivan that's seen better days. The drivers spit at each other, puffing up their chests, and we're pretty much one ice cream cone away from a day at the zoo.

I slow down a bit.

Jamie pulls out his voice recorder, clicks it on, and repeats evenly. 'Suck on my gangrenous, flaky cock, you gigantic pile of skunk diarrhoea.'

'Oi!' I whisper. 'You want a Darwin award with that death wish?'

'Please. These wankers are all bark and no bite.'

'So are you!'

He gives me the once-over. 'I could take you, twiggy.'

'Bark bark.'

The corner of his mouth lifts first, then the full smile.

And just when I'm daring myself to smile back, a patrol swings into the alley, three of them, always three, and the leader, always a leader, calls out at the fighting blokes. 'Oi! Break it up, gentlemen!'

Jamie feels me tense up and leans in. 'Keep walking, they won't stop us.'

'Twenty quid, they will.'

'You have twenty quid?'

'Jamie . . .'

He touches my arm. 'Don't hum.'

We're almost clear of the street when one of them detaches from the group. 'Gentlemen! Lovely evening for a stroll, isn't it? Can I see your IDs?'

My hand twitches on my passport.

Jamie's faster. Front pocket of his messenger bag, pulls it out in one swift motion.

'Irish, eh?' the man asks.

Jamie likes to make things worse for himself. 'Aye,' he says, pointedly.

'How long you been on the mainland?'

'Pardon?'

'How long have you—'

'Ten years. I have a visa.'

The man flips through the pages and unfolds the tiny square of paper. 'Alright. Enjoy your stay, Mr Hayes.'

And then it's my turn, and already they're eyeing me up and down. 'And where are you from?'

Look, I keep things quiet. I don't mind much, it's always been the deal. Jamie's teeth, however, can be heard grinding all the way to Scotland.

I hand out the passport and the officer sniffs. 'Manchester?'

'Yes.'

'You don't sound like you're from Manchester . . .' He glances down at the name. '. . . Sidney.'

I'm not sure what answer he's looking for, there, so I just pick one at random. 'Thanks.'

Perfect. I'm staring somewhere between his nipples.

'You're welcome.' He slaps the passport back against my chest and I just barely manage to grab it before it slides to the ground. 'Have a nice evening.'

The boots stomp past. Jamie chuckles once they're gone, as if we just got away with mischief. 'Alright?'

'Yeah.'

'Breathe.'

I light another cigarette.

Jamie casually yanks it away and flicks it to the pavement. 'How about air, instead? Fucking eejit.'

'Dickhead.'

'Gobshite.'

'Wanker.'

He holds up the recorder and presses play. 'Suck on my gangrenous, flaky cock, you gigantic pile of skunk diarrhoea.'

I laugh.

He laughs.

We both sigh.

'You owe me twenty quid,' I say.

It takes Jamie exactly five words and a grin, that grin, to convince the bloke mopping up the chippy to take our order and then we're sat under flickering neon lights, sniffing against the temperature change.

'I'm starved,' Jamie says.

'Well, we could be home right now.'

'We could be, if you'd bring back normal pizza.'

'Why did you want to come out tonight?'

He shoves an elbow on the table to hold up his head. 'I don't know. I guess . . . I don't know.'

A kid in a hoodie paces out front like he'd come in if only he had more than a quid in the pocket of his ripped jeans. The condensation rises from his mouth and I think that maybe he'll die out there in the cold. Then he shivers and I avert my eyes and think of my dad.

'You know why they call us "gentlemen", right?' Jamie says.

'Why's that?'

'It's the "gentle" in there. They use it to reinforce the idea that we're to remain docile. Well-fucking-behaved.'

'That's a bit far-fetched, isn't it?'

He picks up the chips and pours half a bottle of vinegar on them, as if that's any better than pineapple on a pizza. 'Word choice matters, Sid. Come on.'

The mid-October chill hits as we step down onto the street, the kind that seems manageable right up until you're tired. And it's been a long day, what with the double shift.

The sounds bounce off the walls and ricochet straight into my skull like bullets. Blaring car horns and sirens. Whistling wind. Voices. I pull my hood up and wish I'd brought earphones.

'Want one?'

That's when it happens. When Jamie's got his hand

out and he's holding the bag loosely. That's when the chips are there, and suddenly they're not, and I catch a glimpse of hooded silhouette disappearing around the corner.

'Shit!' I say.

Jamie doesn't say anything. He sprints after the kid.

'Shit,' I say again, and curse a couple more times as I run after him even though I can barely pull in enough air to keep up.

Fuck the wanker who sold me that first packet of cigarettes. Fuck me for buying it with Dad's loose change like the stupid sheep I am. And fuck Jamie for running after a hungry kid as if this is some sort of mad action flick. Fucking drama queen, seriously.

Twenty years. That's about how long we're running, no kidding. That kid has some legs on him and an impressive pair of lungs. I can't make out Jamie's shouting over the buzzing in my ears. My brain's gone numb but some other bloke must be in charge of the body cos somehow I'm managing not to fall over.

I slam into Jamie's back after a sharp right turn. 'Just eat . . . the fucking . . . pizza. Jesus Christ, I'm dying.'

Jamie's doubled over too, but we've got him. The boy's cowering in the dead-end he ran into, with his back against the bins and his hood pulled low over his face.

'Look, mate, if you're that hungry I'll buy you something, just fucking ask.'

The kid holds out the paper bag, looking away, bracing himself. Does he think we'll hurt him? Does he think we'll get violent over a three-quid bag of greasy chips?

Jamie doesn't reach out for it. He squints. 'How old are you?'

Too young, I think, and something's not right. I squint too, angle my head to see beneath the hood, and in a flash of movement, the boy chucks the bag at Jamie and tries to dash past us.

Jamie grabs him and wrestles him back into the corner, onto the pavement, what is he doing? The kid elbows him in the stomach as he flails about. It's like watching a fly stuck in a web and Jamie's the spider, hunched over him, fangs out, what is he doing?

'Let him go,' I tell him.

My phone has found its way to my hand and I'm not sure whether to turn on the camera or dial 999.

'No!' the boy shouts, and something's not right, and it takes me a second to realise the voice came from him.

Jamie yanks the hood off and all at once the struggle dies down. They pant and stare at each other.

'Do you know him?' I say.

Too young, I think. Fifteen? He couldn't be.

'Please,' the boy says.

'How?' Jamie says. 'How did you—'

'Please.'

Jamie nods. 'Sid, put the phone away.' He stumbles back up and helps the boy to his feet, the boy, something wrong with the boy.

I mumble. 'Is he okay?'

'She's bleeding,' Jamie says.

'What?'

'Do you have a tissue?'

'What did you say?'

He catches my eyes. His brain's ahead of his mouth again, and ahead of mine. 'Sid,' he says. Then, lowering his voice, 'She's a woman.'

When I look at the boy again, I see it. There it is. It's been seen. It can't be unseen. She's a woman. I recoil, in fear, mostly. 'You touched her,' I tell Jamie. 'You touched her.'

'I don't think she's ill.'

'No, but . . . how can you know, you can't know, and you t— you touched . . .'

'She's fine! Look at her!'

'N-no, I don't, I don't want . . .'

He searches his pockets, then his bag, and pulls out a crumpled tissue. 'Here. It's clean. I'm pretty sure. Yeah, it's clean. Sorry about that.'

The boy pushes the tissue against his bloody nose. 'Thank you.'

'Come on. It's cold. We'll get you something to eat.'

He sniffs. No, she. She sniffs. 'Are you sure?'

Jamie's eyes soften. He's absolutely transfixed and I'm almost certain I don't like it.

And suddenly, Dan Lucas starts belting '*Hot Stuff*' and all three of us jump out of our skins.

'My phone,' I say.

Jamie laughs. 'Fuck me, that was some timing.'

Caller ID: Tom.

'Just reject it,' Jamie says.

I stare at him for a while, and accept the call. 'Yeah?'

Tom's voice slices through the situation like Earth pulling us back from whatever fucking twilight zone we were in. 'Where the bloody hell have you been?'

'Right. I, uh . . . pub closed down.'

'I know it closed down, hophead, I'm there. Had to get the information from Patrick. And you know I do not enjoy talking to that man.'

Jamie starts talking to the woman under his breath.

I step away. 'We meant to call you, it's just . . . we, uh, we went home. Jamie wanted to hear the address so . . .'

'Oh, for Christ's sake. Are you home now? I was hoping to get smashed.'

'We're . . .' I glance over at the woman in the hoodie, and Jamie standing too close to her. 'Yeah, we're home.'

'I'll come get you.'

'No! No, um . . .'

A puff of condensation rises from her mouth and mingles with Jamie's own breath. *Barometer's getting low.* I bring my hand up to cover my face.

'Tom?' I say, into the phone. 'I'll meet you. Where are you?'

Jamie's head snaps up.

'There's this other bar, couple of streets down,' Tom says. 'Mellow atmosphere.'

'Sounds good.'

'You're going?' Jamie asks, as I hang up.

'I need a drink.'

'You're not supposed to be drinking.'

This is what he says. What he means, though, is 'What are you doing? Don't leave me now.'

I shrug, and what I mean is 'I'm sorry. I can't.'

2

Mellow atmosphere apparently translates to purple lighting and a crowd of blokes looking for a shag to go with their drink. It's been two minutes and already Tom's turned down three candidates, the handsome git. Number four – skinny, dark hair, bit of an emo vibe – is eyeing us from the other end of the counter. Tom's pretending not to notice, but he's watching, weighing the pros and cons.

'So? What happened at the usual place?' he asks.

I'm downing my second shot of cheap booze.

'Hophead?'

'Hmm?'

'What happened at Kelly's?'

I wave for another shot. 'Guy played inappropriate music. There was a snitch in there. They took the barman in for questioning.'

'Listen to yourself. "A snitch".'

I shrug. 'Well, there was.'

'Sure, there was.'

'Fuck you.'

He takes a sip of whatever fancy wine he's got. I down half my pint and the third shot.

'What kind of inappropriate music?'

I hum a bar or two and a few heads turn.

Tom looks around and draws his stool closer to mine. His warm breath hits the side of my face. 'How was it, then?'

'Are you wearing a fucking waistcoat?' I ask.

'The voice, hophead, go on! Was it beautiful?'

'Fuck off. I'm not discussing this here.'

'Come on, hophead, give me something! What, you don't like me anymore?'

I sigh.

'Fine,' he says. 'Don't tell me. I don't care.'

He turns back to his drink. I suppose this should be awkward, but I'm getting pleasantly buzzed and concentrating hard on the placement of my tongue.

My phone chimes. Text from Jamie. '*Taking him home for the night.*'

Not him. Her. He's taking her home, to our home, into our home, taking her home for the night *cos tonight for the first time, just about half past ten, for the first time in history, it's gonna start rainin—*

'Ah, I see.' Tom's looking over my shoulder.

I shove the phone back into my pocket but it's too late. 'What?'

'I see why you didn't want me to come to your place. Funny, that. I always had Jamie pegged for one of those guys.'

'What's that supposed to mean?'

'You know, just one of those "not interested" guys.

Well, good for him!'

My blood's doing something inexplicably funky. Tom's face is getting a smidge blurry, which I'm thankful for at the minute.

Meanwhile Number Four seems to have finally worked up the nerve to walk over.

'Hi,' says Number Four.

'Hi,' says Tom.

'Yeah,' I say.

Number Four smooths down a stray lock of hair more or less successfully, turns to me and smiles a shy smile. The penny drops. This guy's not Number Four.

'Oh,' I say.

'Fancy nipping out for a bit?'

He sounds like he's heard the line in a film and now he's repeating it, only it doesn't have quite the same ring now as it did then. A slight blush rises to his cheeks as he rests his hand on my knee. I'd say he means business, but I'm not sure he knows exactly what the business is.

I glance sideways at Tom. He's shocked that I pulled. Shocked that someone chose me when he's sitting there looking all gorgeous and blurry.

I blink the scene back into focus.

Not-Number-Four searches my face for a hint, thin lips stretched into a teasing smile, hand inching its way up my thigh. He's not half bad at this game. I catch myself looking him up and down, assessing, like Tom does, and entertaining the idea. An endearing little crease has appeared between his eyebrows. I grin at him. The shots and pints are hitting pretty hard, if I'm honest.

I shouldn't, really. It's a bad idea. I should go back

home and make sure Jamie's okay. But then he palms at my groin and now I'm stiffening in my bootcuts. Fuck's sake. I close my eyes and let out a shaky sigh.

'What do you say?' he asks.

And as much as it pains me to admit it, what I say is, 'Your place. Let's go.'

After a quick 'See ya' in Tom's direction, and a 'Have fun then' in response, Not-Number-Four grabs my hand and we're out.

He pulls me down the street and I think we're off to his flat but then he's pushing me into a side alley and the next thing I know his tongue is in my mouth. I grab the back of his head with one hand, his arse with the other, and take control.

'Colin,' he says.

'Sid,' I say.

'Pleasure,' he says, fumbling with my fly and sinking to his knees.

I let it happen for a while. I focus on the sensation, the wetness, the heat. I moan a bit, gasp a bit, but this is not going to cut it. Not that it would be my first blowjob at the back of a club, by any means, but tonight I need an all-nighter. I need a safe place. I need a roof.

I pull his hair. 'Wait, wait, wait.'

He springs back up and mumbles an apology, his well-rehearsed air of confidence crumbling like a week-old biscuit.

'Your place,' I say.

His pride has taken a hit. He's staring down at his DMs. I reach for his shoulder. What I want to do is reach for his cock but what I do is reach for his shoulder, like I'm his fucking boyfriend or something. I work the charm. I stroke his neck, look deep into his eyes, drop my voice a bit. 'Not in the street, come on. We've got all night, yeah? Your place.'

And there's the half smile again. I'm no better than Tom.

The flat is large. Larger than ours.

'You have a flatmate?'

'No. He left.'

He makes it sound like there's more to it. I kind of want to ask, but I don't because it's really none of my business, and soon we're kissing again, sloppy, drunk, shedding our clothes as he pulls me towards his bedroom and onto his bed. When I start getting serious about it, though, something like fear flickers in his eyes. I wonder if this is his first time. I ask if he wants me to stop and he says no.

We fuck. I think it's his first time. We don't look at each other, we don't talk beyond the usual 'Fuck' and 'Is that good?' and 'Oh God'. I fuck him from behind, thinking about something else, and then not thinking at all. It's definitely his first time.

A few minutes after, we're panting next to each other. He came hard and fast, I'd barely even touched him. Took me forever to manage a mediocre finish. Not the boy's fault, mind you.

I cough.

He chuckles.

Then he starts crying. I mean really crying. Tears come pouring out of his eyes. His chest stutters up and down. I watch him gasp and sniffle. Fuck, he's young.

I roll onto my side and put my hand on my arm.

It doesn't help. He opens his mouth like he wants to say something, but the air won't stay in his lungs long enough to form words. So instead he just continues to cry and cry until I start worrying that we might both drown. Eventually I roll onto my back again and look at the ceiling. It's cracked and damp. Neighbour's shower must be leaking.

The next thing I know, I'm wincing and turning away from the sun. Nodded off, I suppose. I yawn and start to stretch and notice a warm weight on my hand.

Colin's still lying next to me. His hand is over mine, his fingers interlaced with mine. Like I'm his fucking boyfriend. He's fast asleep. Young Colin, with his eye sockets all red from the crying. The tears have left trails across his cheeks. He seems peaceful enough now, although his breath still hitches every now and then. I consider leaving, just like that, without waking him. Then I consider not leaving, and settle on that.

What time is it? What day is it? Sunday? I think it's Sunday. Colin shifts on the mattress. His head lolls onto his shoulder and he lets out a little groan. It's cute. I think of waking him up and fucking him again, but now it feels almost indecent. Like an old man fucking a teenager, even though I can't possibly be more than three years his senior.

I badly need a smoke.

I untangle my fingers from Colin's, carefully. I pad over to my jacket, naked, and fish out the packet of fags from one of the pockets and the lighter from the other. I bring the cigarette up to my lips and the lighter up to the cigarette.

'You leaving?' Colin's propped himself up on his elbows.

'No. No, I just . . .' I show him the cigarette. 'Sorry, do you mind?'

He shakes his head.

'Do you want one?'

'No, ta.'

I pull on the curtain a bit, open the window and sit on the ledge. People only have to look up to feast their eyes on my nudity, but really I don't give a flying fuck. In the street below, they're all going about their morning errands, unaware that everything's changed.

'I'm sorry about last night,' says Colin.

I smile. 'It's alright, don't mention it.'

'I honestly don't know what came over me.'

'No worries.'

He nods thank you, gets up and starts searching the room for his clothes. I watch his pale arse as he bends down. Boxers at the foot of the bed. Black skinny jeans halfway under the dresser. He scratches his head. I chuckle and a puff of smoke rises from my mouth.

'Hallway,' I say.

He disappears into the hallway and reappears with his t-shirt. I watch him get dressed. Layer by layer, he becomes Not-Number-Four from the bar again. Except for the ruffled hair and the puffy eyes. Except for the fact that I know, now, that he's not that guy. I know he's Colin, who cries his heart out in the middle of the night. Colin, who doesn't know what came over him.

He puts on the final layer, the smile, and leaves again. When he comes back, I've slipped into my own clothes. He hands me one of the two mugs he's carrying. Instant coffee. Disgusting stuff.

I stub out the cigarette, fish into my back pocket and pop a pill in my mouth.

'What's that?' he asks.

'Antipsychotics.'

'What's it for?'

'Stuff.'

That shuts him up for a while. We sip coffee in silence. I notice he's not sitting down.

'Did I hurt you?' I say.

'What?'

'Last night. Did it hurt you?'

'No,' he lies.

I nod and he shuffles about awkwardly and this is getting really uncomfortable so I down the coffee and stand up.

'I should go.'

'Stay for breakfast?'

'Can't,' I lie. 'Work.'

'Oh.'

He's disappointed. I feel a pang of guilt, but it's not enough to keep me from putting my socks and shoes back on and heading for the door. I have to see Jamie now because I'm a selfish wanker and I shouldn't have fucked off last night.

'Wait!' Colin runs up to me. He takes my hand and slips a piece of paper into my palm. 'My number. Call me.'

He leans up and kisses me. He tastes of salty tears and weak coffee. His number joins the meds in my pocket but I'm never going to use it.

I'm dripping on the doormat.

The key shakes in my hand, and it could be the cold seeping through my wet clothes, it could be the fucking tardive dyskinesia finally catching up to me, but somehow I doubt it. I have to bring my second hand in as backup.

Jamie's asleep on the settee, curled up with his arm over his face. Shielding himself.

Something twists in my gut. I kneel down and let my hand hover just above his chest. I hold my breath until I see the gap closing, until I feel his shirt brush against my palm.

'What are you doing?'

My stomach jumps up to my mouth, and I jump to my feet.

She stands by Jamie's room, halfway hidden in the dark. There are no monsters, pet, go back to bed. There are no monsters. Without thinking, I move between her and the sofa.

'What are you doing?' she asks.

Her voice is odd, low, far back in her throat, like she's been training herself to talk deeper.

'He has sleep apnoea,' I say.

She tilts her head to the side like a bird.

I catch myself looking at her body, and there must be some sort of ancient rule about that, but it seems rules went out the window, so there you go. Not that this type of body is entirely new to me. Not that I'm completely uneducated.

Instead of the dirty hoodie, she's wearing one of Jamie's shirts. It hangs loosely on her shoulders, narrow shoulders, she didn't seem that frail last night, last night, when I fucked off and left Jamie alone with her, *with it*, with her.

'What, uh . . . what's your name?' I try.

Her head tilts to the other side.

The breath catches in my throat. The thoughts catch in my brain and it won't untangle, it's stuck, I'm stuck.

The low voice sounds again. 'Sid?'

I shudder. 'Yeah.'

She extends her hand. 'Olivia.'

I look at the hand, dirt under the fingernails, she bites her nails, like Jamie. Then I look at her face, then at the hand again, and she takes it away before I have time to decide whether or not it's safe to touch her.

'Are you sick?'

She shakes her head and I catch a glimpse of something that looks like blood on the side of her neck.

'Are you sure?'

Nod.

Nil by mouth, do not touch, keep out of children's reach.

'Where did you come from?' I ask.

She doesn't say anything. She just stares with those giant eyes like she can see through my clothes, like she can see through my skin and into my bones.

'How are you not dead? Did you escape?'

She steps back and I step forward.

Cos tonight for the first time

'Do they know you've escaped?' I ask. 'Are they looking for you? Say something!'

'No, they're not.'

'Were you alone? Did you escape alone?'

'No!'

'Who else was with you, where is she?'

Her eyes narrow just above my left shoulder and I turn. And I can't believe I just fell for such a simple trick. I run after her into Jamie's room. She's already got the window halfway open and her leg over the ledge.

'Wait!'

Suddenly Jamie's hand closes around her arm and pulls her back inside.

Just about half past ten

She backs away into the corner, eyes on the door, eyes on the window, eyes on the door again.

'I'm sorry!' Jamie says. 'I'm sorry, but please wait.' Then, to me, 'What did you do?'

His voice goes up and down like it's coming from a faulty radio. Something is crumbling inside my skull and I think it's my brain, I think it's my brain falling apart. I clasp the sides of my head, keep it together, hold it together, don't let it fall to pieces.

For the first time in history

The hair at my temples is damp with rain and sweat.

For the first time in history

It's gonna start . . .

'. . . raining men! It's raining men! Hallelujah, it's raining men!'

'Ah, shit.'

'I'm gonna go out t-t-to run and, and . . .'

'What's happening?' she asks.

'Sid, stay with me, mate.'

'Run and, run and l-let . . .' My voice barely in control, barely mine, off-key, keep going, keep going.

'L-let myself get . . . absolutely soaking wet!'

'What's the matter with him?'

'Just give us a minute.'

The sound of her voice drills into my head, what's the matter with him, what's the matter, what's happening, I need to scream, I'm screaming.

'What's the m—'

'Just shut up for a second, can't you see you're making it worse!'

I feel myself being dragged a few steps. The room spins horribly. I move my feet, disoriented, not sure where the floor is.

'Don't, don't touch me!' I say, and immediately cling to him, and he pulls me into a hug.

And then he's singing. 'It's raining men. Hallelujah, it's raining men. Every specimen.'

'T-tall, blond, dark, lean.'

He's singing louder. 'Rough and tough and strong and mean!'

'It's raining men! Hallelujah it's raining men!'

'Amen!'

My heart thrashes in my ribcage, but I'm breathing and the fog starts to roll back.

Jamie hushes, strokes my back, holds me up.

'I'm gonna go out to run and let myself get . . .'

'. . . absolutely fucking wet!'

'Soaking,' I say.

'What?' he says.

'It's soaking wet, not fucking wet.'

'Oh, soak off.'

I snort with laughter and collapse on the bed, like I've run a marathon.

Jamie turns and stops in his tracks. 'Fuck me.'

'What?'

'She's gone.'

We both run to the window, just in time to see her halfway down the fire escape.

'Fuck's sake!' He strides out of the room. 'Sid, you coming or what?'

'Where?'

'What do you mean where? Down! We're getting her back here, come on!'

'Wait.'

'What?'

'It's not our problem anymore,' I say.

He freezes and looks at me like he can't believe I just said that. To be quite honest, I can't believe I just said that.

'Thanks very much, Sid. Well done.'

The front door slams behind him.

Fuck.

I run after him, tripping over my feet, and catch him on the second floor.

'Jamie, wait!' He doesn't. 'It's not my f—'

'It is! It's your fault! You're scaring h . . . im!' He corrects himself just in time as we run past the neighbour, giggling in his bright-yellow Hawaiian shirt.

'Ooh, having a little fight, are we?'

'Piss off, Gettleman!' I say.

I hear him giggle some more behind us.

And we're outside.

'What now?'

Jamie inhales like he's about to dive into deep water, and walks up to a middle-aged man in a blue suit. 'Excuse me, sir?'

The man doesn't even spare him a glance. Jamie

curses under his breath and walks up to another guy.

'Excuse me, sir?'

The guy stops and grins. He looks a bit of a hippy.

'Have you seen a young bloke come out of here? Short blond hair, Led Zep shirt, about five-seven?'

'Sorry, man,' says the guy, and moves on.

I grab Jamie's arm and pull him aside just as he's about to stop someone else.

'What the fuck are you doing?'

He shakes me off. 'Do you have a better idea?'

Do you?

I let him go.

'No, I'm afraid I haven't seen anyone fitting that description,' says the next guy, old, dapper, newspaper under his arm. 'Why? Have you lost someone?'

I tense up but Jamie doesn't miss a beat.

'My cousin. We had a fight and he ran away.'

The man sniffs and waves dismissively. 'Give the young man some space, he'll be back.'

'Don't patronise me, you English c—'

I pull him away again. 'Whoa, Jamie, Jamie, come on. Let's move on.'

He runs down the street, checking in random alleyways.

I call after him. 'Stop that!'

'Fuck off!'

'It's over.'

'Fuck off, Sid!'

And all at once, he seems to deflate and sinks to the pavement. I sigh. Thank fuck.

As I walk up to him, though, my eye catches some movement to my left, in a dead-end behind a deli. And sure enough, there she is.

I look at Jamie, curled up with his legs folded against his chest and his face buried in his arms. If there ever was a battle about this, I just lost.

'Here,' I say.

'What?'

'Here.' I nod to my left.

And just like that he's on his feet again, mouth stretching into a smile, that smile.

She jumps up at the sound of our footsteps, it's like she's on springs. Her chest heaves, fast, her eyes dart left and right for an escape plan.

Jamie raises both hands in surrender. 'Please don't. Don't run. Please?'

Her bony face turns on me and my blood runs cold. *The street's the place to go*, keep it together, *let myself get absolutely soaking wet*, come on, breathe.

Jamie reaches back and touches my shoulder. 'I know, that was a bit scary and . . . possibly confusing,' he tells her. 'Sid sometimes has episodes like that. You get used to it. And it's not your fault.'

My fingernails dig into my palms.

'He's not okay with it,' she says.

She's keeping an eye on me, like I might suddenly pounce and devour her.

'He is,' says Jamie. 'He's okay with it. Right, Sid?'

I grit my teeth and nod. At the moment, it's the best I can do.

'He'll call them,' she says.

'He won't. I can promise you that. Sid's a good guy.'

My fists loosen a bit, but the voice snickers in my left ear.

She bites her lower lip. 'It's dangerous.'

'Look,' Jamie says. 'However dangerous you think

it might be with us, it's going to be ten times worse out here on your own.'

'It's dangerous for you.'

Something softens in Jamie's eyes, like he's surprised and touched, and when he speaks again, his voice is softer as well. 'You need help. Come back with us.'

He extends his hand and for a moment, it seems like she's about to run again. She takes his hand. She reaches with her bony fingers and touches him and I can almost see the illness spreading to him.

'Alright,' he says. 'We have to cover you up a bit more.'

He looks around. He's still holding her hand. Why is he still holding her hand?

The voice laughs harder.

'Sid, give me your jacket.'

Oh, come on.

'Come on, Sid, please.'

Well, if you're going to say please.

I'm in danger of being the pettiest person in the world here, so I take the jacket off and hand it to him. It's still damp. She slips it on. I'll have to throw the fucking thing out.

'Right. We're walking straight to the building, straight up to the flat. Don't look around too much. Pretend we're having a conversation. If anyone tries to talk to us, just . . . you know, nobody will try to talk to us. It's fine.'

It's fine, my arse. Jamie talk for 'I am scared out of my mind'. He's smiling. If that's not a sign that he's losing his shit, I don't know what is.

'Let's go,' he says.

Out on Wardour again. People pass by us, again and again.

Someone brushes against my shoulder. The hair rises at the back of my neck.

Jamie squeezes my arm, how did he notice this, and leans in close. 'Don't run.' Don't run, don't run, keep it together, *soaking wet, absolutely soaking wet*.

And into the building.

Up the stairs.

In the apartment.

I lock the door and then we're just standing awkwardly in the living room.

Olivia shivers in my jacket.

'Would you like a change of clothes?' Jamie asks. 'Warm yourself up a bit?'

'Thank you.'

As he goes around getting the clothes and showing her the bathroom and chattering all over the place, I let myself fall on the settee, heart still pounding, tremor in my right arm. Home.

Home.

Broken images and sounds from Manchester pop into my mind. Usually, when I think of Manchester, it's only Dad moping around the house or coming back pissed from the pub and then moping around the house.

Today, though, the memories are different.

Dad is tucking me in. He may be drunk, but either he's hiding it well or I'm just not old enough to notice yet. He's talking to me but the words don't touch my mind. I'm already half-asleep, lulled by the familiar deep, slightly throaty voice, the one that, years later, twisted into the voice in my head.

Then there's a musical laughter. Where it comes from, I don't know. Maybe something from the playground.

Then I'm a bit older. It's late summer and I'm sitting by the river with Stuart. This would be just before we moved south. My first crush, Stuart. A childish sort of love that I didn't fully comprehend. He was a bright boy, adventurous, trousers perpetually dirty and ripped at the knees.

I lie down and tune into the scene. For something that happened a good twenty years ago, it's quite clear. There's the smell of hot tarmac in the air. Our feet dangling over the water. His blue and white t-shirt. The sunset giving an almost auburn shine to his hair. Even his worried, mildly disgusted tone when he says, 'So you'll be going to school there and that?' I tell him that yes, I will. 'Well, don't let them order you around, yeah?' I tell him that no, I won't. Stuart taps his worn shoe against mine. I choose to assume that this is his way of expressing affection, and reciprocate.

Then something starts to disturb the picture. Distantly, as if it's being brought in by a very slow tide, I become aware of a voice, but not the usual one. It's a woman, singing some kind of lullaby in a language I don't know. For a moment, I struggle to get my mind to grasp it, but it's unwilling to step forward. It remains just out of reach, so that I can't quite place it. With a thrill, I start wondering if the language could be Urdu, if it could be some vague recollection of my mother. Trying to relax and let it come to me, I bring my thoughts to my breathing. I just need to get into the mindset. I'm two or three years old. My mother is there. Mum. She's singing to me, it's probably bedtime.

Just as the memory oscillates on the horizon, the thoughts of breathing begin to drag along thoughts of my body. Suddenly, brutally, I'm in Soho – my confused, tired, mentally ill, twenty-seven-year-old self.

I lie still for a while, a little bit thrown and a little bit lost. A cold, wet tickle runs from the corner of my right eye to my ear. I jerk upright, swing my legs over the edge of the sofa and promptly wipe the tear with the back of my hand.

'Fuck's sake,' I mumble, pinching the bridge of my nose.

'You okay, mate?'

'Probably.'

'She's showering.' Jamie drops down next to me. 'She fell asleep instantly last night. We barely made it up the stairs, she went straight for the sofa and started snoring. I carried her to the third bedroom. I just, I wanted her to have an actual bed, you know?'

'I guess.'

He laughs. 'Jesus, Sid. Can you believe it?'

No, Jamie, no, I don't believe it, I will never believe it, in fact there's no telling when I'll be waking up in the hospital again with restraints around my wrists.

Any minute now.

Any minute now, crazy.

'So,' I say. 'What's the plan, then?'

'We keep her here until—'

'Until we get caught.'

'Exactly.'

He chuckles. I suppose something about the whole ordeal must be funny. I decide to chuckle too, on the off chance I'm missing something.

'We have to tell people,' he says.

'Are you high?'

'Don't you think people should know?'

Something's about to slip out, something bad, and I know it's bad, and I don't care. 'Not necessarily.'

Jamie lets out a sharp laugh. It sends a jolt of anger into my chest.

'Don't do that,' I say. 'Don't try to make out like I'm being stupid or something.'

He sighs. 'I don't . . . I'm not, but come on! You have to see this changes everything. How can you—'

'What do you think is going to happen? Civil war, fires all around the city, storming Parliament? This isn't one of your stories! This? This is "two idiots disappear into a police station never to be seen again"! Please don't let that be us!'

'They are lying to us!'

'We know they're lying to us!'

'Then why is nobody doing anything about it?'

He looks like he's about to cry out of sheer frustration. I'm out of arguments. I start rubbing my temples and wishing I had a cigarette. There's a light behind his eyes that I haven't seen in years.

'You know what they'll do to us if we get caught?' I ask.

'I do.'

'And you're okay with that?'

He blinks. 'Yes.'

He may as well have kicked me in the solar plexus. I might throw up.

'Okay,' I say, and it comes out croaky.

'Okay?'

'Okay.' Croaky again.

He smiles. 'Brilliant, mate. We're doing the right thing.'

I shove him. He shoves me back. And we both sigh.

'Did you not come home last night?' he asks.

Suddenly Colin's moaning in my ear again.

'I, uh . . . no.'

He knows what this means. It's not the first time. I'm not one of those guys who took a vow of celibacy after the quarantine and then went off to buy a pet to compensate. I don't know how a dog can compensate for that, and I sure as shit don't want to know. Obviously, there are some places, online places, where you can get illegal videos if you're desperate enough. Not worth the risk, if you ask me.

'Who was the guy?' He raises an eyebrow. 'Not Tom?'

'God, no! Just, you know, some boy.'

'Handsome?'

'Thanks.'

He shoves me. I shove him back.

'Come on, mate, it's like I'm interviewing a dead turtle.'

I find myself smirking. We're doing this, are we? 'Actually he looked a bit like y—'

But then the bathroom door opens and Jamie jumps to his feet.

She looks different. Clean. Light. Like a few years fell off with the dirt, right down the shower drain. I wonder how old she is.

Jamie's mouth hangs halfway open.

I clear my throat. 'Still got that pizza from work.'

A curious expression appears on her face. It might be a smile. Whatever it is, it looks as though it hasn't been practised in a very long time.

Jamie's frozen on the spot.

I clear my throat a bit louder. 'I'll go and heat it up, yeah? Jamie?'

'Yes. Thank you.'

I go into the kitchen, shove the pizza in the oven a bit more forcefully than necessary and start pacing. Jamie rushes to get plates and glasses.

Soon enough, the heat from the oven becomes hellish. I go to the window, but I'm afraid to open it so instead I go to the sink, turn on the tap and splash cold water on my face. Then I steady myself on the edge of the sink.

'You okay, mate?'

'Probably.'

We eat in silence and I swear I'm getting flashbacks to the psychiatrist's waiting room, with the hyperawareness of the people around you and the great care not to catch anyone's eyes by accident, cos then they'll think you're wondering what's wrong with them. Jamie's picking out the pineapple and arranging it into shapes.

And then, suddenly, Olivia breaks the unspoken rule. 'My dad used to do that.'

Jamie and I look at each other.

She stares down at her slice. 'We had pizza on Wednesdays, after my dance lessons.'

'You're a dancer?' Jamie asks.

Either she didn't hear that or she's choosing to ignore it. 'He was a vegetarian, but he always picked one with ham because he knew I liked it so much. He had to take all the little pieces of ham off his slice, one by one. Like you.'

They're smiling at each other, cos apparently that's a thing we do now. Smiling at people we barely know like they just handed over a puppy.

'Did you . . .?' He trails off, thinks for a while. 'Have you tried contacting your father, since you . . .?'

The head tilt again. *It's raining men*, fuck that head tilt, like an owl, like an alien, *it's raining men, every specimen*. Fuck the smile, the head tilt and fuck Jamie for finding it all perfectly normal.

'Have you tried contacting your father?' he says again.

'No.'

'Why not?'

Yeah, why not? Make it someone else's problem. Perfect, actually. Jamie, that's brilliant, mate. She'd be happier with her dad anyway, if there's any crumb of family instinct left in there. If it's not been beaten out, or zapped out, or whatever the fuck they did to her back there.

She chews on her lower lip. Jamie does that when he's . . . 'I'm scared,' she says.

'Scared of what?'

'I don't know.'

The idea worms its way into my mind and sparks new energy in there, new purpose. The right thing to do, for the wrong reason. But in the end, does that even matter? 'Do you know where he lives?'

'Sid, there's no way she'll rem—'

'Number 43, NW3 2QF.'

Jamie's nose twitches. 'How can you . . .? How old

were you when . . .?'

The energy claws at my brain. My leg bounces under the table. I snap my fingers. 'Jamie, notebook, pen.'

I grab them from the coffee table and lay them in front of her. 'Can you write it down for us?'

She doesn't move. Jamie frowns.

'It's okay,' I say. 'You can trust us. Go on.'

'You can't write,' says Jamie.

She shakes her head.

'Can you read?' he asks.

She shakes her head again.

I drag the pen and paper to myself. 'Can you repeat the address?'

'Number 43, NW3 2QF.'

I turn to Jamie. 'Hampstead. I'll go tomorrow before my shift.'

'What?' he says.

'Maybe we can find him.'

He makes a sound halfway between exhaling and laughing. 'I don't know, Sid . . .'

'He's her father, he would want to know that she's . . .' I'm not sure what word is appropriate. Alive? Safe? I finally settle on 'here'.

Jamie's mouth opens and closes silently a few times. 'Are you sure it's safe?'

'It's her father.'

'I know, but if you start asking around . . .'

'For all they know I'm just looking for an old friend.'

He shifts his weight on the chair and it creaks.

The voice whispers left and right. *Selfish. Bastard. Stab yourself.* I swing my head to shake it loose and fight back the urge to hum.

'We have to try,' I say. 'Don't we?'

'You don't have to,' Olivia says.

Jamie thinks about it. 'Yeah, we have to.'

3

Hampstead. Nice neighbourhood. Pissing down on quaint semi-detached homes. The roofs are red, for fuck's sake, and I see a few white picket fences. Old flaking paint, but still.

Number 43, NW3 2QF.

The door opens on a blue-eyed man, early to mid-forties, white shirt, rolled-up sleeves, quizzical eyebrows.

'May I help you?'

Posh accent. I smell Oxbridge.

'I'm looking for Jonathan Brown.'

'Terribly sorry, I think you might have the wrong address.'

Fuck me, it's pouring down now and this is going nowhere. I run a hand through my hair. It gets stuck in the knots. Should have known she'd have the address wrong. Twenty-five years. I can barely remember two weeks ago.

'Oh dear, you don't have an umbrella, do you? Come in, would you like some tea?'

All the danger signs instantly start blaring in my ears. Red lights flash, loud buzzing, get out of there, Robinson, you suicidal lunatic, get out of there before it's too late.

'Oh, no, thank you, I should . . .'

'You'll catch your death. Let me at least get you a towel, dry yourself off.' He steps aside.

Absolutely soaking wet

And I cross the threshold.

'Darling, we have company!' Blue-Eyes shouts into the room.

'What?' a voice responds.

'Company!'

Footsteps down the stairs. They have stairs. This is a house. There's a fireplace. Pictures on the mantelpiece. Books crammed into shelves, and more piled next to the sofa. A faint lavender scent in the air. The word 'lovely' comes to mind, where it doesn't belong, so I push it right out.

'Pardon the mess,' says Blue-Eyes, even though the place is tidier than our flat's ever been.

'Sally?' calls a voice.

A tall wiry guy trots in. 'Oh. Not Sally. I . . . would you like a towel?'

I'm dripping on the carpet. 'Shit, I'm sorry.'

They both chuckle and I swear they're almost harmonising it.

'That's alright,' says Wiry-Guy. 'Have a seat, I'll put the kettle on.'

'I'm Charlie,' says Blue-Eyes. 'And this is Nick.'

'Hullo,' says Nick, and then disappears into the kitchen.

'Sid,' I say.

'So!' Charlie waves me to the sofa. 'Have you come a long way, then?'

He starts frantically gathering a bunch of flyers from the coffee table and rearranging the cushions.

'Soho.'

'Oh, right? I thought I was picking up on a Northern accent there. Lancashire, maybe?'

I stare. 'I, uh, I grew up in Manchester.'

He nods. 'Right, Manchester. I'm slipping.'

Nick walks back in, lays three empty cups on the coffee table and drops down next to Charlie. He's a little out of breath.

'Alright, love?' Charlie says.

'I'm fine.' He turns to me. 'Asthma, bloody annoying. So, to what do we owe—'

A little click from the kitchen. Nick sighs. Charlie pats him on the leg.

'I'll get it.' And he gets up.

'What brings you here on this . . . day?' Nick asks.

'I'm looking for a man called Jonathan Brown. Seems I got the wrong place.'

'Can't say it rings a bell. Friend of yours?'

'He's just an old family friend, really. Haven't seen him in a long time but, you know, I was in the neighbourhood so I thought I'd visit. This is a lovely house you've got.'

Nick smiles indulgently. It's pretty clear I'm trying to change the subject. Maybe I should have prepared a better lie but, to be fair, I didn't exactly expect to have to make small talk with the new tenants.

'Yes, we like it. It was fully renovated before we moved in so I guess it probably looks quite different from when you last visited.'

He knows perfectly well I was never here before. I shift on the settee. 'Yes.'

'If he asks you anything personal, you don't have to answer.' Charlie's reappeared with the kettle.

'I'm sorry, I don't mean to make you uncomfortable. We don't get a lot of visitors. Apart from Sally.'

'Sally?'

'She lives across the street,' says Charlie, as if that's a perfectly normal thing to say. 'Milk?'

'I'm sorry?'

'Milk?' he repeats.

Nick elbows him in the ribs. 'You arse.' Then, to me, 'Sally's trans. No infection, no quarantine.'

'No recognition,' Charlie says.

'Sadly,' Nick says.

Well this makes no sense. Does it?

'Actually, Sally's been living here for a long time. She might know your chap. Brown, was it?'

'Oh, I don't mean to be a bother.'

'It's quite alright,' Charlie says. 'I have to return a book to her anyway. Come with. Wouldn't hurt to ask.'

Of course, it could very well hurt to ask. It could hurt so bad both Jamie and I would need a eulogy. But fuck me, now I'm curious.

Nick's got his hand on Charlie's thigh, thumb discreetly stroking. Something tightens in my chest. Not unpleasant. Some sort of pull. I avert my eyes and find a book on the table to my right. *Breakfast at Tiffany's*. I pick it up, probably shouldn't, turn it around. Probably shouldn't. No Department for Culture stamp.

My head snaps up.

'Crikey,' Charlie says.

'Ah, yes,' Nick says.

Shouldn't, definitely shouldn't. I open the book and I'm pretty sure I'm humming again. *We're your Weather Girls. God bless mother nature, she's, she . . .* yellow pages, some threaten to fall. I handle the thing like it's an ancient relic.

'Is this . . .?'

'. . . a book? Why, yes, it is.'

Nick elbows him again, and again, the harmonising laughter.

'We've barely met,' I say. 'Aren't you worried I might, you know?'

Charlie slips seamlessly into an American southern drawl. 'We've always depended on the kindness of strangers.'

I clear my throat. 'Is this Sally's?'

Nick gives me the smile of a pusher dangling a bag of heroin in my face. 'This one is.' And nods to the bookshelf.

Next thing I know, my fingers are brushing against the spines of books and videos. I'm buzzing. My hand is shaking. This is not good.

The Age of Innocence. Casablanca. Some Like It Hot. Mrs Dalloway. To Kill a Mockingbird.

'Can I . . .?' I ask, pulling one out at random.

'Be our guest,' says Charlie.

Jane Eyre. Charlotte Brontë. Which one is the title, I want to ask, but something worryingly close to shame holds my tongue.

The book falls open where the page is marked. *'I am no bird; and no net ensnares me; I am a free human being with an independent will.'*

I turn it over in my head, mouth the words, it's suddenly very important that I remember this by heart. All at once, I feel dwarfed, humiliated, judged, and nobody's doing the judging but myself.

I am no bird; and no net ensnares me; I am a free human being with an independent will. A free human being with an independent will. No net ensnares me. The way Olivia grabbed the chips and ran, her life on the line, run, fast, faster, *I am no bird, cos tonight for the first—*

'Are you quite alright there?'

'Yeah, uh yes, I'm . . . I think.'

'Looks like it's cleared up a bit. Shall we?'

I hand him the book.

'Keep it,' he says.

'No,' I say. And slip it into my backpack.

The air outside smells of wet grass. I stop for a bit, close my eyes, and inhale. Everything slows to a crawl. Never knew lungs could hold that much air. I try to inhale some more but that's about all I can take. Exhale. Nick winks as he brushes past, *Breakfast at Tiffany's* tucked under his arm. They're perfectly happy getting caught with pre-quarantine shit lying around the house, perfectly happy brandishing the stuff in the street for everyone to see. Starting to wonder what I've got myself into, and why I'm not running out of it before it gets worse.

The house across the street, Sally's house, is pretty much indistinguishable from the ones around it. Nick knocks, then Charlie knocks harder, and the door opens.

I have never seen such a hippie in my entire life, which includes Jamie dragging me to university parties full of artsy undergrads. From the flowery headband to the plaid shirt to the wide-legged corduroy.

She speaks with the raised voice of someone who's lost part of their hearing. 'Who might you be?' she says.

I forget to reply, right up until it becomes obvious someone should be talking. 'Sid Robinson, ma'am.'

'Mr Robinson! Call me Sally. "Ma'am" isn't as flattering as you might think.'

We shake. The bracelets clink, the rings dig into my flesh.

'Have you brought me a new friend, boys? Taking pity on the senior citizen?'

'Sid's looking for someone who used to live around here,' says Nick.

She pushes the glasses back up her nose and gives me the once-over. I quickly stop massaging my knuckles.

'Hand me the book, Mr Day. Let's have tea.'

'We actually just had—'

'Well, you can have more, can't you? Breathe, Mr Robinson, you're doing fine.'

And exhale.

The house swallows us. So does a heady stench of roses.

Nick leans over. 'You get used to it.'

The walls are covered in black-framed photographs over yellowish flowery wallpaper. Sally and another woman, young, smiling, in love. The smell of roses suddenly becomes nauseating. I'd probably throw up if my stomach wasn't empty. Nick's hand lands on my shoulder and I realise I've stopped walking. He nudges me forward until we mercifully emerge into the living room.

Sally sits in one of the armchairs and waves for me to sit in the other one. Charlie and Nick settle on the arm rests, either side of me. For some reason, my heart slows a bit.

'Tea?' she asks.

'Oh, no, thank you.'

She turns to Nick with flailing arms. 'Well, what am I supposed to offer if you have tea before you visit, Mr Day?'

'You know you don't have to offer us anything, Sal,' says Nick.

'Of course I do. It's polite. Now then you, Mr Robinson, what can I do for you?'

Charlie nods at me like a proud father at a parent–teacher meeting. Don't hum. Don't hum. Don't hum.

'I was wondering if you knew a man who used to live here,' I say. 'Jonathan Brown?'

Sally smiles. 'I do remember Jonathan.' She points at Nick and Charlie. 'He moved into your house thirty years ago with his wife and their new baby. Nice little family, they were. Not long before the quarantine. Did you know Jonathan, then?'

She knows I didn't. *God bless mother nature, she's a single woman too, absolutely soaking wet, it's raining* . . . the air is gone. Choose your words well.

'No, he's an . . . old family friend.'

The bony finger pushes the glasses up her nose again. 'I'm afraid Jonathan's dead, son.'

Nobody speaks for a while. A minute's silence for the man I didn't even know ever existed until yesterday.

I wish she wouldn't keep calling him by his first name. Throwing up is very much back on the cards.

'Are you sure?' I ask, instead of humming.

'I'm sorry, Mr Robinson. Jonathan died at home a few months after the beginning of the quarantine. He had a stroke in his bath and drowned.'

I tug at the collar of my shirt.

'Well they certainly didn't mention that when they sold us the place,' says Charlie.

'Don't be impertinent, Mr Williamson. Jonathan's health deteriorated quickly when they took his wife and daughter.'

This is making me think about my father. I don't want to think about my father.

'I know this isn't what you were hoping for, Mr Robinson.'

'Thank you, thank you for your . . . help . . .'

'Do you need to be alone? Would you like to go?'

Watch out, you're smiling. No, I'm not. *What's wrong with your face?*

'No, I'm . . . It's okay. I barely knew him. I mean, I am sorry, but . . .'

'Finish your tea, then, young man.' She turns to Nick and Charlie. 'Did you like the book?'

They start talking at the same time.

'Fabulously witty.'

'Absolutely gorgeous prose.'

'I could not put it down.'

Their voices weave and swirl together. I close my eyes and just exist next to them for a while.

Loser.

Shut it.

Leech.

Shut it, shut it, shut it.

I stay too long, in the end. I'm going to be late.

Mike's yelling at me. I'm looking down at my feet because that's what you do and also because Mike has issues with personal space and I don't want his yellow teeth inches from my eyes. There's some brown sauce on the floor, right next to his left shoe. I wonder if he'll step into it.

'I don't know how they did things at your last job, Robinson,' says Mike, 'but here you bloody well arrive on time! Get it?'

I mumble an apology.

'No, you don't just say "sorry" like that!'

'Well, what more can I say?'

His voice goes shrill. 'You bloody make sure it never happens again, Robinson!'

He accentuates every other syllable and rolls his 'r's all over the place, sometimes when there's no 'r' to roll. He claims to be Italian on his mother's side. Probably figures it gives him some sort of extra authority. This is fucking Pizza 24, for fuck's sake.

I am no bird; and no net ensnares me. Let me tell you something, though: this, right now, feels a lot like a net.

'You don't think it's important, do you?' he asks.

I lower my head a bit more. No Mike, I don't fucking think it's important. In fact, I think it's about as far from important as you can get.

I'm afraid I have some bad news. Your father is dead. I'm sorry. No, that sounds harsh. It's about your dad. I'm sorry, but he passed away. There should definitely be a 'sorry' in there somewhere. Back in med school, they taught us about delivering bad news. At that point, though, I'd long stopped paying attention.

I was a smart kid, once. Top marks, med school at UCL. And that's roughly when it started. Schizoaffective disorder, bipolar type. In the official parlance. Something to do with genetic predisposition, triggered by stress, they said, but if you ask me, it was my fault, taking all that shit I shouldn't have been taking.

Mike sprays spit in my face.

What now?

Probably shouldn't have taken the book. That was stupid.

Black frames on yellow wallpaper.

Could I possibly hide in the bathroom and read until it's time to go home?

Stupid, really.

Mike shifts and his white trainer lands neatly in the sauce.

'Crap!' he says – and forgets to roll the 'r'.

Over fourteen hours have passed since I left this morning. I need a shower, I need sleep, I need a cigarette. What I don't need is Tom, casually leaning against the wall outside, fake-checking his inbox on his mobile.

I plaster a smile on my face and give him a slap on the shoulder. 'Alright, fancy man? What brings you here?'

'Nothing. I was on my way home, passed by and figured . . .'

'Oh, cheers, mate.'

We start down the street together. Great, just fucking brilliant.

'So, last night, eh?'

'What?'

'Last night? The boy you left with?' He nudges me.

'Oh, yeah, sorry about that.'

'No, no, I mean, good for you, you know?'

I wonder if I could just punch him in the face and run for it.

'Ta,' I say.

'I went back home after you left. Fancied a quiet night anyway. Crazy at work, these days.'

'Is it?'

'Yeah, mental.'

I try to walk faster. He speeds up to match me.

'There's talk about cuts in the budget. Firing people from my department.'

Random laughter, like this is just hilarious. What the fuck is wrong with you, Tom?

We're approaching the junction where we would normally go our separate ways. I slow down a bit, but he's not paying attention. He talks and talks about his job, his flat, his neighbour, his blocked sink. Then the junction is behind us and I'll be fucked if he's going to follow me home.

'You missed your street.'

'Ah, it's fine. I'll walk you.'

Fuck, *hallelujah it's raining men, every specim* . . . What if he asks to come up? Can't, you can't, sorry but no. Jamie's writing and he needs quiet, we're having construction work done, I don't feel well, I think I'll just go straight to bed.

We reach the building and he's still going on and on, the stream of words doesn't seem about to stop, so I try 'See you, then.'

'D'you fancy a drink?'

'I don't think so. We went out yesterday . . .'

'Yeah, well, we didn't really have time to catch up yesterday, did we?' He elbows me.

'I know. I'm sorry. Maybe some other time? I'm kind of broke, right now.'

'That's no problem, I'll buy you a drink. Come on, you're not going to make me beg, are you?' He touches my sleeve.

'Fucking hell, Tom, I said no!'

He looks like I just punched him.

'Sorry,' I say.

Light flush in his face, hands deep in his pockets. *God bless mother nature*, don't hum, *she's a single woman too*, don't hum.

'It's alright,' he says. 'I'll head home. I'm knackered anyway. Mental at work.'

'Tom . . .'

He flashes the smile at me again. 'See you, hophead!'

I stand there and watch him walk away with that spring in his step. Is it okay to leave things like this? Should I run after him? But then my hand is on the door and I was never going to go after him.

'What's new with you?' Jamie says.

I throw my keys on the coffee table.

'Shh, she's sleeping.' He nods to the bedroom.

'Sorry. You still up?'

'Observant.' He sets his laptop down. 'Not getting anywhere though, if I'm honest.'

I chew on my nails. 'Distracted?'

He stretches, arms above his head, yawning like a cat, and grabs an apple from the fruit bowl.

My eyes follow his long fingers as they leave the bowl, stick the apple between his teeth, and run through his hair. It's messy and dark, ash brown, lightly curling around the metal bar in his ear. I let myself wander to his eyebrows, and down, over the straight bridge of his nose, hint of scar from the bad piercing he had done during his brief goth phase, to his mouth, and down again. Before I know it, I'm watching his Adam's apple move as he chews and swallows.

Nick's hand on Charlie's thigh.

'She looks like my mum.'

'What?'

'She looks like my mum,' he says.

'You don't remember your mum.'

'No, Sid. *You* don't remember your mum.'

This probably shouldn't sting as much as it does. Twenty-five years. Jamie occasionally mentions his mother. It's always casual, with a wave of the hand. The same wave he does when his writing gets rejected.

I know nothing of my mum, only that she's the reason kids bullied me in school. 'It's cos of your ma,' Dad said. He said not to take offence. He took offence, though, when we moved south and 'Fuck off back to your own country' turned to 'Piss off, Manc'.

I am no bird; and no net ensnares me; I am a free human being with an independent will. How badly I want to pull the book from my backpack and show it to him right now.

The night I met Jamie, he offered me a joint – some bloke's party he dragged me to. I said no thank you. Jamie said, 'Come on, mate. It's the end of the world anyway.' So I took the joint. And then I took some other stuff, but that's another story. The point is, he was right. After all the promises of a loud, dramatic apocalypse, it'd started to look like this was actually going to be slow and quiet.

All those years, we had time to get used to it. And we did. We adjusted. Now though, now I just don't know anymore.

'Are we sure she's not sick?' I ask.

'She's not sick.'

'How do we know that? We don't know what it looks like.'

'I know what it looks like. She's not sick.'

I run my hand through my hair to compensate for the massive foot in my mouth. 'What do we do about her if they come here?'

'We hide her.'

'Where?'

'I'll find something.'

'Yeah, you do that.'

He doesn't move.

'Now, please. You do that now.'

He sets the apple core on the table, 'Sure, if that'll shut you up,' and starts pacing and I'm seeing dancing spots.

I hear Jamie opening the pantry and closing it again. First place they'd look, the pantry. When the quarantine started, lots of people thought it would be a good idea to hide in the pantry. It's not. It's a stupid idea, and I sort of judge Jamie for even considering it.

I close my eyes and try to shut everything out. All at once, weariness washes over me. I'm falling forward into the void. I am no bird. Number 43, NW3 2QF. Darling, we have company. We've had tea already, Sal. Black-framed pictures on the yellow walls. You bloody well arrive on time, Robinson. Oh, soak off.

'Get up,' Jamie says.

'What?'

He shoves his hands under the settee and pulls up and I half-roll off, half-stand but my feet won't work and I end up sitting on the floor like it was my plan all along.

The sofa swings backwards with a click. It's a sofa-bed. I'd forgotten it was a sofa-bed. We never open it, it was probably the cheapest thing in IKEA at the time. Doesn't even look like a sofa-bed. Under it is a compartment, probably designed to store sheets and blankets.

Jamie smiles. The left corner of his mouth, then the full grin.

'Alright,' I say, 'get over yourself. It's not the Holy Grail.'

'It is a little bit.'

'Whatever you say.'

'You staying down there?' he asks.

I shrug. 'You helping me up?'

He extends his hand, the long fingers, and I reach up—

'D'you hear that?'

Fluttering and bangs, like a trapped bird.

Screaming.

Jamie speeds to the bedroom.

'Wait, wha— Ah, fuck.'

Whether she's asleep or awake is anyone's guess, but the fighting is obvious. She's on the bed, eyes tightly shut, kicking, flailing, screaming. Incoherent words pour out, her throat sounds raw with the yelling.

Jamie calls her name, loud, and the window is open, the faint smell of something barbecuing outside. The window is open and people in the street below and *tonight for the first time, for the first t-t* . . . I watch him climb on the bed next to her, he touches her, he touches her arm and the eyes fly open, wide, round, *rough and tough and strong and mean, it's raining men, hallelujah it's—*

'Sid, shut up!'

She's jumped off the bed and now she's trying to back away into the wall and Jamie's shushing like he does when it's me, like he does when I'm trying to back away into the wall.

'Please. I'm sorry, but you have to be quiet, please. Sid, get the window.'

'Wh—'

'Window, Sid. Come on!'

I stumble over there and pull the thing down. 'What about the neighbours?'

He doesn't hear me. He's looking her in the eyes, the wide eyes, she's looking at me. Jamie's babbling and she's staring at me and pleading for help, I can see it and feel it like we're the same. *I am a free human being with an independent will.* So I pull in a deep breath, hold it for a while, and let it go. She pulls in a deep breath, holds it for a while, and lets it go.

Jamie squeezes her shoulder. 'Are you okay?'

'Can you give me a minute alone?'

'Of course.'

He walks to the door. I'm not following. I'm sorry, your father passed away. I'm sorry. I wish I had better news. I'm sorry.

'Sid?'

I follow him out.

He sinks onto the settee, and sighs. 'Well, not exactly a piece of cake, is it?'

'People will have heard that.'

'Probably, but they'll think it was us. They're used to your panic attacks.'

'I don't sound like that.'

He smiles. 'You kind of do, actually.' And winks.

4

The book feels both small and heavy in my hands. I was never much of a reader. Last thing I managed to get through was *The Atlas of Human Anatomy* and I retained about twenty percent of it.

'I care for myself. The more solitary, the more friendless, the more unsustained I am, the more I will respect myself.'

Well that's fucked up. Let me tell you how fucked up that is.

I was nineteen years old when Jamie took me to the hospital.

It was January, a few weeks before the exams. I fought and screamed and they had to tranquillise me. I remember, as the drugs were taking effect, looking into Jamie's face. He looked resolved and pained, and he held my gaze until I was out.

When I woke up, he was there. I remember thinking, 'What are you doing here? Don't you have better things to do?' I may or may not have said it out loud. The next day, when I woke up, he was there again. And the next, and the next, and the next. He failed the semester, and I never went back to uni.

The more friendless. The more I will respect myself. Fuck off.

The more solitary. The more unsustained. Your father's dead. I'm so sorry. I couldn't bring myself to say it, I couldn't. The way she was thrashing, screaming. I saw myself, alone and scared shitless, trapped in my own mind. I saw Jamie on the chair next to the bed, dozing over an English Lit book. We're her only acquaintances now, Jamie and me. It's on us. *Humidity is rising, barometer's getting low*, and it's on us.

According to all sources.
The street's the place to go.
I care for myself.
Need a break.

I put the book back in my bag and take it out again. Too close, it's too close, it needs to be far, far away, out of the room, somewhere else.

I get up and flail my arms and pace around.

Jamie's asleep on the sofa now, neck at an awkward angle. I watch for a while and almost forget the book in my hand.

His chest goes down and doesn't come up. I hold my breath too. It's not dangerous, doctors said. Just leave him, they said, and he'll start breathing again soon. How soon? I'm getting dizzy already and I haven't been holding my breath as long as he has. Shouldn't I wake him up? Isn't he going to suffocate? I need oxygen pretty badly now but I'm not taking another breath until he does. I'll wake him up. This is not normal. I'll just wake him up. As I step forward, his chest rises again. I allow mine to do the same.

The more solitary, the more friendless. Focus.

Drawer?

Back of the toilet?

Sofa-bed?

Jamie would find it.

What about the pantry?

Oh, you must be joking.

'Shit!' My foot catches one of the loose floorboards. 'Shit.'

Under the floorboard.

I kneel down, perfect, and pull it out, and freeze.

Jamie's recorder sits there, staring at *Jane Eyre*, and *Jane Eyre* stares back at the recorder. Then I stand and stare at Jamie some more. Don't listen to it. What's in there? You know what's in there. What else could it be? You know what it is, *absolutely soaking wet*, focus.

I take the recorder back to my bedroom.

Before I know it, the door is locked and I'm cross-legged on the bed with the drapes closed and a blanket over my head. Not sure what the blanket is for. It does a good job of blocking out the cars zooming down Shaftesbury, the whistle of the wind through the cracked window, the light snoring from the next room.

Click.

'Okay so, um, let me just take— I'll— I'll get some information down and then we'll just jump into it, okay?'

'Okay.'

'Today is Monday, the, um, 14th of October 2019. Could you repeat that for me?'

'Today is Monday, the 14th of October 2019.'
'Thank you. What's your name?'
'Olivia Angharad Lloyd-Brown.'
Click.

Three-thirty in the morning and I haven't moved in hours. I went back to the floorboard, tucked the recorder away and prayed Jamie wouldn't notice. I pulled the blanket back over my head, but this time it wasn't for privacy. I needed the safety. I wanted to disappear. My teeth sank into my lip, down, down, until a warm metallic taste spread in my mouth, then I started attacking my nails.

Everything would have been fine. Nobody would have imagined for one second that we have a woman here. She walked right through the middle of a crowd. She was there, in plain sight, and no one saw her. No one was expecting to see her, so they didn't. She's a ghost, invisible. If Jamie goes stirring the water, though . . .

I hear the voice again.

While soft winds shake the barley.

We went to Kelly's every week. Sometimes more than once a week. Every time, we saw this guy, and we talked to him. Reg. I could never be arsed to ask his name. He was taking a risk, with the sign on his bathroom door, with the music. I admired his bravery from the safe distance of my own cowardice. I could have told him the gesture was appreciated. I didn't. It makes me sick.

I hear the voice again. Ignore it; it's not real. The

soft humming from the third bedroom. It isn't real. I prick up my ears and listen for it, even though it's not real. It stops and starts again, stops and starts again, like the wailing of a hurt dog, the way it plucks at your nerves.

You're hearing voices, Robinson.

I get up and out into the hallway. Jamie is already standing at the bedroom door. I walk up to him.

'She crying?' I whisper.

He nods.

'Has it happened before?'

'Don't think so,' he says.

I force my face to relax, my eyebrows up, brace myself. 'Did . . . did anything happen that could have . . . upset her?'

His face goes as blank as mine, I see him force it. I see through his eyes, into his brain, the cogs turning. 'Nothing I can think of.'

I almost say something.

'Should we go in, do you think?' His hand is frozen halfway to the doorknob.

'No,' I say. 'Leave her alone.'

I wish him a good night and go back to bed.

Fifteen minutes later, she's still weeping and it doesn't sound like it's going to stop anytime soon. I find myself thinking about Colin, in his room, alone, crying too. Or maybe there's another guy with him. Another guy like me, all awkward and unsure how to react.

A huge chunk of my nail comes off. It fucking hurts.

Not that work hasn't always been meaningless, but fuck me, now it's even worse. As I finally, finally exit the restaurant, I grin at Tony like some corporate drone, shout a 'See ya tomorrow, mate' and mumble some curse under my breath, even though Tony's a good lad, really.

'Mr Robinson!'

I spin around and there's Nick and Charlie, standing across the street, and it's like watching a stranger's muddy boots slam onto your coffee table. The incongruity freezes me on the spot. Nick waves. They close in on me as the cold sweat drips from my neck down my back.

'Mr Robinson, hello!'

My heart's in my chest and then out of it.

It's . . . raining men . . .

I picture my bones snapping in half, breaking through the skin. Red. Flesh. Open bits.

'. . . hallelujah, it's . . .' . . . *raining men, every specimen.*

'You broke him, love.'

Every specimen. My hood is down. I want my earphones.

'Goodness, you're shaking. Please don't worry. I know we must be giving off some serious stalker vibes here. We just needed—'

'Oh, I . . . I have the book, if you want it back. I have it.'

I reach for my backpack, but Charlie grabs my arm.

'Crikey, no, no, no, don't take it out here!'

The sudden contact sends a chill up my spine. I yank myself free more roughly than necessary. Nick catches Charlie's hand in his own and interlaces their fingers. I stare at this for a while.

'What he means is, by all means, keep the book. Please.' He flashes me a smile. 'May we talk?'

Talk. I can do that. If that's all, if that's it, if that's all they want, are they alone, did they come alone?

'Alright,' I say.

'Let's walk.'

Walk and talk. I can do that. I can do that.

We walk, and the cool air clears my head a bit. A slight hint of rain.

We walk.

I wait for one of them to speak. There's something familiar in Charlie's face that I can't quite place. An unease. Like he wants to hide but his eyes are only made bigger, rounder, by the thick glasses he's now wearing. You can see all the shades of blue in there, and the spark of intelligence. Nick notices the unease, and takes charge.

'We've been on the receiving end of a rather unpleasant inspection.'

I keep quiet. Anything you say can and will be used against you, anything you say, one minor slip up, one 'I'm sorry' might be proof enough that it was my doing, that I did this to them, did I do this to them?

'It's all well and good, we got away with a formal warning. First offence and all that. Just a day after your visit, though.' He throws Charlie a side glance, casually checking on him, then catches my eyes. 'Mr Robinson, whatever it is, I can guarantee you we've done worse.'

My voice feels wrong, like I'm lying, like I'm audibly lying through my teeth. 'I have . . . I haven't done anything wrong.'

He switches gear immediately. 'I know you haven't.'

Nothing wrong. I've done nothing wrong, except I have. I've done everything wrong.

'Are you enjoying the book?'

I blink. 'Yes.'

'Would you like another?'

'I thought you'd been raided?'

'They only took what they could find.'

I run my hand through my hair.

'You could come over for a movie.'

I'm hyperventilating like there's no tomorrow. He's playing on my addictive personality like a fucking pro, and I want it, God help me, but I'm already knee-deep in trouble.

'Look, far be it from me to force your hand. We only just met, you've no reason to trust us. However . . .' He slips a card into my hand. 'You seem like you might need a friend or two.'

I don't look at it. Just slip it in my pocket.

'It's your call, Mr Robinson.'

'Sid.'

He grins widely. 'Sid.' Then nods as they both start to walk away.

I call after them. 'You've got no reason to trust me either.'

Charlie clears his throat, puts on his American accent again. 'We have always depended on the kindness of strangers.'

Nick offers a final wave, and they disappear around the corner.

I stop at the shop on the way home and it's pouring down by the time I reach our building. As I'm trying to prod open the heavy front door with my shoulder, there's a soft buzz from my pocket, followed by a beep. I grunt. It'll have to wait. I push all my weight against the door and it gives way suddenly, and I find myself on the floor with my hands and knees grazed and the contents of my bags all over the lobby. I ponder. Maybe I could cry a little bit. That wouldn't be too much of an overreaction, would it?

It takes me a few minutes to gather the groceries, gather myself, and gather the energy to climb the stairs, and when I finally close the flat door behind me, there's no telling what's rain and what's sweat. Everything's dark and quiet. A peek at the microwave tells me it's two twenty-one in the morning. I drop the bags in the kitchen as quietly as possible and make a beeline for the bathroom.

I sit on the edge of the bath, then hiss as the burning sting from my scratched palms finally registers. I get the shower running and place my hand under the stream. Nice. I allow my eyes to close and try to bring all my thoughts to the cool, numbing feeling on my broken skin. I strip and get under the water. I let out a long sigh, enjoying it as much as I can. The strong hammering against my back. The little beads running down my body, trickling from my wet hair. I take my time with it. I soap myself up meticulously, rinse, soap up again, rinse, over and over again until a vision of the landlord presenting us with the water bill pops into my mind.

My towel is on the floor under the hook. I pick it up, dry myself and hang it on the hook. Three seconds later it falls to the floor again.

Just as I'm weighing the pros and cons of picking it back up, the door swings open and I'm nose to nose with Olivia. I jump back. My lower back hits the sink pretty fucking hard. Then I remember I'm naked. This would be a prime panic opportunity. In fact, the panic button is right there, flashing red, alarms blaring, but I can't quite reach it, so instead I just stand there with an exposed body and a blank mind.

We stare at each other for a while.

'I have to pee,' she says.

'I was just showering,' I say.

'I know,' she says.

And I watch in semi-horrified fascination as she walks past me, pulls down her flannel pyjama bottoms, and sits on the toilet. I spin around, avert my eyes, but now I'm just presenting my arse to her and this isn't much better, this isn't better at all, in fact it may even be worse.

Towel.

In the most awkward display of clumsiness imaginable, I extend my foot to pull the towel towards me, bend down from my knees with my legs squeezed together so tight it's pressing in uncomfortable places, and quickly wrap the damp towel around my waist as I stretch back up.

'I— I— I am so, so sorry,' I mumble, and slink out like some cartoon ninja.

As fast and silently as possible, I pad over to my

room, push the door closed and slip into clean boxers. Then I sit for a while with my legs folded up, wondering if this was real or not. I let out a dry sob, but swallow it back immediately as a light knock sounds at the door.

'May I enter?' Olivia's voice in a whisper.

'Yeah. Yes,' I say.

Her face peeks in. She hands me something. Plasters. 'You hurt yourself.' She motions to my hand. 'So I thought . . .'

'Oh.' I reach for the box. 'Thanks, that's . . . Thank you.'

She inches her way towards me, lowers herself onto the mattress, right next to me, so close our knees are touching. My heart pounds against my chest. We smile uncomfortably at each other.

Your father passed away. I'm sorry. For your loss. I'm sorry for your loss. Your father . . . I'm sorry about your father.

You coward. Say it.

I can't.

Say it.

'I'm hungry,' I say. 'Are you hungry?'

She nods.

'I bought cereal.'

'That sounds nice.'

On the way to the kitchen, she glances towards Jamie's room and my teeth grind together. Breathe. I pull the box of cornflakes out of my backpack, making eye contact with *Jane Eyre* for a second before carefully closing the bag again.

She's perched herself on a chair and observes as I pour the cereal. On instinct, I pour more into her bowl.

'Milk and sugar?'

Her face lights up and I find myself smiling.

'I'll take that as a yes.'

'I'm sorry about before,' she says, out of nowhere.

'That's alright.'

'Sometimes I don't know what's . . . good.'

'That's alright,' I repeat.

I seal it with a small smile and hand her the bowl. Our fingers touch as she takes it. She's not sick, is what Jamie said. She's not sick. Malnourished, though. I should have filled her bowl a bit more.

'What did they feed you over there?'

She chews slowly. 'Plain porridge. Some bread. Sometimes an apple.'

I grab the box and add some to her bowl. She emits a tiny sound. A giggle. A tiny, sort of squeaky giggle, and wipes milk from her chin with the back of her hand. Do I have to tell her, do I have to tell her now? Can it not wait? Can it not wait a day or two?

I decide it can't. It's not my secret to keep, not my information to withhold. It can't wait.

'There's something you should know.' I clear my throat. 'I, uh . . . I found the, uh, the people who live in your old home. Your father, he, uh . . . he passed away.'

She stares into my face, completely blank, like she's expecting more out of me. My voice waivers, breaks as I push the words out. 'He had a stroke in the bathtub and drowned, I am so, so sorry, I am so sorry.'

She brings the spoon up to her mouth and resumes eating.

'Do you understand?' I ask.

'Yes.'

'Are you alright?'

'Tell me about the people who live in the house now. Are they good?'

There's something defiant in her posture, something noble.

'I think so,' I say. 'I think they're good.'

Laying in bed with my foot dangling over the edge, I scroll down my contacts list.

I told her everything. Once it started pouring out of my mouth, there was no stopping it. I told her about Nick and Charlie. I told her about Sally. I told her about the neighbourhood, described how the house smells. She asked a few questions. I answered as best I could. I retrieved the book from my backpack and showed it to her. 'Please don't tell Jamie,' I said, and she nodded. She had me read some out loud.

I scroll until I see it.

Dad.

It catches me in the throat. Some sort of obsolete but deeply ingrained 'run home' instinct. My finger hovers over the dial button. 'No offence, mate, but your old man's a fucking bastard.' Jamie's voice. Jamie's twenty-two-year-old voice, from back then.

The psychosis, back then, hit like a fucking truck. I had no clue what was happening to me, no clue what to do, and before I could bring myself to mention it to anyone, let alone my father, ecstasy had already become a crutch. I started taking more and more, every day, just to get through. Sometimes, like the flip of a switch, my entire body pulsed with energy. I'd stop sleeping, forget to eat. I pulled all-nighters, multiple, in a row. Then the switch would click back and I'd sleep for two days straight. Other times the voices took over. I'd reply to someone only I could hear. I'd wake up in a cold sweat, thinking I was somewhere else, thinking I was dying, thinking I was dead.

Dad retreated. Stopped calling, then stopped answering the phone when I called. I thought Jamie would pull back too. I thought, 'We've not known each other that long, he'll find new friends.' He didn't.

A fucking bastard. I believed that for a long time. Not anymore. Not a bastard. A coward, yes. A scared, confused, lonely man, yes. A man who can't help me anymore.

'Are you sure you want to delete Dad?' the phone asks.

Yes.

I bask for a while in the self-pity. I bathe in it, drink it, lap it up like a dying man. Fucking delicious.

Then I hear a sound out in the corridor and start worrying it might not be real. *You arsehole, if it's not real, why are you afraid to walk out there?*

Because. Because what if it's real? What if it's not real and I get confirmation that I'm losing it again? Which one's worse? You decide, alright, cos I'm done.

I peek out of my room.

Olivia's on her way out, tiptoeing around the sofa, slipping into Jamie's jacket.

'What are you doing?' I ask.

'I'm going to see Sally,' she says.

'I can't let you do that.'

'I don't think you have a choice.'

'I'm stronger than you,' I say.

'Are you sure?'

'No.'

She moves to the door and I half-jump in her way.

'She won't turn me in,' she says. 'She knows me.'

'But you don't know her.'

'She's a woman!'

'Shhh!'

'I have to talk to her. I need to speak to someone like me. You have no idea.'

I groan.

'You have no idea,' she repeats.

I groan again, and step aside.

'Thank you.'

My teeth grind together as she opens the door. For a second, she's gone, she left, and I feel empty. Hollowed out.

Then the door opens again.

'Come with me.'

I audibly gasp. 'No.'

She extends her hand. 'Sid. Come with me.'

'No, please.'

But as I say it, I feel myself caving. If I'm honest, I want to. I want to go, God help me, and as she insists again, I take her hand. I reach out and take her hand and grab my bag on the way out.

5

Eyes down on the tube, I said. Eyes down, no talking. She waved me off. I don't need your advice, she said, and fair enough. I wondered how long she'd been on her own before we found her. I didn't ask.

The door swings open and a whiff of rose comes rushing out. Sally retrieves the thick round glasses from the collar of her dress, casually unfolds them, and pushes them up her nose. Then she lets out a loud 'Ah!' and slaps both hands on my shoulders.

'Mr Robinson!' Her eyes narrow on Olivia for a second, and she turns back to me.

'This is my friend Oliver,' I say.

She scrunches up her face. 'Are you showing me off to your friends, young man?'

'Oh, no! I'm sorry, I was just . . . I was retur—'

'I'm teasing, Mr Robinson. Dear me, you get so flustered! Come on in, both of you.'

Stepping inside, my stomach heaves. After making

sure that Sally's got her back to me, I allow my hand to fly up and cover my nose and mouth. We walk through the ill-lit corridors, past ancient-looking furniture and dusty mirrors.

'You like tea, don't you, dear?'

'Yes, miss.'

'Well aren't you a gentleman! Your friend gave me "ma'am" when we first met. Didn't you, Mr Robinson?'

I don't know if it's the tone of her voice, at ease, in control, or if it's the 'gentleman'. I start thinking we should leave. I glance down at Olivia's wrist, but I'm afraid to reach, afraid to signal her. So we remain there, exposed.

Behind a sharp turn, my hip slams into an inconveniently placed sideboard.

'Fuck!' I spit out before I can stop myself. I blush to the root of my hair but Sally doesn't react. I catch her glancing sideways at Olivia. I catch her glancing and feel the hum at the back of my throat.

Moments later the corridor throws us into the living room.

A tray sits on the coffee table, with a teapot and a single cup. Sally grabs it. The bracelets clang on the metal. 'That's yesterday's,' she says. 'You don't want that.'

The second she disappears into the kitchen, Olivia turns to me, all giddy, all excited, and it reminds me of Jamie. She's boiling up inside, I can tell, wound up, like a toy, moved to move, moved to hop around, barely in control. A vague bell rings in the distance, light-years away, through thick fog. I've felt that. I know I have, or I wouldn't recognise it in her. I try to touch it. I giggle with her. But it's out of reach. It's too far, and I'd be hard-pressed to remember the last time I felt that degree of genuine enthusiasm, or what it was about. It's far. It's gone. It's lost.

'I was here before,' Olivia says, in a tiny whisper, in a tiny emotional whisper.

It's lost, and for the first time, *for the first time in history*, I want it back.

'I'm afraid I only have a breakfast blend.' Sally glides back in with the tray. Three cups, this time, and a string of steam escaping from the pot. She pours the tea as we watch, quiet, like some sort of weird ceremony.

'Milk, Mr Robinson?'

'Thank you.'

'Liv?'

We both freeze, and shit, fuck, I knew this was a bad idea, I should have told Jamie where we were going, I should have told Jamie. I set the teacup down and push it away from me as discreetly as possible.

Olivia drops her voice as low as it'll go. 'Pardon?'

Fuck knows what she's trying to salvage, because then Sally mimics, '"Pardon?"' in her own lowest voice, which is considerably lower. Olivia startles, and for a fleeting moment before she catches herself, Sally looks almost hurt. 'My memory hasn't failed me quite yet, my dear, and neither have my eyes. Goodness me, you've grown.'

'Please don't tell anyone,' Olivia says.

Sally gives an indulgent smile. 'Take a good look at me, dear.' Then sighs. 'I did miss you. You probably don't remember me. You were so small.'

'I remember a little.' Olivia points at one of the black frames on the wall. 'I remember her. Your wife? Jan . . .'

'Jang-Mi. We never married, but essentially, yes.'

'You're wearing her dress.'

As she looks down at herself, Sally's entire face transforms and it's like nothing I've seen before. It's old grief. A closed wound that still occasionally itches. I choke on it.

'You look lovely,' says Olivia.

And just like that, the wound appears to be soothed. The grief becomes bearable again. 'Thank you, my dear.'

Olivia mouths the words back, my dear, with delight in her eyes. The delight. I want it back.

'She had a keen eye for pretty things. I'm afraid I don't do it justice.'

'It's beautiful on you,' Olivia says.

'Would you like to try one on?'

The delight again, but wary, like she's not allowed. Nick's smirk pops into my mind. Are you enjoying the book? Would you like another?

'Would you like to try on a dress?'

'Yes.'

I follow them upstairs, like a ghost, barely there, barely a part of this. Sally opens her wardrobe for Olivia. They talk. They pull things out. Colourful things. Flowing things. Things I've no clue how to even begin putting on. Olivia seems about as confused as I am, but she's interested. She's engaged. When did I lose that? When did I lose myself? My fingers find the antipsychotics in my pocket and fiddle with the bottle. *Rough and tough and strong and mean.* I want myself back.

'Turn around, Mr Robinson.'

Olivia holds up an admittedly soft-looking green

piece of cloth. 'I've seen him naked before,' she says, casually.

The blood rushes to my face again, and if I could disappear into the ground, if I could, well there's no telling how far down I'd go.

Sally's voice sounds like the gentle scold of a parent. 'Have you, now? Well. It's not the same, young lady.'

'It's not?'

'No. It's not the same at all.'

I screw my eyes shut and press my palms against my eyelids until patches of colour start popping up left and right.

'Young lady, would you look at yourself. Look at her, Mr Robinson.'

I look.

She's wearing the dress over her jeans. A little string hangs at her left side. Sally walks over, loops it around her waist and ties it into a bow.

'What do you think?' Sally asks me.

I clear my throat. 'Are you supposed to wear trousers underneath?'

'I like it that way,' says Olivia.

'Then that's how you should wear it,' says Sally.

I find myself wondering how much Jamie would give to see this. I find myself wishing he could. The way she holds herself has completely shifted. She twirls around and the skirt floats around her.

'There's a big mirror in the bathroom over there.'

Olivia beams with pride, unrecognisable, as she trots over to the next room. The door closes behind her.

Everything falls quiet. Sally pats the spot next to her on the mattress. 'Sit.'

So I do.

'Isn't she a sight for sore eyes?'

I nod awkwardly.

'She deserves to feel like herself. Everyone does. But she especially deserves it.'

'I suppose she does.'

'You're taking good care of her, aren't you?'

'We're not together,' I say, which is probably the stupidest thing I've ever uttered.

'Oh, please, Mr Robinson, I know you're not together. How much has she told you?'

I turn to look her in the eye, then chicken out and stare at her chin instead. 'I'm afraid to ask.'

'She would have been at the O2.'

'How do you know?'

'That's where they took me.'

'Oh.'

I slowly bite down on my tongue. Harder. Harder.

'They took both of us at first. Jang-Mi said, she said "Tell them". She said it in Korean, so they wouldn't understand. "Tell them and save yourself." I didn't tell them.'

I close my eyes and think of Jamie.

'Of course they caught me at the entrance. They had set up for triage in tents outside. It was all very shoddy, very unprepared. Anyway, I had to strip, and that was that. I don't know what I was thinking.'

'What did they do?'

'They took me back out. Jang-Mi said it would be alright. She said "I will be back with you in no time. You will wish you had more time without my nagging, you will see." She called me by my name. She called me her wife, in English, so they would understand.

They called me some really bad things that I don't care to repeat.'

She pauses to look at me.

'I imagine you've been called some bad things too.'

'Yes.'

'People are cruel. You have to know who you are. You have to shout it. Not for them. For yourself.'

A soft giggle rises from the bathroom.

Sally plays with the beads around her wrist. 'You know, Liv was like a daughter to us. We discussed the possibility of children, a long time ago, but we dismissed it. Too complicated. If I have one regret . . . It's never too complicated, Mr Robinson, but it can be too late.'

All at once my chest clenches and constricts. I can't breathe. I jump up. The room sways.

'We should go,' I say, lifting the wrong wrist to look at my watch.

Sally takes my hand in both of hers and I need out I want out get me out of here *it's raining men hallelujah it's raining men hallelujah it's—*

I try to slip away.

She doesn't let me.

'Don't let her waste her life,' she says, making it worse.

I fight against the urge to sing. 'I won't.'

Her face slides in and out of focus. She releases. 'Go. You need fresh air. I'll send her after you. Go.'

I run out. The corridor shrinks and narrows and I run to the door, help me, door, open, outside, down the steps, across the street, on to the pavement on the other side.

I double over, hands on my knees, head between my legs, and start singing.

'It's raining men, hallelujah, it's raining men, every specimen, tall blond dark and lean, rough and tough and strong and mean . . .'

Olivia's voice pierces through two inches of cotton in my ears. 'Are you alright?'

'D-d-don't, don't touch me.'

'You're having a panic attack.'

'I know.'

'What happened?'

'Nothing . . . ahh, shit . . . hallelujah!'

'I should have come alone.'

'No, it's okay, it's . . .' My eyes fall on the green dress in her hand. 'W-what's that?'

'She told me to keep it.'

I let out a shaky laugh. 'You're killing me.'

'I'm sorry.'

'Don't be sorry. Don't be sorry.'

A siren sounds in the distance. Coming closer. Loud. Like it's inside my ear. Like it's inside my head.

'Do you . . . are you hearing a police car?'

'No.'

I pull out a cigarette, but I can't get the lighter to work. Olivia gently pries it from my grip, flicks it on, does it for me. The smoke helps calm me down. I allow my legs to fold, my arse to hit the pavement, and just sit there taking long drags from the fag for a bit.

Olivia sits next to me.

'You know,' she says, 'I think she's my family.'

6

Jamie Hayes: Okay so, um, let me just take—I'll— I'll get some information down and then we'll just jump into it, okay?

Olivia Lloyd-Brown: Okay.

Hayes: Today is Monday, the, um, 14th of October 2019. Could you repeat that for me?

Lloyd-Brown: Today is Monday, the 14th of October 2019.

Hayes: Thank you. What's your name?

Lloyd-Brown: Olivia Angharad Lloyd-Brown.

Hayes: How old are you?

Lloyd-Brown: I'm not sure. I don't know.

Hayes: You don't know?

(pause)

Lloyd-Brown: No. I don't know.

Hayes: Do you remember anything of what happened on the 12th of March 1994?

Lloyd-Brown: Yes.

Hayes: What do you remember?

Lloyd-Brown: All of it.

(pause)

Hayes: Can you tell me about it?

(pause)

Lloyd-Brown: My father cried when the results came in. We watched it on the telly. My dad was crying.

(pause)

Hayes: How long was it between the referendum and the start of the quarantine?

Lloyd-Brown: Maybe two weeks.

Hayes: What did you do in those two weeks?

Lloyd-Brown: We went to Stonehenge.

Hayes: You went to Stonehenge?

Lloyd-Brown: (laughs) We weren't allowed. We were supposed to stay home. My mum had always wanted to see Stonehenge, so my dad drove us at two in the morning. We jumped the fence. Have you been?

Hayes: I have, yes.

Lloyd-Brown: We laid a blanket on the grass and watched the stars. It was nice.

(pause)

Hayes: Could you tell me what happened on the day you were taken to your quarantine centre?

Lloyd-Brown: They sent buses to our neighbourhood and came knocking on doors to escort us. My parents kissed for a really long time, and then one of the policemen said that it was time to go. My dad was holding me by the arm - around here. I remember I tried to pull away because it sort of hurt but he wouldn't let go. They had to pry me away and hold my dad back. They handed me over to my mum, she, she took me in her arms.

Hayes: How w— oh, were you, were you held at the O2? I assume that's where . . .

Lloyd-Brown: The O2, yes.

Hayes: How was the journey to the O2?

Lloyd-Brown: We were the last ones on the bus, because of how my dad . . . so it was full. We had to stand for a while. Then someone offered us her seat. I could sit on my mum's lap. I remember there was someone who was singing. I remember (hums). The lady next to us was complaining about it to my mum. I remember that woman's face because when we got to the centre, she was sorted symptomatic.

Hayes: Sorted symptomatic?

Lloyd-Brown: They had big tents set up at the entrance, in the parking lot. When we got there, they had us go through the tents. You'd enter on one side and leave on the other. My mum pointed at the doctors there and said they were epi— epidemiologists.

Hayes: Oh, they tested you?

Lloyd-Brown: No, they just looked for symptoms. They called it 'testing' sometimes. But they never tested us. There was a lot of paperwork and they asked a lot of questions. My mum said, 'Dwi'n mynd i ddweud celwydd am dy oedran di', 'I'm going to lie about your age.'

Hayes: Why?

Lloyd-Brown: I don't know. But she said it was important that I didn't correct her. We queued up, and the woman in front of us, the one who was complaining to my mum on the bus, she was blonde, with very small eyebrows. I was a little scared of her. They told her she was symptomatic, and she screamed. I was— I was scared of her.

Hayes: Did she look sick to you?

Lloyd-Brown: No, I didn't notice anything. She looked healthy to me. They said she was likely to be sick and she was sorted symptomatic. Then it was our turn. The doctor told us to take our clothes off. There wasn't a separate room so we had to take our clothes off in front of everyone else. They threw the clothes away and gave us these blue scrubs to put on instead. Some of the girls didn't want to get undressed in front of everybody and the police had to force them.

Hayes: Jesus Christ (inaudible)

Lloyd-Brown: What?

Hayes: Nothing. I'm sorry. Please continue.

Lloyd-Brown: They assigned a room to us. G59, it was. G59.

Hayes: Hang on, I think Sid's home. Let's— (recording cuts off)

(click)

(pause)

Hayes: How many women were there per room?

Lloyd-Brown: Six. Our room had my mum and me, Anita, Grace, Sinead and Rebecca. Sinead and Rebecca were sisters.

Hayes: Did you befriend the others?

Lloyd-Brown: My mum encouraged it. Sinead and Rebecca were about my age so we played together sometimes. Anita and Grace mostly kept to themselves. But I liked them. They were nice.

Hayes: How big was the room?

Lloyd-Brown: Not very, but it was okay. There were three sets of bunk beds against the walls and some space in the middle of the room. When we arrived, there was a towel and a blanket and pillow on each bed.

You had to be careful because if you lost those, or if they were stolen, you didn't get new ones.

Hayes: Was that frequent? The thefts?

Lloyd-Brown: It happened. In the winter, it got quite cold and the blankets weren't very warm. The room doors didn't lock.

Hayes: Did you have any other clothes besides the scrubs you were wearing?

Lloyd-Brown: There was a pair of . . . sort of pyjama scrubs, in a slightly different material.

Hayes: And that's it?

Lloyd-Brown: Yes.

(pause)

(clears throat)

(papers shuffling)

Hayes: What did the centre look like?

Lloyd-Brown: It looked like it had been put together very fast. It always smelled like disinfectant everywhere. Some parts of it were abandoned or under construction the whole time. The rooms were in the arena, in the middle.

Hayes: Were you— (crosstalk)

Lloyd-Brown: And the— Sorry, what?

Hayes: No, sorry, go ahead.

Lloyd-Brown: The shower room and the canteen in the outer ring. The medical stuff was downstairs.

Hayes: So you were allowed to walk around?

Lloyd-Brown: Sometimes. We could leave the arena for two hours at noon to have lunch and then two hours again at six for dinner. On Saturdays, we could spend the whole afternoon outside the room, from noon to eight. At eight, we had to be back in the arena. Most of the girls used this time to try and get to the showers, but since everyone was doing the same thing, it was very difficult to find a vacant shower on a Saturday afternoon. What you wanted to do was go on weekdays, eat your dinner very fast and run to the showers before curfew. Or you could share a shower with someone else if they agreed.

Hayes: Were you ever allowed to go outdoors?

Lloyd-Brown: Not really. Everything was under the dome, so it was all covered and closed off. They had covered all the glass windows with plastic tarp so that it let the light in but we couldn't really see outside. There was a small part of the tarp that was ripped off in the canteen, though. I always tried to sit next to that. You could see a bit of the car park through there.

(pause)

Lloyd-Brown: What is it?

Hayes: What?

Lloyd-Brown: You looked sort of . . .

Hayes: Oh, nothing, I'm just, I'm sorry. Go on.

Lloyd-Brown: We got used to it. They gave us a week to get used to it.

Hayes: And then?

Lloyd-Brown: Then they started the tests.

Hayes: Oh. What were the tests?

Lloyd-Brown: No.

Hayes: I'm sorry?

Lloyd-Brown: Not right now. Sorry.

Hayes: No, no, it's okay. Let's talk about something else. Let's take a break, actually. Would you like tea?

Lloyd-Brown: Thank you.

Hayes: No problem.

(click)

(pause)

(click)

Hayes: The other day you mentioned your, um, your mum saying . . . was it, um, y-you— (laughs) I'm sorry about that. I don't know what's wrong with me today. (clears throat) You spoke Welsh with your mother?

Lloyd-Brown: Yes, I did.

Hayes: Can you tell me a little bit about that?

(pause)

Lloyd-Brown: We didn't have much to entertain ourselves in the rooms. There were no books or games or films. So most of the time, we told each other stories. It started with the older girls telling stories to the youngest to get them to sleep and then everyone started swapping stories. They were either stories that the older girls made up or stories that we'd heard from somewhere else. Everyone did it. We shared stories in the canteen, so that they would travel around the centre. There was a girl in one of the buildings – I don't remember which one – who was a, um, a Sh— a Shakespeare expert. She had the best stories. We were always so excited when one of her stories reached us.

So there were the stories and then there were the songs. And my mum, she sang. She had a beautiful, beautiful voice and she knew a lot of traditional songs from Wales. We loved them. Everyone did. Most girls learned them phonetically and they travelled around like that, a bit messed up sometimes. The girls in G59 had them first-hand. And we were very proud of that. And I remember one day Becca asked my mum if she would teach her some Welsh, and I got scared. I was still a bit young and I didn't want to share. My mum said no. I was surprised. I thought she'd want to teach. She was a teacher, before the quarantine, so I thought she'd want to. Now I think my mum wanted to have a way to talk to me so that nobody else would understand. Back then, to me, it was more like a game. It was like a code, or a secret handshake.

Hayes: My mum was a singer, too.

Lloyd-Brown: Oh?

Hayes: She used to sing in pubs, back in Ireland, and she took me with her. I would sit next to her with an apple juice and pretend it was whisky. Probably really inappropriate, but my dad was too busy to . . . I'm sorry (clears throat)

Lloyd-Brown: (laughs)

Hayes: (laughs)

(pause)

Hayes: Any chance you'd sing one of those songs?

Lloyd-Brown: No.

Hayes: Oh, come on. Please?

Lloyd-Brown: Turn the thing off, then.

Hayes: What about posterity?

Lloyd-Brown: No. Just for you. Turn it off.

(click)

(click)

Lloyd-Brown: They said we wouldn't feel a thing. They said it was harmless, that they'd tested it on animals before.

Hayes: When was this?

Lloyd-Brown: Maybe a year after we arrived.

Hayes: And this was the first vaccine, yeah?

Lloyd-Brown: Yes. Well, the first post-quarantine one.

Hayes: Did it work?

Lloyd-Brown: No.

Hayes: What happened?

Lloyd-Brown: One day, they announced that the new vaccine was going to be tested on some of us and that the candidates would be picked based on their medical record and responses to the tests.

Hayes: Could you refuse if you were picked?

Lloyd-Brown: Technically yes, but they made your life miserable if you didn't cooperate. Suddenly you had all the staff against you. You didn't get as much food in the canteen - and the normal portion was barely enough already. You were taken for tests more often. Sometimes they would take you for tests during your free time and not let you go until curfew. And the security men picked on you more. Stuff like that.

Hayes: How many of you did they test the vaccine on?

Lloyd-Brown: I don't know. In our wing they took two girls. One from 93 and one from 201. They took them one afternoon and they brought them back in the evening. At the next check-up, both those girls were sick.

Hayes: How many vaccines did they try while you were at the centre?

Lloyd-Brown: Five.

Hayes: Did any of them work?

Lloyd-Brown: No.

Hayes: How fast was the infection spreading?

Lloyd-Brown: I'm not sure because most of the time we only saw what was happening in our own wing. But I know that when we first arrived at the centre, there were people everywhere. It was packed. I don't think even one bed was unoccupied. And then, in a few years, the rooms started to empty. We were glad, at first, because with fewer people the portions of food got a bit larger. And it became easier to access the showers. I think most girls were quite happy about this – I know I was – until people they knew started to get sick.

Hayes: Did the girls in your room get sick?

Lloyd-Brown: Grace was the first. We'd known it was coming. She tried to hide it from us for a while, but it was obvious. Anita and Grace started fighting a lot. I didn't understand why, because it wasn't Grace's fault that she was sick. I remember I asked my mum, 'Pam bod nhw'n ymladd?' And she said that they loved each other very much and they were very scared and that was why they were fighting. It didn't make much sense to me at the time. I thought it was crazy and I was annoyed because I couldn't get out of the room and I had to listen to it. I didn't understand it at the time.

At the next check-up, of course, they told Grace that she was sick and they took her away. Next Saturday, when we came back to the room, Anita had hanged herself with the sheet from her bed.

(click)

(click)

(pause)

Hayes: Okay, it's recording. You coming?

Lloyd-Brown: Yes.

Hayes: Uh, ouch.

Lloyd-Brown: What?

Hayes: Uh, that's my foot.

Lloyd-Brown: (laughs) Oh, sorry!

Hayes: (laughs) That's okay. I'm— I'm, uh, curious about your thoughts on the quarantine. Were you - are you - angry at the people who did that to you? Are you angry at the people who did nothing to stop it?

Lloyd-Brown: Back at the centre, a lot of girls hated the men for turning their backs on them, for sending them away. They were very angry.

Hayes: Were you?

Lloyd-Brown: No. I understand why they were, but no.

Hayes: Why not?

Lloyd-Brown: I think, when it happened, I was too young to be angry. And I was too scared. When I was growing up, my mum used to say that it wasn't a good thing to be angry. She used to tell me stories about my dad. She told me, and Sinead and Becca as well, that we shouldn't think that all men would treat us the way the men at the centre treated us.

Hayes: And you believed that?

Lloyd-Brown: She was right.

(pause)

Lloyd-Brown: I don't know if I believed her at the time. I asked why the men weren't doing anything. She said they were trying, but it was very difficult to do something because they were scared. I think I said I was more scared than they were. But she was right. It's not a good thing to be angry.

Hayes: I'm not sure I agree with that.

(pause)

Hayes: I'd like to ask you about the tests again. Is that okay?

Lloyd-Brown: It started about a week after we arrived.

Hayes: Oh.

Lloyd-Brown: What?

Hayes: Nothing. Sorry, I just— I wasn't expecting you to . . . Please.

Lloyd-Brown: They started getting people from their rooms.

Hayes: Randomly?

Lloyd-Brown: It seemed that way.

Hayes: What were the tests like?

Lloyd-Brown: At first it was blood tests, MRI scans, things like that. Then they moved on to injections. I don't know what they were injecting. We weren't really supposed to ask. Eventually people started not coming back from the tests. And those who did were not themselves anymore. They took Sinead and when she came back, she couldn't speak anymore. She never spoke again. 'Naethon nhw rywbeth ofnadwy iddi hi.' 'They did something really bad to her,' my mum said.

Hayes: Was there any way to avoid the tests?

Lloyd-Brown: Yes.

(pause)

Lloyd-Brown: The only women in the centre were the inmates. The men, well, sometimes you would find that they were looking at you. And if you just let them do what they wanted, you could get stuff in exchange like extra food or a new blanket. If they were a doctor and they liked you enough, they made sure you weren't chosen for testing. It never lasted long, though. You had to let them come back to you if you wanted to keep the privileges. Lots of girls did that.

(pause)

Hayes: Did you?

Lloyd-Brown: I would be dead if I hadn't.

(pause)

Lloyd-Brown: At first I didn't want to, and I judged the girls who were doing it. But then one day a doctor came to my room and he called my name. I followed him. You didn't have a choice. I thought I was going to die. He led me down to the basement and told me to get undressed. So I took my scrubs off while he prepared the operating table. He was putting instruments on a tray and I noticed that he was sort of throwing glances at me, looking me up and down, you know, and I knew that it was my only chance. When he told me to sit on the table, I sort of brushed up against him and I tried to smile. It can't have been very convincing because I was very scared. But it worked. He didn't say anything, he just undid— Are you okay?

Hayes: Yes. Yeah, I'm fine, I just . . . Actually I th— I think I need a break. Do you mind if— (recording cuts off)

7

I dreamt I was lying in bed and Jamie was sitting on me. Not in a good way. He was pressing his thumbs into my ribcage, hard, until I couldn't breathe. I thought 'He's killing me. I'm dying.' I felt something collapse in my body and there was a soft puncture sound, like a balloon popping in the distance, and I knew that my rib had pierced into my lung. And then, for some reason, I was bleeding out from the internal wound. 'This doesn't make sense,' I thought. 'What do you know?' Jamie said. 'You're not a doctor.' The bed was quickly getting all sticky and warm and red with blood and Jamie was staring down at me with a blank mask of an expression.

3.16 a.m. and I wake up in a cold sweat. I didn't have time to feel the attack coming on. It's there. The pain stabs in my chest, real, intense, I can't move. I squirm on the mattress, whimpering, hoping Jamie will hear and dreading it at the same time. I look at the ceiling and think it will collapse on me, it's about to collapse on me, I can already taste cement powdering in my throat from the debris. I hide under the covers and screw my eyes shut and I stay there, a shivering mess, until the panic eases off and I fall asleep again.

The dream comes back. Again. Again. Again. Every time I start to drift off, my body jerks me back into consciousness. Wrenched from sleep, drenched, with a thumping heart and ragged breathing, I moan.

'Shit. Shit, come on.'

Let me sleep. Please, let me sleep. But no matter how hard I try, I can't. I can't anymore.

With as little awareness as ever, barely in control of my legs, I go to Jamie's room. The door slowly swings open, clicks shut behind me, and I'm standing in the dark where I shouldn't be. I stick my hand over my nose and mouth to muffle the shallow exhales.

Jamie's always looked particularly open and defenceless in his sleep, like the slightest breeze might cause him physical pain. Maybe it's the apnoea, maybe it's because he never projects that degree of vulnerability when he's awake. Whatever it is, it's there, now, making my heart tighten and my body stretch and tense up.

One of his legs pokes from under the sheet, the sheet, *she hanged herself with the sheet from her bed*, she hanged herself. How easy is it to strangle yourself? My hand slides down to my neck. I squeeze. I can still breathe. I squeeze more. What do you know? You're not a doctor.

Jamie's breath hitches, and he sighs. *I think I need a break. Do you mind?* I shuffle closer to the bed, and he moves. I step back. Let's not do this, Robinson. Let's not do this. But I move closer again as soon as he settles. Just a little. Just a little closer.

The first time he fell asleep on the sofa, back at uni, I thought he was dead. He lay completely still, and pale. Of course, he's always pale, almost translucent, that's just him. I wasn't sure back then.

He moves again, and I startle so badly that he moves more, sighs more, and I look around for a place to hide and before I know it I'm cowering in his wardrobe, entertaining the idea of chucking myself out this weekend with the rest of the trash. The door remains open. I vaguely try to pull it shut, but that's noisy, too noisy, and he's moving again, more consistently. Repetitive short motions underneath the sheet. Is he awake? Would he see me if he were to turn around? I'm probably safe. It's dark enough that I can barely make out his silhouette, and the motion, that short rhythmic swishing of the sheet.

Then he emits a couple of soft gasps and it becomes obvious what's going on. Heat rises to my cheeks, and I flatten myself against the wall at the back of the wardrobe. I try to tune it out, but now I know, and there's no mistaking that for anything else. I become able to distinguish little groans, little whimpers, and I start getting hard. With the hand back over my mouth, biting the inside of my cheek, I revisit the idea of throwing my pathetic self in the bin. My free hand hovers between my legs, not daring to touch, not allowed, you pervert, you absolute pervert, not allowed.

Everything accelerates, barely under control, the motion, the quiet panting, then his breath catches and it's just deafening silence for almost ten seconds. And he lets out a louder exhale. It's over.

After a minute or so, he gets up and pads out, yawning, feet shuffling on the carpet. As soon as the tap starts running in the bathroom, I tiptoe back to my own bedroom and roll onto my back, mortified by the prospect of having to look Jamie in the eye tomorrow. I'm still half-hard in my boxers.

4.39 a.m. I notice a twitch in my hand and go to the bathroom, staring, afraid, at Jamie's door on the way. My tired face seems to melt under the neon light. I pop the tablet into my mouth with hurried, feverish gestures, like I did back then, when it was ecstasy and I needed the rush so bad my bones itched.

4.56 a.m. I feel high.

I sit on the edge of the mattress, batting away the occasional invisible spider from my arms and legs. Did I take the right pill? I go back to check. Looks like it, looks like the right pills. Am I going crazy? I rifle through the notice. *'Side effects include: rapid heartbeat, high blood pressure, dizziness, headaches, nausea and vomiting, high body temperature, spontaneous ejaculation, tardive dyskinesia . . .'* On and on, pages of it. My eyes scan to the bottom of the list. 'On rare occasions: seizures. In very rare cases, sudden unexplained death has occurred.'

A vision of my own gravestone appears in my mind, with the inscription in golden letters: 'Sudden unexplained death has occurred.'

6.12 a.m. I stare at the ceiling.

8.45 a.m. A square of pinkish morning light crawls across the kitchen wall. I pick at a piece of toast. Olivia sips her tea.

New shades have appeared on her face since yesterday, new lines, new colours.

'Are you okay?' New notes in her voice.

I smile, and nod.

I feel obscene. I spied, without permission, without consent. The things I know now. The things I know. And then, last night. Was it real? Pervert.

Pervert.

I tear a piece of the toast off and fling it into the bin, and she watches me do it, and says nothing.

Eventually, the lock on the bathroom door turns and a minute later, Jamie joins us, rubbing a towel on his wet hair. He pours himself a cup of coffee, fiddling with the industrial bar in his left ear. The sounds echo in my mind, like I'm hearing them now. Like he's panting in my ear right now, sweating and clenching around me and what the fuck is wrong with you? Get a grip, Robinson.

'Sid?'

I shiver. 'Mm-hmm?'

'May I talk to you for a minute?'

He grabs my sleeve and pulls me aside. I stagger, lose my balance and clutch his shoulder to keep myself from falling. Then I clear my throat and move away, discreetly using the bookcase as a crutch.

'Yes?' I ask, breezy even though I'm picturing his face contorted in pleasure.

'Are you sick or something?'

Pervert.

'Sick?'

'You look like you might be coming down with a cold.'

I shrug. 'I feel just fine.'

'Oh, come on! Look at you, you can barely stand!'

I let go of the bookcase to prove him wrong. My legs wobble dangerously. He catches me by the wrist and sends goose bumps up my arm. I yank myself free.

'Wh— Sid, what's wrong?'

'Nothing.'

He sighs – oh, the sighing – and checks his watch. 'Are you working today?'

'No. Why?'

'I need to go for a walk. Getting pure restless in here. Mind staying in with her?'

'Sure.'

'Thanks, mate.'

He slaps my shoulder on his way to the door.

'Wait!' I say, my voice a bit higher than usual. 'Passport.'

'Right,' he says, checking all his pockets. 'Uh . . .'

'On your bedside table.'

'Oh.' He goes to his bedroom and comes out

brandishing the thing. 'Thanks, dear.' A wink and a click of his tongue, and he's gone.

My knees give in. I collapse on the settee like a drunk eighty-year-old and close my eyes, desperate to sleep, but that's not happening.

Olivia trots in from the kitchen. 'Where did Jamie go?'

'Just for a walk.'

'Oh, okay. Hey, what's this word?'

I open my eyes.

'Oh, sorry. This word?' She shoves a book under my nose and points.

I squint at the tiny font on the page. Think I need glasses, but that's not exactly affordable. 'Uh . . . Sunrise.'

'Thanks.'

'No problem,' I say, slouching a little more into the cushions.

'And this word?'

The book is already inches from my face. 'Afterwards,' I say.

'Was it this frustrating when you learned how to read?'

'I don't remember. I'd imagine it's always difficult in the beginning.'

She huffs and drops down next to me. 'Can I ask you something?' she says.

'Of course.'

'How long have you known each other?'

'Who?'

'Jamie. You've known him for a long time, haven't you?'

'Ten years,' I say.

'Were you in the same course at university?'

'No. He was English Lit and I was med school. We were roommates.'

'Was he always like this?'

'Like what?'

'You know . . .' She gestures emphatically around her and I find myself chuckling. Pretty much dead on, actually. And I can't shake the smile off.

When I arrived at UCL, I was determined not to make any waves, or anything that could be misconstrued as broadly wave-adjacent. I was seventeen, brown, the son of a factory worker. I had a Mancunian accent and a full scholarship. My life so far had revolved around a strict set of rules, of what was done and what wasn't, and Jamie, well, he'd never even heard of those rules. He would find something he cared about and go for it. He stood up, spoke loud and clear, with his hands, to get his point across. Everything he did was the most important thing he'd ever done. It was fascinating to watch, and I couldn't stop myself.

'Effervescent,' I say.

'Yes. Was he always like that?'

'As far as I can remember. Is he driving you crazy already?'

'No. I think it's beautiful.'

Suddenly it's as if I'm naked again and she's inspecting every crease and imperfection, as if she's seeing a lot more than I even want to see myself. I swallow hard as she keeps asking, keeps plucking more out of me, and I don't have the willpower to stop it.

'How old is he?'

'Twenty-nine.'

'And you?'

'Twenty-seven. He had to work for a couple of years to save for the tuition.'

She swings her legs up and her head comes to rest in my lap. I freeze. Should I be touching her hair or something?

'Was his family struggling?' she asks.

'His father had money and offered to finance uni for him, but Jamie wouldn't take it. They're not on the best terms.'

'Why?'

'His dad voted in favour of the quarantine. Jamie never forgave him for t—' My breath catches. I clear my throat. 'For taking his mum away.'

'Where is he from?'

'Small village called Roundstone, in Connemara.'

She thinks about this. 'Ireland?'

'Yes.'

'Does he speak, uh . . .?'

'Gaelic. Don't tell him I told you.'

'Why not?'

'He's not keen on that part of himself.'

'Why not?'

I frown. 'I'm not sure.'

In a weird way, it's like she just scored a point there. Like I lost. I hadn't even realised I was playing a game.

'I wish I could go there,' she says. 'To Roundstone. Have you ever been?'

The thought seems so absurd I laugh. Because why would I have been there? Why would he ever want to take me there? He wouldn't. I laugh. 'No. I haven't.'

Her eyes close. 'We should go there, some day. The three of us.'

Don't let her waste her life. I wonder if Jamie

ever thinks about it, like I sometimes think about Manchester. *Don't let her waste her life.*

'Yes,' I say. 'We should.'

She yawns and sighs. I watch her fall asleep, and for some reason, I want to cry.

8

She's snoring on my lap and I'm looking at her, just looking, just feeling the weight and warmth of her head anchoring my thighs. It must have been an hour. Her hand rests, unaware, against my pelvis.

You should be feeling something.

I am.

No. You should be feeling more. This is intimate, sensual, arousing. Are you aroused? Are you getting aroused, Robinson, or do you only get off on your flatmate, you sick, voyeuristic pervert? Do you only get off on your flatmate wanking in the dark?

Nausea's building up. I gawk longingly at the cigarettes on the coffee table, but would I really wake her? Would I really push her off me, wake her, just for a smoke? I consider it, but really, I wouldn't. The lines on her face, the new ones, the ones that have appeared since I listened to the recording, have relaxed and faded. The frown's gone. The colour's back in her cheeks. I wouldn't.

The door swings open.

'Alright, mate?'

'Shhh!'

Jamie's eyes fall on us and he slaps his hands on either side of his face, beaming. 'Look at you crazy kids getting along!'

'Alright, Dad.'

He's soaking wet, *absolutely soaking wet*, dishevelled, and if I'm honest, almost rugged. I watch a droplet travel down and drip off the tip of his nose. He sniffs, wipes his face with his forearm. I watch his forearm.

'I take it you're not afraid to touch her anymore?'

'She . . . seems fine.'

'Told you she's not sick.'

'So you did.'

He slips out of his jacket and shakes the rain out of his hair. The purple t-shirt sticks to his shoulder blades.

'Would you like me to free you?' he asks.

'Please.'

He leans in and his breath hits my neck as he gathers her up in his arms. *How about now, Robinson? Are you feeling it now?*

I grab the cigarettes on my way off the sofa and, as he takes Olivia to her bedroom, I find myself praying to fuck-knows-who about fuck-knows-what. To make me sane, I guess. To make me normal, maybe. The voice laughs at me.

'My turn to step out,' I say, as Jamie delicately pulls the bedroom door shut.

'It's pissing down.'

'I need a fag.'

'You need some food.'

I put on my worst Irish accent. '"You need some food."'

'Piss off, Brit.'

We nudge each other. His elbow touches my side.

'Alright, go for your smoke. Eejit.'

'Arsehole.'

'Gobshite.'

'Wanker.'

Immediately as I say it, I start blushing furiously. 'I, um, b-back in a few.'

Downstairs, the smoke flows into my lungs. I hold it there, thinking about the damage it's doing. If I hold it long enough, maybe it will kill me. A few seconds later, I release, still alive. Fantastic. Instead of relaxing with each drag, I feel myself shaking with anger, with frustration.

He led me down to the basement and told me to get undressed.

The palpitations begin.

He didn't say anything, he just undid— Are you okay?

I press my palm flat against my heart.

Then my phone starts ringing and the adrenaline pumps harder, faster. The wrong word comes out. 'What?'

'Hophead?'

'Tom.'

'What's with you?'

'Sorry, I just—'

'Are you having some sort of episode?'

'I'm fine. How are you?'

'Never better. How about a drink tonight?'

I pinch the bridge of my nose for a while, but then I picture myself back home with Jamie and the purple shirt clinging to his body. 'Sure, fancy man, I could use a drink.'

'Brilliant! I'll drop by your place—'

'No!'

'What?'

'When are you off work? I'll pick you up,' I say.

'Tell you what, come by my place around nine. We'll go to my usual spot.'

'Yeah?'

'As long as you promise not to ditch me for some twink halfway through the first round. I do have a reputation to maintain over there.'

'Fair enough. See you tonight.'

'See you, hophead.'

As I shove the phone back in my pocket, my fingers catch on something. I pull out Nick's card. Nicholas Day. Producer. There's a home number. I swing my backpack round, open it, and *Jane Eyre* stares at me, and I stare at *Jane Eyre*. I zip it back up, and dial.

There's a package on their doorstep. I pick it up and then, when it's too late, wonder if that was an appropriate thing to do. It's raining, still, and the thing's clearly been there for a while. I ring the doorbell and wait, and notice the lawn, just starting to grow over the paved footpath.

'Mr Robinson, welcome!'

If possible, Charlie's gone even more Oxbridge

since last time. He takes the package as I hold it stupidly in front of me.

'Dear me, you shouldn't have!'

'Oh, that, that's not . . .'

He giggles. 'I'm pulling your leg, Mr Robinson,' and shouts back over his shoulder. 'Package for you, love! The delivery guy looks familiar as well!'

Nick waves from the sofa. 'Oh! He needs a towel again!'

'Yes, I'll get one. What is it with you and standing outside in the rain, Mr Robinson?'

'Sid.'

'Sid.'

He trots upstairs. Nick sits up and takes his feet off the coffee table. 'Pardon me. It turns out I'm terribly uncivilised. Did they leave that outside in the rain?'

I hand the package to him. 'I'm afraid so.'

'Oh, for crying out loud! This thing's delicate!'

I sit next to him. 'What is it?'

'New camera,' he says, pulling it out of the box and checking it for traces of damage. His fingers fall neatly in the right places, thumb hovering over the buttons, left hand adjusting the aperture.

'You seem to know your way around it,' I say.

'I'm a bit of an enthusiast.'

'Did something happen to your old camera?'

'He got it confiscated.'

Charlie's back with a towel. 'Maybe we should keep a spare set of clothes for you here.'

I thank him, and turn back to Nick. 'Confiscated?'

Nick nods. 'The other day, at that sit-in in front of parliament.'

'Sit-in?'

129

'Mm-hmm. We've not all given up, you know.'

I wonder if I've given up, and whether or not I ever had anything to give up on.

Last time I worked the late shift on address night, my third run was a man just a bit older than Nick and Charlie. Fifty years old, maybe, or thereabouts. Extra pepperoni, barbecue sauce on cheese-filled crust, terrible order. Point is, he had the address muted on his telly and I caught myself watching while he went to get a tip. As he rifled through his wallet, he grabbed the remote and switched to a re-run of a Liverpool v Man City game. No hesitation, not a word about it. The screen flicked from footage of people exiting the polling stations to a referee calling a red card and some burly bloke spitting at the ground. I remember not giving a shit. I wanted my tip and I wanted to leave. The place reeked of cigar and I had a dozen more runs to get through.

This man might have had a daughter, a partner, a friend, someone who got taken away. Surely, he had a mother. He'd given up. He'd given up on them. He didn't give a shit anymore.

For a fleeting second, I get smug. We're sheltering Olivia, aren't we? Doing our part. Surely it's more than most people are doing.

'I've never seen any protests,' I say.

Nick laughs. 'I know you haven't seen any. Want to know why? Because the media's not allowed to show it. And I should know. I work at the BT tower. Anyway, some poor bastard was getting pushed around, so I took out the camera. I thought that would force them to tone it down. It usually does. Evidently, I was wrong.'

'You could have been arrested,' I say.

Charlie hands me a mug. 'He almost was. We shouldn't have been there in the first place. It was badly organised. It wasn't smart. It wasn't safe.'

'Well at least they're trying. We're not about to abandon the few people who still care.' Nick gives Charlie a playful nudge as he sits down, and turns to me. 'You should get in on it, Sid. We could use more numbers.'

'Come on now, darling, don't drag him into this.'

'No, no, I'm not dragging anything. Sid's one of the good ones. I'm sure he's interested.'

Soft kindness lingers on Charlie's face as he fiddles with the hair at Nick's temple. 'Not everyone has the strength for all this, love.'

I get the distinct impression that this is code for 'I don't have the strength anymore.' Code for 'Please.' Charlie and I exchange a glance and I can see it. He's tired. He's exhausted. He's done.

Nick's not nearly done. 'Please, it's nothing to do with strength. Most people keep their mouths shut because they enjoy the low rents and big pay cheques. Did you hear that one guy at the protest? "Economy's thriving so clearly we should trust our government because they know what's best for the country" – fuck off! Fuck that right off!'

'Well maybe he had a poin—'

'He did not have a point! For crying . . . God knows I love you, sweetheart, but come on!'

'I'm not an economist, darling, and neither are you.'

'I'm also not a cook, but if I find hair in my soup you can bet your tight arse I'm returning it.'

Charlie bites his lower lip without a word. The

conversation deflates like a disappointing bake straight out of a hot oven.

'I have your book,' I say.

'Oh, thanks. Would you like another?'

Charlie coughs.

'What?' Nick asks.

'Is that smart? We could get him in trouble.'

I start thinking about Jamie again, and being home, with him, with the shoulder blades and the forearms and the purple shirt sticking to his skin. Suddenly it doesn't seem quite as bad as sitting here in the middle of whatever it is I've just walked into.

'That's okay,' I say. 'I probably shouldn't.'

'Okay, but let us know if you change your mind,' Nick says.

Something falls down in the kitchen, maybe a box of cereal, and Charlie startles. Nick puts a hand on his knee. 'It's nothing.'

Charlie takes the hand off. 'I know, it's fine.'

'What's going on with you today?' Nick says, going for Charlie's shoulder.

And Charlie shrugs him off and springs to his feet. 'You know I just, I need the loo, actually.'

Nick stares after him in shock. 'Sweetheart, come on!'

'I should go,' I say.

'Oh, you don't have to. But yeah, I bet you want to right about now. I'm sorry, that's, that was . . . unseemly.'

'Is he okay?'

'Yes. Yes, he's fine.'

'Are you?'

Nick chuckles somewhat bitterly.

'I'm sorry, that's none of my business.'

'No, it's not.'

I stand. 'I'll just, I'll show myself out.'

He calls me back, catches up to me at the doorstep. He's plastered the smile back on his face. 'I'm terribly sorry. I shouldn't have put this on you.'

'Don't worry about it.'

He shuffles about.

'Are you okay?' I ask again, without thinking.

'Yes. I think so.' He hesitates a bit. 'Sixteen years of marriage. There are bound to be some bumps, aren't there?'

'You're asking me?'

'I would never even entertain the idea of leaving him, but lately I've been wondering whether he'd . . . You know what, forget I said anything.'

'I suppose,' I say.

'Pardon?'

'I suppose in sixteen years of marriage, there're bound to be some bumps.'

The smile becomes genuine. 'Two weeks ago, you didn't even know us,' he says.

'I can't remember two weeks ago,' I say.

9

. . . baby this evenin'

For fuck's sake. Leave me alone.

I want some—

My arm shoots out to the bedside table and slams full speed into a wall instead. I scream, snapping awake, and cradle my hand, eyes welling up, breathing hard through my nose in an attempt to cancel the pain. It's pulsing, throbbing, sharp. I check for broken bones, poking carefully and wiggling my fingers, some residual knowledge from med school floating around in my mind, something about carpals and metacarpals. *What's your residual knowledge say about the headache, genius?*

I jerk upright and the room swings forward, a strange room, spacious and sober, all greys and blacks and leather and metal. I'm in someone's bed. I'm in my underwear, in someone's bed. My hand finds a silvery-grey sheet and I pull it up to cover my chest. I stay like this for a long time, empty, humming to myself, and I swear I've developed a rocking motion to go with it.

The door opens and here's Tom, holding a mug, shirtless as well, though the effect is rather different. As is the attitude. He flashes me a perfectly practised smile. 'Hey, it's alive!'

'Morning,' I say, holding the sheet tightly around me.

'Are you quite alright there, hophead?'

'I don't know.'

He points at the sheet. 'You can let go of that. We don't have any secrets anymore, you and I.'

'Oh God, did we . . .?'

He laughs it off, 'Don't flatter yourself,' and hands me the mug. 'Earl Grey. Lemon.'

'Lemon? The fuck is wrong with milk?'

'It's Earl Grey, you twat.'

I put on a posh accent. '"It's Earl Grey . . ."'

He whacks me on the back of the head. 'Say thank you.'

'Thank you.'

I sip, with one hand still on the sheet. The mug says 'I take my coffee like I take my' followed by the silhouette of a rooster. I stare at that for a while.

Tom looks at me with a strange expression. 'Blackout?'

I nod.

'Well, you were fantastically smashed last night. Bathroom's just through here if you need to . . . you know.'

'Are you going to give me any pointers at all?'

He sits down on the mattress, a bit too close. I hide behind the mug.

'Let's see. I took you to my usual haunt where you had, let's see, five pints. For future reference, your limit is three. Two, if there's no peanuts to absorb the brunt of it. It was a lovely evening, really. Karaoke night.'

'Please tell me I didn't sing.'

'Alright. You didn't sing.'

I rub my forehead. 'I am never drinking again.'

'Well, that's a shame. It was extremely entertaining. You got very talkative. No way to shut you up.'

I chew on my lower lip.

'You went on and on about Jamie and university and Jamie. A lot of Jamie talk. We should have invited him. He would have had a ball. Admittedly I didn't understand every word, what with the slurred speech and the strong accent, but there was some delightful nostalgia going on. Anyway, by midnight you could barely stand so I offered to see you back home, but you weren't having any of it, so I brought you here instead.'

I sigh, setting the mug aside. 'Thank you so much. And look, I'm very sorry about—'

'I'm not finished, hophead.'

'Oh.'

'So I'm getting you out of your clothes, right, to put you to bed, and you keep saying that you have something you need to tell me. So I look at you and you're all grave.'

He searches my face, like he's waiting for my reaction.

'And you tell me that there's a woman living in your apartment.'

We stare at each other. And suddenly, I don't know

if it's the lemon on top of the hangover or what, but I'm running to the bathroom, dropping to my knees and puking my guts out.

I remember it now. The feeling of urgency. The pressing need to get it off my chest. The relief once I'd said it aloud.

'Hophead?'

I cough, spit and cough again.

Tom crouches down next to me. 'Sid.' He hands me some toilet paper. 'You want to tell me more about this?'

I wipe my mouth, flush the toilet and fall back clumsily against the bathtub. Tom shifts to sit next to me. He's a little blurry.

'Look, Tom, I was pissed and possibly manic. I was talking rubbish.'

He's dead serious. 'No, you weren't.'

I stammer, avert my eyes. 'Do you have a cigarette?'

'No. Tell me.'

I exhale loudly. 'Fuck. Okay. What do you want to know?'

'Are you sure it's not one of your hallucination things? You've had those before, yes?'

'She's real. I checked. A lot.'

'What do you mean, a lot?'

'Jamie sees her too.'

He laughs. 'Bloody hell.'

'I know.'

'Why didn't you tell me about this?'

I shrug. 'The fewer people know the better.'

'You don't trust me?'

'We didn't want to put your life in danger.'

'Sure, let's say that.'

I pretend I didn't hear.

'How long?' he asks.

'Couple of weeks.'

'Holy shit. And she's not sick?'

'Doesn't look like it.'

We sit in silence. I close my eyes and swallow, trying to control the nausea. My head is killing me.

'What's her name?'

'Olivia.'

He repeats it, twice, then, 'What's she look like?'

I sigh. 'I don't know. Like a woman.'

'Is she tall?'

'Not very. About my height.'

'Eyes?'

'Dark.'

'You sure you weren't looking in a mirror?'

'Piss off.'

'Long hair?'

'Short. Cropped, like. You do realise she's trying to blend in?'

'Well, I'm going to have to meet her.'

My eyes fly open and I almost have to rush for the toilet again. 'No!'

'What?'

'I'm sorry, Tom, but no, you can't meet her.'

'Why not? I used to come by your place all the time. If I stop doing that, that's suspicious.'

I open my mouth and close it again without a word. He does have a point. I search my brain for a plausible excuse, but all I've got is '*Hot Stuff*' and a sudden craving for beans on toast.

'You don't want Jamie to know you've told me, do you?'

I look at him. 'He would kill me,' I say, quite pitifully.

'You're such a drama queen.'

'No, I mean it. He would strangle me with his bare hands.'

'Ooh, kinky!'

'Please.'

He sighs. 'Alright, fine. We don't tell him I know.'

'Thanks.'

He pats me on the shoulder, as if to say 'you poor fool,' and gets up.

'What time is it?' I ask.

He lifts up his wrist to read his watch. I wonder if he ever takes it off. It looks expensive.

'Quarter to ten.'

I think for a while. 'And what day?'

'The twenty-fourth.'

I give him a look.

'Thursday, you twat.'

I groan. 'Shit, I have to go to work. Don't you?'

'They can manage without me for a second.'

He holds out his hand and helps me up, abs working neatly under the lightly tanned skin of his stomach. I sway a little, struggling to find balance.

'Yeah, you're in no state to drive.'

'I don't have a choice, do I?'

'Your shirt's in the wash. Can you wait?'

'Not really.'

'Alright, I'll find you something.'

He goes back to the bedroom. Leaning on the sink for support, I examine my reflection. I look like shit. I wash my face and look again. Not much better but it will have to do. As I walk out of the bathroom, Tom hands me a clean shirt.

I lift an eyebrow. 'Silk? Now you're just showing off.'

He grimaces. 'Well I'm sorry I don't have any tie and dye, hophead.'

'What if I spill tomato sauce on it?'

'Then you owe me sixty quid.'

I put the shirt on. The sleeves are a bit long so I roll them up. He gives me the once-over and scoffs.

'Shut up, fancy man,' I say.

He whacks me behind the head again. 'Say thank you.'

'Thank you. Do you have my jacket?'

'On the chair over there.'

I check both pockets, unsuccessfully.

Tom creeps up behind me. 'Problem?'

'Can't find my meds. I must have left them at home. What time is it?'

'Five to.'

'I don't have time to go back.'

He shrugs. 'So you skip this once. How bad can it be?'

'I don't know. I guess we'll see.'

I grab my watch and phone from the bedside table. I've got eight missed calls and three voicemails from Jamie. This can't be good. I thank Tom again and rush out, dialling Jamie's mobile as I stumble down the stairs.

'Sid, where the fuck have you been?' His voice is trembling. Or maybe it's the bad connection.

'Sorry. I'm so sorry.'

'Where are you?'

'I'm on my way to work. I slept at Tom's place.'

'What?'

'I slept at Tom's place.' I almost add 'Nothing happened,' but manage to restrain myself.

'Jesus Christ, Sid. Didn't do anyone stupid, did you?'

He probably meant to say 'anything'. He might have said 'anything', actually. The line is crackling so badly now I'm losing every third syllable.

'No, I didn't. Look, you're breaking up. I'll see you tonight, okay?'

'Yeah, well just fucking call me, next time.'

And he hangs up. My stomach tightens with guilt. How bad can it be?

I run all the way to the restaurant but still arrive fifteen minutes after the beginning of my shift. I've missed two runs already. Mike yells at me for another ten minutes, during which I miss a third run. He threatens to fire me. I crawl and beg, as you do when you have an extra mouth to feed and no qualifications. Mike finally sends me to work, red in the face and cursing like a possessed man in approximate Italian.

No trace of Jamie when I finally get home, but Olivia's waiting for me in the living room.

'How pissed off is he?' I ask, dropping my bag. 'On a scale of—'

'He thought you were dead.'

She stares me down. I open my mouth and the wrong words come out.

'I'm alive,' I say.

The corner of her mouth twitches. I swear I hear a snarl.

'I'm sorry,' I say.

'Good for you,' she says.

'Is he sleeping?'

She steps between me and the bedroom. 'You're thinking of waking him up to apologise so you can feel better. Ask yourself right now whether you deserve that more than he deserves to rest.'

I hesitate. 'Fair enough.'

She sniffs. 'See you tomorrow.' And disappears into her room.

You really did it now, Robinson. You really did it now.

But as I flick the bathroom light on, her arms wrap around my waist from behind.

'Goodnight,' she says.

I can't bring myself to turn around. 'Goodnight,' I say.

She squeezes tight, and releases.

I tilt the plastic bag and the tablet slides into my palm. Eurythmics blare over the crappy sound system of the union. It's still allowed, won't get banned for another couple of years. I'm nineteen.

'You done this before?' says the guy.

Jamie laughs. 'You mean tonight?'

Unceremoniously, I shove the thing into my mouth and down the rest of my pint. Jamie scribbles something on his notepad, glancing after the guy as he waddles over to another group.

'Moustache?' I ask.

'Eyebrows,' he says. 'Fascinating.'

I snort with laughter and shush myself louder than the snort.

I sigh.

I scratch my nose.

I stare at Jamie's teeth. 'Nice smile.'

He giggles and tucks the notepad in his pocket. 'Jesus, mate.'

'What?'

He giggles some more. So do I. An exciting warmth is spreading through my chest. My shoulders swing to the pulsing rhythm. Louder and louder.

I pull Jamie's arm and, leaning into his ear, 'Get up and dance!'

'Nah, I don't think so, mate.'

'Come on, it was your idea!'

He looks at me. I'm dancing already.

'Fair enough,' he says, getting up.

I whoop and clap, I think, with the music. That shit is going straight up to my brain, and I'm happy. I've forgotten all about the anatomy midterm I barely passed, which – in my family – means failed. I've forgotten the word fail, and I'm happy.

We make our way to the dance floor. On an impulse, I grab his hand and we sway and jump to the beat. It pounds and pounds in time with my heartbeat. Jamie's eyes are closed. He's enjoying the high, lost in it, his hand warm around mine. My heart starts beating faster than the music.

Our moves sync up and we're practically grinding against each other. My heart is about to explode and there's no telling if I'm going to like it or not. The strobe lights pierce through my eyelids, the beat digs into my ears and suddenly it hurts. It's hot. It's too hot.

The music pulses louder and louder and faster and faster and it's too much at once.

'Jamie . . .'

My skull splits open. Bits of brain run down my neck and stain my shirt collar. I can't breathe.

'Jamie, I think . . . I think something's wrong.'

He doesn't hear. I grab his shoulder and shout over the end of the song.

'What?' he shouts back over the beginning of the next.

Humidity's rising. Barometer's getting low.

'Sid?'

I push my way out of the room and somehow manage to find the street, *the street's the place to go, we better hurry up*.

My lungs won't inflate. I'm caving in on myself.

'What's going on, man?'

I spin around and the whole world spins the other way. Jamie steadies me. His face is covered in crawling things, *humidity's rising, barometer's getting low*.

'Something's wrong! I don't know, I . . . Something's wrong!'

'What?'

'I c— I can't b-breathe!'

He laughs. 'Sure you can.'

'Help me!'

The laughter stops. 'Don't be daft.'

I lose my balance and my hands and knees hit the pavement.

'Shit, okay, um, it's going to be okay.'

'The f-fuck d-do you know! What the f-fuck did he g-give us? Was it . . . laced?'

'It couldn't have been. I've had some too and I'm fine.'

I weep and sob on the tarmac, the street, *the street's the place to go.*

'I'm g-going . . . to pass . . . out.'

'May I touch you? Is it okay to touch you?'

Suddenly a really big spider lands on my back. I shudder and shake it off. I scream.

'Sorry, no touching. No touching.'

'Should I call an ambulance?' says a voice.

'No!' I say.

'No,' Jamie says. 'It's okay, I've got this.'

I can't feel my legs anymore. I reach and grab hold of Jamie's shoulder. 'G-g-get it out of me, oh G-God, please, I'm d— I'm dying.'

'You're not. I won't let you die. I promise.'

I whimper and he doesn't say anything for a while. All my concentration is going into breathing in and out, sharp, through my nose, clenched teeth, breathe, clenched, tight, steady, tight, breathe.

Jamie clears his throat. 'Hey, Sid . . .'

'Hmm.'

'It's raining men.'

'Wha—'

'Hallelujah, it's raining men.'

I choke out a sobbing laugh. He hums over bits he doesn't know as the song spills out from the club. Jamie's voice in my ear.

'Tall, blond, dark and?'

'. . . L-lean.'

'Rough and?'

'T-t-tough.'

'And?'

'Ahh . . . strong.'

'And?'

146

'Uh . . .'

'Sid, and?'

'Mean!' I sing.

And then we're singing together. I'm getting more confident and I hear a smile in his voice and then I realise his hand is on my back again.

'Breathe,' he says.

So I breathe.

Psychotic. That's what I am. 'I'm going to up your dosage a bit.' That's what the doctor said. Then, when that didn't work, 'Let's try something else.' Let's try something else. Let's try something else. I'm going to up your dosage a bit more. A bit more. A bit more. By the end of it, I knew what I was. I was dull, disconnected. The voices faded into the background, and I could string two thoughts together again so that others would understand when I spoke. But I had no clue who I was anymore.

I turn the pill over with my thumb.

Sudden, unexplained death.

He thought you were dead.

Am I dead?

What are you thinking, Robinson? What are you trying to convince yourself of? You're not making sense, Robinson. You're sick.

I set the pill on the edge of the sink.

Antipsychotic. Psychotic. Does that mean anti-me?

Don't be stupid. You're sick. You need help. You need a crutch, a crutch, a crutch, you need a crutch for your sickness.

Who are you, Robinson? Who are you?

My index finger pokes at the pill for what feels like an hour. I push it, in the end, I push it into the sink and watch it disappear down the drain.

My reflection smiles back at me as I look up, and I hadn't realised I was smiling.

I strip and examine my body. Is that mine? It doesn't feel like mine. It stands tall, taller than me, I think, stronger. It exudes a confidence I haven't earned.

I'm laughing.

I'm laughing as I step into the shower and run the water.

That's how it was, at first, with ecstasy. I thought, 'Well done. Now it's over and you can move on with your life.' I felt proud and right and strong. The next day, I wanted to die.

10

(click)

Hayes: —that again, please?

Lloyd-Brown: About Lucy?

Hayes: You never mentioned Lucy before.

Lloyd-Brown: I wasn't ready.

Hayes: I'm sorry. I can turn it back off, if you're not ready. I'll turn it off.

Lloyd-Brown: No, don't. I'm ready.

Hayes: Are you sure?

Lloyd-Brown: Yes.

Hayes: (clears throat) Alright, um . . . Tell me about her?

Lloyd-Brown: She was brilliant. She was funny. She was beautiful. She had very dark hair that didn't look soft, but it was. And her face was quite soft, too, a bit delicate. She looked a little like Sid, actually, and she was Indian too.

Hayes: Pakistani, actually.

Lloyd-Brown: What?

Hayes: Sid's not Indian, he's Pakistani. On his mother's side.

Lloyd-Brown: Oh, I'm sorry. I should have asked.

Hayes: That's okay. You couldn't have known.

Lloyd-Brown: You knew.

Hayes: Well, yes, but I've known him forever.

Lloyd-Brown: Forever?

Hayes: Feels that way.

(pause)

Hayes: Anyway.

Lloyd-Brown: Anyway.

(laughter)

Lloyd-Brown: The first thing I noticed about her was she had . . . How do you say . . . this? Like you?

Hayes: What?

(rustling)

Lloyd-Brown: This?

Hayes: Oh, a piercing.

Lloyd-Brown: Yes, a piercing. Except hers was in her nose. A small ring. Her older sister gave it to her before she died, and Lucy put it on herself with a needle she'd stolen from one of the doctors. I admired that. I thought it was beautiful, that she did that on her own, to her own body.

Hayes: Did you want one yourself?

Lloyd-Brown: I did. But I didn't have any jewellery. Very few of us did. Obviously, there was no way to introduce new things into the centre, so whatever we had came from our sisters or mothers.

Hayes: Or grandmothers?

Lloyd-Brown: There were very few grandmothers when I arrived. None when I left.

(pause)

Hayes: How did you meet Lucy?

Lloyd-Brown: I shared my lunch with her. You know, Lucy was very outspoken. There was the nose-ring, which wasn't strictly forbidden, but it wasn't explicitly allowed either. And she had no filter, she was a loudmouth with no filter. The staff weren't keen on her. Some of the other women also weren't keen on her. I think they were scared to be associated with her. She was alone most of the time. I watched, during lunch. I went to the cafeteria at the same time every day because I knew she would be there.

Hayes: Were you attracted to her?

Lloyd-Brown: I was very attracted to her. (laughs) I was a teenager. Yes. I was very attracted to her.

(pause)

Hayes: You approached her?

Lloyd-Brown: One day, she wasn't given food. I mean, she was, but it wasn't a regular portion. It was almost nothing. There was one man working at the cafeteria who really hated her. He would call her some really bad things, most of which I didn't really understand at the time. He wasn't there often, thankfully, but this one day, he was.

She sat at the usual table, alone, and I could see she wasn't herself. She would usually snap back at him, you know, give him attitude. Not this time. I thought something was off. My mum didn't always come to lunch at the same time as me, but this time she was there. I said to her 'Naethon nhw ddim rhoi bwyd iddi hi', 'she didn't get any food,' and I went over to Lucy and I handed her some of my bread.

Hayes: Did you say anything?

Lloyd-Brown: Not at first. I was intimidated.

Hayes: Did she say anything?

Lloyd-Brown: She invited me to sit with her. I remember looking back at my mum. Lucy said 'Is that your mother?' and I said 'Yes.' She said 'You can go back to her if you prefer,' and I said 'No, I'll sit with you. I want to sit with you.'

(pause)

Lloyd-Brown: We didn't say anything for a while. I was probably staring. Eventually, I asked 'What did he call you?' I thought I knew, and I'd heard it before, but I wasn't sure. She didn't hesitate at all. She said 'He called me a dyke.' I said 'What does that mean?' She said 'It means I like to fuck women.' I said 'Do you?' She said 'Yes. Is that a problem?' I said 'I don't think so.' She said 'Thanks for the bread.'

I started talking a bit more. I asked about the piercing. She said she could give me one if we found a ring or something. I asked if it hurt, and she said no. I remember thinking she was lying. She must be lying, I thought, you know, something like that. It has to hurt, right?

Hayes: A little, when it goes through, but not for long.

Lloyd-Brown: That doesn't sound too bad.

Hayes: It's not.

(pause)

Hayes: What happened next?

Lloyd-Brown: She told me a joke.

Hayes: She told you a joke?

Lloyd-Brown: Yes. What do you call a cow in an earthquake?

Hayes: I don't know. What do you call a cow in an earthquake?

Lloyd-Brown: Milkshake.

(pause)

(snort)

(laughter)

Lloyd-Brown: She was so awkward. (laughs) By the time we left the cafeteria, my mum had already gone back to our room. I went back up. And I saw my mum sitting on her bed with this sort of set face. She was angry. She was so angry at me.

Hayes: Why?

Lloyd-Brown: She said I abandoned her, but I don't think that was it. I think she was afraid that what was happening to Lucy – not getting food, getting picked on by the staff – she was afraid that would happen to me. If I became friends with Lucy. She said we had to stick together because she wouldn't always be there. I felt really bad. I hugged her, and I think I cried.

(pause)

Lloyd-Brown: But I didn't stop seeing Lucy. I tried to hide it at first, but that didn't last. Mum never talked to me about it though. Eventually, I think she warmed up to it. Sometimes she would say she had a headache or she was tired, so that I could go to lunch alone, or to the showers, and meet with Lucy. We ate together, showered together. We started to sneak out at night. By this point, a lot of people had died. It wasn't hard to find a vacant room. We would sneak out, meet in one of the vacant rooms. We played games that we invented. We talked. And I . . . I did something that I was very ashamed of at the time.

Hayes: What did you do?

Lloyd-Brown: I taught her Welsh.

(pause)

Hayes: That's nothing to be ashamed of.

Lloyd-Brown: It felt shameful. Welsh was just for my mum and me. It was our secret code. I'd raised a stink when Becca and Sinead had wanted to learn. I felt like a hypocrite. But Lucy . . .

Hayes: You wanted her to know you.

Lloyd-Brown: I did. I really did. I wanted her to know everything. She was very dear to me.

(pause)

One night, we were just talking – I don't even remember what about – and it felt different. It just felt . . . different.

(pause)

And eventually the, uh . . . the conversation sort of died down. And we were just looking at each other. And she kissed me. No one had ever kissed me, not like that. That doctor, before, he had . . . but that, that didn't count. This was different. And she kissed me. And we just sort of . . . took, took our scrubs off, and we . . . we . . .

Hayes: . . . had sex?

Lloyd-Brown: No, it wasn't sex. It couldn't have been. Sex is a horrible, horrible thing. This was . . . it was different. It felt . . . we, we touched and it felt . . . good. It was diff— different. She was . . . she f— (sobbing)

Hayes: Shit. Um . . .

(rustling)

(crying)

Hayes: I'm sorry.

(more crying and shushing)

Hayes: Shit, hang on, I forgot about the—
(recording cuts off)

(click)

(click)

Hayes: (singing *The Wind that Shakes the Barley*)

Hayes: Wait, is it on?

Lloyd-Brown: No. (laughs)

Hayes: Turn it off!

(laughter)

(rustling)

Lloyd-Brown: It's for posterity!

Hayes: Posterity doesn't need that load of shite!

Lloyd-Brown: It was good!

Hayes: Liar. Give it here.

(laughter)

(pause)

Hayes: Well, we might as well get back to it since you've decided to stab me in the back with this.

Lloyd-Brown: (laughs) Sure.

Hayes: Let me just . . . catch my breath. Fuck. Oh, sorry.

Lloyd-Brown: Jamie?

Hayes: Yes?

Lloyd-Brown: I like you.

(pause)

Hayes: I like you too.

(pause)

Hayes: I, um . . . What, uh, what, what— (clears throat) Pardon me. What made you decide to escape?

Lloyd-Brown: I lost my mother.

11

I lost the twelve pounds I'd somehow managed to put on over the past year. That dragged me back from skinny firmly into the grounds of sickly. A hundred and nineteen pounds for five foot nine, and I can barely hold my own head up. Can't eat from the hunger. Can't think from the thoughts. Vomiting around the clock – bile, from my empty stomach. I know withdrawal when I see it.

I dreamt I was kissing her. Jamie was out, for some reason. I pushed her down on his bed and crawled on top of her and I crashed my lips against hers. There was tongue and teeth, sucking and biting, and my nose bending on her cheekbone. We tore each other's clothes off and I fucked her, but I couldn't feel anything of what was happening below my waist.

We were moving against each other and I knew that's what we were doing, but that was it. Like a blind spot. Like missing a piece of information. And then parts of her started to crumble into dust. An ear, an arm, the shoulder . . . disintegrated. Just gone. We didn't stop. We moaned and gasped, like we were enjoying it, even though I couldn't feel a thing, even though she was falling apart. In the end, she called out Jamie's name. So did I.

I smoke at the living room window, and nobody gives a shit. Nobody gives a shit anymore. I'm barely even there, am I, I'm barely even alive. I could get dizzy, dizzier, any minute, and tumble over the windowsill. I could smash my face on the pavement below. I could die, right now. Not that I'm going to. Not that I'm looking down and considering jumping. I'm not crazy.

The cigarette butt shakes between my fingers. My fingers shake. My hand, my arm, my whole upper body. My ribs rattle in my torso. I cough into my elbow and my brain feels loose in my skull and it ping-pongs against the sides and it won't stop, it won't stop. I'm not crazy.

'Sid?'

'Aye.'

He sees the fag and doesn't comment. Doesn't give a shit.

'I'm heading out,' he says.

'Fantastic.'

'You alright?'

'Perfect.'

'Sure? You don't look so good.'

'You going or what?'

He sighs. 'Fine, don't tell me,' and grabs his jacket, and the umbrella – been raining for days. 'Right, well there's leftovers in the fridge. Eat something, will you? And please, Jesus Christ, please take a shower. You stink.'

'Ta.'

'I'm serious, mate.'

'It's none of your business what I smell like, Jamie! Just go for your walk or whatever the fuck it is that you do and leave me be!'

The door slams.

I flick the cigarette butt out the window and light up another, no good, it's no good, so I go to the bathroom and dig out the tablets from the back of the cupboard, where I left them, hid them, from myself. I look at my reflection and see tears stream down my face even though I'm not really crying. I'm leaking like a faucet, emptying myself. There's nothing left. There can't be anything left. I've got nothing. I can't take it.

Take it.

I take out a pill and immediately slide it back into the bottle. Making sure the door is closed first, feeling quite stupid, I mimic the gesture of putting the pill in my mouth. I swallow nothing.

You stink.

I sniff at myself.

I hate you.

I undress, turn the shower on. The tears mingle with the soapy water.

Breathe. I lap up tepid water straight from the shower head. Maybe I'll puke that in a minute.

My keys sink to the bottom of the backpack as I'm groping blindly for them. My mobile starts ringing. Too much at once, it's too much at once, and why haven't I changed that stupid ringtone yet, for fuck's sake, what was I even thinking? I kneel down, put the backpack on the ground and keep searching with my right hand while my left sinks into my jeans back pocket for the phone. My finger reflexively hits reject before I even have time to read the caller ID. I'm about to put the phone away, but I notice I've got a text.

From Jamie at 7.38. *'Tom's here.'*

I drop the phone.

The door opens and Tom's smiling down at me. 'Hello there, hophead!'

I stagger to my feet and give him my very best impression of a normal person. 'Alright, fancy man?' And then I ask him for permission to come into my own apartment and the whole charade goes to pot.

He moves out of the way. Jamie emerges from the kitchen, holding two bottles of beer. He's smiling, but that's just his own impression of a normal person, and when Tom turns his back to him I catch a flash of distress in his face. I look around – no trace of Olivia. I throw a glance at the sofa, then at Jamie. He gives me an almost imperceptible nod and hands Tom one of the bottles.

'Do you want one?' he asks me.

'No, thanks.'

Tom raises an eyebrow. 'Have you gone teetotal, hophead? I know the other night was rather embarrassing for you, but that's a bit extreme, don't you think?'

'Well, he's not supposed to mix alcohol with his meds anyway,' Jamie says, pointedly.

'Bloody doctors. Always rather keen on taking away your toys, aren't they?'

'What brings you here, Tom?' I ask.

He shrugs. 'Just fancied paying you a little visit. I hadn't seen Jamie in the longest.' He nods his head at me. 'I was starting to think you were covering something up, there.'

I take out a cigarette.

'Sid, what the fuck are you doing? Not in the house, come on.'

'Oh, now you care?'

'Yeah, I do, actually. I'm not in the mood for second-hand smoke. Put it away, please.'

'For fuck's sake!'

'Put it away, please.'

'No.'

'Sid, what the fuck has gotten into you lately!'

'Gentlemen, please. You have company.'

'Fine!' I say, tossing the pack on the table on my way to the kitchen.

I find a stray can of Diet Coke in the fridge. I flick it open, idly wondering what it was doing there in the first place. Did I buy this? I don't remember buying this.

As I come back into the living room, Tom's giggling and I swear to God Jamie's suppressing a chuckle. *Laughing at you. They're laughing at you.*

'I was just telling Jamie about your lovely drunken ramblings.'

The bicycle chain in my mind comes loose and now I'm pedalling really fast with no resistance. 'What?'

'He went all blue-collar Manchester and, ooh boy, what a chatterbox, I'm telling you. Is that what you did with that emo boy the other night? Did you talk his ear off about Jamie until he fell asleep on top of you?'

I'm about to punch him in the teeth and I think Jamie can tell.

'Look, Tom, I'm not feeling very well. Would you mind if we cut this short for tonight?'

'You're not happy to see me?'

He puts on a smile. 'Delighted. Catch you later.'

'Not if I catch you first.' He winks, and gets up. 'Well, this has been delightful,' he says, looking at Jamie and emphasising the last word.

Neither of us walks him to the door. He waits for a bit, then leaves.

As soon as the door is closed, I stride over and lock it, and put it on the chain for good measure. Jamie frees Olivia from under the sofa. 'Are you okay? Sorry it took so long.'

'I'm fine,' she says, but there's a slight tremor in her voice. She excuses herself and goes to the bathroom.

Jamie and I sit back down and he downs his bottle. I take a swig of the God-awful coke.

'Shit,' he says.

'Why did you let him in?'

'He was at the door and he could see the light

coming from inside.'

I nod.

'Do you think she gets claustrophobic in there?' he asks.

'I don't know.' I look down at the tiny space between the seat of the settee and the floor. 'Probably, yes.'

I toss and turn and can't figure out when it got so hot. I'm sweating buckets, fuck me, I already took off my shirt and kicked away the sheet, and it didn't help. The heat is coming from inside of me. I roll onto my side, my back, my other side, my back again, sit up with a frustrated sigh. Outside, the sky is already turning purple. It's five-twenty in the morning.

I go to the kitchen. I run the water and wash last night's dishes. I rub the sponge hard against the pans and scrub angrily at the cutlery, long after it's clean.

Then I go to the bathroom, lock myself in there and yank down my pants. I stand over the toilet with one hand on the wall for support and start wanking. *Is that what you did with that emo boy the other night?* I'll fucking well show you what I did with— what was his name, again? His face is a blur, like his name, something plain, two syllables, three? Focus. The dark hair, the pale arse, the pale face, translucent.

Jamie suddenly pops into my head, eyes lightly closed, mouth hanging open, emitting that gasp, that sharp exhale, and I feel a tug in my balls. I try to push the image away, to replace it with another, what is wrong with you, Robinson, but now I can almost feel him, I can almost feel him sliding against me, uttering my name, and you know what? Fuck it. I lean into it, thrust into it, harder, more, why not? His lips on mine, his tongue pressed against mine, oh God the hair falling in his eyes, shit fuck yes come on, his fist clutching the sheet, his face, God, arching his back, whining through his teeth and coming, coming, c—aaahhhh!

I laugh as my own cum hits the toilet bowl, as I empty myself in strong, satisfying pulses. Something is definitely wrong with me, but in the moment, for a blissful second, I don't care.

'What the fuck do you think you're doing?'

I push my way past Tom and into the living room.

'Why don't you come in,' he says.

'What the fuck were you thinking? You had no right to do that!'

He laughs.

'We agreed, Tom! You had no right!'

He's laughing, he's laughing at you, you're stupid and annoying and he's having a go at you, you stupid loser, you shouldn't have told him about Olivia, now he's having a go at you, he's using you for entertainment, he's laughing at you.

'It's not funny!'

'Hophead, you're going all Lancashire again.'

'I don't care!' *Push the consonants out, don't drop your diphthongs, don't give him a reason to take the piss, he's going to laugh, he's going to laugh at you.* 'I don't care. You agreed, you said you wouldn't tell him.'

'I didn't tell him.'

'Don't start—'

'Are you quite alright, hophead?'

I sink onto the sofa, pinching the bridge of my nose.

Why are you like this?

Why are you like this, Robinson?

Why are you like this?

Tom sits next to me. 'Look, I'm sorry, okay? I was just having a laugh. I would never have told him, you know?'

You don't know that, you can't know that, he would have told him, he would have said, screwed you over, he's going to screw you over.

'Yes, well—'

'But I think *you* should.'

What? 'What?'

'Tell him.'

No. 'No.'

'It would be better for both of you. It's like ripping off a plaster, isn't it? You do it quickly and then you feel all better.'

'Or you bleed to death.'

'It's a plaster, hophead, not a fucking dam.'

I'm getting a headache again. Jesus Christ. Going off the meds. Whose brilliant idea was that? *Yours. It was yours, your idea, you deserve it, you fucked up and now you should suffer, you should die, don't you want to die? You want to die, don't you, why else would you have told him, you want him to turn you in, you want them to kill you and Jamie. You want Jamie to die, don't you, you sick bastard.*

'Are you sure you're alright?'

'Yes. I'm just . . . tired. Just tired.'

'I'll get you a drink.'

'I shouldn't.' I don't want to drink, I don't want to drink ever again. 'I have work later.'

'Not alcohol, don't panic. I'll get you a coke or something.'

He goes to the kitchen. Leaves me alone with the voice.

I chew on the string of my hoodie.

The voice hums in my head, it hums and hisses and it's like a worm in my mind. I fear it. I fear the humming, hissing worm in my mind.

'There you go.'

The glass of coke on the table.

That's poison. That will kill you. Don't drink it.

Tom looks at me looking at the glass. Doesn't speak for a while. Then, 'So tell me about her.'

The glass of coke on the table.

'Come on, hophead, don't be difficult.'

I spit out the string. 'I've got your shirt,' I say, ducking into my backpack.

'Where did she come from?'

'The O2.'

'And she's been over there since . . .?'

'The start.'

'Twenty-five years?'

'Yeah.'

'Christ.'

'Yeah.'

'How old is she?'

'I don't know. Twenty-seven. Twenty-eight. I don't know.'

'Is she pretty?'

I consider. 'Yes. She is.'

'Did you shag her?'

I wince. 'Fucking hell, Tom!'

'Well? Did you or didn't you?'

'No! Jesus, she's . . . How would that even—'

'Did Jamie?'

'No!'

Are you sure about that? Maybe he did. Maybe he fucked her, maybe they fucked and oh God it was good, maybe it was fantastic and he was moaning, ahhh, aaahhhh, and calling her name, calling her name as he fucked her.

'Of course not,' I say.

'Why not?'

I spring to my feet. 'Tom, you are sick, mate! This is fucking sick!' *You're sick, Robinson, you're the sick one, you're hearing voices, Robinson, you're sick, dumb and ugly, you ugly, dumb, sick wanker.*

'Alright, alright, don't hurt yourself.' He waves me back down. 'So what's the plan, then?'

I shrug.

'Seriously? You have no plan?'

'Well, maybe Jamie has a plan, but if he does, he's hiding it well.'

'Sid, this is serious. They're probably looking for her.'

'She says they're not. She says they think she's dead.'

'And you trust her?'

'Jamie does.'

He studies my face. 'Can I ask you something?'

I inhale sharply through the nausea.

He leans forward. 'Why are you letting Jamie make all the decisions about this?'

Take the glass and smash it on your own hand, go on, pick it up now and smash it into your hand, put your hand on the table and smash the glass through it, dig the shards into your hand.

'I don't want to have to make decisions.'

I glance at him. My shifty eyes have failed to convince.

And he blows up. 'Come on, hophead! Wake up, for Christ's sake. You're such a wimp! This is your life on the line and you're just happy to let him play with it!'

And I blow up too. 'Don't fucking start, Tom! You don't get to tell me how to live my life!'

'Yes, come on! Get mad! Anything's better than that bloody doormat you've become!'

'At least I'm not profiting from any of that fucking shit! How much is your rent? How much was that telly? How much was that fucking shirt you loaned me!'

'What are you even talking about? Do you hear yourself?'

'Stop pitying me, you fancy twat!'

'You are pitiful! You're just merrily going about your day like nothing's going on until inevitably – and I really mean it, hophead, I really do – inevitably, he's going to get you killed!'

'Better me than him!'

'Pitiful!'

'Fuck you!'

'You first!'

And suddenly it's over. We're all yelled out, and if I'm honest, that felt fantastic. Did I mean any of that? Probably not. Maybe a little. *You yelled about Olivia, you dumb fuck, the neighbours, the neighbours will have heard you, they're coming for you, they already called the police, they're coming for you right now.*

I throw a look at the door, then at the ceiling.

'Don't worry,' he says. 'It's sound-proof.'

I raise an eyebrow. 'Sound-proof?'

'Completely.'

'I think I'm going to be sick.'

'Well, you know where the bathroom is.'

Another minute goes by in silence before we both speak at the same time.

'So how's work?'

'So you managed to survive without your meds the other day?'

Lie to him.

'Yeah, I did. Didn't make much of a difference at all, actually.'

'Good for you. Taking control. You probably don't even need antidepressants.'

'Antipsychotics,' I say.

'Whatever.'

I'm going to kill you in your sleep tonight.

'You don't know how it was before,' I say.

'I know how it was.'

'No, you don't, you . . .' Just thinking about it I'm getting worked up again, I can tell I'm barely making sense. You can't speak, Robinson. He's right, you are pitiful. 'You've not seen . . . I can't go back . . . let, and . . . what I put Jamie through—'

'Oh, there it is.'

'What?'

He laughs. 'Nothing, hophead. Nothing.'

All of a sudden I feel raw and vulnerable and lonely. The voice has gotten unclear, mumbling, like a drone in the background. I check my phone, for no reason.

'Do you want to crash here tonight?'

I look up so fast my neck cracks. 'Why?'

'Just offering. I assume this whole living situation is a bit of a strain on you.'

'Oh. Cheers, but it's okay. Actually my shift's about to start, I should get going.'

'Of course you should,' he says.

I give him his shirt back and he shows me to the door. We stand there for a while.

'Bye,' I say.

'Bye,' he says.

Then he leans in, like he's going to kiss me. Like he's going to press his lips to mine and kiss me. I tilt my head away. 'Tom, no.'

He moves back and I see a smirk. 'Alright, hophead. Just checking something,' he says, casually.

As if my failure to jump into bed with him at the first hint of flirtation proves something.

My first run of the day takes me across Piccadilly Circus, to a building with marble floors, a concierge in the hall and a fucking bell-hop in the lift. I'm underdressed, leaving mud on the tiles, and definitely not white enough. The concierge sniffs. The bell-hop stands as far away from me as he possibly can. Do I still stink?

Repulsive.

Jamie? Yes? I like you. I like you too.

I hate you. I hate you so much. You stink. Repulsive.

The customer – rich fuck, couldn't spring for fancier food? – fumbles for cash in his wallet while I wait there, why are they never ready? I sigh. I cough. I cough more, and I know I should cover my mouth but my arms won't move and I've lost control of my arms and I barely have muscles anymore.

'Are you sick, man?'

'No.'

'You look sick. You're not contagious, are you? Because they shouldn't send you into people's homes if you're contagious.'

'I'm not sick.'

He gives me the once-over.

'You want a picture?' I ask.

'Are you on drugs?'

'No.'

'You look stoned as shit, man, what the fuck, are you serious?'

'Oh, Jesus fucking Christ, I'm not sick and I'm not stoned and I'd already be out of your hair if you'd prepared the fucking cash ahead of time!'

'That's going to cost you your tip.'

'I'm heartbroken.'

'And I'm going to need the name of your supervisor.'

'Mike Mancini.'

He makes a note before I leave.

It's not until I'm back on the scooter that it finally dawns on me what just happened. Fuck knows there's no salvaging that. Lie down and take it. *Take it, bitch, spread your legs and take it.*

The first time I heard the voice, it told me to go fuck myself. Jamie was sitting by my side. I asked 'What did you say?' and he said 'Nothing.' I thought he was lying. The next day, the voice mumbled in my ear all morning. I thought I had an infection or something. Then, in the afternoon, just before sunset, I heard a very clear, very distinct 'Shove your fist up your arse and pump until you're bleeding.' I got scared. I got terrified, but most of all, I got ashamed. I told Jamie, I told him 'I think I heard someone talking to me.' He asked 'What did he say?' I couldn't repeat it. I said 'Nothing.' I said 'Forget it.' I'd never been so embarrassed. By the end of the month, the voice was telling me to kill myself on a daily basis. And on a daily basis, I considered it.

I make a right on Regent Street and suddenly a double decker's coming at me, so close I could count the driver's teeth. I hurl the scooter to the left and manage to get into my lane just before the bus zooms past with a deafening honk. I pull over and dismount, tight across the chest, pumping with adrenaline, and swing the scooter onto the stand.

Why are you fighting? Just die already.

And the nausea comes over me again in swelling waves. I stumble into the restaurant and run straight for the bathroom. Bent over the toilet bowl for a good fifteen minutes, I retch and gag but nothing's happening. Blood rushes to my lowered head. *You're going to explode, Robinson. Can't you feel the blood vessels pumping too hard, trying too hard, you're trying too hard, Robinson, it's not going to work, you're making it worse.*

'It's raining men, hallelujah, it's raining men . . . every—'

My phone starts ringing.

Fuck, shit, leave me alone. Don't want to talk,

can't talk right now, busy. Call back later. Don't call back. I'll be dead later.

'Rough and . . . tough and . . . s-st-strong . . .'

'Sid? Are you alright?'

'I'm alright, Jamie!'

'It's Tony, mate. Listen, you've got to come out. Mike sent me.'

'Okay.'

I look down into the toilet bowl. The liquid inside turns and turns, like the flush is defective. It's getting to me.

'Do you want me to call a doctor? Or an ambulance?'

I turn away and face the wall, palms flat against the cool tiles, but the swirling continues in my head. *Round and round and round and round, take it, bitch, lie down and take it.*

'It's okay, Tony, just . . . just leave me alone, please.'

'Is he still in there?'

'I think he's unwell.'

'Unwell? He's a fucking mental case is what he is!'

'I think he needs a doctor.'

'No, he needs another job.' And then, to me, 'Robinson, you're sacked.'

'Okay,' I reply, like he just informed me that he used up the last of the mozzarella.

I hear him stride off.

'Sid, mate, I'm sorry,' says Tony.

I don't say anything. He leaves too. *Mental case. Fucking mental case.* I slide down against the wall and I start crying because I'm alone and I'm scared and I need Jamie but he's not here. He's not here anymore.

12

The bruise from Sally's sideboard is receding. I poke it. Pain. Nothing. Pain. Nothing. I wonder if it hurts someone else when I do this. Poke. Does it hurt? It hurts me, so why not someone else? There's pain, it's there, existing, so why not someone else? If I'm hurting someone else, should I stop? Do you want me to stop? Poke. Pain. Poke. Pain. Do you want me to stop?

I walk to Olivia's room.

'Can I tell you something? You can't tell Jamie.'

She puts the book away. I sit.

'What is it?'

'You can't tell Jamie.'

'I won't.'

'I got fired.'

'Oh no. What happened?'

I shrug. 'Budget cuts.'

She touches my thigh. I look at her nose and

wonder what she'd look like with a piercing. I think of Jamie's ear. I think of Jamie's cock.

I like you.

I like you too.

'You look—' she starts.

'Don't finish that sentence.'

'I'm sorry you got fired.'

'Thanks.'

'Is there anything I can do?'

'Don't tell Jamie.'

'I won't.'

I yawn. Last night's sleep was broken by empty thoughts and aimless worries. By me, if I'm honest, rolling around in the pain for self-pity points.

'Can I tell you something too? You can't tell Jamie either.'

'Sure,' I say.

'We've been . . .'

My insides catch on fire.

'. . . recording.'

Breathe. I know.

'Oh?' *Liar, liar. Recording what?* 'Recording what?'

'About the O2. How it was. What happened. You can't tell Jamie I told you.'

'I won't.

'Would you like me to play it for you?'

Liar. Pervert.

'Why does he not want me to know about it?'

'I'm sure he's just trying to protect you.'

Protect me. Sure, let's go with that. I pretend I didn't hear. I'm breathing rather too heavily.

'Would you like to listen to it?'

'S-s-sure.'

I follow her to the living room, to the loose plank, and she pries it open. When she turns to me again, she's a shade paler.

'It's not here,' she says.

I'm seeing spots. I steady myself on the bookshelf. We stand there, staring at each other.

'He went out?' she asks.

'For a walk. I think.'

'He went out with it?'

'Why? Did he mention wanting to do something with it?'

'I don't know.'

I start pacing, hand in my hair, both hands in my hair. 'Jesus, fuck me! Fuck me sideways with a fucking chainsaw, Jesus Christ!'

'What do we do?' she asks.

'I don't know! Do I look like I know? I don't know, okay!'

She grabs the mobile phone that was lying on the table and hands it to me. 'Ring him. Make sure he's okay. Make sure he's okay, please.'

I look at the phone, then close my eyes and exhale. 'That's not mine.'

'What?'

There's a notification on the lock screen. 'One new voicemail.' I punch in the pin code and dial the answering machine.

'You know his code?'

'Shh!'

She recoils and suddenly I see myself from the outside. I soften my face a bit and my voice comes out softer too. 'It's his date of birth.'

You have one new message.

I throw her another glance and she looks about as anxious as I'm feeling. I put the call on speaker.

'Yo, Hayes, it's Carter. Listen, um . . . I hope you don't take this the wrong way, but . . . I don't think I can make it today. Or tomorrow, actually. It's just I've got my father to think of, and he's getting on in years, you know, so I can't really afford to . . . take . . . to help you with that, with your project. I hope you understand. I hope you're not already on your way. I hope you understand. Bye.'

About an hour later, Jamie's keys clink down on the coffee table.

'So were you just never going to tell me?'

He hangs up his jacket. 'Tell you what?'

'"Tell you what?"'

'Sid, you're doing it again.'

'Where's your voice recorder?'

He fishes it out of his pocket and waves it at me with raised eyebrows.

'Hand it over.'

'Why?'

I grab it from his hand and jump backwards and then we're sort of chasing each other around the settee as I fumble with the thing.

'Jesus, you're such a fucking child!' he says, but already I'm pressing play and Olivia's voice shuts him up.

'*What do you call a cow in an earthquake?*

'*I don't know. What do you call a cow in an earthquake?*

'*Milkshake.*'

Silence. He sighs. We both do.

I throw the recorder back to him. At him. He catches it on his chest. It makes a thud.

'People need to know,' he says.

'I'm people! I was right here, right here in front of you, and I needed to know, and you just decided not to tell me! What the fuck, Jamie? What the fuck?'

'I was trying to . . . I didn't think you could handle it.'

'I don't need you to decide for me what I can and can't handle! I need you to treat me like I'm normal! Please, can we just pretend I'm normal?'

'Sure, let's pretend! I'll pretend you're not smoking twice as much as you used to! I'll pretend you don't look like a fucking matchstick! Maybe I should pretend I don't see that you're losing your shit right now, even before you knew about the fucking recording! But hey, apparently you can handle it!'

'Alright, you got me! I can't handle it! I can't handle any of it! This is, all of this, this is your thing and I can't, I can't . . . I never agreed to this! You didn't even ask, for fuck's sake, you know I'm schizoaffective, you should have asked!'

'What do you want me to tell you? It's done now! What would you have done? What the fuck do you want from me, Sid?'

The voice screams in my ear, *Say it, say it, say it, you coward, you know you're a selfish wanker, you know what you want so say it.*

'I want her out!'

I can't believe you just said that. Look at her. Look at the look on her face now that she knows you want her dead. I don't want her dead. *You want her dead.*

Gone. Dead. You'd rather she'd never escaped from that place. You wish she'd been killed over there, over there, injected with poison and killed over there.

Jamie's so pale he's practically see-through. 'Go ahead, Sid. Explain your plan, then. We throw her out. Where does she go?'

I can almost hear a growl escape his lips as I open my mouth to reply.

'Tom's flat is sound-proof,' I say.

He waves it away. 'Are you crazy? Tom? If this thing gets out there, we can't stop it. It will spread.'

'You said people should know.'

'Not like that! It has to be safe for her. We have to think about it.'

I blurt it out. 'Tom already knows!'

He falls silent.

'Tom knows,' I repeat.

'Are you sure? How do you know? Did you tell him?'

I nod.

'Jesus, okay, we need to do some damage control.'

'Tom's not going to . . .'

'For fuck's sake, Sid, you seriously trust Tom to keep a secret?'

'I didn't mean to tell him.'

'Oh, well, if you didn't mean to, that makes everything alright!'

I can't feel my legs. 'Don't you think I'm entitled to make decisions about this too?'

'Do you think you should be?'

The words catch in my throat.

Suddenly Olivia makes a beeline for her room and the door closes behind her.

'Do you think you're in a state to make decisions

right now, Sid?'

I stare at my feet. Fucking shame, Jesus Christ.

'No,' I say, and start humming.

He goes for his jacket. 'Thought not.'

'Where are you going?'

'I need a break.'

I follow him to the door. 'Jamie!'

'What?'

The deep, ashy-brown hair curls lightly around his face. His clear eyes, sharp, alert, gleam above the freckles. I want to have him right there on the landing, rough, against the wall, with him screaming my name and the neighbours watching.

'Nothing. Forget it.'

'In the end, we're all selfish bastards,' is what my dad used to say. He made sure I remembered this. Every speech night, he knelt down in front of me, his face close to mine, his eyes watery. His breath forced whiffs of cheap beer up my nose, his hands on my shoulders pushed me down into the ground. 'Selfish bastards, son. All of us. I'm telling you. When it comes down to it, we're all selfish bastards.' He never told me how he voted.

How many people do you think Tom's told yet? Do you think he's called the cops on you?

I don't know. How could I know?

You know Tom, don't you? Do you trust him?

That laid-back, not-a-care-in-the-world, new-boy-every-week guy that Jamie and I met at UCL. He wasn't on either of our courses. He wasn't in our halls of residence. I'd seen him around now and again. He was a drama student, the bohemian artsy type with the pretty face and the attitude. This one time, Jamie and I were having a drink at the union. He arrived with the usual crowd and, about ten minutes in, broke away from them, walked over and asked point blank, 'Can I pretend to know you for a while? Bit suffocating over there.'

He was wearing the loudest purple shirt I'd ever seen. It caught the light in all the right ways and made my head buzz. I was high.

'Tom Foster,' he said, and he might as well have said 'Bond. James Bond.'

Jamie stretched out and shook his extended hand with that casual confidence of his. Then I shook it.

'You're hot,' Tom said to me.

'Cheers,' I said.

'No, you twat. I mean you're burning up. He's burning up, isn't he?'

Jamie put his hand on my forehead, then on his own to compare. He pushed a glass of water towards me and told me to drink.

'Alright, what is it? Mushrooms? LSD?' Tom asked.

Jamie was very open about this. 'MDMA. Want some?'

'Oh, darling, I don't need that,' Tom said.

'Don't call me darling, sunshine,' Jamie said.

I giggled. Tom seemed amused.

'Fair enough.'

He stayed there with us for most of the night.

Jamie acted annoyed but never told him to go away. It became, if not a tradition, certainly a habit. We got used to him. Him, always with the swarm of friends, always patting each other on the back, laughing together. Sometimes more. Sometimes there was kissing and groping, putting on a show, always putting on a show, until he got bored and came to us for a drink or two.

Do you trust him?

I don't know. No. I don't. I don't trust him.

The bag of Tesco's breakfast blend leaks its colour into the water and I watch. It starts with a little cloud of gold and spreads and spreads and soon the whole mug is brown. I take it to the sink and pour it out.

Don't touch the food. Don't touch the food.

I'm taking a piss and not sure how I got to the bathroom. Falling asleep over the toilet bowl. How tired can you get? After I'm done, I vaguely try for a wank, try to wake myself up, but that's not happening.

I'm in bed, reading. Not reading, staring at the words.

Give up, Robinson.

I'm drying the dishes I probably just washed.

Lay down and take it, Robinson.

I'm walking away from the window and dropping onto the settee.

Suddenly I'm remembering what I just saw out the window and I jump up again and run to Jamie's room and bang on the door.

'What? Jesus, what?'

'Police!'

Jamie rubs the sleep out of his eyes. I shake him by the shoulders. Goose bumps rise on my arms as one thumb inadvertently comes into contact with his neck.

'The police are here! Downstairs, just saw them walk in.'

He gets it. I look into his face and he's getting it, he's gotten it.

He calls for her. 'Oliver?' Then to me, 'Are you sure?' Then to her, 'Oliver!'

'Just saw them walk in.'

'What is it?'

'They're here.' He goes to the window and glances down. 'I see a car. Doesn't look like a police vehicle, though.'

'Unmarked?' I say.

'This isn't a regular patrol.'

'They're trying to sneak up on us?' she asks.

'Maybe,' Jamie says.

My mind's going blank, my mind's going. 'I told Tom,' I say. 'I told Tom and they're, they're . . . here, I . . . it's . . .'

'Sid, not now!'

I turn to her. 'I'm so sorry.'

'Not now!'

She strides to the sofa. 'I'll get in.'

Jamie grabs her hand, 'No!' Then lets it go, then takes it again. 'They'll find you. I'm sc . . . They might find you.'

'Then what do we do?' she says.

Jamie and I exchange a look.

'Let's leave,' I say.

'Let's leave,' he says.

She thinks for a moment, and nods.

Jamie's hands fly to the sides of his head. He can't

stop moving, from one foot to the other, again and again, thinking faster than he can talk. 'I'll, um, go, I'll, I'll go down first. The normal way. You go to my bedroom and you wait for— I'll come round the back of the building and signal you. I'll check that no one's around and then you can come down the fire escape.' He takes her hand again. 'Did you get that?'

'Yes,' she says.

He turns to me.

'Yes,' I say.

He steps out.

'Wait!' I call.

'What?'

And I completely choke. 'Nothing.'

As he disappears from my sight, I'm overcome by that free-falling sensation you sometimes get when you're about to fall asleep. My mind's gone. Olivia touches my back. I tear my eyes from the closed door.

'Let's go,' she says.

I black out again and come to in the bedroom, and I'm staring out the window. I need food. *Don't touch the food. Don't touch.*

'Can you see him?' Olivia whispers.

'Not yet.'

'Can you see him now?'

'Not yet.'

From the corner of my eye, I notice his passport on the floor. *He's going to die,* says the voice. *Because of you,* says the voice. *Because of you.* Fucking hell, Jamie. Fucking hell. I stick the passport in my pocket with mine and check the street again. There he is. I exhale after what seems like years of holding my breath.

'Can you see him?'

'Yes.'

Jamie looks up at the window and gives a quick wave.

I pull the window open and freezing cold wind rushes in.

'Go,' I say.

I reach into Jamie's wardrobe for an old shapeless jumper and slip it on and my God, it smells like home.

It takes a while to climb down. The rusty ladder creaks alarmingly with each step. Should've waited for her to get down before adding my weight on there. *What weight?* says the voice. *You don't exist, Robinson, you're gone already, there's nothing left. Good riddance.* More than once, as I put my foot on the next bar, I convince myself that this time it'll break and we'll both fall to our deaths. I get used to the idea. I let my eyelids fall shut and feel blindly for the metal bar. Then I start taking chances. Letting my body fall before I've secured my foot on the next bar. Concentrating on the sharp rush of adrenaline every time, just before I catch myself. I enjoy it, fuck me, I'm getting off on the idea that I might just die, *just die, just end it, Robinson.*

Then my foot hits tarmac and I open my eyes. We're in the street.

Jamie nods over his shoulder and we follow him. We turn a corner, and all of a sudden we're running. We're running along the little streets and alleyways, half-colliding, pushing each other, grabbing each other, tripping all over the place. I'm elated, like we're running so fast no one could ever catch us. Like we're invincible. Laughter rings out. Mine, hers, his, but their faces aren't laughing. It's like I'm losing my mind.

I listen for Jamie's laugh, frank and infectious and unashamedly high. I tune into it. Don't let go. Don't let go. You'll die. You'll drop, drop dead, drop dead. We run until my lungs are on fire and then we run some more and I hang on to my body, I hang on to my bones and my skin and my brain. Jamie leads us through roundabout ways and turns into paths I didn't even know were there and forever, forever, forever.

We emerge in front of the Hungerford Bridge. I double over, reach for a cigarette and I can't light up, I can't light up, I can't get the lighter to work and I can barely breathe, I can barely catch my breath on fire, on fire, fucking dropping dead any second now. I put the cigarette back in my pocket.

Cold wind, winded, frozen. Please don't kill me.

The Eye looms on the other side of the Thames, all pink and blue and flashing lights even though it's not moved in several minutes, it's dead.

'Is it open?' Olivia says.

'It is,' Jamie says.

'It doesn't look open.'

'They only run it when there's people.'

She looks. She thinks. 'Can we go?'

'You want to go on the wheel?' Jamie says.

'I think so. Yes. I do. I want to go.'

Are you going to say something? Wake up, Robinson! You're not going to say anything, are you, wimpy, spineless, doormat, doormat, doormat.

I open my mouth. The wrong word comes out. 'Doormat,' I say.

'What?' says Jamie.

'Never mind,' I say.

And I start throbbing inside.

'Is that my jumper?' says Jamie.

'No,' I say.

I come to on the wheel.

I come to at the top of the world where there's no one but us, where we're lost and alone and safe but not, why, I'm missing pieces, I need food, don't touch the food.

Olivia says, 'It's beautiful. Isn't it?'

Jamie says, 'It is.'

Get me out of here, it's like I'm watching a movie and get me out, I didn't pay, I don't have a ticket, it's not allowed.

I come to in the street.

I come to in a park.

It's gotten dark. What time? Late? Is it late? Siren in the distance, the evening patrols, it's late and we haven't had tea yet.

'Is that snow?'

'It's snowing.'

'So it is.'

She hops around. 'Oh my God!' She flings her arms around Jamie's neck. 'It's beautiful! Oh my God!'

Jamie looks overwrought and he brings his own arms up to return the hug. *Aaaaaaahhh yeah, come on! I don't understand. Did you shag her, did Jamie, ohhh God fuck, harder! Back off, slut, don't touch me!*

'Shit,' I say.

I'm pounding, corroded machinery with a dead bird inside.

'What?' says Jamie.

'It's too early for snow,' I say.

'Not really,' he says.

'September?'

'November.'

'The trees died early.'

God bless mother nature, she's, she's a—

I come to in the street.

Police, the car, on the next street, around the corner, so close, closing in on us and the horn, the siren, blaring, *barometer's getting low* and I can't breathe I can't breathe barometer's getting low.

I tell Jamie, 'They'll stop me.'

He says, 'What?'

I say, 'You know they always stop me.'

He says, 'They—'

I say, 'Cross the street. You're not with me. We're not together. Cross the street with her. Walk the other way.'

He lies. He says, 'There's no one, Sid. There's no one. Are you seeing something?'

I panic, because he's lying, and lying is dangerous, dangerous is wrong, and wrong is bad, so I beg. I beg, 'Please, they're going to kill you! Please! Please, cross the street, stay away from me!'

The street's the place to the street's the place to the street's the place to go cos tonight for the first time for the first time for the first—

I say, 'What time is it? It's too late! It's too late, we're late, come on, cross the street!'

He says, 'Sid, look at me. Look at me.'

The things crawl on his face. The worms, the bugs, on his face, into his face, into his ears, into his nose.

I sob.

She says, 'What's happening to him?'

I'm scared I'm scared. I say, 'Go back to bed, it's

fine, just go back to bed. There's no monsters, pet, there's no monsters, there's no monsters, pet.' I'm scared, but I can't say that, that's crazy, there's no monsters, pet.

He says, 'We need to get him home. We need to get him off the street.'

Get him off the street cos I'm dangerous, they always stop me, I'm dangerous, you're hearing voices Robinson voices Robinson in your head in your mind you're broken Robinson you're falling apart. Die, you fucking fairy wanker, die. Step on it. Go fuck yourself. Get me out. Grab your vocal cords and pull them out of your mouth. Kill yourself, come on, kill yourself, come on. Get me out of here. Get me help me help me help me help me help me I can't breathe and I'm starving to death.

I say, 'Eating's forbidden.' And the world disappears from underneath, and behind, and in front, and I hit the pavement.

'Jesus, shit! Sid? Come on, mate, stay with me.'

His eyes are gorgeous. It burns. Touch me.

'I'm getting you home. I'll help you up, okay? I'll carry you. May I touch you?'

'I asked. How did you know?' *Tall blond dark lean.* 'Sing with me. Sing with me, love. I need help.'

The street comes back home with us. There's rotting meat under the bed. I'll never be alone again.

13

My head hurts. The sheet's drenched in sweat like I'm evaporating, hot, it's hot, cold and foggy, and the sheet's wet. My head hurts.

'There's a spider in my wall,' I say.

Jamie's at my side. 'It's okay,' he says. 'I'll take care of it.'

'I'm scared and you're not real, why?'

'I'm here. I'm real.'

'How do you know?'

'I'm going to touch your head. Don't be scared. It won't hurt. I'm touching your head now.'

He puts his hand on me, warm and a bit rough and a bit soft, I want to see him touch me.

'This is real,' he says. 'Just focus on this, if you want. It's real.'

He starts massaging my scalp, and I let out a tiny moan.

'Is the pressure okay?'

The strain loosens and eases. I purr through a sigh, in relief, in pleasure.

'Thank you,' I say.

'You're welcome,' he says.

Nothing's attached anymore. Just him and me and floating. Just him and me.

'I'm going to need you to take your meds,' he says.

I look into the clear eyes, gentle, above the freckles. 'It's a bit unsafe,' I say. 'I'm not allowed.'

'You're allowed,' he says. 'I'm allowing you.'

He puts a pill in my hand. His, his on my forehead still. His heat against mine.

'It's a bit dangerous,' I say. 'The box is too big for me.'

He smiles, gentle, beneath the freckles. 'You took them before, and you were feeling better then. Remember? Remember how you took them before?'

'I'm not lying,' I say.

'I know you're not lying.'

'I'm not lying,' I say.

'I know you're not lying, love, but I'm going to need you to trust me, okay?'

'Who's that?'

'Trust me.'

And I trust him, I do, and nobody can say I don't. I take the pill.

'Good man.' He strokes my chin affectionately. 'You need a shave.'

'I'm going to sleep again. I'm sorry.'

'Good idea. Get some rest, yeah?'

'I lost my job.'

'That's okay. It doesn't matter.'

■

I dreamt I was being tortured. I was on an operating table. My chest was open and full of silver surgical clamps and scissors. Men in white coats surrounded me. One of them held out his hand and plunged it into my chest. He pulled at something in there and I screamed. When he took his hand out, the latex glove was red with blood and he was holding a small piece of tissue between his thumb and forefinger. 'Put it back,' I said. 'Tell me where she is,' said the man. 'Please, put it back,' I said. 'Tell me where she is,' said the man. And he reached inside my chest again and pulled out a bigger piece. I screamed again. 'Tell me where she is,' said the man. And I told him.

My old rusty body is mine again. I send the command down my arm and watch my fingers wriggle. The restless feeling in my legs tingles up and down. How long since I last walked?

I roll onto my side. A glass of water sits on the bedside table, and the pills next to it.

Rapid heartbeat, high blood pressure, dizziness, headaches, nausea and vomiting, high body temperature, spontaneous ejaculation, tardive dyskinesia.

I'm stuck in a tree, high above the ground, with the pill in my hand. I think if I dropped the pill, just tilted my hand, just enough to let it tumble down and hit the grass beneath, I think I'd be able to climb down. I drop the pill, but I can't climb down. I fall. I hit every branch on the way down and break my neck on impact.

Dangerous, it's dangerous. You're not allowed. Poison, it's poison. Not allowed, not allowed.

I bring a pill to my mouth, and the voice howls like a wild animal.

Take them all, why don't you? It would be so easy to take them all. Come on, wimp, take them all, doormat, doormat, take them all, shut up.

Shut up.

I bring the water up, and swallow, and down the whole glass as the voice gurgles and shrieks. The liquid scrapes against the walls of my throat like sand. I need more.

I push the covers off and sit up carefully, then stand. My blood pressure drops, I almost white out, and fall back down. I try again, slower, with a hand secured on the wall. When I'm reasonably confident I'm not going to collapse in the immediate future, I start moving to the door, hand sliding along the wallpaper, feeling every little bump, every little imperfection in the pattern.

They're talking in the next room.

Olivia says, '. . . all night?'

And Jamie, 'Couldn't sleep anyway.'

'How is he?' she asks.

Silence. I press my ear against the door.

'Jamie—'

'It hasn't been this bad in ages.'

'Maybe we should call an ambulance.'

My stomach churns, but he replies without missing a beat. 'No.'

'If you're worried about me . . .'

'I'm not. I'm worried about him.'

'Not keen on the hospital, is he?'

'Neither am I. Last time wasn't good.'

I want to smoke. I want to smoke.

'Last time?'

'Last time.' He laughs a joyless, dry laugh. 'Last time, I didn't handle it as well as I should have.'

Vague sensations flash into my mind, parasitic, unbidden, distracting. Last time, *for the first time, for the f . . . history . . . hallelujah, it's . . .*

'I called 999. I called the police. He was scared and paranoid, and he was seeing things that weren't there. I said I was going to call for help, and he just panicked. He locked himself in his room. Cops arrived. Immediately I knew it was a bad idea. This one guy, this drill sergeant type, he was just showing off. He was aggressive. They broke down the door. Sid was cowering in a corner. That fucker just grabbed him without a word, pulled him out, cuffed him. I could see they were hurting him. He was looking at me like he couldn't believe I'd betrayed him. He looked so . . . I shouldn't have called them. I know that now. Especially after, when we got to A&E. Fuck me, that place. They put him in a room with cameras. It was a prison. It was four walls, no windows. They forced him to strip naked. When he wouldn't take the medication, they pinned him down and forced it on him. I tried to stop them, but not hard enough. I didn't fight hard enough.'

Hold his legs.

Help me!

Hold his arms, keep – shit! – keep him from kicking.

Let me go!

Let me go, please, let me go!

'Must have been scary.'

'Oh, he was terrified. I could see it in his face. I'd never seen him like that. He was completely lost, with no agency, no sense of what was happening. He'd lost himself.'

'I meant it must have been scary for you.'

He doesn't reply for a while and the silence leaves room for bad shit, I can't stop thinking, I thought I had my mind under control but it turns out I don't. Please let it be over. Please let it be over now.

Is this really necessary?
Don't touch him like that.
No, he doesn't want to.
You're not doing that.
You don't have the authority for this.
I want to talk to your superior.
You can't make me go.
I want to talk to someone in charge.

'He was lucky to have you.'

'I don't know about that.'

My heart starts hammering in my chest, and they can hear it, *they can hear you, Robinson. Be careful.* I put my hand over it. I will it to slow down so I can breathe, so I can listen, so I can breathe.

'Jamie, you know this isn't your fault, right?'

'That's what the hospital staff said, but . . .'

'What?'

'I gave him so much shit, Liv. So much shit. I pushed it on him, the weed and the E and then he started, he st—'

He chokes on it. I don't want to hear anymore. I want to pass out. Go back to bed and pass out, but I can't move.

'When I took him home, they told me the suicide rate skyrockets for about three months after a discharge. I was expecting to find him dead every minute of every day. I'd open his door in the morning with my heart in my mouth.'

I bite down on the back of my hand. Hard. *Bleed, you bastard.*

'He's here. He's right here, Jamie.'

Some sharp sniffling. A mumbled curse.

'You love him very much, don't you?'

He laughs again, and sighs. 'When he's himself, he's just so funny. He's smart. He's insightful. He's witty. And he cares. He was going to be a doctor. He was so good at it.'

I let my head fall back against the door.

'I think I should go to Tom's place,' Olivia says.

'No.'

'I think you need each other. Just each other. For a while.'

'I don't want you to go.'

'I know. But I think I should.'

How badly I want to smoke.

'I think you should, too.'

A long time passes by in stunned silence. Eventually, it becomes unbearable. I go back to bed, pull the covers over my head, and stop my ears with the palms of my hands. I stay like that for hours.

I dreamt I was getting run over by that double decker on Regent Street. I was on the Pizza 24 scooter again, and I made the right turn, and the bus was coming at me. But this time, I couldn't avoid it. It slammed into me, sent me flying across the street. I knew I was dead. I knew every bone in my body was broken. I knew I wasn't getting up ever again. And then it wasn't me, lying in the street with a broken body. It was Jamie, and he wasn't resigned to death. He was fighting it, squirming uselessly on the tarmac, trying to move, trying to get up, and failing, and failing. I was on the pavement, looking at him, listening to the sirens approaching. I tried to walk up to him, but Olivia was there. 'Don't,' she said. 'Leave him.' And then, in a different voice, 'You're hallucinating,' she said. 'I'm not,' I said. She looked at Jamie, writhing on the street like a dying bird. 'I slept with him,' she said. 'I know,' I said. She started singing. I didn't understand the words, but I knew they meant mourning. And Jamie was squirming and writhing on the tarmac with a broken body.

Jamie walks in, sees me awake and smiles. 'Hey.'

'Hey.'

He seems hesitant.

'I'm, uh . . . I'm not sure how long it's been since . . .' My body aches like I haven't moved in weeks.

'Five days.' He takes a seat next to me, crosses his legs on the mattress. 'Are you hungry?'

'No.'

'What do you remember?'

'Not much. It's fuzzy and sort of blending together.'

'You stopped taking your meds.'

'Yes.'

'Why?'

All the reasons I could potentially give swirl around in my head, like he'd blown on a pile of dust and everything went flying. I try to catch one, any one, but it's not happening. I shrug.

'How are you feeling?'

'Dying for a smoke.'

He groans. Then he fishes out my pack of cigarettes from his trouser pocket. I raise an eyebrow at him.

'I was nervous, okay? And they were just sitting there. So, you know, if you think about it, it was your fault.'

'Did I put a gun to your head?' I say, meaning it as a joke. But then his face is falling and it's really not all that funny. 'Lighter?' I ask.

He digs into his other pocket and hands it over. I light up and take a drag. I hold the smoke in for a while, then sigh it out. The knot in my chest begins to loosen up. Jamie goes to open the window and comes back. We don't speak for a minute or so. A bird is chirping outside, but then again, maybe it's not.

'Sid?'

'Hmm?'

'Don't you fucking do this to me ever again.'

'I'll give it my best shot. But you know I can't always—'

'I know.'

He sighs and extends his hand for the cigarette. I hand it to him and he inhales like his life depends on it.

'Fuck yeah,' he says, exhaling a cloud of smoke into the room.

We both chuckle.

'What have I done?' I say.

'Ah, don't sweat it. I can stop anytime I want.' He gets up and flicks the cigarette butt into the empty glass on the table. 'I've some work I should get back to. Try to sleep, yeah?'

'Yeah.'

Arguably, the hardest part is learning to trust again. The first time, after, after the first episode, it took forever. Jamie took me home and I hid from him. I sat in the closet, in the dark, for hours on end, because how can you know, when he's standing there, if he's standing there? How can you know that his voice is his? I couldn't look at myself in the mirror for months. Whenever I caught sight of myself, it scared me. I saw a stranger who would lie to me, lie through my face, to my face, make me believe I was safe and then kick me in the stomach, disappear, morph, change, and make me trip again.

I get up and walk around my bedroom, touching every object, breathing deeply, paying attention to every detail, every smell, everything. I pinch myself. I think about yesterday, about sharing a smoke with Jamie. Don't you fucking do this to me ever again.

I move to the bathroom, pulling on a t-shirt, scratching at my stubble. It's humid, damp. Maybe Jamie just showered.

I start shaving, and suddenly I'm hearing music. Well, that's new. I cling to it, listen for it. If I can't trust what's real, at least this is clearly not, and clarity's hard to come by these days. I time the razor strokes to the waving sounds. Slowly, I make a game of it. I tune in, relax, enjoy, and eventually the music takes on sad tones, soft notes, a meaning. I become shaky and cut myself with the razor. The blood trickles down my chin. I laugh a bit, and return to the living room.

Jamie's writing. Curled up at one end of the settee, laptop on his crossed legs. I sit, gingerly, at the other end.

'What happened to your face?'

'Cut myself shaving.'

He hands me a tissue. I press it against my chin.

'I picked up a few commissions,' he says.

He starts talking about his work and gets animated. Arms start moving, upper body stretches up, and the spark in his eyes. I can barely hear him over the music, but his expression, the passion, the smile at the corner of his mouth, those move in time, in perfect rhythm, they sway and move, and move me. The music swells.

'Sid?'

'Sorry I'm, uh, I'm . . .'

'Are you seeing something? Hearing something?'

I chuckle, almost embarrassed to remind him that he's breaking the rule. You know the rule, Jamie.

'Sorry, I shouldn't have asked. You don't have to tell me.'

I don't normally tell. Once you've said, people start staring. They start thinking, wow, you really are crazy. On impulse, though . . .

'It's music,' I say. 'I'm hearing music.'

'Oh. Are you okay?'

'Yeah. It's not unpleasant. Just a bit distracting.'

'Do you want me to shut up?'

'No, I just . . . actually I'm, I'm, I'll just switch off for a bit, just until it stops. Is that okay?'

'Of course.'

He goes back to his writing as I close my eyes. Colours appear against my eyelids. Patterns of purples and reds, flowers and growing seeds and extending branches. I'm alone with it. The music swells again. I hear an orchestra. I hear a symphony. I hear a first violin, a second violin, soft piano and a full brass section. It draws a yearning out of me that I neither expected nor cared to confront.

I'm lonely.

'Want to dance?'

'Did you say something?' My eyes flutter open to find his hand reaching out to me. 'Oh. You did.'

'I did.'

I stare at his hand.

'So?' he says.

'So what?'

'Would you like to dance, you massive, massive eejit?'

Part of my brain lights up, and the music slows, intense, as our gazes meet. I'm waiting for the blow. He smiles. I take his hand, and I'm waiting for the blow. He pulls me to my feet, and I'm waiting for the blow.

His free hand comes down to hold my waist. The sensation is completely new, oddly reassuring and quietly exciting.

I suppress a gasp. 'What are you doing?'

'Don't bite your nails.'

'What?'

He nods at my fingers, caught between my teeth. 'Those go on my shoulder, not in your mouth,' he says.

'Oh.'

I touch his shoulder.

He gives a short laugh. 'Do we still have a soundtrack?'

'Yes.'

'Perfect.'

His grasp firms, he locks me in and starts waltzing. He dances me across the room at a brisk pace, and I fumble, trip, mess up, step on his feet and mine. My heart rate shoots through the roof, and I blush to the root of my hair, but then he giggles and maybe it's fine. Maybe everything is fine after all.

'You can dance,' I say.

'Mate, I'd love to return the compliment, but . . .' He sucks air through his teeth.

'You arse. Where did you learn?'

'School.'

'They didn't teach that at my school.'

'I grew up in Ireland.'

'This isn't exactly – sorry – Riverdance, though, is it?'

'Don't make it weird.'

I concentrate on my steps, don't make a fool of yourself, Robinson, don't make him laugh at you, he's laughing at you. I survey every muscle in his face, check for signs, but he's not. He's not laughing at me. I catch myself looking at his lips, what are you doing, focus, focus, focus.

'Are we in sync with the tune?'

If I'm honest, we're not. Not even close. The

music is so much slower than what we're doing right now, that it's practically begging for me to pull him close and bury my face in his neck, *what the fuck is wrong with you, Robinson*. If I'm honest . . .

'Yup.'

He dips me and pulls me back up in one seamless motion, and I let out a falsetto yelp. 'Shit, what the fuck!'

'Scaredy-cat.'

I stick my tongue out at him.

'Does that mean the lift is out of the question?' he says.

'Now who's making it weird?' I say.

'What are you doing?' Olivia says.

Jamie twirls us around. 'What's it look like?'

She watches us with an amused smirk.

'Join us!' Jamie says.

'Oh, no.'

'Come on!'

She locks eyes with me, as if asking for permission, and I don't understand why. I nod. She joins in. We hold each other's hands and spin around, in a circle, around and around, and the music's gone by now but I'm not ready for it to end.

Look at you, says the voice. *Look at you go, you lunatic, are you losing it again so soon?* Around and around, laughing, whooping, until—

'I want to move out,' she says.

Everything stops.

'What?'

'Call Tom. Ask him. Please.'

Jamie clears his throat, sniffs, and ducks into the kitchen.

'Is it because of me?' I mouth at her.

She follows Jamie. I stand there for a while. And close my eyes.

They argued. I stayed out of it. I convinced myself there was nothing I could do about it, and maybe there wasn't.

'It's not your decision to make,' she said.

'If something happens to you, I'm responsible,' he said.

'No, you're not,' she said.

'Yes, I am,' he said.

'No, you're not,' she said.

He had to concede, eventually. Eventually we called Tom, explained, and before we knew it, the lift was taking us up to his fancy apartment.

Jamie's trying to hide the panic attack that's bleeding out of every pore in his body. He's sweating, on edge.

He's still trying.

'Believe me, you don't want to live with Tom. You haven't met him, he's . . . he's . . . and what if he calls the cops? We don't know that he's trustworthy. What if he was the reason they were in the building the other day?'

Doormat.

'They weren't in the building,' I say.

'You saw them walk in,' he says.

'Please don't,' I say. 'You know that was my illness, you know they weren't in the building. Please don't try to use my symptoms to justify—'

Tom's voice rises up from the other side of the door. 'Are you done yet, or do you need a minute?'

'Oh for f— We're not getting any younger, fancy man!'

He appears, his usual self, calmer than he has any business being in the circumstances. 'Bloody hell, hophead, you look like shit.'

'Thanks,' I say.

And then we're inside, and there it is.

They stare at each other. She holds her arms around her chest. I almost ask if she's sure about this. I don't.

'Olivia, I presume?'

'Tom, I presume?'

He smiles his brightest, most charming smile and extends his hand. Jamie and I exchange an apprehensive look, but she just unfolds her arms and shakes hands with him.

'How do you do?' says Tom.

'Nice to meet you,' says Olivia.

He giggles. 'Well, fuck me.'

'Tom . . .'

'Yes, lovely to see you too, Jamie,' says Tom, half-turning, eyes trained on Olivia still. 'Would anyone like a drink? I'm parched.'

'Maybe if you closed your mouth,' says Jamie.

'I'd love some tea,' Olivia says.

Tom winks and clicks his tongue. 'I'll pop the kettle on. Your bedroom's through there. Make yourself at home.'

'Thank you.'

The three of us step into Tom's guest bedroom, like we're glued at the hips, like we've somehow merged into each other over the past month and now the separation's going to require some serious surgical intervention.

She takes in the grey sheets, the black leather armchair, the minimalist art on the exposed brick wall, the lit bookshelf in the corner. She sighs.

'The bed's surprisingly comfortable,' I say.

She smiles at me. 'Do you mind giving me a minute alone?'

'Of course,' says Jamie.

We leave her there and I swear it sounds like fabric being ripped apart. Jamie winces, as if he can hear it too. Tom's placing coasters, then mugs on the coffee table. Mine says '*Ceci n'est pas une tasse*' in ornate cursive. Jamie's just says 'Blow me, I'm hot.' I'm beginning to think maybe this was a terrible idea.

'So, hophead. What made you change your mind? Whatever happened to "he'll strangle me with his bare hands"?'

I squirm.

Jamie leans forward. 'We call her Ollie or Oliver if there's a risk someone can hear, and we switch pronouns when on the phone.'

'Straight to business, then?'

'Do you have somewhere she can hide, in case you get an inspection?'

He thinks for a bit. 'Flat next door's been empty for years. Accessible via the balcony. She'll have to climb over the railing to get across.'

'Show me.'

They both stand while I sit there, unable to move, cradling the mug and staring through it. Then I lean back into the sofa cushions and stare through the industrial pipes and slick ceiling lights.

'Fuck,' I say to the empty room.

'Are you okay?'

I straighten myself up. She's wearing one of the jumpers Jamie gave her, and she wasn't wearing it before, I'm sure. I'm sure. I'm also sixty-five percent sure she's been crying. She takes a seat next to me, brings her knees up and drapes the large shapeless jumper over her legs. I hand her a mug.

She looks at the writing. 'What does it say?' she asks.

I tilt my head sideways and squint. 'You don't want to know.'

'Is that a chicken?'

'That's . . . yeah, that's a chicken.'

She smiles. 'I'm going to miss you guys.'

'We'll visit all the time.'

'I know.'

She sighs and puts her hand on my forearm.

When Dad sent me off to school for the first time after we moved south, I must have had that exact same look on my face, that exact same tone in my voice. Dad wouldn't hear any of it. Keep your chin up. You're a grown man. Stand up straight. Don't let them laugh at you. Fight back if you have to. Don't cry. Don't you dare cry. I was eight years old.

I try to decide which piece of advice is the most appropriate, or the least inappropriate. It all sounds like shit right about now, if I'm honest.

Don't let your voice do that thing.

Speak up.

If someone takes the piss, you sock them in the mouth, got it?

Maybe I was nine, not eight.

'Sid?'

'Yeah?'

'I think you guys should go now. I need you to go now. Could you ask Jamie? Could you tell Jamie you need to go home?'

Why do you have to move your hands like that? I swear I could mistake you for your ma sometimes. Stop being such a sissy.

'I'll try.'

Doormat.

'Anyone for a second cup?' Tom says, too breezy, waltzing back in.

Jamie's following, a trace of something different on his face, that I can't quite decipher.

Olivia glances in my direction.

'Actually, I think we should go,' I say.

'Oh,' says Jamie.

He checks in with her, a brief look of confusion. You want me gone?

'Fair enough,' Tom says. 'We'll have a nice evening, won't we? Get to know each other.'

'Yes,' Olivia says.

Tears burn in my eyes out of nowhere. A lump grows in my throat. I swallow it back. *Don't you dare. Don't you fucking dare, nancy boy.*

She comes up to me. 'Can I give you a hug?'

I nod and she wraps her arms around my neck.

'Bye, Sid.'

'Bye.'

She whispers in my ear, 'I'm not leaving because of you.'

I whisper back. 'I don't believe you.'

Then she turns to Jamie and she doesn't ask. She

just embraces him like it's the most natural thing in the world. He inhales deeply, and releases.

She touches the tip of his nose with her index finger. 'Beep.'

Jamie's face slips for a second, a split second, I see a flash of distress, and then it's gone.

'Is fada liom uaim thú,' he says.

'Byddi di'n iawn,' she says.

'What?' says Tom.

I say nothing.

'I'm so sorry,' Jamie says. 'I didn't catch that.'

She nods with some renewed confidence. 'You'll be fine,' she says.

'Yes,' Jamie says. 'So will you.'

Three days later, she was dead.

14

About a week into my hospitalisation, the guy in the room next to mine overdosed. I'd seen him around a few times, nothing serious. Couldn't say I really knew him. The loss barely registered. Staff organised a seminar. 'Seminar' was what they called it, but really it was a dozen of us sat around in a circle while a psychiatrist explained grief to us. The boy to my left wept. He had glassy dead eyes and visible slashes all over his forearms. He didn't need it explained. I stared at the counsellor and thought, fuck off. Fuck right off.

The phone rings on Thursday night, just as my fingers are twisting the knob to turn the oven off. Jamie picks up. 'Yeah?'

Someone mumbles on the other end.

'Tom,' Jamie says. 'What's new with you? How's it—'

The line crackles with a sharp exhale.

Jamie stops moving. 'Tom?'

The mumbling starts up again, and goes on. And on.

As I watch the glassy eyes – the boy's glassy eyes – take over Jamie's face, my hand twists the knob, cranks the temperature all the way up. I don't need an explanation. I need burning. I need the food, the kitchen, the apartment to burn to the ground.

Jamie swallows. 'Put . . . put Ollie on the phone. Just put Ollie on the phone, please.'

And Tom's strained voice, over the phone, 'Did you hear what I said?'

Jamie sits. He gets up. Sits. Gets up. He turns to me.

'Jamie?' Tom calls. 'Are you there?'

Jamie lifts the phone, stares at it for a while, and hands it to me. I don't want to take it, but I already have and Tom is breathing hard in my ear. I wince. 'Fancy man?'

'Hophead, I am so sorry.'

'What happened?' I ask.

I already know.

'They came looking and they . . . they checked next door. It's empty. It's been empty for years. I didn't think they would, I thought they'd only search in here. I told them the place is quiet, that I never hear any sound coming from there. I tried . . .'

I already know, and at this point we're just stalling, just beating around the fucking bush, and it's getting on my very last nerve. 'For fuck's sake, Tom, is she dead?'

The second the word leaves my mouth, Jamie

strides out the front door.

'Wait! Jam— Shit!' I grab my keys. 'Tom, we're on our way,' I say, and hang up.

I follow Jamie down the stairs.

'It's not safe,' I say under my breath. 'Cops might still be over there. They could still be watching.'

He doesn't register.

I watch the back of his head. I watch his hair, ash brown, curling more and more, think he's probably due for a haircut soon. Did I turn off the oven? The utilities bill must be due soon. Dinner's going to be cold by the time we get back. Where did the voice go? It's quiet, it's empty, the voice is gone and fuck me, that's just wrong. Someone talk to me, please.

I follow him all the way to Tom's flat.

I close my eyes in the lift, but the smell pierces through still, and it smells like, it smells like *I'm not leaving because of you*. I don't believe you. I don't believe you.

The door to the empty flat is wide open. A faint antiseptic smell lingers in the corridor. Jamie and I both look in at the same time and I hear his breath catch in his throat and my own voice does something funky as my stomach flips.

A man in protective equipment's tearing bloodied carpet from the floor. Another inspects the walls.

Jamie turns away and blinks, and blinks again, frowning like he's trying to wipe the image from his memory.

Say something. Shut up.

Jamie bangs on Tom's door, rings the doorbell, bangs on the door again.

For a while, we wait and I can't tear my eyes from

that piece of carpet. And suddenly the cleaning man's face snaps up and he looks at me.

Just then, the door swings open and Tom appears, unshaven, in pyjama bottoms and a plain t-shirt, of all things, and that's wrong. That's just wrong.

'I—'

Jamie shoves him back inside, across the room, pins him against the opposite wall. Tom recoils, shrinks, tries to wriggle free and fails, even though he's quite a few inches taller.

'What the fuck did you do, Foster? What the fuck did you do, you absolute fucking rat, I fucking well warned you!'

I shush anxiously, hurrying to close the door, *It's soundproof. Completely.*

'Jamie, I swear,' Tom says. 'I swear I would n—'

Jamie lets out a dry laugh. 'I promise you, if you finish that sentence, you're a dead man.' He's panting, growling, emitting sounds I've never heard come out of him. 'What happened?'

Tom's bottom lip quivers.

Jamie yanks him by the front of his shirt and slams him back into the wall. Tom yells out as his skull hits the exposed bricks. For a second, Jamie seems shocked at his own strength, at his own intensity, shocked at himself, but then the doubt fades out and he's gone again, he's dissolving, burning up. He's burning out.

'What. Happened. Tom! What happened?'

Tom glances over Jamie's shoulder at me. I look away.

Jamie shakes him. 'Where did they take her?'

'They didn't take her.'

'What the fuck do you mean, they didn't take her?'

'Jamie,' I start. 'The . . . You saw the . . .'

'They shot her,' Tom says.

I hear a strangled sob and I think it came from me, but I can't be sure.

Jamie's voice turns raw and heavy. 'Don't lie to me!'

'They tried to take her and she fought back. She was screaming—'

'Shut up.'

'—and people . . . people were starting to hear, so they just, they killed—'

'Shut up! Shut it now!'

Jamie turns to me, looks directly into my eyes, and keeps talking.

'Shut up. Shut up.'

He shrivels.

'Shut up.'

He heaves and hyperventilates.

He looks to me again and I can almost feel him reaching for me, but I can't catch him, I can't reach back, and he looks at me like he's alone, like I've abandoned him and he's alone.

His eyes close and he begins to mumble. 'Ár nAthair, atá ar neamh. Go naofar d'ainm. Go dtaga do ríocht. Go ndéantar do thoil ar an talamh.'

Tom takes a step forward.

I shake my head at him.

Don't.

'I'm sorry,' he says. 'I'm sorry. There was nothing I could have—'

Jamie spins around and punches him in the

face. Tom whimpers. Jamie gasps. I watch blood trickle down Tom's temple, blood collect on Jamie's knuckles as he cradles his twitching hand.

'Shit,' I say.

Jamie hesitates, moves back and forth for a moment, then leaves.

The left side of Tom's head is starting to swell already and the point of impact has gone purplish-red. He stumbles, woozy, to the sofa.

I stand there.

'Go,' he says.

'Do you need me to call an ambulance?'

'Fuck off, hophead.'

And I leave too.

Jamie's nowhere to be found. He's gone, fuck knows where. 'Shit,' I say again.

Mayfair buzzes with late afternoon life. People talking, laughing, zooming past, on their phones, on their way home from work. It's getting dark and the air smells of snow. A shopkeeper across the road busies himself with Christmas decorations, humming cheerfully, the supreme bastard, and I hope the fucking plastic tree falls on him.

I take three steps and double over in the middle of the street as my gut splits into excruciating, searing pain, like someone ran me through with a white-hot blade.

I'm not leaving because of you.

I steady myself on a parking meter, groaning, clutching my stomach, cold sweat running down my back. I think of the counsellor back at the hospital, and wonder if he still works there, because I changed my mind. I need it explained.

'Sir? Do you need help?'

'Is he okay?'

'Are you in pain? Sir?'

I straighten myself up. 'I'm fine.'

'Are you sure?'

'Yes, thank you. I'm fine.' I laugh, astonished, at the throbbing in my abdomen. 'Everything's fine.'

I knock lightly on Jamie's door, call his name in the gentlest voice I can muster.

'Are you in there?'

And when he doesn't answer, I push in carefully, search for him in the semi-darkness. I squint. His shape lies curled up on the bed, facing the wall. His old boots, still on, have dragged mud onto the sheet. Faintly, I hear him recite Gaelic words under his breath in a constant stream. For a while, I stand at the threshold and think of walking up to him, of examining his hand for signs of a fracture, of brushing the hair out of his face. I think of telling him I'm here, and he's not alone, and we'll get through this together. Then I either think better of it or chicken out. One or the other, or maybe both.

I shuffle to the kitchen like some kind of zombie. As it turns out, I did remember to turn off the oven before leaving. The chicken in there's gone cold and dry. I chuck it in the bin, with mechanical motions and minimal awareness. I wash the three mugs and stray fork that have been waiting in the sink.

Once that's taken care of, I go and sit.

Hours go by and I'm just sitting, no sign of life from

Jamie's room. Just nothing. Just sitting and nothing, but it's not quiet anymore.

Guess what? You laughed.

The voice has changed. It used to be deeper, a bit gruff, Dad's strong northern drawl. Now it's almost lilting, and much more androgynous.

'Who are you?' I say, out loud.

You laughed, bitch, and you said everything's fine. Everything's fine, yes?

'No.'

It's not like you're the one who's died, right? You're fine, so who cares about her? Who cares about him?

'I do.'

It's all about you, isn't it, Robinson?

The recorder smirks at me from the coffee table.

Don't you want to listen? Touch me. Go on, touch me, push my buttons, why don't you, you know you want it, you know you're craving it. You want to hear her voice, don't you? You could pretend. You could just pretend she's right here, with her head in your lap, asking about J . . . shhh, or reading out loud from the folktale book. Shhhhh. Once upon a time, yeah, wouldn't that be nice?

I take the recorder and hold it against my ear, nuzzle it, almost. Only just, only just about.

Push my buttons. Push my buttons, Robinson. Push my buttons.

Click.

Jamie's singing voice drowns out the hallucination. He's naturally talented, and a bit shy. The notes come somewhat hesitant at first, but the words ring out like he means them. As time passes, he gains in confidence. I adjust the volume down a few notches, so it's just for me, so it's intimate, and press the thing, his voice into my ear. 'Wait, is it on?' 'No.' And the laughter. Hers. Then his. 'Turn it off!'

I turn it off.

And rewind.

And play the singing again.

And rewind.

And again.

Don't you want to hear her voice, Robinson?

'No. I don't.'

No?

'No.' I want to hear his.

Insomnia leaves a lot of room for positive symptoms, and fuck me, last night they were wild. They pierced through the medication like it was flimsy paper tissue. There was buzzing, ringing, multiple voices. There were bugs crawling on the ceiling and smoke floating in through the cracks in the window. I closed my eyes and hid under the duvet, and waited. I forced myself to stay in bed until sunrise.

It's 8.30 in the morning. Please, please I need to get up now. Let me get up.

You're a grown man. Get up if you want to. The fuck do I care.

It's 8.54 when my feet touch the floor and I find Jamie in the exact same position I left him in, mercifully asleep.

Swallowing through the lump in my throat, I step in, like a fucking responsible, functioning adult all of a sudden. Out of nowhere. Like I can handle it. I untie his combat boots and pull them off. The left sock comes off with the boot, so I remove the right sock too.

He stirs and mumbles, and I shush under my breath. 'It's okay. It's okay.'

He shuffles up on the mattress, half-conscious. I tug at the lapel of his coat and he picks up on the prompt and removes it himself. He turns away from me again, and stops moving.

Vague thoughts of food touch my mind for a second and I want to puke.

'Goodnight,' I say.

Goodnight? You make me sick, Robinson. Why the fuck aren't you sad? Feel, Jesus fucking damn it! Go on! Go on, go on, go on, feel, go on, be sad, Robinson! Be normal!

I stare at Jamie until I start hearing music, and the music swells and demands space so I step out of the apartment.

My feet take the wheel. Before I know it, I'm back at Pizza 24, groaning at myself. The neon 'open' sign, the branding, the door, give me a disgusting whiff of my own shortcomings. *Couldn't keep a job, could you? Couldn't keep it together.*

Fuck me.

The tall buildings close in on me. All around, and above. Anxiety bubbles under the surface. I take out a cigarette.

'Yes, I'll be right back,' says Tony's voice.

I make a sudden move to walk away but it's too late.

'Sid?'

I try to make it seem as if I was just walking by.

'Alright, Tony!'

He's got a bag of pizzas in one hand and his helmet in the other.

'How are you doing, man?' he says, going for my shoulder and ramming the helmet into my arm on the way. 'Oh, sorry.'

'It's fine,' I say, even though there's a fifty-fifty chance my humerus was shattered. 'Everything's fine. How are you, mate?'

'Good, good. Well, Mike's being an ass.' He throws a look behind him like he's expecting Mike to be standing at the door. 'Look, Sid, I'm sorry about . . .'

'Don't worry about it. And, you know, thanks for sticking up for me.'

He blushes a little. 'You'd have done the same for me. Are you feeling better?'

'Yes,' I say.

Get fucked, says the voice.

I almost finish the cigarette in one drag.

'Never better,' I say.

'Good, that's good,' he says, and very nearly knocks himself out with the helmet. I'm not sure what he was trying to do, maybe scratch his forehead or push the hair from his face. Whatever it was, we both pretend it never happened.

'Well,' he says, 'I should get going or Mike's going to burst a blood vessel.'

His mobile starts ringing to Sinatra's voice. He waves goodbye and picks up as he trots over to his scooter.

'Sì, pronto?'

He starts chattering in very fast Italian. His brother, probably. If he wasn't so shy, he could easily put Mike in his place. Everyone would thank him for it as well. I watch with fondness and, I have to say, slight concern, as he hangs up and drives away distractedly into the traffic. Then again, I'm the one who recently just about drove into a bus.

I notice I'm trying to smoke my fingers, so I flick the tiny stub away and take out the packet again. Then I put it back in my pocket without opening it. I walk to the row of scooters along the pavement and let my hand run against the seat of the first one. Hearing some more noise coming from inside the restaurant, I hurry down the street again. If anyone else sees me, I'll officially become the pathetic guy who still hangs around outside the pizza place where he used to work. A few strides and then I break into a jog, just so it looks like I'm going somewhere. Just so it looks like I have purpose.

I rush past groups of men, carefree, just going about their lives blissfully unaware. Colleagues on their way to work. Friends discussing the latest game. A few couples practically leaning on each other. The jog evolves into a run. The run evolves into a sprint. I feel people's eyes following me as I zoom past them. I hate them. Maybe it's unfair, maybe it makes me bitter, but God how I hate the lot of them.

Oxford Circus appears at the end of the street. The light is red. I'm not stopping. I don't care. If it doesn't turn green, I'll just have to run out in front of the cars. I don't care. Only a few metres to go now. A shiver of anticipation tickles my spine, my skin prickles into goose bumps, and I run faster. Come on, just a few feet more, come on. The cars brake. The light turns green. And I make it to the other side, and stop there, wheezing and choking on my stupid weak lungs.

My phone is ringing and it's Tom and I reject the call and switch the phone to airplane mode. Probably as close as I'll ever get to actually being on a plane. I walk around, turning into random streets, until it's a decent time to be coming back home. Sunset, I suppose. Sunset will do.

I dreamt Olivia was lying in Tom's bathtub. Tom was holding her head under the water. She was dead already. She wasn't fighting or moving at all. Her eyes were open and dead and like mine. Tom's hand was on her forehead, pushing her down into the porcelain tub. I stood at the door and watched. I was wet and wrapped in a robe, as if I'd just come out of the bath myself. Tom turned his head to me. 'Want to try?' he asked. I stepped closer and knelt next to him. I plunged my arm in the cold water and the sleeve of the robe soaked and stuck to my skin. Tom withdrew his hand from Olivia's forehead and I replaced it with mine instead. 'There,' Tom said. He stood up. 'I'll come back later.' He poked at his expensive watch and shook his head. 'Not working. It's the water. I'll have them exchange it.' And he left me with her.

The more Tom calls, the less inclined I am to answer. At first, his caller ID on the screen threw a pang of guilt into my chest. But that evolved quickly into annoyance.

Now it's not even annoyance anymore. Now it's getting to the point where my mind replays Jamie punching him in the face in glorious cinemascope with 5.1 surround sound.

The voice has been yelling at me all morning, constantly screaming in my ear, and it's saying things I don't care to repeat, not even to myself. I've decided it's Tom's fault.

Jamie's not eating. I leave food outside his door and find it there hours later, untouched. He's not talking. He waits until I'm asleep – or thinks I am – to step out and use the bathroom. Sometimes I picture myself poking him with a branch. I picture him responding, groaning, swearing, 'What the fuck are you doing?' Then I picture him not responding. I picture him never responding again.

I've decided it's Tom's fault, and he won't stop calling. Why won't he stop calling? I'm not his fucking dad, am I? I'm not his fucking therapist, and it's his fault, and the voice is so fucking loud and vicious I'm losing my fucking shit.

I stick my fingers in my ears.

Shut up, shut up, shut up.

I curl up into a ball and screw my eyes shut.

Shut up, shut up, please shut up.

I see Olivia behind my closed eyelids. I see her smile as she spins around, the green dress twirling around her knees over the distressed jeans. I see her intelligent eyes squinting at the book in frustration. What's this word? What's that word? I see her dirty blonde hair poking out in spikes from under the hoodie, just starting to grow out again, just the beginning of her, and then not anymore. Nothing anymore.

I open my eyes again to make it go away, but that won't stop the screaming. The voice rages on about death and us and me, and when my phone rings again, I barely hear it.

I hit reject once again, and very nearly hurl the phone against the wall. I bury it under one of the sofa cushions instead and press both hands down into it, and picture myself under it. I pretend I'm smothering myself.

You have a voicemail, twig boy!

I grab the cushion and fling it aside. I do have a voicemail.

'Hophead, it's me. Look, uh . . .'

About ten seconds of silence, there, and a weird hiss-like noise. Or a sniffle. Maybe a sniffle.

'Okay, look . . . see there . . . I just, I thought . . .'

I toss another one of the sofa cushions to the floor. Is he drunk? Is he fucking pissed right now, is that what this is?

'Forget it, Sid. Forget it.'

Beeeeep.

The voice booms. I want it to stop. I need it to stop right now or I'll die. Honest to God, I can't take it.

Something has to give. I swallow hard, grab my keys and my coat, and set out. I've decided it's Tom's fault.

Everyone's looking at me on the way to his. Smoke's probably coming off the top of my head. I run my hand over my scalp, just to check, and it gets stuck in the unwashed knots. My breath rises in plumes in the cold. The voice's gone echoey. I growl back at it. Everyone's looking at me.

The run up the stairs gets the adrenaline pumping

and I'm getting angrier and angrier and the rush is fucking brilliant. I'm ready to explode. I'm high.

'Tom!'

I slam my fist into the door. Pain flashes and throbs in my hand and I love it, but then the door swings open and I don't love that.

Unlocked?

Now the anger is going away and I don't want it to.

'Tom!'

I try to hang on to it, to hold it in place. Flail your arms, stamp your feet, just don't let the rush fade away.

'Tom!'

The flat is dark. I move through the living room and think of the empty apartment next door, where it happened. *She was screaming.*

'Tom?'

In the bedroom, my foot meets something sticky like shampoo or syrup. I reach for the light switch and flick it on, and the voice suddenly clams up.

'Jesus Christ!' I say, and then 'Jesus fucking Christ!' and I have to steady myself on the door-frame because Tom is there, lying in the middle of the room, in his underwear. He's white. All his blood is on the carpet. It trails from the bed, as if he was lying there and maybe got up for something but passed out before he could get to it.

I stare at the gory mess. His phone is on the floor next to his left hand.

Are you going to just stand there?

I grab the phone and dial.

'Emergency. Which service do you require?'

'My f— Ambulance.'

'Connecting you right now.'

I watch the blood infiltrate the cream-coloured carpet. The voice that picks up next is deep, calm, with a hint of a lisp over a soft Jamaican accent.

'Ambulance emergencies. What's happened?'

'My friend slit his wrists.'

'Your friend slit his wrists. Both of them?'

'Yes.'

'Are you with him, right now?'

'Yes, I'm at his flat.'

I give him the address.

'We already traced your call, help is on its way.'

I glance at the phone. 'Traced?'

You're fucking useless, Robinson. You shouldn't have called. It's too late. He's dead, look at him, that's a corpse, you're looking at a corpse, Robinson, there's nobody home. Nobody home. He's empty, Robinson, look at him, look at the body. Look at the corpse. Are you happy now?

'I'm going to ask you a few questions. It won't delay the ambulance.'

'Oh God, I think he's dead. I think he's dead.'

'How old is your friend?'

'Twenty-seven.'

'Twenty—'

'Twenty-eight.'

'Twenty-eight, is he?'

'Yes.'

'Is he awake?'

He'll never be awake ever again and you didn't pay attention, you don't even know what colour his eyes are, you don't give a fuck.

'Sir?'

'No, no, he's unconscious. I just . . .'

231

'Do you know how long ago the accident happened?'

'I don't think it was an accident.'

'How long ago did it happen, do you know?'

'I don't know, I just came in and he, he w ...'

'He was already unconscious when you arrived?'

'Yes.'

'Is the bleeding severe?'

'Yes, my God, it's severe.'

'Is he breathing?'

'I don't know, but there's blood everywhere. It's pulsing out, I think ... I think it's arterial bleeding cos it's pulsing out, and he's ... I think he's gone, I ...'

'What's your name, sir?'

Hang up and walk out the door. You wanted him dead anyway.

'His name?'

'What's your name?'

'Robinson. Sid.'

'Sid, listen to me. You have to stay calm and you have to listen to me because this is very time-sensitive, okay? Now, I need you to do something for me. Is he on the floor?'

'Yeah. On ... on his back.'

'Good. I need you to kneel next to him, put your ear to his mouth and tell me if you can feel or hear any breathing. Can you do that for me? Do that right now.'

'Okay.'

I drop to my knees and my jeans soak up the blood. He's cold and heavy and it's like touching raw chicken.

The voice giggles and sings. *Another one bites the dust.*

I choke up. 'Oh, my God, Tom.'

'Is he not breathing?'

'He's gone. He's gone.'

I'm shaking and sobbing as the operator tries to get my attention, get me to focus, but the focus is elsewhere now, it's razor sharp where it shouldn't be. *Another one bites the dust.* Then I hear a tiny wheeze.

'Shit! Tom? Shit, can you hear me, are you still there?'

'Is he breathing?'

'He is, but it's really faint.'

'Okay, I'm going to need you to tell me immediately if that changes.'

'Are they on their way now?'

'Do you have clean dry towels or something to press against the wounds? We've got a team on their way to you with lights and sirens, but in the meantime, I need you to find towels. Right now.'

'I'll get towels from the bathroom.'

I get up, slip, fall, and get up again. Tom's blood is all over my clothes and hands. The towels are in the bathroom, in a cupboard under the sink. *Don't even bother.*

'Have you found them?'

Give up. What are you even doing? 'Shut up!'

'What?'

'Yes, sorry, yes, I've got towels.'

'Right, listen carefully and I'll tell you what to do.'

'I'm listening.'

'I need you to press the towels firmly against his wrists to stop the bleeding. Don't be gentle, really press hard. We need to make sure he doesn't bleed out completely.'

It's too late. You'll make it worse. 'I'll have to put the phone down. Can you still hear me?'

'Yes, I hear you.'

I kneel in the blood again.

You're killing him faster.

I fumble a bit, try to figure out how to reach both wrists. I end up straddling his hips – *pervert* – one towel on each side, and I do it. I cover the jagged wounds along his veins and put my weight on them. His left arm twitches a bit, then settles.

'Are you doing it?'

'I'm doing it.'

'Very good, Sid. Stay there. Help will be with you any minute.'

'Will he be okay?'

'Is he still breathing?'

'Uh . . . yeah, I think so. Is he going to be okay?'

'The ambulance is on its way. Is the front door open?'

'I'm not sure. Should I go check?'

'No, stay where you are. Will they be able to get into the building?'

'It's not locked. We're on the third floor.'

'They know where you are.'

Tom's face is an expressionless mask. The bruise from Jamie's punch has turned a bit yellow at the edges. His mouth hangs slightly open, chapped, dry lips. His sweaty hair sticks to his forehead.

'Please don't hang up,' I say. *Wimp.*

'I won't. Is he still breathing?'

'Yes.'

'Excellent. How about you? Are you okay?'

'What?'

'How are you holding up?'

'Yeah, I'm . . . I'm fine. I'm just, uh, I'm hearing voices.'

'Is someone around? Can you call for them to help you?'

'No, there's no one. I'm, I have, um, psychosis.'

'Oh, I see. How long have you been dealing with psychosis then?'

'Um . . .' I check myself, press harder into the towels. 'Um, about eight years.'

'I see. You're strong, then, yes? You've got this.'

'I don't know.'

'You've got this, Sid. Remember to breathe. Check his breathing, too.'

'It's very weak. God, please hurry.'

'They're just around the corner.'

'Are you lying?'

But he's not, because now I'm aware of distant sirens and, soon after, running steps in the staircase. I call for them at the top of my voice. 'Over here!'

'They're here, are they?' the operator asks.

'Yeah, they're here. Over here, help me!'

'I'm going to hang up the phone, now.'

'Yes, they're here, thank you. They're here.'

The line goes dead.

My body's gone stiff and they have to pull me off and into the living room so they can get to Tom. One of them stays with me.

'You did very well, sir. Do you want us to ring someone for you?'

'No, thanks, I'm alright.'

But I'm not. The adrenaline has melted off. I look down, wide-eyed, at my soaked clothes. The stench of blood makes my stomach churn and my head swim and I think I'm going to faint and then I do.

When I wake up in the hospital again, I panic. I look for Jamie, but there's no one in the room. I think he's finally decided to get on with his life, leave me in the dust, where I probably belong anyway. The mist fades after a couple of minutes, and I remember what happened, why I'm here, and the panic swerves in a different direction. I call a nurse, and as I wait, I bring my hand up to bite my nails, and stop dead. There's blood under my fingernails.

The guy who walks into the room is sporting huge shadows under his eyes and suppresses a yawn before addressing me.

'Mr Robinson, you're awake. How are you feeling?'

'There was another man who was brought here with me? Tom Foster?'

The man scratches his head. 'I don't know. Hold on, let me check this for you, okay?'

And he leaves me in the dark again.

I wait. Every cell in my body fights to keep the hospital smells and sounds out, to concentrate on other things, because otherwise I know I'll shoot right back there, back then, and there's no telling how long I'll be stuck back there, back then. Tom's phone is on the bedside table. They must have thought it was mine, as if I look like I could afford that. My clothes are folded on a chair, a dark stain on the shirt just barely visible in the obscurity. Could almost just be a shadow.

The door swings open again and the nurse enters, eyes down on a file.

'Thomas Foster?'

'Is he okay?'

He adjusts his glasses on his nose and reads the file. I can't think what can be taking him so long. It's easy enough to check if someone's alive or not.

Eventually, he looks up.

'He's okay.'

I exhale loudly and let my head fall back on the pillow.

'He's in intensive care.'

'Can I see him?'

'We'll need to take care of your discharge first.'

It takes a few tests and a fair amount of paperwork before they let me go. I put my clothes back on, wincing. They're absolutely gross, but it's the thought – that came from inside your friend – that makes me want to puke. They ask me to disinfect my hands before entering the ward. I soap up to my elbows, glancing down at the state of myself. But hey, at least my hands are clean.

Tom's dead to the world. 'Resting,' they said, but it doesn't look like resting to me. There are wires and tubes everywhere. I should probably know what they're for, but I don't. His wrists are tightly bandaged, and a lot more delicate than I remember. I can't shake off the vision of the wide cuts under there, squirting red with the pressure of a fire hose. Suddenly sensing I might be about to pass out again, I move my eyes to his face instead.

Fucking hell, Tom, look at you.

I cautiously put my hand on his brow. Clammy and a bit cold. Surely he can't be warm enough in the stupid gown. My fingers slide into his hair. They said it's good to touch him and talk to him, but I don't know. Right now it just feels awkward and more than a little inappropriate. We're not that close.

'Hey, Tom,' I say. 'Hey, fancy man.'

It's all I can manage.

'Are you his partner?'

I spin around.

The tall man, broad shoulders and a kind face, smiles and extends his hand to me. 'My name is Dr Bennani, I'm taking care of Mr Foster.'

'I'm just a friend. Sid Robinson.'

We shake.

'Mr Robinson! The one who called the ambulance. He was very lucky you showed up when you did. You saved his life.'

'Will he be okay?'

'He isn't in any immediate danger. He nicked a tendon in his right wrist. We did our best to repair it, but he may lose some degree of mobility. Is he right-handed?'

I run a hand through my hair. 'I'm not sure.'

'Does he have any family?

'No. He's alone.'

Bennani nods. 'Do you know him well? Would you mind answering a few questions for me?'

He leads me out of the room and through a maze of identical corridors. The air is thick with antiseptic. We walk past a closed door and someone is moaning loudly on the other side. Bennani doesn't even blink. Just continues straight to his destination. We end up in an office so small I wouldn't be surprised if it had once been a broom cupboard.

He waves for me to take a seat and starts moving

papers around on his desk. A bit disorganised, for a doctor. Eventually, he pulls out a pink form and a pen.

'There,' he says.

And he proceeds to ask me all sorts of things about Tom's medical history, his allergies, his childhood, his family, his job, his daily habits. A never-ending stream of questions, most of which I don't know the answer to.

'Did anything happen to him recently that could have triggered this? Tough breakup? Anniversary of a loss, maybe?'

He catches something in my eyes, fear, probably, or shame.

'It's important that you tell me,' he prompts.

I swallow hard. 'A loss,' I say. 'A few days ago.'

Bennani nods. He doesn't ask more about this. He doesn't comment. He makes a note and moves on to the next question.

Hours later, I arrive home, mind blank and completely worn out, to find Jamie pacing the flat with his mobile against his ear. Seeing me, he throws the phone towards the settee, misses, and the thing crashes on the floor with such force that several bits of it break away and go flying across the room. He strides over and hugs me and I just stand there, unable to process it.

'Sid, what the fuck? I told you not to do that! Do you have any idea—' and then noticing the blood on my clothes, 'What happened? Are you okay? Are you hurt? Talk to me.'

'Tom tried to kill himself.'

15

Snow weaves and tumbles in front of my bedroom window. It glimmers white, shimmers, against the red bricks of the building across from ours. Winter cold seeps in from the poorly insulated glass, and the heater at my ankles pushes out hot air frantically along with clanking sounds and a faint smell of burnt dust. I dug out the Christmas jumper Jamie got me as a joke a few years back. I slipped it on, for some reason, and looked at the reindeer winking at me in the mirror. Now all that's missing is a cup of hot cocoa, gingerbread in the oven, and an over-encumbered tree.

I picture Olivia as a toddler, all bundled up in a tiny duffel coat, scarf and hat, running around Nick and Charlie's front yard, tripping over herself. She falls face first into the fluffy snow, and her dad grabs her, lifts her up and plops her back on her feet. Her mum smiles and wipes snowflakes from her face.

Olivia grins, wide, joyful, because it's all good, really, it didn't hurt, and runs off again.

It's snowing.

So it is.

It's beautiful.

Before he let me go, the doctor suggested I call Tom's work to inform them. He offered to do it himself. Fuck knows what possessed me, I said I could manage. I still have his phone, the fancy git with the newest, fanciest gadget I can barely figure out how to turn on. I scroll through the contacts list, vaguely wondering why he didn't set up a pin code, or a fingerprint, or a retina scan, or whatever the fuck these things have nowadays. It's almost as if he wanted me to snoop.

I've been scrolling for ages. Guy after guy after guy. I try not to think too hard about the fact that he felt the need to keep every single one of his hookups in his contacts list. Freddie, Harry, hh4u1987, Hophead, Ian, Jamie, Jon69 . . . Eventually, at the very bottom of it all, I find what I'm looking for. 'Work.' I'm pretty sure he works for an insurance company. In what capacity, though, I have no clue.

A smooth-voiced secretary recites the name of the company and then states his own name, which I instantly forget. I'm focussing hard on what I have to say. I've been preparing this, choosing the words carefully, repeating them in my mind.

'Hi,' I start. 'I'm calling on behalf of Mr Thomas Foster.'

The secretary asks me to hold on and I hear him chattering indistinctly to someone.

'Sir?'

'Yes.'

'I'm afraid Mr Foster no longer works here.'

This knocks my whole speech out of my mind. 'I'm sorry?'

'Mr Foster was let go, two . . . almost three weeks ago.'

Running on autopilot, I thank him for his help, apologise for taking up his time and hang up the phone.

I pad over to Jamie's room, and just as he opens the door, I remember the Christmas jumper. He stares at the reindeer. It would probably have been less embarrassing if I'd just gone ahead and knocked on his door completely nude.

Pervert, says the voice.

'It, uh, looks like Tom got sacked a few weeks back,' I say.

'So?'

'Nothing, I just thought . . . nothing.'

He brings bloodied fingernails up to his teeth. *These go on my shoulder, not in your mouth*. His knuckles are bruised from the punch still. An awkward moment passes between us.

'Can I borrow your laptop?' I ask, on purpose, waiting for 'It's "may I"'. He barely hears me. Fuck knows what I was expecting.

'Sure.'

'I just need to sort out some CVs. I figure I should probably start looking, you know, so I just thought I'd, I'll just send out some CVs.'

'Knock yourself out.'

'I won't,' I say, for some reason, and before I have time to correct myself, he closes the door on me.

I light a cigarette. My fingers click on the keys and I tap my foot in time with the clicking, and it's possible my lips are moving.

The only remotely impressive thing I've got going for me is a stack of 'A's in my exams at secondary school. It's all downhill after that, with some two years of med school, and then months of suspicious unemployment – but I'm not about to explain that one – followed by a string of shitty jobs, some of which weren't even exactly official. I consider putting Mike down as a reference, laugh at myself, and add Tony's name instead, hoping he remembers that we did agree to do this for each other if ever one of us managed to escape.

I light another cigarette.

I feel like a pinball machine, with the bleeps and the clinking and the flashing lights everywhere. I'm high, stoned, wasted and I think my lips are moving, and I'm talking, I'm talking to myself, to the screen. 'Fuck you,' I'm telling the screen. 'Fuck moping around. Fuck mania, fuck depression and anxiety and death, fuck schizophrenia. Fuck you, Mike, with your fake accent and your fake tan and your fake face. I could have been a doctor. I was good at it. I was brilliant at it. I could be making a difference, because I'm smart. I'm a smart fucker, and you're not, Mike, you're the stupidest, most vapid wanker I've ever had the misfortune to answer to, and I can't wait for you to realise your pathetic little life is worthless and empty and nobody likes you. Fuck you.'

I copy the file onto an old USB drive, close the laptop and stare down between my knees with my hands holding my skull in place and my right leg bouncing up and down. Clink clink clink bleep bleep bleep – Whoo, yeah!

'What is wrong with you? Fuck's sake, shut up, you arsehole.'

A cluster of fluff and hair floats around the floorboards.

'Do something!'

I light another cigarette.

I dig the vacuum cleaner out of the cupboard, fumble with the attachments for a minute, and once I've started, I find I can't stop. I launch myself on a quest to eradicate every single fleck of dust in the flat. The noise drowns out the voice nicely enough, and the activity drowns out everything else. I cling to the purpose until my knuckles go white. I hoover the living room, the kitchen, the bathroom. I move the settee and hoover under it. I run down to the basement for a load of laundry, back up to rearrange the dishes more efficiently. I clean inside the fridge and microwave. While the dryer's running, I run to the corner shop and print out some copies of the CV. I come home and bleach the bathtub.

At some point, Jamie pops out and asks what the fuck I'm doing and I've got my sleeves rolled up, my hands full of soap and half a dozen sponges fanned out around me.

'We've been living in filth,' I tell him. 'That's no good, that's terrible for your health, and you know with your sleep apnoea you already have a hard time breathing, and I've seen this documentary where this bloke developed mould in his lungs, like cancer but not cancer, from just fucking living in his house. We have to clean more often. It's okay, you can go back to bed, I'm taking care of it, I'm going to finish up in here and then I'll probably, uh, I'll probably need to go in your room at some point, I can change the sheets it's no big deal, I'll be just a minute, actually I can do it now if you pref—'

And he goes back into his room and slams the door shut.

I just turned twenty and Dad didn't call.

My mind is clearer than it's been in months. Not perfect by any means, and my short-term memory's taken a serious hit, but I can think now, which is more than I could claim when I first landed in the ward.

Some symptoms remain. I've been told they will, probably forever, to some extent. But I am managing.

I feel hopeful, and almost smart.

As hospital staff buzz around, I find myself observing, making mental notes, asking for a pen and paper and making physical notes. I listen in when the doctors discuss work in the hallway. Sometimes I ask questions. Most of them ignore me, but some of them appear mildly entertained by my sudden burst of bubbly interest.

A nurse comes in for the weekly blood test. The new meds they've got me on are working but they have to monitor my white blood cell count. The nurse places the tourniquet on my arm and turns to talk to a colleague. They begin to talk about other things. His upcoming vacation, his new car, his favourite restaurant. I start wondering whether or not that's appropriate in front of patients who've very little hope of ever leaving the premises.

I glance over to my roommate, and he's pretending to sleep as he always does when there's someone else in the room.

It's been more than five minutes. The tourniquet digs into my arm, but I'm afraid to say anything.

Eventually he turns back to me, tugs on my wrist to bring me closer, and wipes the crook of my elbow with alcohol.

He blows on the site.

I pull my arm away.

'What are you doing?' he asks.

'You can't do that,' I say.

He sighs. 'It's just a blood test, son. Give me your arm and let me do my job.'

I tell him I have no problem with the blood test. 'But you can't blow on it like that,' I say. 'It's a huge infection risk.'

His expression shifts into embarrassment, then contained anger, like maybe he'd be tempted to hit me if there weren't cameras everywhere. Begrudgingly, he applies the alcohol again, muttering about charging me for the waste of cotton balls.

'It's not my fault—'

'Excuse me, are you a doctor?'

'No.'

He pokes me a bit roughly and begins to draw the blood. 'Are you a nurse?'

I wince. 'No, sir.'

'That's right. You're a psychiatric patient. Try to remember that, if you can.' He removes the needle and covers the puncture hole. 'Hold this.'

I press my thumb over the gauze and he leaves

without bothering to give me a piece of tape to hold it in place.

For the life of me, I can't recall how I managed to land the delivery job. They must have been as desperate as I was. Either that or I look a lot worse now than I used to.

I flash the manager my best smile, but now it just seems like I'm flirting, doesn't it, and he's looking down his nose at my extended hand and does he think I'm about to pass some sort of disease onto him or something?

'We'll call you,' he says.

'Looking forward to it,' I say, with the grin still clinging to my face like it's died there and stiffened with the most unfortunate case of rigor mortis.

I tell myself one more, one more, every time, just one more and then you can rest, then you can go home and rest.

Always one more.

One more.

The last man to reject me – last one, I promise, just one more, okay? – is in his mid-fifties and the owner of a pub in Shepherd's Bush. 'Achilles' Heel', of all the stupid names. I shake the snow out of my hair at the entrance as a swarm of customers, ranging from the mildly tipsy to the completely shitfaced, push each other around, roaring merrily and slapping each other's backs.

The owner appears to be tending the bar alone. He gives my CV a quick look, not long enough to really read anything, and eyes me up and down.

In the other places, I'd been eagerly pointing out lines on the sheet of paper, elaborating on them in broken sentences until they started thinking I was high, drunk or both. But now things are finally slowing down, like the pinball machine has run out of credits.

Excuse me, are you a doctor?
Are you a nurse?

A particularly imposing brute of a man treads on my foot as he leans over the counter and barks something I don't understand.

'Go home, Larry,' says the owner, unimpressed. 'You're done. Go home.'

The man replies with a grunt-like sound, either an 'aye' or 'agh' or something in-between, and crushes my foot again on his way out. I don't think he was ever aware of my presence. The owner turns to another guy and starts talking and I wonder if he's forgotten I'm here too. I hang around for a few minutes, then give up and walk to the door.

'Mr Robinson, where are you going?'

I turn back, half-thinking I've heard him wrong. He's handing me my CV.

'Oh,' I say. 'Thank you. Thank you for your time.'

I take the thing – a few pence saved on printing – and turn again.

'When can you start?'

Now I've definitely heard him wrong. 'Pardon?'

'Would Saturday be okay? I'm afraid I can't offer much more than twelve pounds an hour at the moment. We could go through the paperwork and training in the morning, when it's quiet?'

A loud burst of laughter blasts out and covers most of my stammering.

'I'm afraid I didn't catch that,' says the owner, pointing at his ear and articulating over the noise.

I step closer, leaning over the counter until my feet are barely touching the floor. 'Sounds perfect!' I shout.

'Can you come in at ten?' he shouts.

'Of course!' I shout.

'That's great. I'll see you then.'

I step out feeling like I've just had an out-of-body experience.

Jamie seems to have shrunk. His tiny frame hunches over the kitchen table where I forced him to sit. The spoon clicks against the bowl of soup I forced him to eat.

I'm on a timer. The soup is disappearing so fast it's obvious he wants out of here.

'I found a job,' I say, trying to make it sound enthusiastic and natural.

'Good.'

'Bartending.'

'Good.'

'Yeah, it is.'

Timer goes off. Soup is gone.

He gets up. 'Well, I'm glad your life's all sorted, mate.'

'What's that supposed to mean?'

'Nothing. I'm happy for you.'

'Are you okay?'

'Sure.'

'You don't seem okay.'

'Yes, well, I'm sorry we can't all be as obviously okay as you are.'

My foot twitches under the table. 'What?'

'Forget it.'

'Jamie, do you want to talk ab—'

'No, Sid! I don't want to talk, alright? Just, just let me deal with this in my own way, okay? Just leave me be.'

'Okay. Sorry.'

'Okay.'

He goes back to his room and I mimic his 'Okay' under my breath like I'm five years old and he just said 'I'm rubber and you're glue.'

I sleep through Thursday and Friday, and walk into the pub at quarter to ten on Saturday. The owner springs from behind the counter. He's all over me in a split second, grabbing my hand in both of his and shaking vigorously.

'Sidney, good morning! Mind if I call you Sidney?'

I think of my dad and become uneasy.

'It's fine, yes,' I say.

'I'm Achilles. Mum used to love all that mythology stuff. My brother's Hector. Must have known we'd end up trying to kill each other.'

He lets out a booming laugh and I chuckle in response.

'Mind if we start right away?'

'Of course.'

We sign the contract first. I pretend to read. The words don't touch my mind at all, but to be fair, it's not like I have much of a choice either way. Then he starts walking around the place with me, showing me everything, teaching me how to pull a pint, work the till, start the dishwasher. It's easy. It's easy enough, in fact, that I barely need to concentrate, and I end up thinking of my dad a bit too much. I don't know why. Apart from the whole 'Sidney' thing, Achilles is nothing like my dad. When I was growing up, encouragement was rough and challenging, and smiles were a once-in-a-blue-moon type of deal.

'Yup, exactly like that. You've got this, no problem at all!' Achilles is saying.

There's something in the way he looks at me, though, that brings back memories of safety. Like my trousers are ripped at the knees and he's teaching me to ride a bike without the training wheels. *You can do this, Sidney. Easy. That's my boy.*

Once we're done with the training, he pulls two half-pints and hands me one. Suddenly the memories of safety fade behind memories of trying to get Dad's attention while he's passed out on the settee with a pile of empty bottles at the foot of the coffee table.

'Oh, I'm sorry,' he says. 'Does your religion prohibit alcohol? Because that's absolutely fine with—'

'No, it's not that, just I'm still on the clock.'

He shrugs. 'It's not strong. And I'm going to need you to relax because the regulars are about to swarm the place like bees on honey, and believe me, those bees sting something fierce.'

I hesitate.

'You deserve it,' he says. 'But you don't have to, if

you'd rather not. I can drink for the two of us.'

He winks.

'Thanks,' I say, taking the glass with an uncomfortable twitch of a smile.

He pulls up a stool. 'So. Never got round to finishing med school, did you? Wasn't all it's cracked up to be?'

I shrug. 'I just couldn't cut it, I suppose.'

'Well, now that's unlikely. You seem like a smart enough lad.'

I chug half the glass in one go.

'You shouldn't give up on your dreams, son.'

'I think I lack the ambition,' I say. 'It's too late now anyways.'

'You say that as if you're old or something. You've got time.'

The alcohol is starting to hit and I find myself a touch bolder than I'd normally be on a first day at a new job. 'Are you trying to get me to quit and go back to school?'

He laughs. 'Fair enough. Please don't. I'd be in a pickle without your help.'

'Might want to wait until after the first rush hour before you decide how much help I am.'

He slaps me on the shoulder as he gets up. 'Ah, you'll be fine, Sidney.'

I down the rest of the beer.

Fine.

Am I fine?

Too fine?

Inappropriately fine, maybe?

Customers start pouring in after five and it gets busy enough to keep me from thinking about anything else.

When the end of my shift approaches, it brings with it a sense of dread.

Achilles comes and slaps me on the shoulder at about half past ten. 'Thank you, Sidney. You can go now.'

'Are you sure? I can stay a bit longer.'

'No, you go home now. I can manage. I've kept you here longer than I should have already.'

16

Dr Bennani catches me on my way to the ICU and diverts me to his office for a minute. He tells me things about Tom, like I'm his person, somehow. Like I'm entitled to know. How desperate can they be?

He tells me they want to move Tom to the psychiatric ward. My skin crawls. They think he's still a danger to himself which, in and of itself, warrants all sorts of skin-crawling, but it's not just that. I touch my own wrist, half-expecting to find the plastic bracelet there again. *Robinson, Sidney. 14 June 1992. Penicillin allergy.* Then the number. The barcode.

I pull on the sleeve of my hoodie and tell him Tom recently lost his job. He makes a note.

'There was something else I wanted to mention,' he says. 'While I have you here.'

I say nothing and wait for him to continue.

'We believe he could regain most of the mobility in his right wrist.'

'But?'

'But he's not willing to work with the physical therapist at the moment.'

I pinch the bridge of my nose, and sigh. 'Yeah, I probably wouldn't be either.'

Bennani gives me a strange look. 'How close are the two of you?'

'Why?'

'I'm just wondering if he might be more inclined to work with you.'

The fucking hilarious spit-in-your-face irony.

'I'm not a doctor,' I say.

He pulls out a pamphlet and slides it across the desk.

'It's quite simple, really, just some exercises for dexterity.'

He starts explaining and pointing at pictures and I chuckle awkwardly. I tell him I'll try, because what else am I going to tell him?

I stop at the door on my way out.

'We're really not all that close,' I say.

'Well, you're listed as his emergency contact,' he says.

I consider this, sigh, nod, and I'm out the door.

Tom's eyes fall on me as I approach the bed. Grey eyes, I think. Don't forget again.

I look at his wrists. I seem to have completely forgotten my manners.

I wonder how they feel. I wonder if the wounds sting or scratch or pull or throb.

Why don't you try it for yourself? says the voice, as my heart rate spikes.

I clear my throat.

'Hi,' I say.

Last night I couldn't sleep. The thought of being in that room again, of looking at him, of looking at it. I just knew it would trigger some seriously shitty stuff.

Why don't you try it for yourself, Robinson?

So I read up. Jamie has books, from back then, in case I ever seemed like I was going to . . . I know what you're supposed to say, how you're supposed to act, what you're supposed to ask. How long have you been feeling this way? What made you feel that you had to do this? I'm here for you. I want to help if I can.

I look two inches below his left ear, and all that contrived bullshit flies out the window.

'Fuck,' I say.

A moment goes by, and he pulls in a laboured breath. 'Did I inconvenience you terribly?'

His face is blank.

I soften the muscles in mine. 'No. You didn't.'

'Oh,' he says. 'Good.'

'Why didn't you tell me you got sacked?' I ask.

He shrugs. 'You didn't tell me when you got sacked.'

Suddenly it's like I stepped on a landmine. Click. Don't move now. Careful now, or it's over.

'How, uh . . . how do you know about that?'

'I came by the restaurant the other day. Looking for you. They mentioned it.'

'Oh. You know I didn't mean to keep it from you. It just . . . it never came up.'

'Never came up either.'

My hand hovers over the pamphlet in my coat

pocket, and I decide now's not the time. Then I decide now's the time to say something painfully idiotic.

'It's all been a bit crazy these past few weeks, hasn't it?'

'I heard it,' he says.

In the sterile blue light of the room, he looks pasty and sick.

'I was standing on the other side of the wall. The window was open. I could have crossed over. I heard them open the door. I heard them find her. She cried for help. She fought back against them. They shot her. I could have crossed over.'

My hand leaves the pamphlet and moves over to his.

He locks eyes with me. 'You should have let me die,' he says. 'You bastard, why couldn't you just let me die?'

He doesn't mean it. That's what the doctors told Jamie, back when he was on the phone with the emergency services and I was screaming and crying and throwing bottles at him across the room. He doesn't mean it. And I'll tell you what, though. I did mean it. Of course, I don't anymore, but at the time? When things were so bad and I just knew Jamie was trying to kill me? Fuck me, I meant it.

'I had to,' I say.

'Why?'

Oh, you're going to insist, are you, Tom? You're going to lie there, all white in the face, all broken, and ask why I didn't watch you bleed out on the carpet?

'You would have done the same for me.'

He gives a sharp laugh. I get a bit scared.

'Yeah,' he says. 'I suppose I would have.'

When I get home from the hospital, Jamie's pacing the living room, arguing into his mobile.

'I don't know what made me think you'd help,' he's saying. 'It's not like you owed me a favour or anything! . . . No . . . No, don't bother . . . Aye, you too . . . Aye, piss off!'

For a second, I catch a glimpse of the boy I met at uni. For a second, he's got that fire again, that bottomless energy. He always got so outraged at injustice. I stare for a second, and think, he could change the world. Effervescent, I think.

He hangs up and tosses the phone on the settee. 'Imigh leat, ya wanker, fuck's sake!'

'Who was that?' I ask.

'No one.'

'Didn't sound like no one.'

'Don't start.' He drops down, then winces, lifts his hips and pulls the mobile from under him. 'Fucking thing,' he says, chucking it on the coffee table.

I try a step forward.

He sighs. 'What?'

'I think we should talk.'

'About?'

I lower myself next to him. A small vein pulses in his neck. I imagine what it would be like to run my tongue over it.

'I went to see Tom,' I say.

'So?'

The voice in my head starts speaking. I tune it out.

'You want me to feel sorry for him?' he asks.

The landmine clicks again.

'I'd like you to show some form of empathy.'

'He called the cops on her.'

'I don't think he did.'

He springs up. 'He did! He called them!'

I spring up too. 'He has huge cuts on his wrists, Jamie, he almost died!'

'I don't care! After what he did to her, he fucking well should be feeling guilty!'

'Who are you?'

'Don't push me, Sid! You should be glad he's the one I—' He catches himself.

'What?' I ask.

'Nothing.'

'What?'

'Nothing. Forget it.'

I know what's on his mind. It's been on mine, a constant whisper since we got that phone call, since he threw that punch at Tom. I'm not even sure anymore if the voice is saying it or if it's just me, saying it to myself, over and over.

'Jamie, we are done with this. Just come out and say it.'

'I don't—'

'Jamie!'

'It's your fault she's dead!'

And there it is. The voice laughs and wolf-whistles.

'I know,' I say.

That throws him for a second before he starts yelling again. 'It's your fault! Why couldn't you just shut your mouth? Why couldn't you just take your fucking meds and shut your mouth?'

I hold his gaze.

He shoves me.

'Why do you have to be like this? You should have told me you weren't taking your meds! You shouldn't have stopped in the first place! You knew this would happen! Why can't you be fucking responsible for two fucking seconds? You're ruining my life, Sid, and I have to hold your hand through it? Fuck that! We trusted you and you got her killed! Deal with that on your own and stay away from me, you nut job!'

He winces, like he wasn't expecting that last part to come out. We stare at each other, and I swear part of me just wants to grab him, push him against the wall and furiously rip his clothes off. The rest of me wants to open the window and jump.

He looks like he's about to speak, but steels himself instead, strides out, and slams the door.

Like a fucking plaster.

The building next to ours has no windows. Not on that side. The pavement is far below and lethal-looking. If I lean out of the window and look right, there's the dark tunnel of the alleyway between the two buildings and at the end, daylight on Wardour Street. The sun doesn't come to my window.

I lock the door. Turn the little key and trap myself. Jamie's bedroom doesn't lock. He moved in a few weeks before me. Once or twice, I wondered why he set me up in this room. Maybe he wanted the opportunity to lock me up if it ever got bad again.

Nut job.

Psycho.

I find Tom's phone in my pocket. Forgot to give it back to him. I'll have to go back. I'll have to go back anyway. But now I'll really have to go back, won't I?

I lie down and, without thinking, take my own phone out and scroll down the contacts.

Tom.

My thumb hovers over the name for a while. And then I'm calling. Tom's phone, in my other hand, starts buzzing.

Incoming call: Hophead.

My thumb moves over Tom's touch screen like it's not really part of my body, like my brain isn't in control of it.

Accept.

I put my phone to my ear.

'Tom, it's me.'

My own voice comes echoing back at me, feeble, from the other phone.

My throat tightens. I push through it.

'I'm sorry. Please, I'm so sorry. I'm . . . I fucked up, you know, and . . . you know, I fucked up really, really bad, and I'm s— I'm sorry. I never meant to . . . but . . . You didn't kill her, Tom. I did. I k— I . . . and I never even cared and I am so, so sorry. I don't want you to die, Tom, please don't die. Please don't die.'

And then I can't speak anymore, so I just sob over the phone, and listen to the pathetic echo on the other end.

It lasts about five minutes before I realise that the echo has stopped. I've been disconnected.

I drop my right arm onto the mattress and just lie there, a phone in each hand, staring at the ceiling.

17

Lloyd-Brown: We knew the infection was particularly bad in older people. Aggressively contagious, they said. Aggressively contagious. There wasn't much they could do about it at the start, but once the place started emptying, they organised for the older women to move to a separate wing. At first I didn't think much of it. Then they came for my mum.

(pause)

Lloyd-Brown: She wasn't that old, I didn't think, and I told them. I told them, 'She's not old enough.' They took her away.

Hayes: I am so sorry.

Lloyd-Brown: Don't apologise.

(pause)

Lloyd-Brown: I ran to Lucy's room. I cried. She said we'd find a way to go see her at night. She said we'd find the wing and go see her every week. I said 'Can we go tonight?' She said yes. It was easy enough to sneak around. At that point there wasn't much security anymore. The staff was pretty bare-boned.

Hayes: Langley's been pulling funding from the quarantine relief.

Lloyd-Brown: Who's that?

Hayes: Prime Minister. Not too keen on investing in things that don't directly benefit him.

Lloyd-Brown: Oh. Well, if he hadn't done that, we might not have been able to escape.

Hayes: True enough. I'll send over a thank-you card. Anyway, sorry. You went to see your mother that night?

Lloyd-Brown: We tried. We walked around the arena. We went through every corridor, every floor, every way we could think of. We couldn't find where the older women were. The other wings were all dark and empty. There was no power and nobody, not a sound. I remember getting a bit scared, it was so quiet. Lucy was always braver. She held my hand and led the way.

Eventually we left the arena. You know, around the living quarters used to be a shopping centre. Now that's all abandoned, too. We walked past all the old stores. I remember there was, there was one store, a shoe store. And there were still shoes in there. They were covered in dust and there were boxes everywhere on the floor. I remember, there was one pair that I noticed because my mum used to wear shoes like that. It was brown with a small heel, and it had a ribbon going up like a ballerina's shoe. Lucy said I should take them, but I was too scared to get caught with them in my room.

We weren't getting anywhere looking for my mum, so we ended up in the cafeteria. Lucy stole some old bread from the kitchen and we huddled up next to the tear in the plastic tarp. She said 'We'll find her tomorrow,' and she moved her foot a bit so that her toes were on top of mine.

There was a street lamp shining through the tarp, and it made it a bit difficult to see out of the window, but I looked until my eyes adjusted and eventually I noticed that there were trucks outside on the parking lot. Like caravans. Three of them. I'd never seen them before. Maybe they weren't there or I just hadn't noticed. I pointed it out to Lucy, and she hadn't seen them either. We took turns looking through the hole. Then Lucy said 'There's people.' I pushed her to see for myself. I saw a couple of doctors escorting a group of maybe five women, and I couldn't be sure but I thought one of them was my mother.

Hayes: You couldn't be sure?

Lloyd-Brown: It was dark and we could only see the back of them from where we were. But I was pretty sure it was my mum. The doctors had the women enter one of the caravans and closed the door. I remember I wanted to call out to my mum. She wouldn't have heard, and someone else might have heard and caught us outside past curfew, but I wanted to call out to her. I ended up pulling at the hole in the tarp to make it bigger, so I could see better. Lucy asked what I was doing, and I didn't reply, and she started helping me. The thing ended up torn enough that we could fit through it. We had our hands flat on the glass. We could

look outside like we were there, almost.
Like we were outside.

Lucy said 'Do you feel that?' and I noticed
a rush of cool air coming at my ankles from
somewhere on the left, between the tarp
and the window. I said 'Is it open over
there?' Lucy didn't reply. She slid through
the tear and started shuffling towards where
the air was coming from. I followed her. It
was a tight fit and we were sort of pushed
against the glass to avoid moving the tarp
too much. It smelled like plastic and it
was a bit hard to breathe. It took maybe two
minutes before we reached an emergency exit
door. The air was coming from underneath.

Lucy and I looked at each other. She reached
for the bar to push the door open, and I
got scared that it would set off an alarm
or something, but I didn't try to stop her.
The door opened and there was no alarm. We
got lucky. We got out.

(pause)

Hayes: What did you do once you got out?

Lloyd-Brown: Lucy was staring up at the
sky. She wasn't moving. I just ran for
the caravans. I wanted my mum. There were
hedges separating different sections of
the parking lot. I hid behind that. I

wasn't sure where the doctors were, so I waited and kept my eyes on the caravan door, because I figured they would have to come out eventually. Lucy joined me after a while. We waited for a long time, but nobody came out.

Then it started smelling.

Hayes: Smelling?

Lloyd-Brown: We snuck around to the other side of the caravans and there was a back door we hadn't been watching. And it was open. And behind the caravans there, there was a sort of, a pit. Dug in the middle of, and there was smoke and fire, and it smelled really, really bad.

Hayes: Jesus fuck.

(pause)

Hayes: I shouldn't have asked, let's, let's take a, a break or just, just stop—

Lloyd-Brown: Once I'd seen that, and I knew, I knew we were leaving. I wanted to go right there and then. I wanted to jump in the river and just put as much distance as possible between me and the smell. Neither of us could swim. I thought we'd figure it out because we had to. Lucy saved me. She said no. She said 'We need to think it through.' I didn't want to think it through. She said 'Cariad, we're going to leave, I promise, but we have to at least get some food and blankets.'

She took my arm and pulled me back to the emergency door, but we couldn't go back in. The door had shut behind us and it couldn't be opened from the outside. I was shaking, I remember, I think I was in shock. Lucy took charge completely. I would have just stood there. She took charge. She had me crouch down behind the hedges and said 'Aros fan hyn,' *wait here*, 'I'm going to look around.'

I waited for her. I don't think it was particularly cold, but I was freezing. I thought she wouldn't come back and I would die there. It took a long while. But she did. She came back. She said she found a tunnel that seemed to cross the river and it wasn't guarded. We went for it. The tunnel was closed so cars couldn't go in, but on foot it was easy enough to enter. So we went for it. We could barely see anything the whole way through. We held onto each other and we walked in the dark for maybe a half hour, and eventually . . .

Hayes: You made it out.

Lloyd-Brown: We made it out.

(click)

(click)

Hayes: Where did you go once you'd made it out?

Lloyd-Brown: We talked about it a lot that first night, and then the next day. We were sleeping outside. Stealing clothes. Stealing food. We had no money, no identification. We didn't exist, really, and I thought it had to stay that way. Lucy wanted to find her family. She asked about my dad, and I said I wasn't sure. I wasn't sure I wanted to go back.

Hayes: Why not?

Lloyd-Brown: Well, my dad . . . you know, he wasn't really mine anymore. Or I wasn't really his.

(pause)

Lloyd-Brown: It was twenty-five years, Jamie.

Hayes: I— Yeah . . . (inaudible) Yes.

Lloyd-Brown: It's not coming home. That man,

my father? I don't know. What if he didn't recognise me? What if I didn't recognise him? It's not coming home. You understand?

Hayes: I do.

(pause)

Lloyd-Brown: To Lucy, though, it was coming home. She had very strong memories of her granddad. He'd been taking care of her and her sister. She would often tell me stories about him. Once we'd left the O2, she started talking about him every day. Every day we would wake up and start walking. We walked west, towards the centre of London, as best as we could tell. And Lucy would start talking about her nana – that's what she called him. I started getting scared that we wouldn't find him. I thought he might have passed away. I thought we might never find him.

Hayes: Did you?

Lloyd-Brown: Yes, we did.

(pause)

Hayes: Liv?

Lloyd-Brown: It took us a few days to reach Lucy's old home, and by the time we got there . . . You know, Lucy, she was stronger than me, and a bit older, I think, but sometimes she was like a child. She was so excited, and I think part of it was because she wanted me to meet him. Or she wanted him to meet me. I was nervous.

(pause)

Lloyd-Brown: At first I was nervous that he wouldn't be there. Once we reached the door and it was time to ring the doorbell, I, I had a bit of a stupid thought.

Hayes: And what was that?

Lloyd-Brown: (laughs) 'I hope he'll like me.' (laughs) I was disgusting. We both were. It had been a week and we hadn't been able to shower. I wanted to make a good impression. (laughs) I swear, Jamie, you would have run away screaming, we were so gross.

Hayes: Not a chance.

Lloyd-Brown: Well, Lucy's granddad didn't run either. He answered the door, this tiny old man with white hair and very thick glasses, and he looked at Lucy. And he said, 'Amaya?' Lucy said 'Nana, it's me.' And he looked at her again. And he started crying. With, with his hand in front of his mouth. He hugged her and waved us in.

He kept saying things like 'I thought I saw the ghost of my daughter,' and 'I've been praying for this.' 'I was praying for this.' I remember noticing that he wasn't wearing shoes, and thinking maybe we should have taken our shoes off at the door. But at the same time, taking off your shoes, it leaves you vulnerable. I didn't know this man.

Hayes: You thought maybe he would call the police?

Lloyd-Brown: Yes, and I was very ashamed that I thought that. Lucy trusted him, and he seemed genuinely happy to see her, he looked so relieved.

Lucy introduced me. She said 'Nana, this is Liv. We're together.' I'm not sure he understood what that meant, but he came up to me and touched my face. He said I had a pretty face. (laughs)

Hayes: (inaudible)

Lloyd-Brown: What?

Hayes: Nothing, I (inaudible) sorry. (clears throat) How, uh, how long did you stay with Lucy's grandfather?

Lloyd-Brown: A few hours.

Hayes: What made you leave?

Lloyd-Brown: We were in the shower. Lucy's granddad had given us some of his son's old clothes, that he'd left when he moved out. We went to the bathroom to cut each other's hair and shower. Lucy went back to the living room first and then she came back and she looked different. She said 'You have to go now.' She said her uncle was here and, the way she said it, I could tell it wasn't good. Apparently he came by every day to help his dad with household chores and cooking. Lucy said 'I'll take you out through the back, you have to go.'

I asked 'What about you?' She said it was too late. That they'd seen her. I didn't understand. We were running anyway. I didn't understand why it mattered that they'd seen her. I argued, while I was putting on the clothes and my shoes. I said she had to come with me. She pulled me to the back, to the kitchen, and there was a backdoor there. I kept arguing. She looked me in the eyes. She said 'Cariad, I love you, but I can't leave him again.'

I said some really bad things. I told her she couldn't abandon me. I told her this man was not her family and it wasn't worth getting caught. I said I was her family and we were in this together, and that I, that I had to be more important than someone who hadn't been part of her life in twenty-five years. I think I really hurt her. I didn't mean it. I didn't mean any of it. Of course she wanted to stay with her nana. Of course she did.

(pause)

Lloyd-Brown: Anyway, I don't, I don't think I want to talk about this anymore. I left. We kissed and hugged. And I left.

(pause)

Hayes: I'm sorry.

(pause)

Hayes: For what it's worth, I'm glad we found you.

Lloyd-Brown: So am I.

(pause)

Lloyd-Brown: I was jealous that Lucy got to see her nana and talk to him and hug him, and I . . . you know. I had no one. I know it's ugly. It's very ugly. I should have been happy for her. I was jealous and

I kinda hated her for it. I think. Not really, but a little. You know?

(pause)

Hayes: Liv?

Lloyd-Brown: Yes?

Hayes: Would you like to learn Irish?

(pause)

Lloyd-Brown: I would love to.

18

The wall of near-identical houses stares me down. Sally's, in the middle, dares me to walk up to its door, dares me to touch it, ring the doorbell and enter even though last time was before. Even though, between then and now, I fucked up and destroyed a life.

Go on. Ring and destroy another.

I draw in a breath, not quite as deep as I'd hoped. The brass knob pushes back against my index finger, but I'm stronger, I press it in until the sound echoes inside. I take another breath.

Sally opens, sees me alone.

'Where is your friend?'

I close my eyes for a moment. It was going to be just a blink, but my eyelids sort of give up halfway through.

Where's your friend, Robinson? Did you kill her, by any chance? Did you kill her?

'She's gone,' I say, clearing my throat first so it comes out properly.

Sally's face remains blank. She takes me by the arm, pulls me inside, and the door closes. With the new privacy, she allows herself a sigh. She's moving along the hallway towards the living room, but I'm not going in any deeper than strictly necessary. She turns back and we look at each other from either end of the corridor.

'What happened?'

'I broke down. We moved her to a friend's house. Police gunned her down.'

'She deserved better than that.'

'Yes.'

She weighs the pros and cons before the next words leave her mouth. 'You promised.'

'Yes, I did.'

'Are you going to apologise?'

I say nothing. A heavy silence sets in. I look to the right at the old pictures of Jang-Mi and Sally. Both of them smile at me like nothing bad ever happened. My hand runs through my hair before I have time to notice it.

'I know what happened at the O2,' I say.

She follows my gaze for a second, to Jang-Mi's grin.

'Do I want to know?' she asks.

'Yes.'

She takes a moment to consider, then waves me in. 'Come sit. Let's talk.'

With a lump in my throat that I'm not about to give in to, not now, maybe not ever again, I sit with her and tell her everything.

She hears me. She believes every gruesome, unbelievable detail. A thought of disclosure floats into my mind. If she knew my history, the paranoia, the hallucinations, would she still hear me? Or would she morph and twist into the faces of the doctors, back then, casually mocking as I desperately argued that someone was planning to smother me in my sleep? I'm no liar. I'm not lying, but then again, I never was.

I tell her everything about the O2. The abuse, the experiments, the tests. The fire pit. Once I'm done, I let it sink in. And I get up.

'I should go. I have to go.'

She doesn't move. 'You know, I was going to paint today. Maybe paint her. In that green dress.'

Her face hangs towards the floor. I'm seeing a tired old woman who, in another life, might have been Olivia's grandmother.

'You should,' I say.

'I don't know.'

'You should.'

I take my leave, and as I reach the door, she calls me back.

'Mr Robinson?'

She stands at the other end of the hallway, smaller, I think, than before.

'Come here,' she says, and opens her arms for me.

I freeze a while. I'm not sure, and she's frozen too, waiting. Eventually I move over to her, move in, and time slows as I indulge in the hug. Her bony hand holds my shoulder in place. The scent of roses and musty clothes seeps into my own shirt.

'I'm sorry for your loss,' she says.

It hits me like a ton of bricks. My vision blurs and my eyes start frantically darting around. These aren't words I've heard before. Not addressed to me. *For the first time. For the first time in history.* I manage to regain some degree of composure with a few shallow inhales.

'I'm sorry for yours,' I mumble.

I dial Jamie on the way out. As it rings, my eyes fall on Nick and Charlie's house and a pang of guilt squeezes my insides. I wasn't planning on visiting them. I came to Hampstead fully intending to sneak to Sally's, then sneak back to Soho without so much as a 'How do you do?'. I told myself they've got their own shit to deal with, and they probably do.

'Sid?'

My stomach does a flip. Fuck me. *God bless Mother Nature.*

'Let's do it,' I say. 'Let's get that story out there. I'll help.'

The other end of the line almost pulses with stunned silence.

'Jamie?'

'Sid?'

That flip again.

Pathetic. Loser.

'Yes.'

'Look, Sid . . . about yesterday . . . I, uh, you know, I don't, I didn't—'

'Do you have any leads?'

'What?'

I heave a sigh, hand in my hair, then plunging into my coat pocket for the cigarettes. 'For the story?'

'Not really,' he says. 'My contacts like to talk a

great deal, but they aren't exactly lining up at the door to risk their careers and-slash-or lives.'

Without thinking, I walk to Nick and Charlie's door as I'm talking. 'We only need one.'

'Well, so far I haven't been able to find one.'

'Let's talk about it when I get home.'

'Where are you?'

'Running errands. I'll talk to you tonight, yeah?'

'Yeah. And look, Sid, I'm—'

I hang up and knock on the door, humming over the 'You're ruining his life' that's been playing on repeat in my left ear. I hum over the voice, *gonna go out to run and let myself get absolutely soaking wet*, but it doesn't help much.

I knock again, and stop singing with a jolt when Sally's voice calls out from the other side of the road.

'They're not here.'

'Oh. Do you know where they are?'

She hesitates. 'Why don't you give Mr Day a call? It's not really my place to say.'

19

I find Nick in front of Charlie's hospital room. He's talking to an old, bearded, bespectacled man in a white coat who looks so much like the archetypal doctor it doesn't seem right, like the beard might come off with one good tug.

I give him a sympathetic smile and a little wave as the doctor leaves, and Nick comes up to me.

'You didn't have to come. That's kind of you.'

'What happened?'

Nick brushes the hair from his face and keeps his hand sort of there, around, covering his mouth, flicking at his nose, scratching at his cheek.

'He, uh . . . he woke up in the middle of the night. I think he woke up. He screamed. He kept screaming. I tried to calm him down. I said it was just a bad dream, but . . .'

He swallows. His face reflects intense effort, controlled concentration to keep himself in check.

'But?'

'But it bloody well seemed like more than just a bad dream.'

Charlie's demeanour last time I'd visited them worms its way back into my mind. I see the exhaustion, the anxiety. The look in his wide eyes appears clearer than I was willing to notice back then.

'I sort of, uh, stroked, stroked his back, and eventually he stopped screaming. He stopped moving. I called his name. He didn't reply. He just stared at the wall. I went to get him some water, and when I came back he hadn't moved. Hours later, he still hadn't moved. He didn't take the water. I couldn't even get him to take the water.'

I suddenly want to see him. Call it morbid curiosity. Certainly it can't be professional curiosity.

Excuse me, are you a doctor?

'Catatonic?' I ask.

'That's what they said.'

'You called 999.'

He nods.

'You did the right thing.'

He laughs. His nostrils flare beneath his fingers. 'The right thing would have been to get rid of the books and flyers and all that stupid stuff. The right thing would have been to stop going to the protests. I knew he was worried about it. Now they say he's having a breakdown or something. Jesus Christ, Sid.'

He looks at me like I can do something about it, like I can make his mistakes go away. I look at him and feel weirdly resentful. Because he did ignore the signs. Because yes, he should have gotten rid of the illegal shit.

Then I start thinking about Tom, just upstairs in the psych ward, and maybe I don't have a leg to stand on.

'He's sick right now,' I say. 'He'll get better. And when he does, he's going to be so grateful that you were there for him.'

I manage a half-sincere smile.

He shrugs. 'Thank you. Thank you for coming, you really didn't have to.'

'Don't mention it.'

'It's just been a bit difficult lately, you know?'

'I know. I'm sorry I wasn't there more.'

This is what I'd meant to tell Tom. Seems to fit quite an array of situations these days.

'Don't be ridiculous. We just met you and I'm dragging you into this. You must be desperate for friends.'

'Something like that.'

'Oh,' he says. 'Well that makes two of us, then.'

His mobile starts ringing. He glances at it and sighs. 'Programme director. I have to take it.'

'Of course.'

He walks a few steps further away from the rooms.

'Hello? . . . Yeah, I know . . . I said I can't . . . No, I can't, my husband's not well . . . Look . . . Well, he's in the hospital . . . Yeah, thanks . . . I thought Peter was doing it . . . Well, Peter can do it . . . No, not me . . . No . . . Look, why can't Peter do it? He's good and he's an engineer as well, so really you'd be trading up . . .' He closes his eyes and lets his forehead fall against the wall. 'I'll think about it. Thanks for understanding.'

He hangs up, but doesn't move. Dead on his feet. I walk up to him.

'How long have you been here?' I ask.

'I don't know. I can't go home without him.'

I'm not sure if he means that he can't leave Charlie or that he can't be alone in their house.

'You can stay at my place for a while,' I try. 'Come home with me.'

His eyes open in surprise. 'Oh, no, thank you but I don't think so.'

'Look, stay until the end of visiting hours, that's another . . .' I check my watch. '. . . thirty minutes. Then you're coming home with me. You shouldn't be alone.'

He considers. He's beginning to wheeze a little. 'You don't want to wait around for a half hour,' he says.

'I have a friend here. I'll visit him. Do you have an asthma inhaler?'

'In my coat.'

'Okay. Let's get it.'

I take his arm and pull him from the wall and together we shuffle into the room.

The inhaler clicks as Nick takes a sharp breath.

Charlie's sedated face seems peaceful enough now. The hair at his temples is greying and a few lines run across his high forehead.

Nick sits on the edge of the bed. He reaches over and brushes the hair from Charlie's face, and there it is again, the squeeze in my chest, the longing. Then he leans in and I look away.

'I'll, um, I'll go see my friend,' I say, slipping out.

Jamie frowns when Nick walks into the flat with me.

I braced myself on the tube back. To be honest,

I could have warned him with a text, but every time I took my phone out I ended up putting it back in my pocket without sending anything. I was afraid he would say no. I thought that if Nick was already there, it would be harder for Jamie to send him away. I tried to justify myself by remembering how he asked Olivia to stay without talking to me first, but the mere thought of her made me nauseous, so I spent the remainder of the journey pretending to forget to text.

'Hello,' Jamie says.

I blurt everything out in one breath. 'Jamie, this is my friend Nick. Nick, my flatmate Jamie. Nick is going through some stuff right now, so I invited him to stay here for a few days. Since we do have a spare room. Just for a few days. Hope that's okay.'

Jamie rises to his feet, eyes moving slowly between Nick and me. He shakes Nick's hand.

'Nice to meet you.'

'And you,' Nick says. 'I've heard a lot about you.'

'Have you?'

I let out a highly unconvincing fake laugh.

'I don't mean to intrude,' says Nick. 'Maybe this was a bad idea, I should just—'

'No, no,' Jamie says. 'No problem at all. Sid, may I talk to you for a minute?'

I follow him to his bedroom. He gives Nick a stiff grin and closes the door behind us.

'Who's this?'

'Nick.'

'Yeah but who's Nick? Do we know him?'

I tell him everything. Olivia's old house, Charlie and Nick, Sally, the books, the movies, the flyers, and when I'm done, he gives a loud sigh.

'Jesus, Sid—'

I snap. 'Trust me!' And that defuses him instantly.

He rubs the short hair at the back of his neck. 'You're right. You're right, it's just I thought we were going to . . . you know?'

'We will. We will, okay? I promise.'

'If you say so.'

I touch his shoulder. 'Trust me.'

We both look at my hand on his shoulder. Something's boiling in my chest and the blood pumps in my fingertips.

'I'm tired,' he says.

My cue to leave.

Nick stands in the middle of the living room, abandoned and all inwards on himself. I wave him to the settee.

'So this is the friend, then?' he says, and you can hear the inverted commas in his voice.

'Yeah,' I say, casually, like I'm not admitting to anything here.

'Cheerful fellow.'

'Give him a break, he's had a couple of rough weeks.'

He smiles playfully.

I cough and check my watch. 'Are you hungry?'

'Starving, actually,' he says.

We make an omelette and eat in the living room, cross-legged on the sofa with the plates balanced on our laps.

We talk about random things, unimportant things. Our jobs. The weather. It's unspoken but intentional. We both need a break. I'd almost forgotten how pleasant such a simple chat could be. There's no tension between us, and the relief is intense.

Eventually the plates lie empty on the coffee table, and we're cradling mugs of tea. It's gotten dark. Now would probably be a good time to flick the lights on, but I can't quite bring myself to get up.

Nick stretches his legs out in front of him. 'So, your other friend. At the hospital. What happened to him?'

My heart rate picks up. I say nothing, praying my agitation isn't too transparent.

'Sorry,' Nick says. 'Possibly none of my business. Charlie's usually there to keep me from prying.'

'Wrist injury,' I say. 'I'm helping him with physical therapy. Trying anyway.'

Tom was more receptive today. I brought up the exercises and was met with minimal resistance. It occurred to me that he might be so dreadfully bored over there that any distraction would be welcome. In a psychiatric ward, time crawls.

That was the hardest part. Making myself step into the ward. Making myself walk among these people – *your people, Robinson, did you miss them?* – shuffling along the corridors. I tried to hide how scared I was, how terrified, and how monstrous the hospital felt in that moment.

As I describe the exercises to Nick, my focus returns. I grab his hand and demonstrate, and point at the different muscles in there, the different tendons.

Nick's sporting a quiet smile. As soon as I notice it, I become self-conscious and fall silent again.

Why are you like this?

Don't gesticulate like that, boy, don't let your voice do that thing.

'I can see why Jamie likes you,' Nick says.

I frown. 'He doesn't.'

'Doesn't he?'

'I'm pretty sure he hates me.'

Nick's face softens. 'Why would he hate you?'

'Because I'm responsible for the death of someone he loved.'

He's obviously surprised if not shocked, but he doesn't ask any questions. He just looks at me and, matter-of-factly, 'I don't know what you did or didn't do. But the man I met earlier does not hate you.'

He blinks a few times, gets up and carries the plates back to the kitchen.

A floorboard creaks behind me. Jamie stands at his bedroom door, in his pyjama bottoms, shirtless. We gaze at each other and something almost intimate passes between us. I watch his shoulder blades work under his skin as he turns away.

20

The adrenaline drained out of me overnight. Is this normal? I cover my eyes and groan. Is this adulthood? I'm not sure if this is a lot to deal with or just the regular amount. I can't decide if I need a break or if I just want one. We're just getting started, aren't we? I did promise.

I promise.

With my hand still covering my eyes, I start singing to myself. Not as I usually sing. Not in a panic, not frantically to keep myself sane. I sing like Jamie sang. I sing a bit raw, a bit shaky, with the memory of his voice playing in my ear.

I sat within the valley green,
I sat me with my true love.
My sad heart strove the two between,
The old love and the new love.
The old for her, the new
that made me think on Ireland dearly.
While soft wind blew down the glade

And shook the golden barley.

My voice isn't as clear, as expressive. Not as good, really, but it's surprisingly calming, and it manages to get rid of everything else until eventually there's nothing left. Just the song, just the way my voice vibrates in my skull, in my throat, in my chest, just the slight tightening of my stomach muscles as I expel the air. And then it's over and my voice wavers and dies out.

And the doorbell chimes.

The flat is eerily still as I come out of my room. It appears to be early. Nick and Jamie must still be sleeping.

I put my eye against the peephole. The man's standing too close to clearly make out but the white hair held back in a ponytail's all I need. I clear my throat, inhale deeply and plaster on a smile as I swing the door open.

'Mr Lennox, sir, hello!'

He leans forward like he's been invited in. The tips of his shoes plant themselves across the threshold.

Tell him to step back.

'Good morning, Mr Robinson!'

Tell him to get out of your face.

'I'm terribly sorry, did we forget the rent? What, uh, what day is it?'

'No, no, you're fine.'

His large hand rests on the door-frame, and I swear his grin widens as he feels me tensing up. *Close the door. Close the door on his fingers.*

'What . . . what can I do for you?' I ask.

'Well, it's a bit of an awkward situation for me. I'm in a bit of a pickle.'

He shifts his weight closer and I draw back an inch or two.

'A pickle?'

'You see, my nephew's moving to London for his PhD. Very driven young lad, very promising, he is. My late sister's youngest.'

'Oh?'

'Yes, and well, you know how it is. I did promise my late sister that I'd take care of the lad. And well, he's going to need a place to stay.'

His Old Spice wafts over as he stretches his neck to gawk past me into the flat.

I put two and two together. 'You want the apartment back?'

'It pains me to ask, I'm sure you understand. My late sister would have done anything for this kid.'

Tell him to shove his late sister where the sun don't shine.

'I understand.'

Oh, you fucking doormat, you.

'When will you be n—'

'In a month.'

'Sh . . . sure, I, uh . . .'

His massive bear paw lands heavily on my shoulder.

'You know I wouldn't normally ask, Mr Robinson, but as you can see, I'm in a pickle. It shouldn't be too difficult to find new accommodation, should it? What with the lovely economic climate we're enjoying these days?'

Loser.

Homeless loser. Fucking doormat. Always letting everyone walk over you. Are you gonna cry? Are you gonna cry, nancy boy?

I stammer.

Suddenly Jamie's arm drapes around my shoulders,

pushing Lennox's hand off of me.

'Top of the morning to you, sir!'

I half-turn to whisper at him. '"Top of the morning?"'

He elbows me in the ribs and I turn my attention back to the landlord.

Lennox's demeanour has adjusted. He's outnumbered now, and I'd always had the impression that Jamie intimidated him.

'Mr Hayes, how are you?'

'Can't complain, sir. And yourself?'

The landlord puffs his chest out, scrambling for the upper hand.

'You look a bit peaky, son. You need to get some of that beautiful winter sunlight we've been having! Bring some colour back to those cheeks!'

Jamie gives him his most charming smile. 'Yes, sir, I'll bear that in mind.'

An awkward moment passes during which Jamie suppresses a yawn.

'I was just telling Mr Robinson here that I'm going to be needing the apartment back quite soon, unfortunately.'

'So I heard,' says Jamie, 'but you have to give us at least three months' notice. We do have a contract.'

Lennox deflates. 'Of course. Of course. How about if I give you until the beginning of February? Would that be okay?'

'Well, three months would be February 27th, wouldn't it?'

'Yes, of course it would. February 27th it is, then.'

Jamie nods. 'Thank you. That's very kind of you. Bye now!'

He releases my shoulder, shuts the door and we

both lean back against it, exhaling in unison.

'Wonderful,' says Jamie.

Nick emerges from the third room.

'You know, if you're in a tight spot, you can always stay with us for a while. I mean, you'll have to share the sofa, but . . .'

He looks in my direction and gives a discreet wink.

'Thanks, but we couldn't,' Jamie says, talking for the two of us and for some reason I don't mind.

'Fair enough. The offer stands, if you change your mind. It's the least I can do.'

And he disappears into the bathroom.

Jamie and I exchange a slightly embarrassed look.

'It'll be fine,' he says. 'We'll find another place.'

'I know,' I say.

He follows me to the kitchen. I busy myself with breakfast, popping the kettle on and bread in the toaster, and he helps. I'm trying to decide whether or not he hates me. Whether or not he heard me sing earlier. Our fingers touch against the mugs. We steal glances at each other, just checking in, maybe, or maybe more.

'You alright?' he mumbles.

'Yeah,' I mumble. 'You?'

'Yeah.'

But he's lying, he's biting things back, and then things escape anyway.

'I had this editor friend,' he says. 'Well, not a friend, really. A contact. Christopher Carter. Published a couple of my pieces in the past. Was involved with this underground paper a few years back. Didn't amount to much, they only printed three issues before the group was dismantled, but I thought he might be interested in the story. I was wrong.'

The morning light slicing through the window hits his profile, his nose dipped forward, and casts intricate shadows in the shell of his ear.

'I'm starting to think it's just you and me. Other people are either too scared or they recently happened upon outrageous amounts of money and a new-found loyalty to the establishment. I just really thought Carter was one of the good ones.'

'He didn't seem like a bad guy,' I say.

He raises an eyebrow.

'I listened to your voicemail. A while back. I'm sorry.'

'Ah, don't sweat it.'

'We're asking a lot, you know.'

'I know we are.'

The tip of his sock rubs at a spot on the floor. I take him in, all of him, and find myself physically, viscerally pulled.

'Am I interrupting?' Nick asks, all polite and formal and definitely interrupting.

'Not at all,' says Jamie.

'Tea?' I offer.

'Thank you.'

I motion for him to sit at the kitchen table and catch Jamie's eye as I pour him a mug.

'Be nice,' I mouth.

Jamie clears his throat. 'So . . . Nick, right?'

Nick's head snaps up, like that might be a trick question. 'Yes.'

'I'm sorry if I seemed a bit out of sorts before.'

'Please, I barged in uninvited.'

'You are invited,' Jamie says.

He extends his hand across the tabletop and they

shake once more, with infinitely more warmth than last night.

'I'm sorry about . . . whatever it is that you're having to deal with.'

Nick nods thank you as I offer him milk. 'My husband is currently hospitalised.'

'Oh dear, what happened?'

Nick goes quiet. At first he seems like he might just be thinking about his answer or weighing his words, but after a while Jamie mercifully picks up on his discomfort and changes the subject.

'So what do you do?'

'I'm a producer at the Tower.'

Interest sparks on Jamie's face. 'Radio or television?'

'Radio.'

He begins to sip his tea, unwinding a bit. 'Mostly documentaries, but recently I've had to diversify to some extent.'

'Did you get the "entertainment value" speech as well?'

'Oh, yes. Sid tells me you're a journalist?'

I hide behind the box of cereal.

'If you can call that stuff journalism.' Jamie nods at the newspaper in front of him.

Nick grimaces. 'Well, you have to make your rent one way or another, don't you? We're still paying for the house, Charlie and I.'

'It's a bit of a tightrope walk, isn't it? Maintaining a career without selling out completely.'

'You can say that again. They're asking me to do the next address. God knows how I'm going to get out of that one.'

'Not keen on the address, are you?' Jamie says.

Nick hesitates.

'Oh, don't worry, neither are we.'

He gestures between the two of us, like there's something there.

I offer Nick my best attempt at a reassuring smile. It occurs to me that he would never have thought twice about speaking against the address before. *We have always depended on the kindness of strangers.* He doesn't seem to be depending on much anymore. Without Charlie there, he looks naked in a snowstorm.

'Did, uh, Sid, did you show him the book?' Nick asks.

'The book?'

'Jane Eyre,' I say.

'You have a copy of *Jane Eyre?*'

Nick sighs. 'Among other things.'

'Among other things?'

'Jamie . . .' I warn, but it's too late.

He's rising from his chair, walking around the table. One-track mind and impossible to derail.

'Other things as in more books?'

The words come out slow, measured. 'Books, movies, newspapers. My husband and I, we . . . participate . . . in the pushback effort.'

'Participate?' Jamie repeats.

'Used to.'

'Used to?'

'Jamie, leave him alone.'

'It took a toll on Charlie. A really big toll. I—'

Jamie grabs my sleeve. 'I need to talk to you. Now.'

He drags me to the living room before I have time to protest and we break into frantic whispers.

'We need to show him the tape,' he says.

'No,' I say.

He knew I was going to say that.

'Okay, see, but hear me out. He works at the Tower. You obviously think he can be trusted and I am trusting you right now. This is me trusting you, okay?'

'That's not the problem, Jamie. He doesn't need that in his life right now.'

The frustration bursts out of him in wild gestures, the flailing and ranting, the sizzling intensity that I can't look away from.

'We need this! This is our way in! He works at the Tower, maybe he can help! Maybe he knows someone who can! Sid, please, you know this is bigger than him or either of us. We have to try. We have nothing. I have nothing. Please?'

I wrestle down a surge of sheer, hair-raising want.

Keep your head.

Focus.

I stammer for a while. *We have nothing.* I can hear Olivia's voice, and see her face, and I owe her. The question is, do I owe her more than I owe Nick? How much more?

'Look, Sid, I won't tell him if you don't w—'

'Okay.'

'Okay?'

I push the hair out of my face. 'You're right. This isn't our information to keep. We owe her.'

'Yes! Yes, oh my God, I could kiss you!'

'Yes, well . . .'

'Thank you. We can do something really good here.'

'I hope so.'

'I know so.'

I give him a small smile. He returns it with a nod

and goes to retrieve the recorder from his messenger bag.

'So what is it?' Nick says, as I walk back into the kitchen.

He sits like a statue, mind halfway to elsewhere, the only movement his thumb playing with the golden band on his left hand.

'I'm not an idiot, you know. What is it that you have, that you're not supposed to have? Is it a book? A video?'

I pull up a chair, close, to get his full attention.

'Before we show you, you have to know this is . . .'

'Big?'

'It's big.'

He seems doubtful. I'm unsure why, or what can be said that would even come close to preparing him for it.

Jamie draws his own chair between us and holds up the recorder.

'Brace yourself.'

Nick offers him the gently amused look of a tired teacher who's just been asked a particularly naive question.

'With all due respect, if I had a penny for every time someone's come to me thinking they've found the most novel, incredible—'

Jamie presses play.

'Okay so, um, let me just take— I'll— I'll get some information down and then we'll just jump into it, okay?'

'Okay.'

And I watch Nick fall silent.

'Today is Monday, the, um, 14th of October 2019. Could you repeat that for me?'

'Today is Monday, the 14th of October 2019.'

And I watch him understand.

'Thank you. What's your name?'

'Olivia Angharad Lloyd-Brown.'

The stupor melts off his face, his body thaws and heats up. The gears start spinning again.

Fifty-seven minutes and forty-one seconds later, the recording clicks to a stop.

Nick reaches out with shaking fingers. 'May I?'

Jamie hands him the recorder. Nick rewinds a bit and presses play again.

'Liv?'

'Yes?'

'Would you like to learn Irish?'

'I would love to.'

Rewind. Play.

'I would love to.'

Rewind. Play.

'I would love to.'

And stop.

'Where is she now?' he asks.

Jamie spits out a piece of nail. 'Gone.'

Nick looks at me. I look at my feet.

'What are you planning to do with this?'

'Trying to find someone to publish—'

'That's not good enough.'

Jamie stiffens. 'Pardon?'

'This isn't something you write about, it's not something you publish. Jamie, this isn't a story, and it certainly isn't yours.'

'So, what? We do nothing?'

'Of course we do something. Are you joking? Of course we do something.'

'What do we do?' I ask.

'We broadcast it.'

I feel Jamie's leg start bouncing up and down and discreetly touch his knee under the table.

He clears his throat. 'I know a few underground publications, but I never heard of an underground radio station.'

Nick chuckles. 'No, no, you don't want some fifty guys holed up in their basements hearing this. You want everyone to hear it.'

He delicately sets the recorder back on the table.

'We jam the address.'

Jamie moves my hand away and his legs resumes the bouncing.

I clench my jaw and power through. 'How?'

'I know someone.'

'Who?'

'A colleague. His name is Peter Davis. He's an engineer. All the technical know-how you could ask for, and he's been working at the Tower for years, so he knows exactly what equipment they use.'

'How do we know we can trust this guy?' Jamie says. 'If he works at the Tower —'

'I work at the Tower,' Nick says.

'Most people who work at the Tower are government zombies.'

'Jamie . . .' I say.

'You'd be surprised,' Nick says.

Jamie sighs. 'Can you vouch for this guy? Do you know him personally?'

'We've been out for drinks after work a couple of

times. When he's had a few, he can get pretty loud about his feelings towards the authorities.'

'He could be pretending.'

Nick pulls a tired smile from the corners of his mouth. 'Well, that's just the way they keep you from acting, isn't it? You can never be one hundred percent sure. At some point, you just have to take a chance.'

He stands.

'I should go. Visiting hours. Look, it's your tape, so the decision is yours. Think about it.'

We exchange a few pleasantries and he heads for the hospital.

With the return to privacy, Jamie begins to shake.

'I know that you'd have preferred to write about it,' I say. 'I know that sharing her voice with . . . I know it's not easy for you.'

'We have to,' he says.

'I think we do,' I say.

He strides over to the window and yanks it open, and then he's breathing hard through his nose and I'm wrapping my arms around my torso to shield myself from the cold.

He groans. 'Is this what a panic attack feels like?'

'Yeah. It is.'

'I don't like it so much.'

'Yeah. Me neither.'

21

Home is up. The staircase faces me like a wall, like an impregnable fortress. Home is up, and I'm down here.

At first I thought it was just a routine check. It wasn't. They went straight for me, like they knew I would walk through here. Like they were waiting. At first I thought it would be over in a matter of minutes. It wasn't.

'Sir, may we have a moment of your time?'

They pulled me aside.

'I didn't do anything wrong.'

'We need to confirm your identity, please.'

He was built like an ox. He towered a whole foot over me. The leader, always a leader. The other two, to my left and right, breathed in my face. It smelled like old gum. He held out his hand for my passport and looked at the information at the same time as he asked for it.

'Name?'

'Sid Robinson.'

'Short for Siddhartha?'

'Short for Sidney.'

'Where are you from?'

'Manchester.'

'No, I mean . . .' He gestured at his own face, meaning mine.

I stared. 'Manchester.'

'Right. Here's what's going to happen. You're going to accompany us to the station.'

After that my mind went blank with fear. I think I said no. I think I said please, and no, and I haven't done anything wrong. They didn't care. The panic mounted, and the voice in my head, reacting to stress, seeing an opportunity, got louder. *You're dead. You're dead.* It hissed, vicious, obscene, like it was enjoying it. *They'll cut you open. They'll spill your guts in a back alley behind the station and you'll die staring up at the sun, you'll die blinded and choking on your own blood.*

'Shut up!'

'What did you just say to me?'

'N-nothing.'

Then he pulled out handcuffs, and I did the most idiotic thing I could have possibly done. I tried to run.

He caught me, yanked me back. His fist pulled on my hair until I lost my balance. I yelped so loud people must have heard. No one intervened. The skin on my side scraped against the tarmac as he dragged me. I could feel it peeling off.

'You're hurting me!' I called.

He barked something I didn't understand.

'I'm not resisting,' I said. 'I'm not resisting!'

He rammed his boot into my stomach, then let go, and my head slammed against the kerb. I stayed down, winded, hand hovering over my throbbing side, not daring to touch. The large hand closed like a vice on my shirt collar and pulled me, half-strangled, to my feet. I shook, buckled, fell back down. He pulled me up again.

'Stand!'

'I can't.'

'Stand!'

I knew falling again was a death sentence, and for a second, I was okay with it. It was the thought of Jamie, alone and uncertain, wondering why I never came home, that sparked my survival instinct. I clung awkwardly to the man's bicep and managed, somehow, to stay upright all the way to the car.

I put my foot on the first step. Everything has to come to an end. Five flights of stairs. Come on.

The ride took forever. I felt nothing but the burning pain along my right side. I watched the back of the men's heads from the backseat, stewing in my own blood, hands cuffed on my lap, unable to tilt my head down and examine the damage. My shirt, damp, stuck to the scratches.

'Pub tonight?' said one of them.

'You know it,' said another.

I closed my eyes.

First-floor landing. You're doing great. You can do this. Come on.

The car pulled up in front of a plain brick building, old and a bit shabby. The ox man dragged me out and shoved me through the door. The receptionist sitting behind a desk in the first room didn't even look up as we walked past.

'Alright, mate,' he said. 'See the game last night?'

'Nah, I was on duty.'

And we dove into a string of neon-lit corridors. Left, left, right, left, right, into a lift, right, right.

Second-floor landing. If you make it home, you never have to go out again. I promise. You can lay in bed forever. Come on. Come on.

We stopped in front of a door.

'We'll come get you,' said the ox man.

He shoved me inside and, as I stumbled forward,

the door swung shut and clicked, and it was pitch black, it was oppressive darkness, oppressive silence. I felt blindly in front of me and found the door inches from my face. My elbows hit the walls on either side as I tried to move. I called for help. I pleaded, I'm claustrophobic, please, I'm dying, please, God, have mercy. I begged.

Third-floor landing. What were you thinking? Give up. You can't climb any more. Give up.

When the door opened again, ages later, I wept. The ox man was chewing slowly on a sandwich.

'Out you go.'

He walked me to an office and knocked on the door.

'Come in,' said a voice.

We came in. The ox man removed the handcuffs and walked out and I was left standing in an ill-lit office with dirty windows.

The man behind the desk had a clean-cut face and clear intelligent eyes. He wore a businessman's black suit. He took his time before looking up from his paperwork.

'Have a seat,' he said, with a quick smile. 'Legs uncrossed, please, hands palms-up on your thighs.'

As I sat on the single chair in the middle of the room, he drew a packet of cigarettes out from a drawer.

'It says here you smoke, Mr Robinson. Do you want one?'

'No,' I said.

It came out hoarse, barely more than a whisper, but you could have heard a fly in that room.

'Well, do you mind if I have one?'

He lit one and stared at it for a while, absent-mindedly.

'These things will be the death of me. Have you ever tried quitting? I probably should, but there never seems to be a good time. Stressful job.'

He took a drag, slowly, and looked down at his papers again.

'Now then, Mr Robinson. Any idea why you're here?'

I shook my head.

'Speak up, please, when you reply.'

'No,' I said.

'No idea?'

I shook my head again.

'Speak up.'

'I haven't done anything.'

He laughed. 'Well I should hope not, otherwise you'd be in quite a lot of trouble here, wouldn't you?'

He looked at me like he was expecting me to speak, but I didn't know what to say. He got up and walked around the desk. The red tip of the cigarette flashed and I startled, but he just leant back against the desk casually.

'Hands on your thighs, please. Palms up.'

I put my hands back.

'I need the restroom,' I tried.

'In a moment.'

He smoked for a while. Then he reached back for the ashtray and stubbed the cigarette out. 'Do you know a gentleman by the name of Oscar Jones?'

'No,' I said.

'You may know him as Sally. Does that ring any bells?'

I stared at my lap.

'Charles Williamson? Nicholas Day? Do you know these people?'

'I need the restroom, please.'

He chuckled. 'You're right not to answer that. It's not a real question. I know you've been in contact with them.'

I should have kept my mouth shut, but the way he let it hang in the air for a minute made me so uncomfortable I had to hear the sound of my own voice.

'Is that bad?' I asked.

'Well, that very much depends on the outcome of our little chat. You see, Mr Williamson and Mr Day are unimportant. They're a nuisance, but not a priority. As for your involvement in this, consorting with dissidents is a minor offence that we don't usually preoccupy ourselves with. However, it is enough to justify an arrest, should we decide to revise our priorities. Do you understand? Speak up, please.'

'Yes.'

'Good.'

He crouched down in front of me. I tried to pretend I couldn't feel his breath against my open hands.

'I don't mean to scare you, Mr Robinson. To tell you the truth, we have no grudge against you and no particular interest in your activities. It's your flatmate we're worried about.'

My head snapped up. Our eyes met, and he saw something that he wasn't expecting.

'Ah.'

Fourth-floor landing.

'Hardly an ideal place for a nap, is it?'

Pardon?

'Lad?' Gettleman gives me the same look Dad gave me that one time I was sent home from school with a temperature when he had planned to get pissed in front of the telly. The Hawaiian shirt makes it marginally less intimidating, a touch more incongruous.

'Sorry,' I say.

'Had a few more than you could handle?'

'No.'

He sighs. 'Going up? Need a hand? Or a shoulder?'

I start shaking my head no, but it turns into a nod.

'Alright, up you go, lad, up you go!'

I thought I would pass out.

He scribbled a note in the file, and turned to me again. 'Mr Robinson, we believe your flatmate Mr Hayes is in danger of becoming an agitator. Now, agitators are worse than a nuisance and they are very much a priority. Do you understand?'

'Yes.'

'Good. We don't want this to get out of hand, and it seems you don't want that either. So, to keep this under control, we believe Mr Hayes should be provided with a chaperone. Someone who watches over him and lets us know how he's doing. That's where you come in.'

'Jamie hasn't done anything wrong,' I said. 'He hasn't done anything.'

Suddenly his face transformed. He glared. 'Mr Robinson, we are trained to recognise the bad apples at a glance. Are you telling me I'm bad at my job?'

My hands were shaking on my lap. 'No.'

And then, just as suddenly, he went back to his casual tone. 'We'll make it worth your while, of course. We're not ungrateful. For instance . . .' He had a look at the file. 'It says here you require antipsychotic medication. We can help you pay for that. We can help you find a new place to live and pay your rent. We can make sure you never have to pull a pint again for the rest of your life.'

He whipped out a cigarette and handed it to me. I was gasping. I took it.

Fifth-floor landing.

'You know, my brother's kid used to have a bit of a drinking problem, too, and he went to one of those whatchamacallits. Rehab places. Did wonders, that. Maybe your, uh, boyfriend could look into that for you.'

'Not my boyfriend, and I don't have a drinking problem.'

'That's what my brother's kid used to say.'

'Thank you for your help. I should . . .'

'Of course, do what you have to do, lad. Try some aspirin.'

'I will.'

Somehow, I find my way to the bathroom, strip, take a piss, shower. I scrub myself frantically. The soap stings in my broken skin and I relish it and want more. I press on the bruises. It hurts so bad I want to puke. Fuck, yes.

'You know where to find us, Mr Robinson.'

Clean pair of boxers and a t-shirt to cover the bandages. Brain completely fried. I collapse on the sofa and fall asleep, but none of it goes away.

22

'There's always been someone in the flat, there's no way they'd have had an opportunity to do this! You know that!'

I'm ripping strips of wallpaper off with my bare hands. The bandage at my side threatens to fall off as sweat soaks the tape. I try my best not to grunt at the stabbing pain in my thorax, to appear reasonable, but it's hard, it's hard, and I think I've got a cracked rib.

'I'm just checking,' I tell him. 'It won't be long, I just need to check, I'm just checking, you have to let me cos you, you, you have to let me check.'

'I know it's scary,' Jamie's saying. 'I'm scared too. But you have to see that this is paranoia, Sid, and you're having a panic attack.'

He grabs me by the wrists. I think of the handcuffs and yank myself free.

'No, I'm not!'

'Yes, you are.'

'It's fine, it's fine. I just have to check. I just have to make sure before he gets here. I'll be, uh, I'll be, I'll be twenty minutes tops. An hour tops. It won't be long, I just have to make sure, cos you know they do that, they put mics in and it could have been done, they could have done that when we were out, you don't know until you check, it's just good sense, it's sensible.'

'Sid, come on. If we were tapped, they'd have come for us ages ago! We talk about the tape all the time. We played it five days ago!'

'Oh, shut up, please, just . . .' I bring my index finger to my lips. 'Shhh, okay?'

Keys jiggle in the front door and I jump out of my skin.

Nick takes in the situation. 'What's going on?'

'Noth—'

'I'm checking for wires.'

'No, no he's not,' Jamie says.

'Yes, I am!'

'For fuck's sake! What's gotten into you all of a sudden? You're taking your meds, right?'

'Is he unwell?' Nick asks.

'"Is he unwell"?' I repeat, before I can stop myself. 'Jesus Christ.'

'Should I call Peter and cancel tonight? We can cancel if it's too much.'

'No! No, it's fine,' Jamie says.

'I'm sorry about that,' I say. 'That was uncalled for.'

I resume the task, tearing off paper along the doorway, running my finger underneath, panting and wiping the sweat from my brow with my sleeve, narrating as I go. 'They usually run the wires along the skirting boards, sometimes it's in the lighting, in the fixtures, we have to check there too.'

'You think you might be bugged?'

Jamie sighs. 'We're not tapped! He's being unreasonable.'

'We do have a few hours before Peter gets here,' Nick says. 'We could check.'

Jamie shakes his head and I feel a sob stuck somewhere between my diaphragm and my throat. He comes up to me again and looks for eye contact.

'Sid, this has happened before. You know these thoughts you're having are a part of . . .' He glances at Nick. '. . . of the deal. This idea that we're under surveillance? It came out of nowhere. You weren't worried when we played the tape for Nick. What's changed?'

I almost tell him, but instead I just hold my arm around myself, over the bruises. 'Nothing, nothing, I just think it'd be better if we made sure cos—'

'Nothing's changed,' Jamie says, almost tender. 'Come on, Sid, think rationally.'

'I can't.'

Everything inside me's gone and there only remains a deep pit of cold terror where my stomach should be.

'I can't, okay?'

I blink a few times through the blur.

'Humour me. Please. Just humour me.'

He thinks for a moment, then disappears into the cupboard and comes back with his tool bag.

'I'll get the switches. You check the skirting boards.'

I sniff. Hadn't noticed I was weeping again.

'Thank you,' I mumble, wiping the tears away with the back of my hand.

It takes us most of the day to unscrew the switches and peel off the wallpaper along the skirting boards, along the corners and the door-frames.

We're blasting a Pink Floyd CD to cover the noise – Jamie's idea – and it drills into my head and I hate it, I hate it so much, but it works. It's just shrill enough that any of our sounds blend right in. The disc has already looped twice.

As it's about to go back to track one again, Jamie takes off his rubber gloves and throws them on the settee.

'Done.'

'Yes, I'm done too,' says Nick, struggling up.

'Have we checked behind the heating?' I ask.

'Yes,' Jamie says, turning off the stereo.

'Under the settee?'

'Yes.'

'The shower?'

'Yes! We checked everywhere, for fuck's sake, there's nothing!'

'This is good,' Nick says. 'There's nothing. Feel better?'

I chew on my lower lip. 'Yeah, that's . . . it's better. Yeah.'

'I need a fucking drink,' Jamie says, and right as he says it, there are loud footsteps up the stairs outside.

We share a sideways glance and move to the door as one.

'Is it him?' I ask.

It's not. This is five or six pairs of boots.

'Jesus,' Jamie says. 'It's okay. Stay calm. They won't find anything, but you have to stay calm. It's going to be okay.'

'How did they know? Do you think Davis could have sent—'

'Wait, wait,' says Jamie, looking through the peephole. 'They're not coming here.'

He laughs with relief, then catches himself laughing and goes stern. 'It's the neighbour.'

I push him out of the way to have a look for myself.

They're pounding on Gettleman's door.

'Police! We know you're here, Mr Gettleman, open the door!'

It takes a while, but eventually the door opens and out comes Gettleman, partway between rattled and resigned.

'What's going on?' he says, with an empty smile.

'We're going to need you to come with us, I'm afraid.'

'I have nothing to hide. You can search my house if you want.'

'That won't be necessary.'

They drag him away from his home as he looks over his shoulder at what he's leaving behind.

'Do you think it's because of us?' I whisper.

'Of course not,' says Jamie. 'Don't be daft.' But he doesn't sound convinced at all.

'What if they just had the wrong flat number?'

Jamie turns to Nick. 'How confident are you that your guy isn't responsible for this?'

Nick gives a pained shrug.

'Jesus fucking Christ, seriously?' Jamie turns to me again. 'Is it a mistake?'

'What?'

'Are we making a huge mistake? Should we call it off? Let's do it. Let's call it off.'

'Okay.'

'Are you crazy? We can't call it off!'

'Oh, fuck you!'

'We can't call it off, we have to do something and we need this guy's help! We don't have a choice!'

Nick shushes us, 'Hey, boys, boys,' and waves at the door.

I look again. As the patrol escorts Gettleman down the stairs, another figure appears. I tense up. The man crosses paths with the officers, breezy, saluting them as if he were crossing paths with a couple of colleagues. They disappear around the corner, and Davis knocks on our door.

I jump upright.

Jamie opens it.

'Hi!' Davis exclaims, like we're old friends.

'Hi, come on in!' Jamie replies, like we're old friends.

And he closes the door behind us.

Davis looks to be in his mid-forties, strong-jawed, nearly six feet tall and cockney as fuck. His hair is prematurely greying but he's fit enough to beat any of us to a pulp if the mood takes him.

He stalks into the room and spits his consonants at me. 'What the fuck was that? You might have mentioned your building's crawling with pigs! Why not meet directly at the station while you're at it?'

I stammer and Jamie steps between us, but he's already moved on.

He nods at Nick. 'Day.'

'Peter, these are my friends—'

'Define "friends".'

'This is Sid,' Jamie says, 'and I'm Jamie. Nice to meet you.'

'Delighted.'

'The place is safe, Pete,' Nick says. 'We just checked for wires.'

Davis's eyes shift between the three of us expectantly. 'So what's the deal, here?'

'We're looking to broadcast something.'

'What?'

Jamie hesitates.

Davis rolls his eyes. 'Nick?'

'Nick isn't in charge of this,' Jamie says.

'Look, mate, I don't know you and I don't know your mute friend here.' He waves in my general direction. 'If I'm going to do this, Nick is damn well going to be the one in charge.'

'No, I'm not.'

We all turn to Nick.

'I'm sorry, Pete. I'll be around, but I can't be too involved and I can't bring this back to my home.'

'Why the hell not?'

'Because my husband is unwell.'

Davis's shoulders rise to his ears like a bird ruffling its feathers. 'Right. Husband.' The word comes out an embarrassed mumble.

'Yes,' Nick says.

Davis clears his throat. 'Well, I'm going to need to see what you've got before we get into any kind of agreement here.'

Jamie doesn't miss a beat. 'Well, I'm going to need a kind of agreement before I can show you what I've got.'

'You must be joking. You go "I have stuff" and expect me to piss myself with excitement? The way I see it, mate, you need me a hell of a lot more than I need you.'

'Look, "mate"—'

Nick's softest voice interrupts. 'Jamie. He deserves to know what he's stepping into. Doesn't he?'

Jamie checks in with me, and I nod, and he nods too.

'Alright then,' Davis says. 'Show me.'

23

By the time we make it to Tottenham Court Road, it's morning peak. Nick and I cram ourselves into the train, pushed around by strangers sweating through their winter coats, rushing in and out with their eyes fixed on their phones. People are tetchy, tutting at their neighbours, hissing snide remarks when they think they can't be heard. It's so mundane it's practically obscene.

Peter said we would need a portable transmitter. He talked about splicing and frequencies, satellite and signal intrusion, and I understood very little of it. Professional know-how radiated from every one of his pores, with a healthy dose of arrogance on top of it. He said to trust him. He said he'd build whatever we would need from scratch, that he'd procure the pieces from different sources to avoid suspicion. 'I've got this,' he said. On just one condition – he'd get to listen to the tape again whenever he wanted.

'Isn't it a bit risky, though?' I ask Nick, picking vague words for the benefit of the commuters and hoping he'll understand.

'It's a business transaction,' Nick says. 'It'll always carry some degree of risk.'

I say nothing.

'How are things between you and Jamie?'

My hand runs through my hair on instinct. I catch myself humming under my breath.

'Yesterday he yelled for ten minutes because I spilled tea on the sofa,' I say.

'Goodness. Remind me never to bring mugs into the living room.'

'Wasn't about that, really. The other day he dropped my toothbrush in the toilet. Complete accident. I nearly bit his head off.'

'A tad tense, aren't we?'

'See, that's the thing. We're already on edge and I don't want . . . If Peter starts coming round all the time . . .'

'It won't be all the time.'

'He said whenever he felt like it.'

Nick gives me a small smile. 'I don't think you understand what this means to him. Wanting to listen to it again, well, it doesn't strike me as that outlandish of a request.'

'Even if he suddenly fancies it in the middle of the night?'

He shrugs.

'We have to have some boundaries,' I say. 'This isn't his.'

'No, it's not. But is it really yours?'

I concede with a half-grunt.

When we arrive, the hospital entrance pushes memories into the light like some sick flashback, and I feel my stomach heave. The cold blue glow, the long corridors. The handcuffs. A massive hand gripping my collar. Sharp pain in my side.

I palm at my ribcage and wince.

Nick knocks lightly on Charlie's door and a soft voice calls us in. I stand awkwardly a few steps back.

Charlie extends his hand almost desperately. 'Darling?'

Nick goes to sit on the edge of the bed and their fingers intertwine. 'Hey, handsome.'

I attempt a shy wave, clearing my throat to signal my presence. Charlie's eyes focus above Nick's shoulder for a second, and he pulls a weak smile from the corners of his mouth, but soon his attention is back on his husband.

'I don't want to be here,' he says, in the familiar flat tone of voice brought about by strong mood stabilisers.

'I'm so sorry, love. You were very unwell. I didn't know what to do.'

Charlie reaches out and touches Nick's chin to tilt his head up. 'Here's looking at you, kid.'

Nick lets out a breathy chuckle.

'I want to go home,' says Charlie.

'I know. But they need to keep you here a bit longer, okay? Just a bit longer, I promise.'

'I miss you.'

'I miss you too.'

They kiss and I look. I stare.

Pervert.

I know what you're thinking. I know what you want.

They exchange gentle touches and murmur terms of endearment.

They wish you weren't here. It would be better if you weren't here. They know you're watching and they hate it and they hate you, they hate you for staring like a voyeuristic, perverted outcast.

You can't stop yourself, can you?

I can't stop staring.

You can't control yourself.

I stare until the door opens, snapping me clean out of it, and the bearded doctor squeezes past me.

Nick gently pulls away. 'Darling, we have company.'

Charlie throws a fearful glance in the doctor's direction.

'Don't leave me,' he whispers.

Nick's smile almost slips away. 'Sweetheart, are you—'

'Good morning, Mr Williamson! How are we feeling today?'

Charlie fidgets with the hospital bracelet. 'Fine.'

The room falls eerily silent as the doctor busies himself with Charlie's vitals and IV drip. I vaguely wonder why they even put him on an IV in the first place.

'I'll go check on my friend,' I say.

Nick nods, and I'm on my way to the door, but then Charlie speaks in a sleepy voice.

'It hurts.'

Nick shifts his weight on the mattress, checking he's not crushing Charlie's leg.

'It hurts,' Charlie mumbles again.

'What hurts, love?'

'I'm drowning. You're drowning me.'

This time, the smile slides clean off Nick's face. 'What?'

'Please. I can't breathe.'

Handcuffs.

Scraping.

Blood.

Catch the game last night?

We'll come get you.

'Charlie? What do you mean, love, who's drowning you?'

But Charlie's already drifting off.

'I wouldn't pay too much attention to that, sir,' says the doctor.

Nick and I exchange a look.

'Did you just force him to sleep?' Nick asks.

'He seemed to be getting somewhat agitated.'

'He was fine before you entered the room.'

The doctor gives us both a quick smile. 'Well, you know how it is. Some people get nervous around doctors.'

'He doesn't,' Nick says, standing.

The floodgates burst open and I'm fighting against the memories and it's like trying to stop a tsunami with a stern look.

'Did he mention something to you about being drowned?' Nick asks.

The doctor seems hesitant for a second. 'He did.'

'Why didn't you tell me?'

The humming buzzes in my chest.

It's raining men

I'm claustrophobic, please, please let me go, I'm dying, please have mercy.

Hallelujah, it's

The doctor sighs. 'Look, sir, your husband is going through a psychotic episode. He may cling to the belief that something happened to him, but you have to understand these delusions, powerful as they may be, are just that. We'd normally prefer to move him upstairs to the psychiatric ward, for more specialised care, but I'm afraid we're currently at capacity.'

'You think he's crazy,' Nick says.

I blink.

The voice bursts out laughing.

Focus.

'You're not even entertaining the idea that something might have happened to him?'

'Nothing happened to him.'

The doctor moves closer and Nick interposes himself.

'I need to access the patient.'

'I don't think I want him here anymore.'

'Sir . . .'

'I want him discharged.'

'I wouldn't recommend it. He's not well enough to leave the hospital.'

He tries to approach again, and Nick shoves him back.

'Hey, come on, now,' I try.

'Stay out of it, Sid!'

'Respectfully, sir, don't make me call security.'

Charlie's frowning in his sleep, breathing fast and shallow.

'Step away from my husband before I respectfully shove your stethoscope up your—'

I spring forward. 'Hold on, hold on! Nick, just . . . let's not make this worse.'

I glance at Charlie's distressed face, then turn to the doctor.

'You're not allowed to hold him here against his will. He's not technically a psychiatric patient and you have no reason to believe he's a danger to himself or others.'

I brace myself as the doctor thinks. Nick's eyes ping-pong between us.

'He'd have to sign an AMA,' says the doctor.

'What's that?' Nick asks.

'It's a form,' I say. 'Confirms he's leaving against medical advice.'

'He can't sign anything right now.'

I consider. 'Fair enough. In the meantime, we'll be needing a different doctor.'

'But—'

'We're requesting a different doctor.'

Blood pounds against my eardrums and the voice hisses over it.

'Yes, sir,' says the doctor.

'We'll call a nurse if we need anything,' I say.

His shoulder catches mine as he leaves.

Nick sinks back onto the bed and brushes the hair back from Charlie's forehead. I think of Jamie.

'That was rather impressive. Thank you.'

I chew on one of my hoodie's strings for a while.

'I don't think he's having a psychotic episode,' I say.

Our voices both drop low. It almost feels like attending a wake.

'What do you think it is?'

'I'm not a doctor.'

'But you're thinking something.'

I spit out the string. 'I think it's post-traumatic stress disorder.'

'You think they really hurt him?'

'Not here. Not them. I think they're covering for the people who did.'

'Police?'

I say nothing. I just give him a look.

He swallows. 'He said he was drowning.'

Once again, I say nothing.

He searches Charlie's face, as if he's trying to read something in a foreign language.

'I didn't even notice. How did I not notice?'

My fingers gingerly check the bandage under my shirt.

'I'll, uh . . . I'll go up now. We'll get him home to you. We will.'

'Yes, please.'

I take an alternate route to get to work. It's probably stupid and utterly fails at making me feel better, but God help me it's the only way I can bring myself to go.

Achilles yells at me for a while. Not like Mike used to yell. He scolds like a scared parent, with a crease between his eyebrows, trying to make me understand why this is a serious matter, and why I shouldn't do it again. When they took me, I didn't call to explain. I couldn't. He was waiting for me all evening.

I apologise. It'll never happen again. The events of the day, coupled with the constant brush of fabric against the bruises, have left me drained and queasy. Achilles pulls a bar stool behind the counter for me to sit on. Later, when the pub's calm enough, he comes up to me.

'Everything alright, there, son?'

'Pardon?'

'You're a bit out of it.'

'God, I'm sorry. I didn't sleep well last night.'

Which isn't really a lie.

'Why don't you go home and have a rest?' he says. 'It's pretty dead tonight anyway.'

'I'm messing everything up, aren't I?'

'Well. Yes. You are.'

I sigh and rub my eyelids.

'Don't worry too much about it. We all have days like this.' And, slapping me on the back, 'Go on, then. Get your jacket. I'll take it from here.'

So I do. I get my jacket and prepare to leave, and then I turn at the door.

'You're nice to me.'

'Suppose I am, yeah.'

'Why?'

He looks strange for a second, and then he smiles. 'I guess you remind me of someone.'

I fish into my pocket and remember I smoked my last one earlier. 'You don't happen to have a cigarette, do you?'

'Yes. But I'm not giving you one. Go home, son.'

My phone starts ringing as I step out.

'Peter.'

'Get the tape ready, I'm coming over.'

'Right now?'

'Forty minutes.'

And he hangs up. Fuck him.

I try Jamie's mobile twice before diving into the tube, and finally manage to get him as I'm exiting the train.

'Did Davis call you?' I ask.

'I don't know,' he says. 'Maybe. I wasn't at my phone.'

'He's on his way over.'

'It's fucking midnight.'

'I know.' I check my watch. 'He should be there in fifteen . . . ish.'

'Jesus fucking Christ, English prick, I swear to—'

'Oi.'

He sighs. 'I'm stepping out.'

'What?'

'I need some air.'

'Is Nick there?'

'No, he went home. Said he had to get stuff done.'

'Jamie, you can't just take off—'

'I'll be back before he gets here, okay? Jesus.'

And he hangs up too.

Barely five minutes after I make it home, Peter's knocking 'shave and a haircut' on the door and Jamie's not back yet. I open the door and fade aside and he barges in like he owns the fucking place.

'Davis.'

'Robinson. Where's the chief?'

'Out. I can't play you the tape right now.'

He spins around, arms out, and eyes me up and down. 'I don't see that you have much of a choice.'

'That's right, I don't. I can't play you the tape because I don't know where it is.'

He frowns. 'You don't know where it is?'

I pinch my lips and shake my head.

'Why not?'

'Because.'

'Chief doesn't trust you or you don't trust yourself?'

I run a hand through my hair. 'Look, it's not happening right now, so . . .'

He plops himself down on the sofa and his shoes land heavy on the coffee table. 'It's fine. I can wait.'

So we do. We wait. I text Jamie and we wait for an hour in uncomfortable silence. I check my phone every now and then. Jamie's leaving me on read and it's causing my insides to twist and my heart to pound against my ribcage. I dial his mobile. It rings a few times and goes to voicemail.

'Shit!' I mumble into the answering machine.

'Maybe they took him,' says Peter.

I jump up. 'You should leave.'

'What?'

'I have to go look for him.'

'I'll wait for you.'

'No. Go back home. Come back tomorrow.'

He opens his mouth.

'Fuck off, now!' I say.

He closes his mouth, and stands. 'Well, look who suddenly grew a pair.'

I concentrate hard on not blinking. 'Now.'

He nods. 'I'll be back tomorrow.'

I wait a few seconds so we're not walking down the stairs together. He doesn't need to see my hands shaking, he doesn't need to hear my ragged breathing.

Out in the street, I try Jamie's mobile again. No luck.

'Jamie, you bastard! You better have a fucking good reason to not be answering your phone right now! You better be dead, you hear!'

And I hang up and stifle a sob. This is London. It's huge and loud and pushing me to the very edge of the panic attack. He could be anywhere. I head down the street, half-running, but then which way? Maybe they did take him.

My phone buzzes. I fish it out of my pocket.

'*Pub. J.*'

I swear I can feel my bone marrow vibrating. I try to call again but he won't pick up. So I text. '*Pub where?*'

Buzz. '*Wardour and Shaftesbury.*'

I make a left on Wardour and run down to the shabby pub at the corner of Shaftesbury Avenue.

And there he is, slumped over a table, clutching a pint. I march over, ready to yell, but then he moves his head and I see red eyes swimming with tears and the anger evaporates into the dusty air.

He doesn't notice me until I'm lowering myself down opposite him and then he quickly wipes his cheeks with the heel of his hand. I pretend I don't see. He's got the hazy, slightly lost air of someone who's had a few already. I try to make eye contact, but he's having none of it.

'You know,' he says. 'I can't stop thinking about her.'

He chews on his knuckles and sniffs, fighting against his runny nose. I put my hand on the table, halfway between us, wanting to touch him, not wanting to force anything.

'I dream about her,' he says. 'All the time. It's too much, and I just want . . . I want my mother.' He sighs and laughs at himself, like this is the stupidest thing he's ever said. 'I just want my mum, Sid. You know?'

I look at him and it briefly crosses my mind that he has to be the most beautiful person I've ever seen.

'I can play him the tape if he wants to hear it,' I say. 'I can do that. You don't have to keep listening to it.'

His hand drops onto mine. Like it's casual, bordering on random. Like maybe my hand just happened to be on the spot where his just happened to land. That's fair enough. I'll take that.

We sit in silence for a few minutes. My arse is freezing on the wooden bench. I shift a bit on the seat and he squeezes my hand convulsively, as if he thought I was going to leave. Then he clears his throat, sniffs again and mumbles something about getting a cold.

'Let's go home,' I say, eventually. 'Let's go home, yeah?'

He nods at his Guinness.

I pay the barman with my last tenner – seventy pence change – and we leave.

He doesn't say a word on the way home, and when the door finally closes behind us, he sits and stares directly ahead as I remove my shoes and coat.

He doesn't move when I sit next to him in the semi-darkness.

He's drowning.

I get up again. His eyes follow me around as I fumble with drawers looking for a piece of paper and a pen that still works, but he doesn't ask. I find a bag of tea lights at the back of a cupboard. With the pen in my mouth, one of the candles in my palm and the paper tucked between my index and middle finger, I walk up to him, take his hand, and pull him up.

I drag him to the kitchen and we settle down at the table. I set everything down, pop the cap off the pen and draw a big arch on the paper. I close it at the bottom to turn it into a gravestone. It looks like absolute shit. I add some little tufts of grass around the base.

Jamie raises an eyebrow.

I scribble in the middle. '*Olivia Lloyd-Brown. ? - 2019. Dearly missed.*'

Jamie stares at it, and at me, but I'm not quite done. My hand reaches into my pocket for the lighter and I bring it to the candle to light it. Turns out it's scented, and that's a bit too much, but now I've committed to it and it's too late. The flame flickers in the centre of the table and the kitchen fills with a whiff of cinnamon.

Jamie's fingertips brush against the sheet of paper.

'You have a doctor's handwriting,' he says.

'Thanks.'

'I'm sorry I dropped your toothbrush.'

'I'm sorry I spilled tea on the sofa.'

24

As December crawls along, the world splits neatly down the middle.

Everything outside is a shade darker. Maybe it's the shorter days. Maybe it's just me. It has been tougher to go out since they took me. The snow's melted into dirty puddles. London appears to have settled into its customary piercing humidity.

Thankfully, however cold it gets out there, home feels that much warmer by contrast, and the strain appears to have loosened between Jamie and me. We always did tend to get closer during the winter months. It's in little things. Softer looks. Offers of mugs of hot coffee. Quiet 'You alright?'s every once in a while.

Over dinner, on the 24th, Jamie's head snaps up. 'Tomorrow's Christmas.'

I tell him that yes, it is.

'We didn't even get a tree,' he says.

'Who cares,' I say, and he shrugs in agreement.

But the next morning, he knocks on my bedroom door with a carton of eggnog and rattles the chessboard under my nose. A bit of a Christmas day tradition. Eggnog and chess. We both suck at the game. I smile. I tell him to hang on, and I slip into the ugly Christmas jumper. The reindeer one that, years ago, he gave me as a joke. We share a laugh at the state of the thing. For a few hours everything is well, then Peter calls and it's back to reality.

He comes over every three or four days. Jamie retrieves the tape from wherever he's keeping it and I send him out on a walk before Peter even gets here. I can take it. He did ask, that first time, when I begged him in a frenzy not to tell me where he hides the recorder. He asked me why, and I sunk to my knees and pleaded. He doesn't ask anymore.

Sometimes singing happens while the tape's playing. It's fair to say at this point I know it by heart. Olivia's voice has been drilled into my mind, so deep that I occasionally mistake memories for symptoms. I turn around, just in case she's here, just in case she's back. Peter keeps an eye on me as if I'm, well, exactly what I am. Last time he had me play it twice for him, then went and locked himself in the bathroom for fifteen minutes. It made my skin crawl.

January first.

Charlie went home a week ago. I think of him every day on my way to work. I think of his head underwater because of me, and I wonder when they'll appear on a street corner and shove me into a car again. So far, nothing. I can take it.

'Happy New Year,' I say.

'Happy New Year,' Nick says.

He comes over every Wednesday while Charlie's in therapy.

'How's he holding up?' Jamie asks as I lock the door and put it on the chain.

Nick drops onto the sofa.

His hand dips into his pocket for his phone. He checks it, begins typing, and appears to change his mind.

'Nick?'

'Huh? Oh, sorry, pardon me, that's terribly rude.'

The phone disappears into his coat again.

Jamie chuckles. 'Don't worry about it. I'll pop the kettle on.'

'Sorry, what was your question?' Nick asks, turning to me.

'Would you rather not talk about it?'

He crosses his legs and uncrosses them immediately. 'No. You can ask.'

'How are things with Charlie?'

'It's not easy every day, but we're working on it.'

His jaw clenches. He glances over at the kitchen where Jamie's busying himself with the tea, and when his eyes meet mine again, all of a sudden it's like he's at a confessional.

'I feel like I want to kill someone.'

I hold everything in.

'You know,' he says. 'I was thinking. Maybe we don't need Peter. I can do this myself.'

'What?'

'They want me to work the next address anyway. It'll be easier if I'm on site. I can keep an eye on the broadcast. Splicing is more reliable than—'

'No.'

'No?'

'You can't get involved.'

'They did this to him specifically so we would stop resisting. If we let them win—'

'Remember when I said he'd be grateful you were there for him?'

'Yes.'

'Well, funny thing. In order for that to happen, you have to actually be there for him.'

He inhales sharply, but he's got nothing. I've won.

'Sometimes he wakes up in tears in the middle of the night and he doesn't even remember where he is.'

'I'm sorry,' I say.

'I'm just so afraid that it'll never be the same again.'

I don't say anything at first. Embarrassment and, to a certain extent, self-preservation hold me back. But then he draws in a shaky breath and something else – call it instinct – kicks in.

'I have schizophrenia.'

Nick sits up. 'You what?'

Go on. Tell him you were so far gone that your father gave up on you. Tell him even Dad is scared of you.

I force myself to swallow.

'Well. Schizoaffective disorder. I've had it since I was nineteen.'

He stammers. 'You, but you, you look . . .'

'Normal?'

'Well. You look well.'

I chuckle. 'You did see me tearing the paper from the wall that one time, didn't you?'

'Oh.'

'Sometimes I believe things, and it's like . . . I

know that I should know that they can't be true. But at the same time, I can't stop myself just sort of . . . just completely believing them.'

Suddenly, even though it's not coming from him, I feel judged.

I swing my head to the side to shake the thoughts out.

'I'm not dangerous,' I say.

'I know you're not,' he says.

'I'm sorry,' I say. 'It's just I'm not . . . I'm not used to—'

Jamie sits next to me. I hadn't realised he was back. He doesn't say anything, but lets me know with a glance that he heard. That he knows.

'Nineteen?' Nick asks.

'Yeah. It w— it was . . .' I pause to breathe. I'm bit dizzy, a bit high and unfocused. 'Scary. Lonely. At first. Still, sometimes.'

Jamie extends an arm along the back of the settee and his hand settles discreetly between my shoulder blades.

Rough and tough and strong and
Bite your tongue, nancy boy.

I stop talking for a while. The sheer stress of disclosure's making it hard to think.

Eventually, I manage a slow 'I forgot why I told you.'

'Look,' Jamie says. 'Here's the thing. You're right. It will likely never be the same again. But that doesn't mean you'll never laugh together again. It doesn't mean you won't connect anymore. You'll get there. Trust me.'

Nick looks between the two of us and smiles and I

know what he's thinking and he's wrong. He's wrong.

The next minute, 'shave and a haircut' sounds at the door.

'Did you hear that?' I ask.

'Yeah,' Jamie says. 'Yeah, we did.'

'Is that Peter?' Nick asks.

'Sounds like it.'

'Doesn't he usually call ahead?'

'My phone's off. Sid?'

I look up. 'What?'

'You okay?'

'Yes.'

'I could probably convince him to come back later,' Nick offers.

'No,' I say. 'It's fine. I'm fine.'

I hear a swarm of people flooding the streets outside. I hear angry shouting, desperate screaming, sharp gunshots.

'Just let him in. It's fine.'

He does, although I've clearly failed to convince him.

Peter pushes in like he owns the place. 'Who's the man?'

He drops next to me, slaps me on the back so hard it sends pain all the way around to my ribs, and slams his muddy boots on the coffee table.

'You have to be kidding me,' says Jamie. 'We eat at that—'

'Transmitter's ready. Merry Christmas. Or, you know, happy New Year. Whichever.'

I look at Jamie and Jamie looks at me, and then we both look at Nick.

'Really?'

'What, you didn't think I could do it?'

Something's off with him, though. Slurred speech, like he's had a few. Like he's had more than a few.

'Are you pissed right now?' Jamie asks.

'Feck off, Paddy.'

Jamie sighs. 'Do you have it with you?'

Peter pats his backpack.

'Show me.'

Jamie goes for the backpack but Peter pulls it away.

'Play the tape.'

'Show me first.'

'No.'

Nick clears his throat gently. 'Come on, Pete.'

A threat appears in Peter's eyes, behind the drunken haze.

'They know the deal.' And then, to Jamie, 'Haven't seen you in a while, Paddy. Thought this was all too much for your sensitive—'

I stand. 'That's enough. Show us the thing. Then I'll play the tape.'

He stands too, and advances on me, and Dad pops into my mind. I step back.

'You think I don't know what'll happen once you've got what you needed me for? I have leverage now, but what then? How can I know you'll play it after I give you the gizmo? I'm not your friend. It's obvious you don't like me. What keeps you from just kicking me out and never letting me in again?'

I shrug. 'Well you're just going to have to trust us on that.'

'But I don't! I don't trust you as far as I can fucking throw you!'

Stand your ground, I tell myself, but my feet shuffle

back, and back, and back, even as my voice rises.

'You've heard the thing a hundred times already! You know every word by heart! Fucking hell, I knew every word by heart the second time I heard it! Why could you possibly need to hear it again right now?'

'Because I need to hear her voice!'

I open my mouth but I really haven't thought it through. Peter's face has flushed and distorted and I'm legitimately worried he might jump at my throat.

'You know how long it's been since I heard a voice like that?' he shouts. 'Twenty-five years, four months and two fucking days! You don't understand! None of you!'

He moves as if to shove me. Something flashes in my peripheral vision and Jamie springs between us, grabs his forearm and pushes him back. 'Oi!'

'They took my wife! She was ill, she was going to die and she just wanted to die at home and they took her from me when she was barely conscious! You have no idea!'

'We've all lost people we loved here,' says Nick.

'No! This thing did nothing to you compared to what it did to me!'

Jamie growls. 'Excuse me?'

'It's not a competition, Pete,' says Nick.

Peter's boots drag on the floorboards as he turns. 'This is all you kids have ever known, but not me! Okay? It's all you remember, but not me! This isn't my fucking world!'

'Certainly not all I remember, "kid",' says Nick, voice rising a bit as well.

Peter gives him a dismissive wave. 'Yeah, but you're a poof. Probably your ideal world, this!'

'Thank you very much for that, Pete.'

'You have no idea how hard these twenty-five years have been on us normal people!'

'Normal people?' Jamie says.

'You heard me, you unnatural f—'

Jamie lunges at him and I hear myself yelling. 'Fucking stop that right now!'

And miraculously, they all freeze.

I catch Peter's attention and force myself to hold it and he holds too.

'I am so sorry about your wife,' I say. 'I can't even begin to imagine. We're on the same team, Peter. We'll get them. We'll get them, yeah?'

He blinks.

I hold.

He goes to his backpack. 'Come and see that, Paddy, you'll like that.'

The thing looks like a digital alarm clock with an antenna sticking out of it. The casing is an aggressive shade of pink.

'So?' says Peter, with some pride.

'Well, Jesus, could you have made it any more conspicuous?' Jamie says.

'Fuck you.'

'How does it work?'

His hand slides over it. 'Plug your input in there – that would be your dictaphone thing, whatever the fuck you want to call that monstrosity – it's mini jack, let me know if you need an adapter – then power on, power off, volume control goes to eleven, wavelength control – 300 GHz to 300 MHz – battery compartment at the bottom. You'll need four double As, make sure you've got spares on D-day.'

Jamie reaches for the machine and Peter slaps his hand away.

'Wh— look, I'm going to have to touch it at some point.'

'Be careful or I'll send you the fucking bill, alright?'

'Alright. Jesus.'

'How much did it cost you to build?' Nick asks.

'About a month's salary.'

'Crikey.'

'Most of it was delivery fees. I wasn't about to order every component from the same place, was I? I'm not stupid.'

Jamie turns the transmitter around in his hands. 'So just plug in, turn it on and press play?'

'Pretty much.'

Nick frowns. 'Won't they have forward error correction?'

'They don't. I checked. You're welcome. They're cheap and arrogant, and that's how we get them. Right, Robinson?' He elbows me in the ribs.

'Right,' my mouth says.

Humidity's rising
Barometer's getting low
According to all sources
The street's the

My body tries to rock back and forth but it's not happening. I'm not letting it happen. It's contained. It's fine.

I tuck my hands underneath my thighs to hide the shaking.

'So how do we do this?' I ask.

'The range on this isn't fantastic, but it'll do. Their signal is directional, which means one of you boys will have to plant yourself near the Tower, aim the transmitter at their receiver, and tune into the right frequency.'

'I'll do it,' says Jamie.

You're going to die.
Cos tonight for the first
Choke on it.
for the first

'Won't they stop us straight away, though?'

'It's a big machine. Takes time to react. By the time they realise what's going on and do something about it, people will have heard enough. Plus if we're lucky, some of the tech people might be more interested in what they're hearing than in stopping it.'

Nick's looking at me. It's under control, right?

Just about half past ten
For the first time
in history

'Next address is in, what, two days?'

'Three. Saturday.'

'Saturday. Okay.'

'Saturday?' I say.

My head under the water. Smoke in my face. The glowing tip of a cigarette inches from my neck.

Hands palms-up on your thighs, Mr Robinson.

'You're not going on Saturday, though,' he says. 'You're waiting until next month.'

'Next month,' I say.

The nerves just beneath my skin. Electricity, like a shock, whenever the cloth of my shirt moves against me.

It's raining men, hallelujah, it's raining men, amen.

'Why not now?'

'Because we're not ready now. We have to test it, see how close exactly you need to get to the tower. No point getting too close if we can avoid it.'

'Too close,' I say.

Blurred shapes briefly turn on me again. Their faces are lost now, and something presses on my eardrums, fucking hell, *God bless Mother Nature, she*

'We need to study the terrain, see where you can hide, make sure it's as safe as possible. I have a few ideas—'

'Wait, wait, wait, one second. Sid?' Jamie's looking at me.

'Yeah?'

'What's wrong with your boyfriend, Paddy?'

'Not your business.'

'I'm fine, I'm fine.'

The pavement peels the skin from my side.

'Sid, mate, you're shaking like mad. Plus, I'm right here.'

Something moves in the dark, back and forth, like he's waving. I try to follow it, but everything's getting away from me and the boot kicks into my stomach and my rib splits open.

'We should stop talking about this for now,' he says.

I jump up and my shin hits something hard. Coffee table. 'No— um, ouch . . . I'm fine, really. I just need some . . . some fresh air, that's all. Keep talking, I'll . . . I'll . . .'

I move in the general direction of the door. They're talking, probably protesting, but it's all jumbled and none of it makes any sense.

I'm not sure how I get down the stairs without breaking my neck, but a minute later I come to in the street, singing in half-gasps and slowly getting my mind back.

You're weak.

I stumble into the nearest shop for cigarettes.

You're dependent.

The bloke at the till watches me fish into my pockets until I realise I'm skint. I curse loudly, apologise, and leave empty-handed.

You're addicted.

I sit on the kerb.

You're pathetic.

Next month.

You know where to find us, Mr Robinson.

I don't think we have a month.

You're fucked.

'Hello, hophead.'

'Hey, fancy man.'

I grab the putty from his bedside table and he whines.

'Aw, come on, not today. Can't I have one day off?'

'Say "please".'

'Please?'

'No.'

His head falls back on the pillow.

'Sit up,' I say. And when he doesn't move, 'Up. I'll

count to three. One. Two . . .'

'Okay, okay. Christ!'

'Good man.'

He grimaces but takes the putty from me and we fall into the motions. Press, move, press, move.

It has to be Saturday, right?

Legs uncrossed, please, hands palms-up on your thighs.

Without thinking, I uncross my legs.

Next month will be too late. It has to be Saturday, but does it have to be Jamie?

'You okay?' Tom asks.

'I need a cigarette.'

His hand twitches. He groans with the effort. 'If I can write my name in cursive, you can quit smoking.'

'Your name is three letters.'

'So is yours. You know these'll kill you.'

I think, and sigh, and as it turns out it doesn't have to be Jamie. Not if he thinks he's going next month.

I cross my legs again.

'Lots of things could kill me. Next one.'

I tuck the putty between his thumb and index finger and help him press. Then I stop helping. He struggles.

'Go on,' I say, running a hand through my hair. 'Push it, push it, harder, come on.'

The putty slips away, tumbles from his lap and thuds on the floor as he winces.

'Shit! I'm done, forget it! I'm done!'

He's cradling his hand against his chest.

'Give us a look.'

'Why?'

'Come on.'

I take his hand into mine and gently stretch his

fingers one by one. Extension, retraction. Back and forth. Carefully. Things are coming back to me, from so far away it's like another life.

'Some Lovers Try Positions That They Can't Handle.'

'What now?'

'Your carpal bones. Scaphoid, Lunate, Triquetrum, Pisiform, Trapezium, Trapezoid, Capitate, Hamate. Little trick we learned in med school.'

He makes a show of giving me the once-over. 'For a second there, I thought you were propositioning me.'

'Don't flatter yourself, fancy man. Push against my palm with your fingertips.'

I catch a slight tremor in the abductor as he presses and decide to work on the thumb some more.

'Hophead?'

'Yeah?'

'Thanks.'

'Mm-hmm, no problem.'

'No, Sid.' He pulls his hand away and I find myself almost magnetically drawn to his eyes instead. 'Thank you.'

It takes me a while. 'You're welcome.'

A minute later, and I swear I have no idea how this happened, I've got him pinned against the bathroom wall and he's spouting the dirtiest stream of filth I've ever heard come out of a guy's mouth. I laugh a bit, 'Fucking hell, Tom,' but somehow it's a huge turn-on and at this point I'm too worked up to try and figure out what that might say about me. I fumble with my fly, shove my jeans and pants midway down my thighs. I turn him over, grab his hips.

'Alright?'

'Yes, keep going, keep going!'

I press in easily enough, sighing, only just now realising how badly I craved the sensation. He chokes out something that vaguely sounds like my name, followed by an urgent call for more. I wrap my fingers around his weak hand and help him jerk off as I fuck him. We both moan and buck and it doesn't take long before we're coming hard and surprisingly in sync.

His left hand is braced against the tiles, arm shaking. I let my forehead fall on his shoulder and exhale a chuckle. My ears are ringing and I can feel a low buzz still at the back of my throat.

'Christ, hophead,' he mumbles. 'That was something else.'

'Mm-hmm. You okay?'

'Fantastic.'

I pull out of him and tuck myself back into my pants. He takes his hand off the wall and I have to catch him before he collapses.

'Shit. Tom?'

'I'm fine, just . . . bit light-headed.'

I help him sit on the toilet, 'Keep your head down,' get some toilet paper and clean him up.

Maybe there's a stupid wanker competition I could enter. Fuck knows we could use the prize money. Tom looks about to faint again from sheer exhaustion.

I throw the paper away, put his arm over my shoulder and guide him back to the bed. He's shivering. I pull the covers over him and tuck them under the mattress.

I clear my throat. 'Look, Tom, this . . .' I clear my throat again.

'Right,' he says.

'I don't know what I was thinking.'

'"Oh God, I'm not going to last much longer"?'

'Something like that. Are you hurt?'

'No.'

I check his bandages anyway. No bleeding, thank God for that. He's nodding off. I make sure he's comfortable and leave him to rest. On my way out, I realise this is the first genuine smile I've seen on his face since we lost Olivia.

Down in the street, I stop a passerby for a cigarette. I fumble with my lighter for a minute before giving in and stopping someone else.

'Excuse me? Got a light?'

The man reaches into his pocket.

'Cheers.'

'No problem.'

And I lean on the wall and smoke like my life depends on it. Then I turn around and bang my head repeatedly against the concrete. Fucking stupid bastard. Jesus Christ.

'That won't turn back time, mate.'

I look just in time to see a young bloke zooming past on a bike, laughing. I raise my middle finger at him, but he's already gone. Maybe he was never there in the first place.

25

Forty-five quid a month. That's how much it costs to muffle the voices and iron out the distortions. It's not so bad, I'm told. Could be worse. Way back at the start, when I voiced a timid complaint, I was bombarded with horror stories about the United States, and debt, and thousands of dollars' worth of medical bills. It succeeded in making me shut up and hand over my credit card, but really, if we're honest here, who gives a fuck about the United States?

'This was your last refill. Would you like me to fax your doctor?'

'No, that's okay.'

I stare at the card reader and pray that the money Achilles sent has already made it to my account. Eventually it spits out a receipt and I let go of the breath I was holding.

The pharmacist smiles apologetically. 'Technology, eh?'

'Yeah.'

On the way out, a rack full of nicotine patches stops me in my tracks: *'Two for one. Don't let addiction control your life.'*

As my hand reaches for one of the boxes, an image of my life starts to build. The guy living in it looks like me, only healthier. He's not gaunt, not run-down, but groomed, clean and alert. He stands a bit taller, more confident. Almost desirable.

I never did anything for that guy, in twenty-seven years, not a single thing.

With a swing of my head, and as the blond man next to me takes a cautious step back, I take the box to the self-checkout and pull out my card again.

What are you doing? It's too late now.

I don't care. Just let me have this.

The audacity of this boy.

Just outside the door I roll up my sleeve and stick a patch on my skinny arm. The blond man gives me a wide berth as he exits the building with a pack of loo paper tucked under his arm, and I giggle.

Oh, the humanity. The arrogance.

What now?

On Thursday evening, I go to Hampstead, which is a terrible idea. Laying low would be the safer move, three days from the address. But I can't stop myself. I take the bus instead of the tube, as if it'll save me, as if I'll be invisible.

The pre-recorded announcement calls out every stop and my own voices repeat everything in my left ear, then my right. 603 to Swiss Cottage Station. The next stop is Hillcrest Estate. 603 to Swiss Cottage Station. The next stop is Highgate School. 603 to Swiss Cottage Station. The next stop is Stormont Road.

An old man sits across from me, stammering into his phone, explaining something about a surgical procedure that went wrong between shocked gasps. Winter sun falls through the window and projects a square of light on the bald dome of his head.

I rest my head against the glass and try my best to tune it out.

The next stop next stop is Kenwood is Kenwood House. 603 to Swiss 603 to Swiss Cottage Station Cottage Station.

I pull my hood up. I look at the sky, at the birds. I wonder how it is in the rest of the world, where none of this has happened. Are children loud? Are the streets crowded? The rents higher? Do people remember us, out here on our closed-off islands? Have they given up on us yet? As far as I'm concerned, across the Channel might as well be on Mars. Maybe that goes both ways. Maybe we're just not essential anymore, or never were.

The old man hangs up. His eyes dart around, wild, as if searching for some sort of anchor. On instinct, I decide to provide it. I raise my head, gaze steady, until he notices me, and hold him there. Something passes between us. Without a word, he tells me he's lost, and I tell him I'm a little lost too, I suppose. He asks for forgiveness and I tell him it's okay. I tell him he's forgiven.

It lasts for a minute or so, and then I misstep.

'Who did you lose?' I ask.

The connection breaks. He gets up and gets off at the next stop.

603 to Swiss Cottage Station Swiss Cottage Station. The next stop is next stop is Hampstead Heath Hampstead Heath.

My thumb finds the button as I swing out of my seat.

During the short walk from the bus stop to number 43, I do a relatively good job of staring at my feet. It's only when I reach Nick and Charlie's doorstep that Sally's house grabs my eyes. And it won't let go.

Knock, says the voice. *They'll see you looking. Knock.*

But Sally's house won't let go. The place looks dark. Is she home? Sun's barely starting to set. Surely she wouldn't already be in bed at six-thirty.

Would she?

Flick a light switch, Sally. Come on. Show me you're safe.

You may know him as Sally. Does that ring any bells?

'Come on,' I mutter. 'Come on, Sally. C—'

Suddenly a light turns on upstairs, and even though I was hoping for it, it sends my heart rate through the roof. The jolt of energy shoots down my arm and I convulsively knock on Nick and Charlie's door.

She's fine, I tell myself. But for how long?

Charlie opens with a tired smile below messy greying blond hair, and the subdued expression of someone who's finally made it home after trudging through a snowstorm, but I think it's the casual openness of the striped green socks that prompts me to throw my arms around him.

He chuckles, a bit stiff. 'Oh. Goodness.'

'Sorry,' I say, stepping back and extending my hand instead. 'Sorry, um . . .'

We shake awkwardly.

'Goodness. It's nice to see you too. How are you, Sid Robinson?'

'Fine,' I say. 'You?'

He waves me in, but keeps his arms around his torso. 'Fine. Better. Brain's a tad foggy. Blame the medication.'

'I know the feeling,' I say, without thinking.

We dance around each other for a moment as we approach the dinner table. Whatever's going on in his head looks a lot like what's going on in mine.

'I'm on antipsychotics,' I offer.

'So am I,' he replies.

We pull up a couple of chairs and sit quietly. Nick can be heard messing around in the kitchen. I glance back, wishing he'd come and break the silence, but then Charlie leans in.

'Is it normal that my mouth is constantly dry?' he asks.

'Oh, God, I know. It's terrible. I keep getting cracks in my lips.'

'I've taken to carrying lip balm in my pocket at all times, but having to interject some variation of "Pardon me, darling, I need to reapply" has a way of ruining romantic moments.'

He laughs with his mouth closed, a coy, sing-song exhale of a laugh.

I beam across the table.

'I thought I heard talking!'

Nick traipses in from the kitchen and places a roast in the centre of the table.

'I know it's not Sunday, but we so rarely have company over for tea. Thought I'd make it special.'

He shakes off the oven mitts and I watch his fingers run lightly across the back of Charlie's neck.

'I probably should have asked about any dietary requirements.'

'No, no, it's perfect,' I say. Then I add 'It's lovely,' and I'm still staring at their casual gestures of affection and it's anyone's guess at this point what exactly I'm talking about when I say 'It's lovely.'

What do you want? says the voice.

I stroke the nicotine patch through the sleeve of my shirt.

I don't know.

'Wine!' Nick exclaims.

'I'll get it,' Charlie says.

They share a quick kiss before Charlie trots off. I look down, but it's brief, it's too late.

What do you want, Robinson?

'He seems well.'

Nick smiles. It looks like relief. 'This is definitely one of the good days.'

I nod. My wandering gaze finds an old picture sitting on the mantelpiece. The boy in the picture must be six or seven years old. He's staring into the camera, electric blue eyes taking up most of his face, a grin – a few teeth missing – occupying what little space is left.

'Charlie, he's looking at the crazy eyes picture!' Nick shouts over his shoulder.

Charlie emerges with a bottle in one hand and

three wine-glasses in the other. 'Goodness. Don't worry. It's more scared of you and all that.'

'No, it's cute,' I say. 'You were quite cute. Not that you're not now. No, wait. I mean, I didn't mean, I just, you know I meant, because the, um . . .'

What the fuck are you saying? Shut up, shut up right now.

He twists the corkscrew in. 'Mr Robinson, you're trying to seduce me, aren't you?'

'What?' The cork pops out and I startle. 'Oh, what, uh, no, I'm just, I, um—'

'Sid, relax,' Charlie says, pouring the wine. 'It was just a joke. Not a particularly funny one, I'll readily admit, but in my defence, I am quite heavily medicated.'

His lips stretch, friendly, and I recognise the boy in the picture.

Nick's wearing a strange expression though. 'May I ask you something?'

I signal to Charlie before he fills my glass too much because, frankly, I probably don't need alcohol on top of whatever the fuck that was just now.

'Sure,' I say.

'Are you religious?'

'Why? Do I look religious?'

'I don't know.'

'I'm not, no.'

'So you don't believe in God?'

'No. I don't. Do you?'

'Used to, I think. Both of us. Nowadays, though . . .' He shrugs.

'Not so much?' I say.

'Not so much,' he says.

After some more wine and the best meal I've had in longer than I can recall, Charlie excuses himself.

'He puts on a good show,' Nick says, as we settle in the living room with a night cap. 'But he's tired. He's drained.'

'I should go,' I say, not wanting to go.

'No rush. I'll call you a cab in a bit.'

He leans forward, scanning the room as if this isn't his home. It does look different at night, almost too silent. I'm used to the constant drone of traffic.

'Place looks empty, doesn't it?' he says. 'Without all that stuff?'

There's no denying it does. The bookshelves have taken on a skeletal quality, and I can make out some lighter spots on the carpet where piles of magazines and leaflets used to be.

'Did I do the right thing?'

I swirl my Bailey's around in its glass. The ice cubes clink gently together.

'He does seem better,' I say. 'Overall.'

'Yes, he does, doesn't he?'

I want to tell him that this doesn't mean they've given up. That they haven't been beaten. The words won't come out.

I look at his wedding ring, instead, as he swivels it around with his thumb. It's engraved. An intricate olive branch runs around the gold band, a few leaves here and there.

'It's beautiful,' I say, pointing it out. 'I hadn't noticed before.'

He smiles. 'Thank you. My mother was a jeweller.'

Oh, for fuck's sake, Robinson, shut up, just shut up, shut up.

362

'Sorry.'

'No, it's alright,' he says. 'This was one of her last creations. She made one for me, and one for my sister.'

He reaches into his shirt collar and pulls out a smaller ring on a delicate chain. Cold sweat runs down my back.

'It's alright,' he says again.

'Was she your younger sister or . . .?'

'My twin, actually.'

'What was she like?'

Nick thinks for a bit. 'You know how, when you lose someone, as the years go by you build them up in your mind? How you can only think about how amazing they were, how they made the room light up just by walking in?'

I nod.

'She was obnoxious,' he says. 'She was a self-absorbed teenager, embarrassingly arrogant, and a bit of a bully. And I miss her.'

The small ring disappears under his shirt again.

'It's so strange,' he says. 'Coming back here after listening to that tape. Almost like the place is haunted now.'

'Yes.'

We don't speak for a while. The house weighs on us. I can almost see little Olivia, three or four years old, running around, climbing the stairs on all fours. I can almost hear her laughing.

'Sid?'

'Hmm?'

'Can I ask you something?'

'Of course.'

'When you told me you were responsible for the death of someone Jamie loved, you meant her, didn't you?'

I down half the Bailey's. 'Yes. I did.'

He considers. 'So, you think he was in love with her?'

A dry laugh escapes me. I thought he'd want to know how I did it. If I called police on her or just took care of it with my own two hands.

'Did he tell you he was in love with her?' he asks.

'No. It was obvious.'

And down goes the last of the Bailey's. The alcohol is going straight to my head.

'And, you know, it makes sense.'

'Does it?' Nick asks.

'Well, I suppose. More sense than . . .'

I suddenly realise I'm about to cry. I can still smell the hospital on my skin. I can still feel Tom's body against mine.

Nancy boy.

'More sense than what?'

Oi, nancy boy!

I shrug.

'You've noticed him, haven't you? Jamie?' he asks.

'Of course.'

He chuckles indulgently. 'No, I mean you've really noticed him. When you look at him, you see details. You see the curve of his mouth, the shape of his jaw, the line of his eyebrows. You've noticed the way he moves, the sway of his hips. You hear the lower notes in his voice. You try not to think of it too hard at night. Sometimes you fail, perhaps?'

I swallow. Something's stirring deep inside. I

364

become scared it might escape. 'What are you talking about?'

'You can conjure up his scent like—' He snaps his fingers.

'I don't—'

'What I don't understand is why you're fighting this so hard. You said you're not devout, and you're certainly not conservative. You've been with men before, haven't you?'

'I've been with people.'

He shakes his head. 'I know guys who've "been with people". You? You've been with men.'

I think of Tom's desperate whine as I grabbed him by the hips.

Don't you dare. Don't you fucking dare.

'Why is it so hard to admit?' Nick asks. 'Why is it so hard, Sid?'

I briefly consider blaming it all on Dad.

'Were, uh . . . Were you and Charlie together before the quarantine?'

'No. We met a few years after.' His eyes gleam like he knows something I don't. His brow twitches. 'But if your question is did I prefer men before, then the answer is yes. I did.'

I look at him for a moment, and burst into tears.

He puts his hand on my thigh.

'Sorry,' I choke out. 'I-I just . . . Everything's . . .'

He pries the empty glass from my fingers. 'Could you do me a favour? Close your eyes.'

I sniffle. 'Why?' But already, my eyelids droop and flutter, as if he's hypnotising me. I'm drunk, shit, I'm so drunk.

'Close your eyes. There you go. Ready?'

He snaps his fingers again and all of a sudden I can smell Jamie like he's right there, like he's sitting two inches away. Strong sandalwood. He always did use a bit too much aftershave. If he'd just reach, just once, reach over and touch me. If he'd let his hands roam over my chest, over my back, just brush his lips against my neck, if I had the nerve to ask . . .

'You're smiling,' Nick says. 'Are you happy?'

'Yes,' I say. And I laugh and sob and shake and it's all breaking loose.

26

I'm a skinny eighteen-year-old and I've somehow managed to pull a postgrad at a dance mixer. We've worked up quite a sweat together in the semi-darkness of the union, he's brought me back to his dorm and it's happening.

He stretches me with his fingers for barely a minute before reaching for a condom. I'm panting hard, excited, nervous, vaguely wishing it could be the other way around, vaguely picturing my own fingers massaging between his buttocks, but too shy to ask. I watch him give himself a few tugs and roll the condom on.

I am entranced.

Feeling bold, daring, improper in all the best ways, I take his cock in my hand and squeeze a bit, and the wet hiss that comes out of his mouth sends a thrill up my spine.

I've played on my own before. I've practised,

prepared, explored. This is nothing like that. It's been five minutes since we got started and the sheet is already damp against my back.

He straddles my chest, pulls himself up, holds the bed-frame. 'Suck,' he says. And I do. I suck, eager, with a pounding heart, while he moans things like 'Ahhh God' and 'Fuck yeah, bitch'. One of his hands tangles in my hair, slows me down, and the other reaches for the lube. I awkwardly try to finger myself a bit, because I know what's coming and I don't think I'm ready for it.

And it's happening.

My legs wrap around his back. He pushes in steadily. I recall reading something about how you're supposed to bear down in response but I'm barely in control of my muscles.

He moans. 'Fuck, that's tight. Ahh yeah, you little cunt.'

He keeps his eyes closed and I wish he wouldn't, I wish he would look at me the same way I'm looking at him. I am in awe. I run my hands all over him. I find purchase on his shoulders, on his back.

He starts going faster.

The sounds become obscene, rhythmic creaking, wet slapping, and then he shifts his weight and touches my prostate, and the intensity catches me completely by surprise. I hear myself squeal. His hand clasps over my mouth. He grazes the same spot again and I want to scream how good it feels but I'm choking against his moist palm.

'Shut the fuck up!'

I look him up and down and up again. The toned abs, the dark hair trailing from his navel to his groin, the contact, God, the friction, the heat. The air smells of exertion and his grunts pulse in my head, in my gut, in the pit of my stomach and I'm coming too soon and his hand muffles my shout.

He keeps thrusting furiously as I'm coming down from the high and now it's too much.

I gasp. 'St— ohh, stop, stop.'

He groans, 'Come on!' but pulls out, tosses the condom aside, and then he's frantically stroking himself in front of me until he comes all over his fist. I let my head fall on the pillow, replaying the whole thing in my mind, biting my lower lip at the phantom sensation in my arse.

He wipes his hand on my stomach, 'Fucking virgin,' and goes to the bathroom, leaving me aching and exhausted on the bed with a huge grin across my face.

On Friday morning, I pop an aspirin.

Are you happy?

Bright and early, sunrise hits the bathroom tiles and ping-pongs off the mirror and into my hair. My feet, still wet from the shower, leave prints on the tiles as I pad over to the shelf. I rummage in every cupboard until I find an old comb, wash the thing with hand soap, and drag it through my damp hair. It hurts a bit. I haven't done this in years, but today . . . well. Today feels different.

'Come on,' I mumble. 'Come on, you bastard.'

I bring my fingers up to help the comb.

Are you happy?

Eventually I'm able to get it through without too

much effort. I try to tie the hair back but it's not quite long enough. After a couple of attempts, the hair tie gets tossed back into the drawer where I found it. Fuck knows what it was even doing there in the first place.

I open a brand-new pack of disposable razors and shave carefully. I take my time with it, make it clean, make it good, and then I rinse and examine myself.

I smile.

Yes.

I try a few different smiles. It turns into grimacing, then into pulling on my skin, on my face, to smooth out stress lines.

What are you doing?

The coffee machine slurps and rattles. I steady my hands on the mug and inhale the steam, and my eyes travel around the living room.

There's your answer. That's what Nick said, when he asked if I was happy, and I said yes. There's your answer. I'm not sure it's much of an answer, though, and it's certainly not a solution.

I start making faces at nothing. My lips start moving, and then the sound comes on like someone bumped up the volume a notch or two.

'Oh, for the love of God, it's not that hard, is it? What's the worst that could happen? You might get caught tomorrow. You might die. Do you really want to die knowing you never even tried your luck? Okay, so it's a little bit hard. So it's the hardest thing anyone's ever had to do. How do people do this? You're such a coward. You are such a coward, I swear to God. Just tell him. Just, you know, open your mouth and tell him you want his fucking—'

'What's up?'

I startle and spill coffee all over my lap. 'Jesus, fuck!'

Jamie snorts with laughter as I spring up from the settee, licking the drops off my fingers and the side of the mug.

'Oh shit, sorry,' he says, giggling some more.

'It's not funny!'

'I'm sorry.'

I set the mug on the table. '"I'm sorry."'

'I am!'

'Well tell your face then!'

He pulls an exaggerated pout and now I'm laughing.

'Alright, don't hurt yourself.'

We chuckle together, and then something changes behind his eyes. I get nervous.

'How long were you standing there?' I ask.

'Oh, no, I just walked in.'

'Okay. Good.'

But he's still looking at me all weird.

'Do I have something on my face?'

'You look different. What did you do?'

'Uh, showered?'

He approaches. 'No, but you did something to your hair. What, do you have a date or something?'

I scoff. 'Of course I don't have a date. Don't be ridiculous.'

'And you smell different. Is that my aftershave?'

'No.'

'It's okay, I don't mind. You can use it.'

'I didn't.'

'You look good.'

Heat rises to my cheeks. 'Did I look that bad before?'

'No, I didn't say— wait, is that a patch?' He grabs my arm. 'Are you wearing a nicotine patch?'

'Yeah.'

'Oh my God, look at you! I'm so proud of you!'

I suppress a shiver as he ropes me into a tight hug. His hand slaps flat against my shoulder-blade and keeps me there for a while.

'That's definitely my aftershave.'

'Yeah. Sorry.'

'It's fine.'

'I'm going to soak my trousers.'

'What?'

'Trousers. Stain.'

He lets me go. 'Oh. Right, yes.'

As I change into a clean pair of jeans, Jamie shouts from the other side of the door. 'Seriously, mate, what's gotten into you? What's the occasion?'

'There's no occas—' I swing the door open and he's standing right there. 'Jesus, you're nosy.'

'A bit, yeah. I like to think it makes me a good journalist.'

'It makes you a pain in the arse.'

He follows me around as I bring the trousers to the sink and scrub at the stain, but he doesn't ask again. I glance at him in the mirror and he wiggles his eyebrows.

The words almost spill out right there and then. They stir in my gut, swish around. I don't understand why it's suddenly so hard to keep them in when it's all I've been doing for near on a decade.

'Where's the tape recorder?' I ask, instead.

He frowns. 'I thought you didn't want to know.'

'Maybe I changed my mind,' I say, flicking the tap

off and wringing out the trousers.

'It's under my mattress.'

'It's like you want to get arrested. Just put it back under the floorboard.'

'You think they wouldn't look there?'

'I think they'd definitely look under your mattress.'

He blocks my way out of the bathroom, arms stretched either side of the door-frame. 'Is everything alright?'

I blink. 'Yeah.'

He doesn't move.

'I have to go to the hospital,' I prompt.

He hesitates, but eventually slopes aside, and then he's rubbing the back of his head awkwardly as I get ready to leave. 'So how, um . . . how's Tom?'

Christ, Sid, right there, yes, ahh God, fuck me that's—

'Good.'

'Oh, good. That's, uh, that's good.'

Yes, ohh yes!

'Yeah.' I point over my shoulder. 'I should go.'

'Sid?'

'Yeah?'

'I really am proud of you, yeah?'

Once again, I think I'm about to tell him, but then he says 'Talk to you later,' and I say 'Yeah. Later.'

Tom's asleep. I knock lightly on the open door.

'Hey, fancy man.'

He stirs and wakes up, and when he sees me a faint smile appears on his face. 'Hophead.'

'I can come back later if you want to rest.'

'No,' he says, suddenly snapping up.

I adjust the pillows against his back and he shifts his leg to allow me to sit on the edge of the mattress. I'm not sure where to put my hands. They end up awkwardly on my lap, sweaty as fuck.

'How are you?' I ask.

'A little bored, if we're being honest here – and I think we should be.'

'Sorry I've missed a few days. It's just, I've been—'

'Ashamed?'

'Busy.' I chew on my lower lip.

'Look, hophead, it's not the first time someone's regretted shagging me.'

'No, I don't regret – well, yeah, I do, but it's not – I mean, you're perfectly – I don't . . . ah, fuck.'

I bury my face in my hands. Ashamed sounds about right, actually.

'It's alright,' he says. 'It was just a shag, come on! No big deal.'

I let out an embarrassed grunt and he chuckles. Then I look up at him through my fingers. 'I'm so sorry, Tom.'

'You're such a sissy.'

I relax a little. 'I should have called, at least.'

'Nah. It's not like we went out for a candlelit dinner or anything.'

'I should have called.'

He shrugs. Instinctively, my hand moves over to his.

'Easy there, Casanova,' he says. 'Last time that happened . . .'

I wrench my hand away and miserably try to save

my dignity by running it through my hair.

'It was good, though,' he says. 'Wasn't it?'

'To be honest, I don't really remember much,' I say, and think of my hips rocking against his buttocks.

'Oh, that's classy!'

I manage a shy, apologetic laugh.

'Well trust me,' he says. 'It was bloody brilliant. I rocked your world.' He gives me a wink and quietly adds, voice a bit husky, 'You certainly rocked mine.'

We stare hard at each other. I'm barely breathing.

'So. Still in love with Jamie?'

For a second, I think about denying it, but there's only so many times you can revert all the progress you've made, and at this point it just needs to come out.

'Yes,' I say. 'Yeah.'

'Mm-hmm. And have you told him yet?'

'I'm . . . working on it.'

He sighs loudly. 'Hophead, he's never going to figure it out on his own.'

My head tilts back and before I know it I'm letting out another groan. 'Ugh, why not?'

'Because he's thick.'

I laugh again, and so does he.

'He's unbelievably, head-up-his-arse thick as a brick.'

But then the laughter fades and he suddenly seems exhausted.

'Probably belong together, the two of you.'

I frown. 'What do you—'

'Jamie,' he says.

I turn around, and sure enough . . .

'Jamie,' I say.

Jamie clears his throat and takes a hesitant step forward. 'Is . . . is this a bad time?'

It takes Tom a while to process the question and form a reply.

'No,' he says. 'No, come in.'

Jamie shuffles over and sits on the other side of the bed. There's something in his hand. He sets it on the bedside table. It's a little purple teddy bear, horribly flashy.

'That's just a stupid . . . thing.' And he clears his throat again.

'Thank you,' says Tom.

'So, uh, how've you been?'

'Good.'

'Good. Look, you know . . . you know I'm glad you're not . . . uh, Sid, can you give us a few minutes?'

I exchange a look with Tom and he gives a quick nod. With everything I've got, I try to convey 'Please don't tell him'. Tom's face remains set. I get up and leave.

In the end they talked for what felt like an hour, but was probably only around twenty minutes. I waited in front of the door. Twice, I thought about nipping downstairs for a fag. Twice, I shook the craving out of myself with slippery willpower and some flailing of the extremities.

Why do you even care?

Tom and I went through the physical therapy after Jamie left. Once more with feeling, I suppose. I allowed myself to feel like a doctor. He can hold a pen now, and write slowly, laboriously, with a tiny crease between his eyebrows. 'You're doing so well,' I said. 'Thank you,' he said. He smiled, and suddenly it all felt a bit dangerous again, so I stared at my feet for a while.

It's six-thirty and already the sun has set. As the light changed outside, anxiety descended on my chest, and the voice, the voice became excited about it. As I fiddle with my keys, it bursts out laughing, out of nowhere, and I can almost feel moist, hot puffs of breath against my ear. I wrench my head away from it.

There's a pile of newspapers on the coffee table, an empty mug precariously balanced on top of that and a notebook on the floor. Jamie's nodded off on the settee, his hand still loosely holding the pen.

I set my backpack on the floor and the pizza bag I brought back on top of it, and kneel down next to Jamie to pick up the notebook. It's full of his tiny cramped handwriting. I put it on the table. Then I carefully take the pen from him and place it on the notebook, making sure it's not going to roll off, taking my time with it. And then I'm just watching him.

He's troubled, mumbling indistinctly in his sleep. His head tosses on the cushion and a dark lock of hair falls over his eyes. I reach over and brush it back, and he seems to subconsciously welcome the touch. I'm calm and tense, happy and sad, strong and weak, all at once.

'Hey,' I whisper. 'Hey. I have to tell you something. Tonight. It's kind of big, and I'm scared that, um . . . well, I'm not sure what I'm scared of but I'm, I'm really scared. So, uh, please go easy on me, okay?'

He exhales a sigh, stirs and his eyes flutter open. I freeze.

'You, uh, you weren't breathing,' I say.

He's looking up at me with a soft expression.

'Oh,' he says, still fuzzy with sleep. 'You know you don't need to worry about that. It never lasts long. Doctor said I'm fine.'

'I know.'

I bite down on my tongue, hard, as he scrambles to his feet.

'I'm starved,' he says.

'I dropped by the pizza place.'

I grab the plastic bag and pull out the box.

'Feeling nostalgic?' he asks.

'Bite me,' I say.

'What did you get?'

I slide over to the kitchen without a word.

'Sid, what did you get?'

'Pizza.'

'Sid, I swear to God, if you brought home another pineapple monstrosity—'

'I didn't! No pineapple, I swear.'

He splashes water on his face and dries himself with a tea towel. 'I shouldn't have fallen asleep. I have work to do.'

'You probably couldn't help it.'

'Were you saying something? Before?'

I make a face at the plates I just retrieved from the cupboard. 'About what?'

'About—' He opens the pizza box and lets out an exasperated sigh. 'What's that?'

'Pineapple.'

He stares at me like I'm a complete monster.

'What do you want me to say? Just pick them off.'

We grab a slice each and he carefully removes the

cubes of pineapple before shovelling them onto my plate.

'You know,' I say, 'for all the shit you give me about this, I don't think I've ever seen you try it before.'

'Don't even think about it.'

'I'm just saying, don't knock it till you've tried it.'

I take a piece from my plate and hold it up in front of him.

'No.'

'Come on. My hands are clean.'

'I certainly hope so.'

I picture myself placing the pineapple between my teeth, and moving closer, and closer. I picture it passing from my mouth into his, and my tongue following. My chest cavity flutters and pounds from the inside out, like there's a trapped bird in there.

As it is, his fingertips barely graze mine as he nabs the cube of fruit and sticks it in his mouth.

'So?'

'It's revolting,' he says.

But he smiles at me, the left corner of his mouth and then the full grin. He just smiles and I can't hold it in any longer.

27

He's chewing on the pineapple and I think I'm about
to say it, I think I'm about to.

'Jamie, I've been falling—'

And the psychosis won't let me finish.

Bang! Bang! Bang!

I flinch. 'Shit!'

Bang! Bang! Bang! Bang!

'Shit, fuck, come on!'

I hit myself. I clench my fist and hit myself in the
head, in the skull. I try to beat it out of me.

Bang! Bang! Bang! Bang!

'Police, open up!'

My eyes go wide and I finally look at Jamie.

'Is that real?'

He nods and he's frightened, he's frightened, he's
frightened.

We're your Weather Girls

'Open up! Now!'

And have we got news for you

He gets up and runs to the door.

'Wait!' I call.

He pulls a face, puts his index finger across his lips.

Humidity's rising

Barometer's getting low

I glance over to the loose floorboard.

He nods.

I wait for him to signal me to breathe, but he's too distracted, he's too frightened, scared, and I'm late, it's too late, I can't believe I had a plan and it's too late, and I haven't done anything yet.

Five of them march in and spread out in the flat. A sixth man steps in after them, the leader, and with a cold thrill I recognise the ox man who picked me off the street.

He turns to Jamie. 'Mr Hayes?'

'Yes,' says Jamie.

'Mind if we look around?'

'Go ahead.'

The man steps towards me and I start saying 'no' over and over again under my breath and I can't stop it.

He gives me a nod. 'Mr Robinson.'

My arm shoots out searching for a wall but there's nothing there and it's like falling down a flight of stairs.

I can't breathe.

According to all sources

The street's the place to go

Cos tonight for the first time

I can't breathe I'm not breathing I'm not b—

They turn everything upside down.

Living room.

Kitchen.

Bathroom.

My bedroom.

Jamie's.

They flip the mattresses.

I pant through it.

Don't look at the floor, don't look at the floor! You just said that out loud, no I didn't, I didn't, you just said!

The anxiety mounts like someone opened a tap. It fills me up and I can't get it out how do I get it out you said that out loud you're getting it wrong you're getting it wrong sh-shut up!

Just about half past ten
For the first time in history

'It's g-gonna – gonna start raining men, it's raining men, hallelu . . . jah, it's ohh God . . . J-Jamie . . .'

He's with me in a split second. I find his shirt, his neck. I grab him and hold on and cry through the fog.

'Jamie!'

'It's okay,' he says. 'It's okay. It's okay.'

'What's wrong with him?'

'I'm gonna go out to r-run and – and . . . no, no, I need help, I can't, I can't . . .'

'It's okay,' Jamie's saying. 'It's okay. Shhh, it's okay.'

I'm getting light-headed, I'm losing consciousness, I want – 'I want to go outside!'

'Just keep singing. Absolutely soaking wet! Come on, Sid.'

'Please, it's not working.'

I try to steady my voice, to appear reasonable, normal, but I'm whimpering through chattering teeth.

'It's not working. I need to go out. Please.'

'Oi, Mick, what's going on? What is he, crazy or something?'

'He's having a panic attack.'

Fuck, fuck, 'Fuck! Let me out! God, let me out, let me out!' I break free and push at the walls. It's like I'm buried alive with tons and tons and tons of dirt on top of me.

'Look, can I just take him outside for a few minutes?'

'Nobody's leaving the apartment until we're done.'

'He's not well!'

'Nobody.'

Jamie huffs. 'Can I at least crack a window?'

'He could use an open window to pass on a message outside.'

'Oh, for fuck's sake!'

I sink to the floor and curl up into a ball. 'I can't, I can't, I can't.'

Jamie crouches by my side and carefully touches between my shoulder blades. 'Sid? Sid, we can't go outside right now. But it's nearly over. They're leaving soon, then we'll go outside, okay?'

'He shouldn't have anything to fear if he hasn't done anything wrong.'

Jamie strokes circles on my back.

'Come here, Sid, come here.' His arm wraps around me. His hand is on my brow, then in my hair, reassuringly.

'Look at me. Forget about them. It's just you and me. Just you and me, nobody here but us, yeah?'

I trust him. I trust him and nobody can say I don't.

One of the men sneers. 'Oooh, yeah baby, why don't you give him a kiss?'

The others laugh and wolf-whistle.

I feel a sharp exhale on my neck and Jamie hisses. 'Mind your fucking business.'

The laughter stops.

'What did you say?'

'Just do your fucking job, aye, and then fuck off!'

'Alright. Come here, Mick.'

They pull him away from me.

'No!'

One of them grabs Jamie's arm, twists it around and drives it up his back. Jamie bites back a cry.

'I think I'll have you in for contempt. What do you think, lads?'

This gets a wave of approving grunts from the others. I try to stand and immediately two of them hold me back as I half-collapse on them.

'No! Let him go!'

'It's okay, Sid,' Jamie says.

I'm seeing white around the edges. 'Please, I'll do anything you want! I swear he's not doing anything wrong! I swear!'

Jamie does a bit of a double take on me. His expression shifts into a frown.

'That's enough,' calls the ox man, emerging from my bedroom.

The others turn to him expectantly.

'Let him go,' he says.

Jamie keeps staring at me with that strange look on his face even as they release him, like he doesn't care about anything else anymore.

'Come on. Let's not overstay our welcome.'

He snaps his fingers, and they march out one by one.

'Always a pleasure, Mr Robinson. Mr Hayes.'

And the door closes behind them.

I collapse on the settee and sing, loud, at the top of my voice, to regulate my breathing.

'Cos tonight for the first time. Just about half past ten. For the first time in history, it's gonna start raining men. It's raining men. Hallelujah, it's raining men.' I press my palms against my eyelids until colours pop up. 'Hmm. Oh God. Oh my God.'

Jamie doesn't move. He towers over me, and when I look up, the colours superimpose on his face.

'What did they do to you?' he asks.

I don't reply.

'Did they hurt you?'

They're grabbing me, pulling me, I'm falling backwards, my side scrapes against the tarmac.

'I should have told you. I'm sorry.'

'Just tell me now. Tell me now. What did they do?'

They shove me into the cell, it's dark, it's a coffin, the ox man chews on the sandwich.

'I was on my way to work, a couple of weeks ago, and they came at me.'

I bring my hands up to shield my face because all of a sudden I can't look at him, I can't look at anything, and the lights are too bright.

'I tried to run. I don't know why. There was no way I could have lost them. There were three of them. They took me. They drove me to a station. They asked me questions. About you.'

He cuts me off. 'What they did to Charlie. Did they do that to you?'

'No. No, but they asked about you. They wanted me to report, they wanted me to spy on you.'

'A couple of weeks ago?'

'Yeah.'

'Fuck. You should have told me.'

'I know.'

'It's Friday.'

'Yes.'

'Fuck.'

'Yeah.'

He drops down next to me. I angle my head just enough to discreetly check him out.

'Okay,' he says. 'Look, you're not going to like this, but I don't think we have a choice. They'll be back. They'll come for you again, they'll come for me, they'll come for everyone we know. Sid, I don't think we can wait for next month's address.'

I hesitate. I look at my hands. I look at the room. I look at the industrial bar in his ear.

'I was going to go tomorrow,' I say.

'What?'

I give him a small, skittish smile.

'Without me?' he asks.

'Yes.'

He jumps to his feet. 'Are you fucking crazy?'

'Don't call me crazy.'

'Well, what do you call this, Sid?'

And I spring up too. 'I call it—'

'I can't fucking believe you!'

'Oh, Jesus fucking hell, quit interrupting me!' I pull on my hair like he's right and I'm actually going crazy. 'Why is it so hard? Why are you making it so hard?'

He's fuming. His accent's as thick as it's ever been, and he's yelling at me, and I'm not even sure why or what's happening anymore. He was so soft, so gentle, just five minutes ago.

'Let me make it really easy,' he says. 'If anyone's going on their own tomorrow, it's me.'

'No, fuck that. I'm going.'

'Why? I made the tape, this whole thing was my idea, Sid, why shouldn't I go?'

'Because it's not logical, alright? It doesn't make sense!'

'Why not?'

'Because look at you! Look at your life, look at your potential, and then look at . . .' I falter. My voice cracks as I push out the words. '. . . look at mine.'

I scratch at the nicotine patch, for fuck's sake, what are you thinking, who do you think you are, and I start peeling the fucking stupid thing off.

The anger melts off Jamie's face.

'Leave it,' he says.

I protest, vague mumbles, barely coherent, and keep clawing at the patch.

'Come on, Sid, leave it.'

He tries to pull my hand away. I yank myself free and shove him. Hard.

'What the fuck is the matter with you?'

Say it! Tell him, tell him now, just say it, you fucking coward, say it!

I come at him and shove him again.

He grabs my collar, tries to hold me back.

I push him away and swing my fist at him and he dodges it.

'Sid, Jesus Christ!'

We push and pull at each other all at once. I grab his hair and tug his head back until his neck is exposed.

The small vein pulses just above his clavicle and I watch the pulsing and I'm boiling, I'm boiling over, I'm going crazy and he sees it, he looks into my eyes and sees and I'm dizzy and heaving and he's looking into my eyes.

I press my mouth into his.

Ten years of accumulated tension come flooding out of me. My hands take fistfuls of his hair, angle his head. I feel drunk out of my mind. I suck at him, pry at him, bite at him. I pour my heart into his mouth until there's nothing left.

Then I let out a heavy moan and he gasps and it's too much. I'm about to pass out. And come. Not necessarily in that order.

I pull away, breathless and hard as fuck, wiping my mouth with the back of my hand. He stares, wide-eyed, the shine of my saliva on his lips and a twitch in his thigh muscle. I suddenly fear I've broken something.

'I'm sorry,' I mumble. 'I shouldn't have.'

And I rush to my room.

It's raining men
Hallelujah, it's raining men
A – fucking – *men.*

When I first arrived at my dorm room, he was already there. The boy. He clocked me, tossed the book he was reading on the sofa as he sprang to his feet. It was as if he'd been waiting for me. The left corner of his mouth rose first, before the smile spread to his entire face, and already something at the back of my mind was whispering, 'You're fucked.'

'Med school?' the boy said.

Irish, bright-eyed, a hint of freckles. Oh, you are so fucked.

'I'm English Lit,' said the boy. 'Suppose they wanted to broaden our horizons.'

He extended his hand.

'How are you? I'm Jamie.'

We shook.

'Sid.'

I fucked up. I really did. I pace around in a tight circle, clockwise, anticlockwise, clockwise, anticlockwise. Wonder if I could plead temporary insanity. Go back and apologise properly. Tell him it was all a terrible misunderstanding. Push him into the sofa and climb on top of him, *rough and tough and strong and* oh God.

Just as I'm whimpering into my hands, the door opens and shuts behind me. I turn and say something like 'Look, Jam— hmm—'

Well, he's talented, with the arm around my waist and the hand at the back of my neck and that thing with his tongue. If he keeps that up, my heart is going to bust out through my ribcage and splat on the carpet and it's going to be so hard to clean.

'We'll never get our deposit back,' I say.

'What?'

'Nothing.'

We make out for a while. I tune into the heat of him, clutch the front of his shirt and lose myself. He's passionate, purposeful. He tastes like everything I've ever wanted. We draw each other closer and closer and I want him to know how perfect this is. After a few minutes, he gives a sharp exhale and reaches beneath my t-shirt, and it turns out that's the kick-start my brain needs. I start thinking of that guy, my first time, with his eyes shut, pretending I was someone else, wanting someone else.

'No. Jamie, no.'

I give his shoulders a small push and look him up and down. Half his shirt has come untucked and exertion flushes his cheeks bright red. He's sexier than he's got any right to be.

'Don't you want this?' he whispers.

'No!'

Then again, it would be more convincing if my hard-on wasn't pressing against his leg right now.

He blinks.

'Okay, I do! I do want this! Sue me! I've wanted this for fucking years, and you . . . we can't because I just, I want . . .' I trail off. 'I love you, okay? For fuck's sake, Jamie, I love you.'

And there's my heart, all over the carpet.

The wheels turn in his head. 'I love y—'

'Don't lie,' I say. 'Don't lie, cos I swear I am this close to believing you.'

It takes a second before he drops the act with a sigh. He gives me a sad look and I shoot it right back at him. I'm not sure where that leaves us.

'I'm sorry,' he says.

I force a chuckle. 'Me too.'

'May I hug you?'

I open my arms and he moves in. My chin rests on his shoulder, his on mine, and we just stand there for a minute. Maybe that's where that leaves us. Maybe that's okay.

Then he clears his throat. 'Is that an illegal tape recorder in your pocket or . . .?'

'Oh, soak off.'

We share a laugh, but this is still a bit awkward so I sit on the bed and cross my legs for a while.

'How did I not see this?'

I shrug. 'Tom seems to think it's cos you're an idiot.'

'Tom knew before I did? Fucking perfect.'

'He's not that bad.'

'I know.'

'I fucked him.'

'Aw, mate, that's gross. When?'

'Few days ago.'

Both his eyebrows shoot up. 'At the hospital?'

I nod. 'Bathroom.'

'You slut.'

'I was thinking of you the whole time.'

'Thanks.'

'No problem.'

He looks at me like I matter. For the life of me, I can't figure out why.

'You're gorgeous,' I say. 'It's not fair.'

'You're blind as a fucking bat.'

'I can see just fine.'

'How many fingers am I holding up?'

'I don't care.' Against my better judgement I'm leaning in again and then I hear myself asking. 'Can I?'

His eyes flicker to my lips, and back up. 'It's "may I" . . .'

I kiss him. Softly. Deliberately. I touch his jaw, his neck. I brush the tip of his tongue with mine. For a blissful moment, everything is quiet. His heartbeat flutters against my palm.

He mumbles. 'I, um, I have a bit of a confession to make.'

'Hmm?'

'I've never actually kissed anyone before.'

I yank my head away. 'Fuck off.'

'Way to kill the mood.'

'What mood? Fuck the mood! Did I just steal your first kiss away from you? Oh my God, I'm such a wanker!'

I fling myself backwards onto the mattress and stay there with both hands over my face. A clock's ticking somewhere nearby, even though there's no clock in the room and I took the batteries out of the one in the living room ages ago because it was driving me crazy.

Eventually the bed creaks and I feel Jamie's presence to my right. Years go by without a word, until I finally ask.

'Were you in love with her?'

He squirms. 'I don't know.'

'Liar.'

'Yes, well, I'm not the only one keeping my feelings close to my chest, am I?'

'Oi!'

'Why didn't you say anything?'

I search the ceiling for something to stare at. 'I guess I figured, if it was going to happen, it would have happened years ago. And I was right.'

'I do love you, but . . .'

I mimic taking an arrow to the heart. We exchange a look.

'I don't know if I was in love with her yet,' he says.

'But I think I was headed that way, you know? I really think I was.'

Something sinks in the pit of my stomach. I quietly acknowledge it.

He clears his throat. 'And you, you didn't, you never . . . felt . . . anything? For her?'

'No. Not like how I feel about you.' I cross my arms behind my head. 'Can I ask you something?'

'"May I".'

'If that was your first kiss, does that mean you've never . . . had . . .'

He shakes his head.

'Why not?'

'Suppose I never wanted to.'

'What about before, when we were . . . Did you want to then?'

'I think I just wanted it over with.'

A few tears roll down my cheeks. I don't move, I don't try to stop it, and he pretends not to notice.

'Maybe I just missed out.' He gives a short laugh, then seems to deflate a bit. 'Did I miss out?'

I'm starting to think I must have angered someone important in a past life.

'How does it feel?'

I turn my head and he's blushing. Cute.

'How does what feel?' I ask.

'You know . . .'

'Yeah, I do know. Do you?'

'Give me a break, come on. This isn't my area of expertise.'

'And you think it's mine?'

'You tell me. How's Tom, by the way?'

'How dare you?'

He laughs. I laugh. We giggle and nudge each other like a pair of teenagers. The sound, the scent, the warmth make me want to pounce on him.

'Is it nice?' he asks. 'I'm assuming it's better than just being . . . you know . . . on your own.'

I swallow through the lump in my throat. 'Nice? Yeah, it's nice. It's really fucking nice. Would you like me to show you?'

'Hey, you're the one who pushed me away.'

'Bear with me, I'm trying to remember why.'

The conversation dies out for a few minutes. It's gotten late. It's gotten very late and my body feels like it's made of lead.

'How do you think it'll go tomorrow?' Jamie asks, out of the blue.

I think about it. 'We'll get up late, after noon maybe, and have breakfast. We have bread, don't we? And eggs? Then we'll pack the transmitter in my backpack, the recorder in your pocket, and we'll head out together.'

'Forecast says it might snow.'

'Oh. Nice.'

His hand finds mine on the mattress.

'And then what?'

'We'll go to the Tower,' I say. 'The entrance is on Cleveland Street. Across the road is the university. Cavendish campus. There's a small square to one side, with trees, benches. We'll sit there.'

'You've thought about this.'

I keep going in the same calm breath, in the same monotone. I've never been so sure of what I was doing.

'We won't take the transmitter out of the backpack. We'll just have it open, not too much. We'll wait for the address to start. And then we'll play the tape.'

'You've really thought about this.'

'I was going to go on my own.'

'Well, you won't.'

I smile.

'And then?'

'It'll be strange to hear her voice outside of home. It'll be hard, but you'll be okay. I'll be there. People will start showing up in the streets. More and more. They'll come flocking to the Tower. They'll have heard enough to want an explanation. They'll take over, and you and I, we'll just . . . sort of . . . disappear. We'll slip away, maybe go for a drink or something.'

'What if we get caught?'

'We won't.'

'What if we get caught?'

'I don't know.'

He suppresses a fearful sob, and I just keep holding his hand.

'Sometimes I wonder why it fell on us,' he says. 'Sometimes I wish she'd never come here. I wish it was somebody else's problem. Is that awful?'

I attempt a smirk. 'Yes.'

He sighs and turns away from me and for a second I think I pushed it too far. But then he reaches back, finds my wrist and pulls my arm around his waist. I scoot closer until my chest presses into his back, my nose against the crook of his neck. We fall into place like puzzle pieces and we fit remarkably well, only the picture doesn't match the one on the box.

I love you so much, I think. So much. And I smile, and squeeze him tighter instead of saying anything out loud.

We stay like this until sleep begins to take hold, and longer.

'I hope it snows tomorrow,' I say.

'Yeah,' he says. 'That would be nice.'

In a haze, I hear myself utter something that distantly resembles the word 'elephant', and Jamie laughs, that laugh, his.

'Yeah, you too, mate.'

28

It's Saturday morning, the pillowcase smells like Jamie, and I fancy beans on toast. I breathe everything in. I stretch into the domesticity, eyes closed, unwilling to let go of it just yet.

'Is it snowing?'

I hear a sleepy purr to my right, and chuckle.

'Have I mentioned how much I like your voice?'

I slip underneath the duvet. 'We should probably get up. You first.'

It occurs to me that I'm still fully dressed in last night's clothes. Those need to come off. I need a shower. I need food. What time is it?

'Hey, any chance we've got a can of beans laying around somewhere? Jamie?'

I open my eyes.

'Jamie?'

I'm alone.

'Oh.'

Psycho. I scoff at myself.

My meds sit on the bedside table, where I don't recall leaving them. I pop a pill into my mouth, but there's no water so I end up swallowing it dry and gagging a bit as it sticks on the way down.

Flicking my tongue repeatedly in an attempt to coax out more saliva, I shuffle to the door.

'Jesus, why would you let me talk to myself like—'

You're locked in.

'Uh, Jamie?'

I twist the doorknob and it won't budge. I pull, push, tug, tug again. The key's not sticking out of the lock anymore.

'Jamie?'

You're locked in.

'Jamie!'

I pound on the door.

'Oi, Jamie, come on!'

I drive my shoulder into it and pain shoots through the arm all the way to the fingertips but everything feels dull and far away. The door doesn't budge. I press my ear against it.

'Are you still there? What time is it? Are you still there?'

I run to the window. The sky's a pale mauve. Looks like late afternoon. Three, maybe four.

And it's snowing.

My legs go numb. Suddenly I can't tell which way I'm facing.

'Are you there?' I whisper.

He left you, says the voice. *Would you like me to tell you why?*

'No!'

I tug on my hair, swing my head sideways to shut it up. I grab the desk chair and hurl it at the door and a piece of it flies off.

'Jamie! For fuck's sake, stop doing that, you can't do that!'

I slam my fists against the wood.

'You can't decide for me! You c— you can't keep' – I slide to the floor – 'deciding for me.'

Stand. I can't. *Who decides for you, Robinson? Who decides?*

I scramble to my feet.

Get out of my way, get out, get out.

I search frantically for my mobile. I check my pockets. I tear the pillows off the bed. As I pull the duvet down, the phone thuds onto the floor.

4.18 p.m.

I ring Jamie, and of course he doesn't pick up. I open my mouth. All that comes out is a weak, pathetic, 'Did you even try to wake me?'

And I hang up.

I ring Nick. Nothing.

I ring Peter.

I ring Tom.

'Hophead?'

The rush of relief disappears as fast as it came. He's stuck in the hospital. I almost hang up, but then he calls my name and my thumb moves away from the button.

'Sid?'

I gasp. 'Oh my God, there's nothing you can do. There's nothing you can do.'

'Talk to me. What's going on?'

'I'm trapped, I'm, I'm trapped in my room and Jamie's gone and I can't get out, I'm trapped, I—'

'Is the door locked?'

'Yes.'

'He locked you in?'

'Yes.'

'On purpose?'

'Yes! Fuck, I'm trapped and I have to find, I have to get out, somehow, I have to get to him.'

'Where is he?'

I stare at the phone for a while, thinking, wondering.

'I can't tell you,' I say.

'Okay,' he says.

'It's not a delusion.'

'Okay.'

'What do I do?'

'I assume calling the police to come free you is out of the question?'

'Tom!'

'Alright, alright. Um . . . there's definitely no way you can break down the door?'

I throw myself against the door again, and again, with all my weight, with desperate energy, and I hear a distant 'Christ' over the speaker. I put the phone to my ear again, winded and shaking.

'I'm not strong enough.'

'Bobby pin? Paperclip?'

'I wouldn't know what to do.'

'Fire escape?'

'Oh!'

I yank the window open. Cold wind whistles on its way in. I shudder. The rusty ladder zigzags down from Jamie's bedroom to the left. It's far, but not too far. I'll have to walk along the ledge to reach it.

'Sid?'

'I can make it.'

'You— Well, hold on a minute, let's not do anything stupid.'

I toss the phone on the bed and sit to tie my shoes.

'Sid? Are you safe?'

'I can make it.'

'Are you safe?'

I grab the phone and hang up. As the freezing air sends another shiver down my spine, I slip into the ugly Christmas jumper that Jamie, years ago, gave me as a joke.

My right leg swings out, then my left. I sit on the windowsill with the heels of my shoes tapping against the bricks outside. My hands brace against the frame.

The ledge below is a few inches deeper than my shoe size, and barely in reach when I angle my hips, stretch out one leg and extend the tip of my foot.

You'll have to drop.

I huff a few times and try to conjure up the song but I've got nothing. The wind howls in my ears and I've got nothing. And the voice repeats: *You'll have to drop. You're going to die.*

Have I mentioned how much I like your voice?

Okay. Okay.

'Don't look down. Just don't look down, okay?'

I close my eyes – don't close your eyes! – and open them again, and look down.

'Fuck, shit! Okay. Oh God. Okay.'

I secure one hand on the windowsill, the other flat against the bricks, and lower myself down. My arm strains with the effort of controlling the movement. I become hyperaware of my fingers.

Just as the sole of my shoe touches the ledge, I push

too hard on the wall and my entire body swings around.

I yelp.

The bricks drag the jumper up my torso as I slide down, scraping a deep burn into the skin on my side. My second foot catches the ledge and my back hits the wall. My free hand twists awkwardly behind my shoulder to grab the window.

I bite down on my lower lip. 'Ow.'

That was the hardest part.

'Oh, you liar. You liar.'

Snowflakes freeze on my eyelashes. I blink to clear my vision.

The ladder seems farther away than it was a minute ago, maybe seven feet away. I grit my teeth and begin to inch my way over, exhaling sharply with every shuffle. I keep my eyes fixed on the building across from ours. No windows. A pigeon flies by. A car alarm blares in the distance.

Halfway there, I almost slip on a patch of ice that's formed where a pipe was leaking. At the exact same moment, my phone buzzes in my pocket. I stop for a second with my heart in my mouth. I wait it out. The buzzing repeats a few times, then stops.

I step over the patch of ice.

Keep going.

Keep going.

The railing glints in the light, like it's covered in a film of water. I hold out a clammy hand and feel my palm stick to the cold metal as I clasp the bar.

'Yes!' I hiss.

Compared to the ledge, the ladder feels almost as safe as stable ground. I clamber down, the icy railing tugging at my fingertips with each step, almost as if it doesn't want to let me go.

When I finally reach the tarmac, my legs instantly give up. I crumple to the pavement and just heave and quiver on my hands and knees for a while.

My mobile starts buzzing again.

I pull it out of my pocket.

Tom.

I answer.

'I'm alive.'

And hang up.

4.56 p.m.

Sun's going down. I run to Leicester Square, hoping to catch the Northern line, but just as I'm sprinting down the stairs into the station, I notice I don't have my wallet. I curse under my breath and steal a glance at the turnstiles. There's people around. Police. There's no use even trying.

5.12 p.m.

It's too late. Sun's going down and it's about to start. Just run.

I race back out and dive onto Charing Cross Road.

5.21 p.m.

I cross Shaftesbury.

5.28 p.m.

I cross New Oxford Street. A car to my left runs the red light and nearly slams into me. The driver's eyes dart to his radio, frowning, as he raises a hand in apology.

My lungs are on fire.

5.32 p.m.

As I rush past a pub, Olivia's voice stops me.

'They sent buses to our neighbourhood and came knocking on doors to escort us.'

I shake my head. I try to shake it out. It doesn't work.

Soon enough the street speakers along Tottenham Court Road start blasting out her voice.

'The doctor told us to take our clothes off. There wasn't a separate room so we had to take our clothes off in front of everyone else. They threw the clothes away and gave us these blue scrubs to put on instead. Some of the girls didn't want to get undressed in front of everybody and the police had to force them.'

I approach a group of guys chatting excitedly under one of the speakers.

'Do you hear that?'

'What?'

'That, the voice! Is that real?'

'Sure sounds real to me, man, but Benji here says it's a hoax!'

'I stand by it. There's no way that's real.'

'How could you possibly know that?'

'Because, you child, I was there before the quarantine. That's not a woman's voice, it's too deep.'

'It's not a hoax,' I say.

'That's clearly a man,' he says. 'Trust me.'

'Well, either way, someone's getting fired tonight,' says the other.

'Sure, let's go with "fired",' Benji says.

They shout after me as I sprint away.

'I wouldn't go over there, man! They'll be sending riot control in a minute.'

'It's a fucking hoax!'

5.45 p.m.

The recording echoes in the streets, and people have stepped out of their buildings. They've gathered

406

in clusters to gossip and listen and gossip some more. Some weep. Some yell at the speakers.

I pretend I can't see.

There's two voices now, three, four, screaming at me to hurry up, to give up, to go home, to kill myself.

I reach Howland Street and right as I turn a brick crashes into a shop window barely two feet in front of me. I shield my face from the flying shards.

Someone shouts 'What the fuck do you think you're doing?'

Two men restrain a third.

'That's my daughter! That's my fucking daughter, you bastards!'

No, I think. No, it's not.

Shattered glass crunches under my feet as I push past.

'They did what they had to back then,' says someone else, 'and it could have been a lot worse, believe me!'

5.50 p.m.

The crowd around the Tower drifts forth like a giant flock of birds. Olivia's voice bounces off the walls, all crunchy and echoey behind the whirring of the tape recorder.

'We went for it. The tunnel was closed so cars couldn't go in, but on foot it was easy enough to enter. So we went for it. We could barely see anything the whole way through. We held onto—'

Click.

The breath catches in my throat.

'. . . each other,' I say.

5.53 p.m.

I squeeze my way through, extending my neck to

407

try and see something, anything. I mumble apologies on the way, even though no one gives a shit. Pardon me. Sorry. Excuse me. Pardon.

The building itself appears to be cordoned off, but that's not the focal point. Noses and faces and index fingers point across the street at the university – Cavendish campus – and the small square to one side, with the trees and the benches.

'What's going on?'

'They're taking someone?'

'I think they found the guys.'

'How many people?'

'Is that woman with them?'

According to all sources

'Jamie!' I call.

A man with a mohawk and multiple piercings in his eyebrows turns. 'Yeah?'

He's holding his phone above his head to film. On the tiny screen is Jamie.

Jamie and two other guys, probably students, backed up against the wall, cowering with their bags cradled to their chests. Jamie's arm reaches across to shield them. He talks to the cops – three of them, always three – arguing, passionate, effervescent.

The street's the place to go

I push.

Can you hear him?

I push to the front of the crowd just in time to see one of the officers slapping one of the kids across the face with the back of his hand.

The boy cries out in pain.

People film to my left, gawk to my right.

I take a step forward, break away from the crowd,

and my carefully practised received pronunciation slides clean off.

'Oi, thug lord! Back off, yeah?'

The leader – always a leader – stalks up to me and it's like he's being pulled forward by his puffed-up chest. He catches me around the arm and drags me over to the others.

Jamie and I exchange a look.

I'm sorry, he says.

I'm sorry, I say.

'Let him go,' he says.

'You want a fucking taser in the neck?'

A baton strikes the back of my knees and I sink down.

'Let him go!' Jamie shouts. 'Don't hurt him! He hasn't done anything!'

I flail. I fight back. I'm not nearly as scared as I should be. They wrestle me down until my cheek's pressing into the gravel. Jamie strains to reach me, but they've got him pinned to the wall.

'Stay down, don't fucking move! I'll smash your fucking face in!'

One of them spits in my face. I flinch.

'Don't move!'

They drag my wrist up at a wrong angle.

'Ow, my arm, you bastard!'

'Shut it, Bollywood!'

'Don't try anything, mate, it's not going to end well for you!'

Jamie scans the mob. 'You're just going to fucking stare? Wake up, Jesus Christ, wa—'

'Shut it!'

A stranger's voice rises from the crowd. 'Maybe

ease up a bit, man.'

And another. 'He can't move when you've got your foot on his back, can he?'

'That's excessive, mate.'

'He's not armed, is he?'

The circle around us draws in. The leader pulls out his gun.

'Back! Stand back!'

He leans into the radio at his shoulder and calls for backup, and then I can't see anymore. A boot bears down on the side of my neck and I gasp and choke and I'm desperate to see Jamie's face one last time and tell him again, tell him again, make sure he knows.

He calls my name, then calls to them.

'Wait, no, wait! It was me, alright? It was me! Look, I've got the transmitter in my backpack! It's right here!'

'On your knees! Drop the bag!'

'I'm trying to show you.'

'Drop it right now!'

'Alright, just, just let me just show you the—'

6 p.m.

The gunshot cracks like a whip through the cold. My eardrums shatter. Voices pop left and right, behind the ringing, and I can't tell which are real and which are in my head.

'What happened?'

'Did it hit someone?'

'What did you do?'

Movement flashes. The pressure on my neck releases.

Jamie looks like he's in the middle of a powerful bad trip and someone just asked him a complex maths question. His coat is turning red.

'Oh my God.'

'What happened?'

'He wasn't armed!'

'You shot him!'

'Fucking pig shot him! He wasn't even armed!'

The cops wave their guns around, unsure where to aim. Their eyes dart from one angry face to the next. The one who fired the shot's got his hand clasped over his mouth.

'Put the fucking guns down!' someone shouts. 'We're not armed!'

'Stand back!'

'Are you happy now?'

'Someone take the gun away from him!'

A young man in a tracksuit touches Jamie's shoulder. 'You should sit down, brother.'

Jamie pulls away. 'I'm okay,' he says. 'It's, uh, it's fine. I'm okay. My friend's, um . . .'

He takes one step towards me and drops like a stone.

Handcuffs glint in the light of the street lamp.

The crowd breaks into screams and raging threats. A mass of bodies charges at the cop. I fight against the movement with everything I have, scrambling onto my hands and knees, wincing as someone's foot catches my chin.

I throw my upper body over Jamie's head, tuck my own face into my arms, and wait as the wave swells and crashes over us.

When the onslaught finally dies down, he's already going into shock. He looks up at me, disoriented, hands clasped to his stomach.

'Sid, what's, what . . .'

I pry his fingers away.

'Let me see it, love,' I say. 'Let me take a look.'

He stares and whimpers as I open his coat and drag his shirt up. The hole is almost as wide as my thumb. Blood leaks out black and thick, in pulses, like it's being heaved out.

I start humming to myself. Jamie's sobbing and moaning and I have to block it out, I have to block out the sounds. I take off my jumper, the ugly Christmas one that he gave me as a joke, and press it into the wound.

'Ahh, God fuck!'

'Somebody call an ambulance!'

Nobody moves. I turn and the commotion hits me. Most of the crowd is pushing back against rows of riot control in a cacophony of thuds and hollering. A smaller group stays back and just ogles us. Some of them still have their camera phones out.

'Ambulance, you fucking arseholes, now! Now!'

The guy in the tracksuit dials and starts talking and I shout over my shoulder.

'Twenty-nine year old, gunshot wound to the abdomen!'

He repeats it into the phone.

'Where in the abdomen?' he asks, after a short pause.

'Upper right side, just below the ribcage.'

A pause again. 'Is there an exi—'

'No exit point. I think it's in the liver. Are they on their way?'

'How do you know it's in the—'

'I don't! I said "I think"! I think it's in the liver, for fuck's sake! Are they on their way?'

The jumper's already soaked and heavy, and that's when Jamie starts mumbling. His voice comes out higher than usual, incoherent, blurting out syllables between short inhales.

'Are you in a lot of pain?' I ask stupidly.

'Mm— mm-hmm.' He gives a quick nod and mumbles again and the terror is plain in his face. 'An— ahh! An f-f-feidir linn dul abhaile anois?'

Something in my stomach that I didn't even know was there starts sinking.

'Sweetheart, I can't . . . I don't understand.'

He looks at me like that doesn't make sense. Like I should have understood.

'I won't let you die,' I say. 'I pro . . .'

It stays inside me. I can't get it out. It lingers there and fizzles out.

I take a deep breath and think. I saved Tom. I can do it again. I can save Jamie like I saved Tom. I press the jumper down harder but the blood is coming out of his mouth now.

I turn and see the young man still on the phone.

'Come on, fuck, are they sleeping?'

'He says . . . try to block the bleed—'

'I KNOW!'

I know.

I know what I'm doing isn't good enough. I know he's bleeding out. So I remove the jumper.

Jamie lets out a breath and it almost sounds like relief. I can do this, I think.

'Jamie?'

He blinks at me.

'It's raining men . . .'

He blinks again.

'Hallelujah, it's raining men . . .'

It takes a while. 'Amen,' he says.

I run my fingers across his stomach, petting, soothing as best I can.

'Tall, blond, dark and?'

'L-l-lean . . .'

My thumb finds the bullet-hole.

'Rough and?'

He grits his teeth. 'Tough.'

I press my thumb in. 'And?'

'S-s— ahh! Strong!'

'And?'

Tears run from his eyes down to his ears. He tries to swallow but just gags and more blood collects on his teeth.

'Jamie, and?'

'. . . mean. . .'

I push my thumb down until his skin feels tight around it.

His head tosses about. His blood is all over my hands but the wound seems plugged. Something in there is pulling at my finger, suctioning it in place. For a stupid second, I think everything will be fine.

Then he starts breathing fast and shallow. I try hushing him. He struggles, frantic, like he's drowning.

'Ár nAthair, atá ar neamh. Go naofar d'ainm.'

His skin has gone yellowy-white and he's sweating and shaking like I've never seen before.

'Go dtaga do ríocht. Sid, it's . . . it's not snowing anymore.'

I see the distress in his eyes and my heart slows. I smile. I put my free hand on his cheek and stroke and look at him with all the love I can't say.

I tell him I've stopped the bleeding. I tell him it looks better. I tell him I can hear the sirens approaching.

'I promise,' I say.

29

When the ambulance arrived, Jamie had been dead for fifteen minutes. They pronounced him at the scene. I watched in silence, with strangers rubbing the back of my neck and reciting condolences. I clutched in my hands the ugly Christmas jumper that, years ago, he gave me as a joke.

The following week I got sick. Dead of winter, hours outside in nothing but short sleeves. I was in bed for days, almost delirious, with a temperature of forty-one, chattering teeth and a savage headache. I could barely move. Nick and Charlie didn't leave my side, no matter how hard I screamed for them to get lost.

The illness came and went. January passed in a daze. When Nick asked if I wanted to move in with them, I told him to fuck off back to his own home and pulled the sheet over my head.

On the fourth of February, exactly a month after, I dreamt Jamie was touching me. It started off slow. His hands cupping my face for a while. Then he slid closer and rubbed his nose against my cheek. I laughed and so did he, and I dipped my head back to allow him to stroke my neck. I leaned into the deep rise and fall of his chest. My shirt came off. His hands moved over my torso, over my back. I felt a low hum at the back of my throat and it became loud, cutting through the haze, and I realised I was awake, in bed, staring at the ceiling, and it wasn't a dream. It was something else.

I got up. Took my meds, showered, got dressed. I peeked out the window and took in my very first glimpse of the consequences of what we'd done. There wasn't much to see, if I'm honest. The sounds, though. I've no clue where the original tape ended up, but as it turns out, that didn't matter. It's out. It's everywhere. God knows that's a good thing, but sometimes, fuck me, sometimes I wish it wasn't.

February 27th. My keys clink on the coffee table and I stand there for several minutes and maybe I'm stuck there, on that square inch of living room, forever. The apartment looks dead. Smells dead. Tastes dead. My entire life, in two large suitcases, sits in the middle of the room.

Move.

I walk around and flick all the lights on.

I wash last night's plate and leave it in the rack to dry. I briefly consider taking the bottle of dish soap – there's a decent amount left – but Tom's probably got something much fancier at his place. Eco-friendly, hypoallergenic, or some shit.

I walk around and flick all the lights off again.

Groaning, I bend down and unzip one of the suitcases. Wasn't thinking. I dig out a towel and a few pairs of socks fall out. I shove them back in. Fuck's sake.

I spread the towel out on my bed and line up my tools on top. Alcohol wipes. Hollow needles. Saline solution. Paper towels.

Breathe.

I pull the industrial bar out of my pocket.

Nick held it out to me outside the morgue on the day of the cremation. It was sunny and the silver caught the light between his thumb and index finger.

'Coroner thought you might want it,' he said.

I shook my head.

He opened my hand and placed the little metal bar in it anyway. It was cold.

'There is nothing worse than regret,' he said. 'Trust me.'

I felt a thickness in my throat, and wished he'd chosen different words.

My phone vibrates against my thigh. I pull it out, put it on speaker and set it down at my side.

'Tom.'

'Hophead. Just wanted to make sure you were still coming.'

I pull one of the alcohol swabs from the box, tear it open and wipe my left ear.

'Yeah.'

'Sorry. It's just they won't let me leave on my own, you know?'

'I know. I'll be there.'

I tilt my head at the mirror on my wardrobe and

mark two spots on my ear.

Tom doesn't speak for a while. I glance at the phone, thinking maybe he hung up.

'How are you?' he asks, and my nostrils flare, and I suppress a sigh.

I don't reply. I busy myself with the needles and say nothing until the silence eats him alive.

'That, uh, that was bad, wasn't it? I'm sorry, that was—'

'I'm fine, fancy man. I'll be there, and then we can just . . . I don't know. Get takeaway or something.'

'Sounds good.'

'Talk to you later, yeah?'

'Yes. Yes.'

The speaker clicks.

I press the needle against the first mark on my outer helix. I draw in a deep breath and, as I exhale, I drive the needle in. My jaw clenches. It pops once, the skin. Twice, the cartilage. Thrice, the skin on the other side.

I swallow and hum softly. My hands fumble a bit with the jewellery. I finally manage to slide it through, and it pinches a bit when the needle comes out.

I screw the barbell end on and check my work in the mirror. Decent.

The ear's gone red with the rush of blood. Second one will hurt more.

It has to hurt, right?

A little, when it goes through, but not for long.

That doesn't sound too bad.

It's not.

I swing my head sideways. Pain shoots from my ear down to my jaw.

'Shit!'

I blink at the phone screen to reassure myself that Tom's not on the line anymore.

Then I take out a second needle, breathe in again, one, two, three, and push it all the way through the second mark in one quick motion. I wince, panting sharply through my nose. Not too bad, my arse.

My shaky hands make it a bit harder to get the metal bar in, but eventually, it's done.

I pop the cap off the bottle of saline solution, pour a healthy amount on a paper towel and clean everything up. My ear buzzes with the sting and through the buzzing I can almost hear Jamie's twenty-year-old voice in the musty intimacy of our tiny dorm room.

'Hey, welcome back, what's new with you?'

He'd stayed on campus over the holiday break. He always did. I dropped my suitcase at the foot of my desk and he gave me the biggest smile, the biggest hug.

'How did it go with your dad?'

I must have said it went fine, although I'd be hard-pressed to remember the exact wording. I recall the physicality of his presence. I recall being keenly aware of him in that moment, to the point where my voice broke as I answered whatever it was that I ended up answering. I know I didn't tell him about Dad drunkenly sobbing on my shoulder as I quietly gave up on mentioning the anxiety attacks.

He seemed to know anyway.

We sat on his bed, shared a joint, and talked for hours. We had plans, I think, although we quickly forgot about them.

'Is that new?' I asked, pointing at the industrial bar.

He exhaled a cloud of smoke into the room. 'Oh yeah! Had it done over the weekend. Christmas present or something, I guess. What do you think?'

He moved his face closer to give me a better look. It was completely innocent. I stared at the shell of his ear. The details in there, the light curves, the soft skin, made saliva build up in my mouth.

'It's nice.'

'Oh good! I thought maybe it made me look like that hipster who runs the pub quiz at the union.'

I chuckled. 'That guy . . .'

He laughed. 'Fucking poser, you know?'

'Yeah. No, you, it looks good on you. It suits you.'

His eyes brightened, like it mattered to him that I liked it.

'Anyways, glad you're back!' he said. 'Happy New Year, Sid.'

'Happy New Year,' I said.

Before heading out, I stop in front of the mirror again. I tuck a lock of hair back.

It doesn't look as good on you.

I check the time, grab my jacket and keys, and scan the room as I dial. I can't tell if I'm sad or not.

'Yes, hello. I need a taxi. Corner of Old Compton and Wardour Street. Ta.'

One last glance over my shoulder, and I struggle down the stair with the suitcases.

The street blares and howls. Protesters chant in the distance. It's Piccadilly Circus today. Leicester Square tomorrow.

The cab swings in from Wardour and I wave it down. The driver eyes me as I settle in the back seat.

'Moving day?' he asks, nodding at the luggage.

'Yes.'

'You look familiar. Have we met?'

I give him a small smile, a small head shake. He squints at me, as if that'll help him remember, and gives up with a shrug.

'Reckon you've got one of these faces.'

'Mm-hmm.'

As he pulls the car out of neutral, I text Tom – '*On my way*' – and get a near-instant thumbs up.

The cabbie twists around, arm over the headrest, and flashes me a grin.

'So. Where are you going, then?'

ACKNOWLEDGEMENTS

I want to extend my deepest thanks to all the wonderful friends, colleagues and partners in crime without whom I'd have cracked long before Sid found his voice.

Daniel, you know this book would not be what it is today if it weren't for you. Thank you for being my sounding board, my writing buddy, and my brother – not that you had much of a choice on that last one.

Mum, Maxwell, Raphy, thank you for reading things that were nowhere near ready and cheering me on regardless. Riley, your invaluable input saved me from nosediving into a pit of self-publishing despair.

Grateful thanks to Kate and Nadhira, the best editor and sensitivity reader I could have hoped for. I can't wait to work with you both again.

Amalas, you know how much I admire your work. Thank you for breathing life into that quiet moment of affection. Kaz, thank you for giving Sid the face he will forever have in my mind's eye.

Diolch, Elen, for Olivia's Welsh. Stephen, for Jamie's Irish, go raibh maith agat.

And to you, Phil, sweetheart, thank you for my life. I love you.

RESOURCES

If some or all of Sid's experiences resonated with you, please know that you are not alone. Here are some places where you might find guidance, support, and a community.

STRONG 365
strong365.org
Advice and resources for people living with psychosis

BEYOND
wearebeyond.org.uk
24/7 crisis support messenger across the UK
Text Beyond to 85258

SCHIZOPHRENIC.NYC
schizophrenic.nyc
Podcasts, videos, and a beautiful line of clothing to break through the stigma associated with schizophrenia and schizoaffective disorder

The following organisations offer support to LGBTQ+ people. You will be listened to. You will be heard.

SWITCHBOARD LGBT+ HELPLINE
switchboard.lgbt
Based in the United Kingdom
Helpline open every day from 10 a.m. to 10 p.m.:
0300 330 0630
Or email chris@switchboard.lgbt

THE TREVOR PROJECT
trevorproject.org
Based in the United States
24/7 helpline: 1-866-488-7386

If you or someone you know is in immediate danger, please call your local emergency services.

ABOUT THE AUTHOR

Alistair Caradec grew up on the stories his dad read him at night, classical music whenever his mum sat at the piano, and the role-playing games he made up with his brother and cousins. Much of his childhood was spent exploring the fields behind his parents' house and the forest on the outskirts of their village.

He left France in his early twenties to study creative writing in Glasgow, Scotland. Those were two of the most formative years of his life. He produced more writing than he thought himself capable of, honed his narrative voice in a second language, and fell in love with the Scottish countryside.

In the midst of a pretty severe depressive episode back in the summer of 2014, he met his partner Phil, who was going through a lot of the same things at the time. Their long-distance relationship – from the UK to Hawaii – eventually brought them to Canada where they established their home and eventually got married.

Nowadays Alistair's time is split between his family, his day job at a video game services company and his budding writing career.

Alistair began medically transitioning to male in 2019 and came out as gay the next year.